Prague Nights

Prague Nights

BENJAMIN BLACK

VIKING
an imprint of
PENGUIN BOOKS

VIKING

UK | USA | Canada | Ireland | Australia
India | New Zealand | South Africa

Viking is part of the Penguin Random House group of companies
whose addresses can be found at global.penguinrandomhouse.com

First published 2017
001

Copyright © Benjamin Black, 2017

The moral right of the author has been asserted

Set in 11.5/13.5 pt Dante MT Std
Typeset by Jouve (UK), Milton Keynes
Printed in Great Britain by Clays Ltd, St Ives plc

A CIP catalogue record for this book is available from the British Library

HARDBACK ISBN: 978–0–241–29785–8
TRADE PAPERBACK ISBN: 978–0–241–19737–0

www.greenpenguin.co.uk

MIX
Paper from
responsible sources
FSC® C018179

Penguin Random House is committed to a
sustainable future for our business, our readers
and our planet. This book is made from Forest
Stewardship Council® certified paper.

I

December 1599

I

Few now recall that it was I who discovered the corpse of Dr Kroll's misfortunate daughter thrown upon the snow that night in Golden Lane. The fickle muse of history has all but erased the name of Christian Stern from her time- less pages, yet often I have had cause to think how much better it would have been for me had it never been written there in the first place. I was to soar high, on gorgeous plumage, but in the end fell back to earth with wings ablaze.

It was the heart of winter, and a crescent moon hung crookedly over the bulk of Hradčany Castle looming above the narrow laneway where the body lay. Such stars there were!—like a hoard of jewels strewn across a dome of taut black silk. Since a boy I had been fascinated by the mystery of the heavens and sought to know their secret harmonies. But that night I was drunk, and those gemlike lights seemed to spin and sway dizzyingly above me. So addled was I, it's a wonder I noticed the young woman at all, where she lay dead in the deep shadow of the castle wall.

I had arrived in Prague only that day, passing under one of the city's southern gates at nightfall, after a hard journey up from Regensburg, the roads rutted and the Vltava fro- zen solid from bank to bank. I found lodgings at the Blue Elephant, a low establishment in Kleinseite, where I asked for nothing but went at once to my room and threw myself onto the bed still in my travelling clothes. But I could not sleep for a multitude of lice making a furtive rustling all round me under the blankets, and a diamond merchant from Antwerp, dying in the room next to mine, who coughed and cried without cease.

At last, bone-weary though I was, I rose and went down to the taproom and sat on a stool there in the inglenook and drank schnapps and ate *bratwurst* and black bread in the company of an old soldier, grizzled and shaggy, who regaled me with blood-boltered tales of his days as a mercenary under the Duke of Alba in the Low Countries many years before.

It was after midnight and the fire in the grate had died to ash when, far gone in drink, the two of us had the idea, which seemed a capital one at the time, of venturing out to admire the snowbound city by starlight. The streets were deserted: not a creature save ourselves was fool enough to be abroad in such bitter cold. I stopped in a sheltered corner to relieve my bursting bladder and the old fellow wandered off, burbling and crooning to himself. A night bird swooped overhead through the darkness, a pale-winged, silent apparition, no sooner there than it was gone. Buttoning my breeches—not an easy thing to do when you are drunk and your fingers are freezing—I set off on what I thought was the way back to the inn. But at once I got lost in that maze of winding streets and blind alleys below the castle, where I swear the stench of night soil would have driven back the Turk.

How, from there, I managed to end up in Golden Lane is a thing I cannot account for. Fate, too, is a capricious female.

I was a young man still, barely five and twenty, bright, quick and ambitious, with all the world before me, ripe for conquest, or so I imagined. My father was the Prince-Bishop

4

of Regensburg, no less, my mother a serving girl in the Bishop's palace: a bastard I was, then, but determined to be no man's churl. My mother died when I was still a babe, and the Bishop fostered me on a childless couple, one Willebrand Stern and his shrew of a wife, who bestowed on me their name and sought to rear me in the fear of the Lord, which meant half starving me and beating me regularly for my supposedly incurable sinfulness. I ran away more than once from the Sterns' cheerless house on Pfauengasse, and each time was captured and brought back, to be thrashed again, with redoubled vigour.

I had from the start a great thirst for knowledge of all things, and in time I became a precocious adept in natural philosophy and an ever-curious if somewhat sceptical student of the occult arts. I was fortunate to have got a sound education, thanks to my father the Bishop, who insisted I attend Regensburg's Gymnasium, although foster-father Stern had preferred to apprentice me straight off to a farrier. In school I excelled at the quadrivium, showing a particular bent for arithmetic, geometry and cosmological studies. As a student I was both hard-working and clever—more than clever—and by the age of fifteen, already taller and stronger than my foster-father, I was enrolled in the University of Würzburg.

That was a happy time, maybe the happiest of my life, up there in gentle old Franconia, where I had wise and diligent teachers and soon amassed a great store of learning. When my years of study were done I stayed on at the university, earning a living of sorts by tutoring the dull-witted sons of the city's rich merchants. But a life in the academy could not for long satisfy a man of my wilful and single-minded stamp.

5

The Sterns had been sorry to see me leave for Würzburg, not out of fondness for me but for the reason that, when I went, so too did their monthly stipend from the Bishop. On the day of my departure I made a vow to myself that my foster-parents would never set eyes on me again, and that was one vow I kept. I was to return to Regensburg once only, a decade later, when the Sterns were dead and there was an inheritance to collect. The legacy was a matter merely of a handful of gulden, hardly worth the journey from Würzburg, but it was enough to pay my way onwards to Prague, that capital of magic towards which I had yearned all my life.

The Bishop himself was recently dead. When with ill grace I had fulfilled my duty and visited his last resting place and, with greater unwillingness, that of the Sterns, I quitted Regensburg as fast as my old nag would carry me. In a calfskin pouch lodged next to my breast I carried a letter of commendation, which I had requested of His Grace when he was dying, though with small hope of being obliged. But on his deathbed the great man summoned a scribe to draw up the document, which he duly signed and dispatched post-haste to his importunate son.

This favour from my father was accompanied by a substantial purse of gold and silver. The letter and the money surprised me: as I was well aware, I was by no means the best-loved among his numerous misbegotten offspring. Perhaps he had heard what a scholar I had made of myself and hoped I might follow in his footsteps and become a prelate. But if that was what the old man thought, then by God he did not know his son.

He also sent me—I found it only by chance in the bottom of the purse—a gold ring that I think must have

6

belonged to my mother. Could it be that he had given her this plain gold band as a secret token of fondness—of love, even? The possibility disturbed me: I had determined to think of my father as a monster and did not wish to have to think again.

And so I came to Prague, at the close of the year of Our Lord 1599, in the reign of Rudolf II, of the House of Habsburg, King of Hungary and Bohemia, Archduke of Austria and ruler of the Holy Roman Empire. That was a happier age, an era of peace and plenty before this terrible war of the religions—which has been raging now for nigh on thirty years—had engulfed the world in slaughter, fire and ruin. Rudolf may have been more than a little mad, but he was tolerant to all, holding every man's beliefs, Christian, Jew or Mussulman, to be his own concern and no business of state, monarch or marshal.

Rudolf, as is well known, had no love for Vienna, the city of his birth, and he lost no time in transferring the imperial court to Prague in—ah, I forget the year; my memory these days is a sieve. Yet I do not forget my aim in coming to the capital of his empire, which was no less than to win the Emperor's favour and secure a place among the scores of learned men who laboured at His Majesty's pleasure, and under his direction, in the fabulous hothouse that was Hradčany Castle. Most were alchemists, but not all: at court there were wise savants, too, notably the astronomer Johannes Kepler and the noble Dane Tycho Brahe, Rudolf's Imperial Mathematician, great men, the two of them, though of the two Kepler was by far the greater.

It was no easy goal I had set myself. I knew, as who did not, Rudolf's reputation as a disliker of humanity. For years His Majesty had kept to his private quarters in the castle, poring over ancient texts and brooding in his wonder rooms, not showing himself even to the most intimate of his courtiers for weeks on end; he had been known to leave envoys of the most illustrious princes to cool their heels for half a year or more before deigning to grant them an audience. But what was that to me? I meant to make my way into the imperial sanctum without hindrance or delay, by whatever means and by whatever necessary stratagems, so large were my ambitions and so firm my self-belief.

Thoughts of royal favour were far from my mind that night in Golden Lane. I stood swaying and sighing, my mind fogged and my eyes bleared, peering in drunken distress at the young woman's corpse where it lay asprawl in the snow.

I thought at first she was old, a tiny, shrunken crone. I was unable, I suppose, to conceive that anyone so young could be so cruelly, so irreclaimably dead. She lay on her back with her face to the sky, and she might have been studying, with remote indifference, the equally indifferent scatter of stars arched above her. Her limbs were twisted and thrown about, as if she had collapsed exhausted in the midst of an antic dance.

Now I looked more closely and saw that she was not old at all, that in fact she was a maid of no more than seventeen or eighteen.

Why had she been out on such a night? She had no cloak, and wore only a gown of embroidered dark velvet, and felt slippers that would have afforded her scant protection against the cold and the snow. Had she been brought from indoors somewhere nearby and done to death on this spot? She had lain here some long time, for the snow had piled up in a drift against her at one side. It would have covered her all over had not, as I supposed, the warmth of her body, even as it was diminishing, melted the flakes as they drifted down on her. When I touched the stuff of her gown I instantly drew back my fingers, shuddering, for the wetted velvet was brittle and sharp with ice. I was reminded of the frozen pelt of a dead dog I had held in my arms when I was a boy, a house dog that my foster-father, old man Stern, had shut out of doors all night and left to perish in the cold of midwinter.

But this poor young woman now, this slaughtered creature! I could do no more than stand there helplessly and gaze at her in pity and dismay. Her eyes were a little way open, and the pallid light of the stars shone on the orbs themselves, glazing their surfaces and giving them the look of hazed-over mother-of-pearl. They seemed to me, those eyes, deader than all the rest of her.

For long moments I leaned forward with my hands braced on my knees, drunkenly asway and breathing heavily. Now and then I let fall a shivery, rasping sigh. I wondered what strange power the creature possessed, dead as she was. How could she hold me here, even as I was urging myself to flee the spot and fly back to the sanctuary of the Blue Elephant? Maybe something of her spirit lingered within her even yet, a failing light; maybe I, as the only living being round about, was required to stay by her, and be a witness to the final extinguishing of that last flickering flame. The dead, though voiceless, still demand their rights.

Her head was surrounded by a sort of halo, not radiant but, on the contrary, of a deep and polished blackness against the white of the snow. When I first noticed it I couldn't think what it might be, but now, bending lower, I saw, just above the lace ruff she wore, a deep gash across

9

her throat, like a second, grotesquely gaping, mouth, and understood that her head was resting in a pool of her own life-blood, a black round in which the faint radiance of the heavens faintly glinted.

Yet even then I tarried, in hapless agitation, held there as if my feet were fastened to the ground. I urged myself to turn away, to turn away now, this instant, and be gone. No one had seen me come, and no one would see me go. True, the snow all round was fresh, and my boots would leave their prints in it, but who was to say they were the prints of my boots, and who was there to follow my track?

Still I could not shift myself, could not shake off the impalpable grip of the dead hand that held me there. I thought to cover her face, but I had no cape, or kerchief even, and I was not prepared to relinquish my coat of beaver skin on a night of such killing cold, no matter how strong the natural imperative to shield her, in the shame of such a death, from the world's blank, unfeeling gaze.

I knelt on one knee and tried to lift her by the shoulders, but rigor mortis and the frost had stiffened her; besides, her gown was stuck fast to the ice on the flagstones and would not be freed. As I was struggling to raise her—to what purpose I would have been hard put to say—I caught a heavy, sweetish fragrance that I thought must be the smell of that dark pool of blood behind her head, although it, too, like the rest of her, was frozen and inert.

When I let go of her and stood back, there came up out of her a drawn-out, rattling sort of sigh. At Würzburg I had studied doctoring for a twelvemonth, and knew that corpses sometimes made such sounds, as their inner organs shifted and settled on the way to dissolution. All the same, every hair on my head stood erect.

I crouched again and examined more closely the wound in her throat. It was not a clean cut, such as a sharp blade would make, but, rather, was ragged and gouged, as if some ravening animal had got hold of her there, sunk its fangs into her tender flesh and ripped it asunder.

I also saw that she was wearing a heavy gold chain, and on the chain was a medallion, gold too. It was circular and large, with flaring edges, a Medusa head, it might have been, or an image of the great disc of the sun itself.

At last I broke free of whatever dead force she had been wielding over me. I turned and stumbled away up the lane, in search of help, although surely the poor creature was far beyond all human succour. Death is death, whatever the priests or the necromancers—if there is a difference between the two—would have us believe, and there's an end of it, our mortal span done with.

The little houses as I passed them were shuttered and silent, with not a chink of light showing in any of the windows, yet despite the deserted aspect of the place and the lateness of the hour, I had the impression of being spied upon secretly by countless waking, watchful eyes.

My feet were numb from the cold, while my hands, cold too, nevertheless burned under the skin, with a sort of feverish heat. I felt strangely detached, from my surroundings and from myself; it was as though death had touched me, too, had brushed me ever so lightly with an icy fingertip. I thought of the glasses of schnapps—how many?—that I and the old soldier had downed, sitting by the hearth at the Blue Elephant, and I longed now for a mouthful, the merest mouthful, of that fiery liquor, to warm my blood and calm my confused and racing thoughts.

After I had trudged for some way along the base of the

castle ramparts, the snow squeaking under my boots and my breath puffing ghostly shapes on the air, I came to a gate with a portcullis. To the right of the gate was a sentry box, inside which a lantern glowed weakly, although in the midst of such darkness it seemed a great light. The sentry was asleep where he stood, leaning heavily on his pike. He was short and fat, with a belly as round and tight as a beer keg. In a brazier beside him there glowed a fire of sea coals, a little of the welcome warmth of which reached to where I stood.

I called out a halloo and stamped my foot hard on the ground, and at last the sentry's eyelids fluttered open. He goggled at me blankly, still half asleep. Then, coming more or less to his senses, and remembering who and what he was supposed to be, he hauled himself to attention with a grunting effort, his coat of mail jangling. He straightened his helmet and made a great show of levelling his lance and brandishing the blade of it at me menacingly, while demanding in a thick, slurred voice to know who it was that went there and what business I was about.

I gave my name, but had to repeat it, the second time fairly shouting it in the fellow's face. 'Stern!' I bellowed. 'Christian Stern!'

I should admit that at this time I had a high notion of my own name, for I could already see it embossed on the spines of a row of learned tomes that I had no doubt I should some day write.

The sentry stood gazing up at me, dull-eyed and blinking. I recounted to him how I had chanced upon the young woman, lying on the stones amid the snow under the castle wall, with her throat torn open from the point of one earlobe to the other. Upon hearing my story, the fellow hawked and spat over the half-door a gob that landed with a splat just short of the toe of my right boot. I pictured myself using that toe to deliver the rascal a good hard kick to the soft underpart of his pendulous belly.

'What's it to me,' he said scornfully, 'if a drab had her windpipe slit?'

'She was no drab,' I said, thinking of the velvet gown and the gold medallion on its gold chain. 'On the contrary, she was a gentlewoman, as I believe.'

'All the whores in Prague fancy themselves high-born ladies,' the sentry said with renewed scorn.

My temper in those young days was high and hot, and I considered wresting the lance from the fellow's grasp and giving him a whack of it upon his helmet to repay him for his insolence. Instead I controlled myself and told him that someone in authority should be notified that a grave felony had been committed.

At this the sentry laughed, and replied that someone in authority had been notified, for hadn't I just told him, and wasn't he someone in authority? It was apparent he considered this a rare turn of wit.

I sighed. My feet were almost entirely numb by now, and I could feel hardly anything of them from the ankles down. What, I asked myself, was that young woman to me, and why was I so concerned for her, who after all was no more than a corpse?

Now another guardsman arrived; I heard his boots crunching over the ice before he appeared out of the mist and the snowy darkness, like a warrior's fresh-made ghost emerging from the smoke of battle. He looked not much of a warrior, though, being thin-limbed, gangly and gaunt. A rusty arquebus was slung over his shoulder. Come to relieve his fat counterpart, he bent on me an eye wholly indifferent as to who I might be and wiped his nose on a knuckle. The two exchanged some words, and the newcomer took up his place in the sentry box, putting down his firearm and offering his scrawny backside gratefully to the brazier and its glowing coals.

Once more I urged the fat sentry to come with me and view the corpse of the young woman and decide what was to be done.

'Leave her to the night watch,' he replied. 'He'll find her on his rounds.'

If he did not come with me now, I said, I would straightway fetch an officer of the guard and lay a complaint against him. This was mere bluff, of course, but I put so much authority into my tone that the fellow, after another hesitation, shrugged and grunted at me vexedly to lead on.

We made our way back down the lane. The sentry walked with a bow-legged waddle. He was so stunted that the top of his head, as round as a cabbage, hardly came much higher than my elbow.

The young woman's corpse was as I had left it, and no one had been there in the meantime, for mine were still the only boot-prints visible in the snow.

Beside me, the fat fellow made a harsh noise at the back of his throat and shut one eye and sucked his teeth. He stepped forward and, with a grunt, squatted on his heels. Lifting up the medallion, he held it on his palm and examined it by the faint light of the stars. He gave a low whistle. 'Real gold, that is,' he said. 'Feel the heft of it.'

What is it about gold, I wonder, that all men imagine themselves masters of the assayer's art? The same is true of precious stones, yet any old chunk of carved glass can be passed off as a gem of rarest quality, as every jeweller, and every cutpurse, will tell you.

Suddenly the fellow let drop the medallion as if it had scorched his palm. He struggled to his feet and stumbled an unsteady step backwards in alarm. 'I know this one!' he muttered. 'It's Kroll's daughter, his girl. Christ's blood!' He turned to me with a wild look, then peered all about in the darkness, as if he feared a skulk of murderers might be in hiding out there, ready to pounce.

'Kroll?' I asked. 'Who or what is Kroll, pray?'

The sentry gave a desperate sort of laugh. 'You don't know Dr Kroll,' he said, 'the Emperor's sawbones and one of his chief wizards?' He laughed again, grimly. 'I daresay you soon will, friend.'

And soon, indeed, I would.

2

Dawn was still a good way off when they came for me at my lodgings. It was a great shock and a greater fright, yet I found that in some deep part of myself I was not entirely surprised. I suspect there lurks in every one of us, since Adam ate the apple, the guilty expectation of just such a distant hammering on the door at dead of night, of curt voices in the hall and the tramp of heavy boots on the stair. No man in his heart believes himself entirely innocent.

Hearing the violent commotion now, I sprang up on my bed and cast about in a panic, but I had not even a blade to defend myself. I wondered confusedly how they had known where to find me. In the night, after the fat sentry had identified the dead young woman for me, I had accompanied him to the gate, where he had conferred in urgent mutterings with his companion-in-arms over the half-door of the sentry box. That was the moment when I finally came to my senses—by now the effect of the schnapps had almost worn off—and I stepped back cautiously and turned and made off into the night, leaving the two guards to their anxious colloquy.

At the Blue Elephant I had to wait outside in the cold for a long time, knocking at the door and peering anxiously up and down the street, before the innkeeper's wife came down at last and let me in. She had risen from her bed and was in her nightclothes, her hair gathered under a dainty nightcap of white muslin. I had taken note of her already, when I first arrived. She was a pretty thing, with ruddy cheeks and shining black curls, though she looked to be somewhat on the mature side, to my young man's eye.

Taking up a candlestick, she lit me to my room. When we got there she tarried in the doorway, giving me a brazen smile and the benefit of the view down the loose front of her shift. I caught her womanly fragrance and even fancied I could feel the warm glow of her skin. The candlelight softened her features and smoothed the fine fans of wrinkles at the corners of her mouth and eyes. I'm sure I would have taken her up on her unspoken offer and drawn her with me into the room and into my bed, lice or no lice, had there not at that moment come back to me clearly, like an awful warning, the hazy glitter in the half-open, lifeless eyes of the young woman lying in the snow under the castle wall, with that other, terrible, mouth below her chin bloodily agape.

The merchant next door had quietened by then—he might have succeeded in dying at last, for all I knew—yet still I hardly slept, and when I did, my sleep was plagued by dreams, presently to be proved prophetic, that were loud with shrieks and alarms and shot through with wild rushings in darkness from one patch of stark lamplight to another.

When I'd heard the soldiers downstairs, my first thought had been to leap out at the window and flee, but the room was on an upper floor: had I jumped I would have ended up broken and bleeding in the street below. Sluggish with fright, I was hardly halfway out of the bed before the door burst open and a squad of helmeted figures, sashed and booted, came crowding in. A mailed fist grasped me violently by the shoulder and hauled me to my feet.

Now I was pummelled and cursed and shouted at with

17

incomprehensible commands, and my clothes were flung at me and I was ordered to dress myself at once. I hopped on one leg about the floor pulling on my hose, and took a ringing blow to the side of the head for not being quick enough about it. Then I was hustled down the stairs amid a mingled fug of sweat and steel and the raw breath of rough men-at-arms.

As I was being led out at the front entrance, I glanced back over my shoulder and saw the innkeeper's wife, in her nightcap, peeping out fearfully from behind the taproom door. It was to be my last sight of her, but even now, all these years later, I recall her image often to my mind, with painful clarity, and experience yet again a fond and sad regret for that opportunity lost. Is not old age incorrigible?

Fortunately I had managed to snatch up my coat, for the still-dark sky was laden with sagging, big-bellied clouds, and a biting wind dashed flurries of snow into my face, like half-frozen spit.

When the soldiers had first broken into the room, it had seemed to me there must be a dozen men at least, but I saw now that they were no more than four. They clanked along, unrelenting and wordless, in a square formation, a sort of moving cage, with me inside it, stumbling and panting. They marched as one, in matched step, which made me feel all the more clumsy and helpless in their midst.

We passed through a gate, wider and loftier than the one where, hours before, I had come upon the sleeping sentry, then across a cobbled yard greasy with soft snow, to ascend three broad stone steps. Imprisoned by that box of armed men, I entered a bare hall with a roof immensely high and lit by rushlights in iron holders set halfway up the walls. How strange it is, the things that fear chooses to fasten on:

those lights, flickering and smoking and making a sound like a conflagration raging afar, seemed to me the very image of bleak foreboding and fright.

I was led to a broad oaken door, with metal studs the size of a man's fists set into it. The door opened onto another hall, somewhat smaller than the outer one, and there the ceiling was lower. A big table with high-backed chairs ranged around it stood in the middle of the floor, square and stolid, planted heavy as an ox on its four massive legs. Something in this arrangement, too, seemed uncanny, the table bare and gleaming and in a queer way baleful, the big chairs crouched motionless yet seemingly aquiver with intent, like hunting dogs poised and waiting on their master's whistle.

Opposite the door was a fireplace with an open hearth tall enough for a man to stand up. A single blazing log of beechwood was supported between two tall bronze andirons that were decorated with the moulded figures of porpoises, Nereids and writhing mermen. No torches burned there, and the only light in the room came from the fire.

The squad of soldiers withdrew, swinging the door shut behind them.

I stood before the table, as if it were the Judgment Seat, waiting for I knew not what. All that could be heard was the crackle of the flames in the hearth and the sound of my own laboured breathing. I was glad of the fire's glow, and had moved to approach it more closely when a voice spoke, making me start back—I had thought there was no one but myself in the room.

'Stern,' the voice snapped out. 'That is what you call yourself, yes?'

I peered into the leaping shadows thrown by the fire-light, searching for the source of the words that had been delivered with such sharpness and rude force.

In the gloom to the left of the hearth I made out a large, elderly man, who had been mostly hidden from me by the back of the richly upholstered, throne-like chair in which he was seated, facing the fire. He seemed to be asleep, from the slack way he was reclining, with his chin slumped on his chest and one arm hanging limply by the side of the chair. As I saw, however, his eyes were open, the pupils reflecting the busy flames of the fire.

But he was not the man who had spoken. Another figure was standing off to the right of the hearth, far back, where the light of the fire hardly reached. I had the impression of a slight, lean frame, a small head, a sharply pointed beard above a silk ruff, its whiteness glowing eerily in the gloom. I recalled another ruff I had seen lately, though that one had been dark and stiff with blood.

'Yes,' I answered, and had to pause to clear my throat. 'Yes, that is my name.'

The man in the shadows gave a soft and, for some reason, disbelieving snort, and came forward into the light.

His eyes seemed black in the fire's glow and were set close together, like two tiny bright black beads. He had greyish hair, cut short and coming far down on his forehead in a narrow peak that found an echo in his sharply pointed beard. He was dressed in doublet and hose; his legs were curiously slender and delicate, more like a woman's than a man's. He was of middle years, and in aspect quick and keenly watchful. I did not at all care for the look of him, with his piercing eyes and widow's peak and that satanic beard cut in the fashionable Spanish style.

'And you claim to have travelled here from Regensburg,' he said, his tone this time of sceptical amusement.

'Yes,' I answered. 'I set out from Regensburg a week ago and came to Prague last evening.'

'Regensburg,' the man repeated, with a soft, sarcastic laugh.

I was puzzled: from this fellow's responses, it seemed I might have been claiming to have arrived here a moment past from Atlantis, or the fabled city of Ur.

'Regensburg is the city of my birth,' I said, speaking slowly and clearly, as to a child, 'although I have been away from there for many years, first studying and then tutoring at the University of Würzburg.'

'Regensburg!' the man said again, with yet another snicker. 'Würzburg!' He turned to the man seated in the chair. 'How plausible he makes these westward places sound, eh, Doctor?'

I was by now thoroughly bewildered. Plainly the man in the ruff was convinced I was lying—but why would I lie about such simple matters as my name and birthplace? And, besides, why was he questioning me in this truculent fashion? I had done no wrong, or none that I knew of. Surely it could not be a violation of the city ordinances to happen upon a corpse by accident. And yet, deep down, I had again the vague and guilty sense of unsurprise I had felt when I first heard the noise of the soldiers' boot heels on the stairway at the Blue Elephant.

I tried again.

'My name is Christian Stern,' I said, speaking even more slowly now, and with a heavier emphasis. 'I came to Prague last evening, by way of Regensburg. Regensburg is where I was born and where I lived until I went away, at a young age, to study at the University of Würzburg, and it's at Würzburg that I have been a scholar and a tutor for some years past.' I hesitated, and then added: 'I shall not be long in Prague, for I am on my way to Dresden.'

This was not true, and I regretted it as soon as I had said it. I had no intention of travelling on to Dresden, or to anywhere else. Prague had been my yearned-for destination, and in Prague I meant to stop. Given this man's suspicious and threatening manner, however, it had seemed wise to present myself as a passing stranger who would soon be safely gone from the city. Now I chided myself for the falsehood, for later, I bodefully thought, it would probably get me into further trouble. But what business was it of this officious fellow whether I stayed on in Prague or not? And what, further, had any of this to do with the dead girl in the snow?

'Step closer,' the man said brusquely, 'where we can see you clearly.'

I walked around three sides of the table and stopped in front of the fireplace. The man considered me for a long moment in silence, inclining his small, neat head at a sharp tilt, like a blackbird stopping in mid-forage with one ear cocked.

'Do you know who I am?' the man asked.

'No, sir,' I said, 'I do not.'

He drew his head upright, and lifted high his chin. 'I am Felix Wenzel,' he said, 'High Steward to His Majesty the Emperor Rudolf.'

Ah! I thought, and my heart made a skipping little beat. Felix Wenzel, as all the world knew, was one of the cleverest, most cunning, and most feared of the Emperor's advisers. I was as much impressed as alarmed. Felix Wenzel!

'I am honoured to make your acquaintance, sir,' I said, with a stiff bow. Bowing, I am not ashamed to say, is a thing I have never got the hang of.

Wenzel smiled coldly and stroked the corners of his mouth with a finger and thumb, making a faint rasping sound in the grizzled stubble there. Still he regarded me with his bright, hard gaze. 'Tell us why you did the young woman to death,' he said.

The log in the hearth crackled and hissed, the light of its flames glinting on the naked breasts of a sea nymph leaning out from the base of one of the bronze andirons. For a moment I was so taken aback I could not speak. This was a notion it had not occurred to me even to consider, that I should be accused of the young woman's murder.

I cleared my throat again. 'You are mistaken, sir,' I said. 'I found her dead, where she lay. She had been so for some time, for her limbs were set and stiff.'

Wenzel nodded, though it was no more than a flick of impatience, as if he were dismissing an irrelevant and irritating detail. 'You are lying, of course,' he said.

Now the man seated in the chair before the fire, who had seemed to be lost in his own thoughts and not attending to us at all, suddenly spoke. 'Würzburg,' he said, in a low and weary-sounding growl, lifting his head and turning to glance up at me. 'You come from Würzburg, you say?'

'That's so, sir,' I replied. 'Würzburg is where I have resided this ten-year, and where I have my work, at the university.' I turned to Wenzel again. 'If you doubt it, there are people there—colleagues, professors, men of learning—who will vouch for me.'

'Oh, certainly!' Wenzel exclaimed with scorn. 'The wise men of Würzburg would vouch for their grandmother's goat!' He turned away and walked off into his shadowed corner.

Ruefully now, I recalled my father the Bishop's letter of attestation—why had I not thought to take it with me when the soldiers were dragging me out of my room at the Blue Elephant? I could have produced it now and proved my identity. Forgetful fool that I was, I had left it under the stinking straw mattress, where, on arriving at the inn, I had tucked it for safety.

The man in the chair was looking up at me still. He had a large head with a high, domed forehead, a prominent nose and a full beard. His eyes were slack-rimmed and inflamed. 'She was my daughter,' he said, so quietly that I barely caught the words. 'The one you found.' He heaved a long, softly falling sigh. 'Magdalena, she is called—was called. My daughter.'

I nodded. I had already guessed that this must be the Dr Kroll whom the fat sentry had spoken of as the dead young woman's father.

Now Wenzel addressed me again from the shadows. 'And the renegade, Madek,' he asked, 'what do you know of him?'

Dr Kroll, in his chair, gave a strange start, of surprise, it seemed, or even shock, at hearing that name. He stared at Wenzel, then turned back to the fire.

To Wenzel's question I could offer no reply. I knew of no Madek, papist, renegade, or otherwise. Indeed, I could make nothing of any of this—the murdered woman, these high officials, this baffling, nightmarish interrogation. I felt like a man who, setting out on horseback at evening, had fallen asleep in the saddle, and now had woken to find himself on an unknown road, in deepest night, lost and confused.

Wenzel approached into the firelight again, pacing slowly with his eyes lowered and his hands clasped behind his back, setting one slim foot in front of the other with nice judgement and care, as if he were keeping to a line traced, straight but invisibly, along the floor. His slippers were made of soft calfskin, with silver threading and even a scrap of scarlet ribbon in the lace holes. A vain fellow, then, and not a little in love with himself. Note that well, I told myself: a man's weaknesses are always useful to know and keep stored away.

But if Wenzel was vain, he was dangerous, too. This was the man who, when no more than a stripling, had ordered, so it was said, the assassination of his two brothers in a dispute over their father's will.

Reaching the fireplace, Wenzel stopped, raised his head and squinted at me with what might have been an executioner's measuring eye. 'I could have you broken on the rack,' he said. 'I could have you blinded and thrust out into the night to stumble off in search of whatever hole it was you crawled out of. I could do anything to you, *Christian Stern*, so-called.' Despite the harshness of the words, he had spoken them in a mild, almost playful tone, suave and amused.

Beyond his shoulder, through the diamond panes of a window on the far side of the room, I saw the darkly agitated flicker of blown snow. From far off in the streets of the city came faintly the night watch's mournful-sounding cry.

Wenzel was regarding me still with a narrowed eye. 'Well?' he said. 'Have you nothing to say?'

'I can say, sir,' I answered, 'that whoever it is you think I am, you are mistaken. I am a travelling scholar, late of Würzburg. I came to this city last evening, as I have told you, and lodged at the Blue Elephant in Kleinseite, or Malá Strana, as I believe that part of the city is called in the Czech tongue. Being sleepless, and having drunk overmuch, I wandered from the inn out into the darkness and the snow, and found myself under the castle wall, and there happened upon the corpse of this unfortunate man's daughter—'

'This man,' Wenzel said, brusquely interrupting, 'is Dr Ulrich Kroll, court physician to His Majesty the Emperor.' He paused, and drew back his head and looked at me with rich contempt along the side of his nose. 'Listen, fellow,' he said, 'have you any notion of the enormity of the crime you have committed?'

'My lord steward,' I patiently replied, 'I have committed no crime. If I had murdered the young woman, would I have gone to alert the sentry at the gate and led him to where the body lay? Would I not have hurried back to the inn and gathered up my belongings and fled the city altogether, instead of returning to my room and to my bed, where the soldiers that you sent discovered me with such ease?' I paused. 'If you knew anything of me, sir,' I said, 'you would know that whatever else I may be, I am not a fool.'

I turned to Kroll, who, his chin sunk again on his breast, was gazing bleakly into the fireplace and the throbbing white heart of the flames. 'I swear to you, Doctor,' I said, 'I never saw your daughter alive. She had long since drawn her last breath when I came upon her. I might have made off and left her corpse there in the snow, alone and uncared for. Surely it's a pledge of my innocence that I did not.'

The log in the fireplace broke apart in the middle, where the flames were strongest, and the burning ends of the two halves slumped at an angle to the stone floor of the hearth in a shower of crackling sparks. Kroll, a muscle beating steadily in his jaw, watched the agitated flames as they shot up from the ashy stubs only to fall back again as quickly as they had risen.

'Yes,' he said, in his deep, slow, weary way. 'Yes, yes.'

Wenzel made to speak again but Kroll lifted a hand, gesturing for him to be silent. One of the broken parts of the log sank further, sending up another spurt of sparks.

'This is not the man who murdered my child,' Kroll said. 'He is not lying.' He glanced up sidelong at me again. 'She was already cold, you say?'

'She was, sir,' I answered. 'Her agony was long past, and she was at peace.'

Yet even as I said this I recalled how the young woman had kept a grip on me somehow, as if her dying were not done with, as if something of her spirit were still there in her, for all that she was frozen and for ever beyond stirring.

Kroll put up his hand again, this time to cover his eyes. 'Yes,' he said, as heavily and with the same finality as before. 'Yes.'

Wenzel made an impatient sound and turned away, plucking at the silken ruff at his throat. He looked about him ill-temperedly here and there, as if calling on invisible others beyond the firelight to be witnesses to the folly of the moment.

Dr Kroll set his hands tremblingly on the padded arms of the chair and rose to his feet, heaving the sorrowing burden of himself upright with an effort. Wenzel, turning towards the stricken man, put out a hand to help him but at once withdrew it, looking to see if I had seen the gesture, and turned aside again, biting the back of his thumb. He had seen me note the kindly impulse and its hasty withdrawal; he had seen me spot a weakness, and he would not forget.

'I must go home now and rest,' Dr Kroll said.

'Stay a moment,' Wenzel said. 'I'll have your carriage brought up to the door.'

Kroll ignored him and instead bent his red-rimmed gaze once more on me. 'Leave here, and travel on,' he said. 'Go to Dresden—go anywhere. Prague is no place for you.' He glanced briefly in Wenzel's direction. 'Here everything is tainted and sick.'

Then he walked heavily out, the hem of his dark robe trailing along the floor behind him.

3

Once more I was fenced within a square of men in clanking armour, once more I was marched across the cobbled square and thence out through the tall gate where, a little while before, I had been led in. It was snowing still. The spinning flakes might have been the tattered fragments of a celestial catastrophe, a sort of wet white ash sifting down upon the world.

In that room, before the fireplace, after Dr Kroll had departed, Wenzel had paced again for a little while, stroking his beard and seeming lost in thought, then had crossed to the door and summoned the guard and handed me again into their custody, without so much as another glance in my direction.

Having passed through the gate now, the detachment, with me in its midst, wheeled to the right and marched along under the castle wall. Soon we came to a squat round tower set on a corner of the wall, like the stump of a severed finger pointing skywards in pained protest. Here I was half pushed, half pulled up a flight of stone steps, to arrive, light-headed and giddy, at another studded door, this one narrow and low.

The door was kicked open and I was thrust into a tiny cold evil-smelling cell. All gaol cells smell the same, as I can well attest, after a life of greatly mixed fortunes.

When the door was shut the darkness was total, a medium to itself, dense yet dizzyingly penetrable. I stood and listened to the slow, dull beating of my heart. Then I took a cautious step forward, with arms outstretched, my fingertips tingling in awful expectation of what they might meet. All they met, however, was a curved, continuous and coldly sweating wall, the stones of which had been polished smooth through countless centuries by hands like mine, feeling their way over them in blind helplessness.

The little space, I soon discovered, was unfurnished, save for a wooden bench of sorts, on which I sat down. I set my elbows on my knees and rested my head in my hands. In the utter darkness it made no difference whether my eyes were shut or open; the quality of the blackness before me remained the same. This gave me a sensation of queasy lightness, as if I were afloat somehow, motionlessly drowning, in a soft dark silent sea.

Presently a grey glimmer began to creep down from what I saw was a barred window set high up in the wall at my back. The window was square and small, and I could reach it only by standing on the bench and taking hold of the bars and drawing myself up with my toes scrabbling for purchase on the slippery wall. Outside, a sombre dawn was breaking over the roofs and spires of the city. I hung there, gasping from the effort, the muscles of my arms quivering, wanting to let go but loath to lose sight of even that deserted, wintry prospect.

Bells in countless churches were tolling the hour; it seemed to me I had never in my life heard so bleak and comfortless a sound. The thought came slithering into my defenceless consciousness that I might never be released from this foul dungeon, unless it was to be taken out on a freezing midwinter morning much like this one and marched to some grimy corner of the castle keep and made to kneel there with my neck on the block, where my last sight of this world would be that of the hooded headsman testing the edge of his blade with a thick thumb.

I was still hanging there at the window with arms aquiver, my fingers numb and my wrists creaking, when I heard a sound at the door, a metallic clatter. I released my hold on the bars and dropped down to the bench. Cowering, I sat with my back pressed to the wall, expecting the soldiers to come crowding in again and haul me off to some new encounter just as menacing and bewildering as the one I had lately endured.

But the door didn't open. Instead a panel at the bottom of it was pushed aside, with an abrupt *clack!* that made me think of the confessional: nowhere like a prison cell to recall a man to his sins. A battered pewter plate with a lump of bread on it was pushed in, followed by a clay mug.

These rations I pounced on almost joyfully. The bread was mouldy and hard and dry as chalk, but I gnawed at it nevertheless, hunched over like a starved rat, mumbling the dough into sticky pellets in my mouth and washing them down as best I could with gulps of foul-tasting water from the mug.

When I had eaten, if eating it could be called, I lay down on my side on the bench with my knees drawn up to my chest, pulling my coat close about me. After a little while I began shivering, the shivers coming in spasms that started at the nape of my neck and flowed swiftly downwards along my back, like waves running upon a shallow shore. Gradually the daylight strengthened, though it brought me no consolation, as it is supposed to do. Somehow it only made stronger the sense I had of drowning, as if it were not that light was falling, but that something else, some thick, transparent liquid, were welling up all round me.

31

At last I fell into a nightmarish half-sleep. I suspect a delusioning philtre had been slipped into the water in the mug, for in my dozing I entered upon a strange state in which I seemed to be not in the cell but merely dreaming that I was, while yet knowing full well that I was wholly there and that it was no dream.

In the depths of my delirium a face appeared and hovered over me in the glimmering dawn light, a face I recognised from the countless likenesses of it to be seen throughout the empire, painted on canvas, carved in stone and stamped on coins. The face was heavy and broad, with a pendulous jaw, a sagging nether lip, and large, dark eyes brimming with an infinite melancholy. For some time it hung above me motionless, a visage stark and pale, like a floating moon, regarding me with the moon's cold, remote and unreturnable gaze.

I can't say how many hours passed before I emerged at last from that hazy torpor. The light seemed not much stronger than it had been before I fell asleep. The cold, however, was more intense. I could barely stir my limbs, they were so stiff, and there was a cramp in the pit of my stomach as if a stone were lodged there, which was no doubt the persisting presence of the crust of indigestible bread I had unwisely consumed earlier. I raised myself on the bench, my stiffened joints protesting, and sat shivering with the collar of my greatcoat clutched close about my throat.

Strangely, I began to be convinced that there was someone else in the cell along with me, a figure without substance yet ineluctably there, crouching beside me on the bench. It had no moonlike face, no mournful eyes, no soft brown beard; instead, it seemed to be another version of myself, a conjured, invisible twin. This other me was no company or comfort but wholly alien, my terrifying and hideously knowing insubstantial double.

How long, I wondered, would it take, in this place, for me to lose my mind?

I had never, up to then, been able to entertain seriously the prospect of my own death—it had seemed a bad joke, crassly told—but now I thought it entirely possible that I would die, that even if my head were not to fall under the axe the numbing cold alone would kill me before night came again. It is a measure of my desperate straits that I fancied I would welcome death as a happy release. I thought of the numbness spreading over all my flesh and penetrating through muscles and into bone; I thought of my heart fluttering inside me as a hawk hovers, before folding its wings and sinking down in stillness. Would something of me persist for a little while, a tiny, failing light such as I had sensed glimmering still in the corpse of Magdalena Kroll? If so, there would be, for me, no one here to witness its final extinguishing, except for that formless phantom at my side, although he, surely, would die the instant I did.

Unlikely as it may seem, I found myself harking back with longing to the days of my childhood, days that, in the present gloom, all at once seemed to me to have been nothing but happy and bright. Even that dismal house on Pfauengasse became in my memory of it a haven of tranquillity and loving-kindness. And the Sterns, what of them? Why, were the cell door to be thrown open at that moment and they to come scowlingly in, chanting prayers and loudly upbraiding me, which was ever their way, I believe I would have fallen to my knees before them and kissed their hands for joy at the familiar sight of them.

The snow was still falling outside: I could see the shadow

33

of it moving at the window. In my mind I pictured the city huddled as though in mute submission under that soundless lapsing, succumbing, like me, to the merciless, creeping cold.

At length, shamed by these self-pitying maunderings, I made myself get up from the bench and pace vigorously up and down the floor, stamping my feet and flapping my arms to get the blood moving in my veins, all the while drawing in long, slow, strength-giving breaths, though the icy air seared my lungs. After a time, however, I succumbed to a renewed deathly weariness and was forced to lie down. Again, I was half in a doze when suddenly a key rattled in the lock and the door was thrown open. I sat up, knuckling my eyes and blinking, certain this time of more soldiers, more shouted commands, more cuffs and kicks. I had chafed in my solitude, but now my only wish was that it might not end.

It was not soldiers who entered, but only the gaoler, a sad-eyed, crooked fellow with a hump high on one shoulder and a big bunch of keys jangling on an iron hoop attached to his belt. He motioned me to my feet and led me out.

We descended the winding stair, I going first and the hunchback lurching clumsily from step to step behind me. Two guards were waiting below, and I was set between them and marched away. The guards spoke not a word, to me or to each other, only strode stolidly along, swinging their halberds. The snow had stopped, taking a brief rest, as it might be, after so much swirling effort. Under a low, leaden sky the daylight had the look of water in which a drop of ink had been dispersed. Few folk were about, and of those few, none paid me the slightest heed; I might have been a walking ghost.

Along the way I happened to glance into a little sloping

yard enclosed by three blind walls. A gibbet stood there, and dangling from it at the end of a short, thick rope was the fat sentry, his face purple and his swollen tongue stuck like an apple in the round O of his gaping mouth. I recalled the fellow toddling along sullenly beside me through the darkness and the snow in Golden Lane, after we had finished viewing the corpse of Magdalena Kroll, and I thought, with a shudder, of how those bandy little legs of his must have kicked and wriggled when the hangman was hoisting him aloft.

We passed through other gateways, doors, antechambers; rooms giving onto yet other rooms. In one of these the soldiers at last halted.

The place had, curiously, the look of a monk's cell. There was a prie-dieu of polished dark oak, a small table with a stack of bound books on it, and two wooden armchairs before the fire. What light there was came in by a single small window with many leaded panes. In the fireplace a few damp logs smouldered, giving off the barest glimmer of warmth, which nevertheless I was grateful for. Shutting off entirely the back wall, or so I thought, a faded tapestry depicted the slaying of Actaeon by his own hounds. Gazing at it, I felt a sudden pang of sympathy for the unfortunate hero horribly dying there, and I would not have been much surprised if the sentries had stood back now and a slavering pack of dogs had come bounding in to rend me to pieces. This vision, or hallucination, was so vivid that I think I must have been suffering still from the effects of whatever potion it was that had been put in the water I had drunk in that prison cell.

Time passed. The escort pair exchanged words in a language I did not recognise—I presumed it was Czech or some dialect of it—and laughed wheezingly into their fists. I watched them grimly, wondering if I and my likely fate were the object of the joke that was amusing them so. They loitered by the doorway in slovenly fashion, squeaking in their dully shining Spanish tunics and their hinged leather leggings. When a step sounded outside, however, they sprang to attention smartly enough.

The person who entered wore a black habit, all of a piece and reaching almost to the floor, so that at first I took him for a cleric of some kind, a priest or monk. He was tall and thin, a man all of angles, with a narrow face and a somewhat swarth complexion. He would have seemed the very essence of the ascetic but for his dark and darkly passionate eye and the carnal look of his mouth, which was scarlet-lipped, strikingly wide, and curved like a sickle.

He waved a hand in a dismissive gesture and the soldiers hurriedly withdrew, almost elbowing each other in their eagerness to be gone from the presence of that tall thin person in his long black robe. He did not so much as glance in my direction but crossed swiftly to the little table and fingered the books there, frowning and moving his lips without sound, like an actor silently rehearsing his lines. I waited; for all the man's seeming to ignore me, I had the impression of being circled about and sniffed at by a sleek and gleaming creature—a panther, say, or some such sinuous, burnished beast.

Now the man turned, giving an elaborate, histrionic start, as if he had just that moment noticed me standing there. He smiled, if a panther might be said to smile.

'So, Herr Doktor Stern,' he said, 'you have come amongst us at last!'

4

Once again I was put in mind of the clammy intimacy of the confessional. There was the man's priestly garb, there was the prie-dieu with its suggestion of penitential kneeling, there were the books on the table that might be the sacred tablets of ritual forgiveness and absolution. And there was the man himself, with his unctuous and softly suggestive manner.

He had brought forward one of the chairs and set it by the fire, inviting me, with a wide and almost comical swoop of his arm, to be seated, then had fetched the other chair and sat down himself. Now we were facing each other, and so close together that our knees were almost touching.

'My name, by the way,' he said, as if it were a matter of the least significance or interest, 'is Philipp Lang.'

He wore a flat black felt hat with four corners to it, somewhat like a cardinal's biretta; a ring on the middle finger of his left hand was set with a ruby the size of a thrush's egg. His hair under the hat was cut short in tight, gleaming black curls, like shavings of coal. He was still smiling.

Philipp Lang, or Lang von Langenfels, as he was pleased to style himself, was the Emperor Rudolf's chief man, all by his own making. He was also a liar, an extortionist and a shameless embezzler, yet he was untouchable, and remained so for a very long time, before eventually he fell. He had been brought up a Jew in the Prague ghetto, but had lost no time in renouncing his faith and converting to the Church of Rome. After early adventures that would have put any other man in chains, if not a noose, he had wriggled his way into the imperial court, where he found immediate favour with the Emperor. His Majesty took him on first as his valet, then brought him into his bed, for Rudolf, as all the world knows, had a taste for young men, especially when he was young himself. Soon it was that wherever the Emperor went, there, too, at his shoulder, Lang would be—the royal familiar, tall, slender, smiling, and robed habitually in black.

Lang's enemies, who were legion, charged that the former Jew was a sorcerer who held his imperial master in thrall with spells and potions supplied to him by demons. But whether by means of magic, buggery or both combined, the young man rose with smooth swiftness through the ranks of the royal household to attain at last the lofty and, as he made sure it should be, supreme position of Court Chamberlain, in power and influence far above even the likes of Felix Wenzel.

Half the court, the half he hadn't yet succeeded in winning over with bribes, threats or seduction, strove tirelessly to topple him. Countless conspiracies were mounted against him. Spies were set to spy on him, assassins were sent to assassinate him. Everything failed. The Chamberlain swept serenely through his days as if enclosed within a suit of impenetrable crystal armour, beyond the touch of all save those he deemed useful to him and his purposes.

His greed was boundless. From all who sought his patronage, and they included some of the closest among Rudolf's innermost circle, the Chamberlain extorted payment in large sums of gold, fine houses, parcels of land. He oversaw the collection of tithes and rents, and made of it another route to enrichment. By the time of his greatest days he had amassed a fabulous fortune in gold, along with vast properties and numerous profitable benefices throughout the empire.

And yet, for all his crimes and corruptions, he was possessed of a subtle and well-nigh irresistible charm. Only the most implacable among his foes were immune to his humorous and self-mocking way. *Yes, look at me,* he would seem to say, *look at me perched up here in this lofty place. Isn't it absurd? Who would have thought a ghetto Jew could scale such heights?*

As I was to find, I was no less susceptible than anyone else to his honeyed words and ways. When he sat down by the fire and laced his fingers before him and leaned forward, with that smile of his, it seemed to me that, far from menacing me with his panther's claws, the Chamberlain was brushing up against me, sleekly, sinuously, with soft, persuasive purrings.

Straight off, and with an expression of deep concern, he enquired as to my well-being. He was aware of the events of the night, he said, and gave a little grimace of regretful distaste. Had I been beaten by the soldiers, had my gaolers mistreated me? No? Ah, good, good. And what of my journey from Regensburg? Had that been difficult, in such harsh weather? I had braved the cold, I had surmounted all hurdles? He was glad, so glad to hear it.

'And what a shock it must have been, to find that poor young woman who had been so cruelly destroyed!'

From the start I had found myself responding to him with a fluency and ease that even I was surprised by.

Presently, and to my greater surprise, I moved on from immediate matters to speak of the general circumstances of my life. I heard myself telling him of my father the Prince-Bishop and my mother and her early death, of my foster-parents and their harsh and loveless ways. I spoke of the Gymnasium in Regensburg and of my studies there, and dwelled, at some length, on my happy years at Würzburg. I boasted of my love of learning and of my fascination with the alchemical arts, into the arcana of which, as I did not hesitate to assert, I had delved deeply, uncovering much that was valuable and an enhancement to my intellect.

By now the light in the room seemed brighter than it had been, the listless fire warmer, while the image of the fat sentry dangling like a sack of pork from the gibbet in that cold, blind yard had faded entirely from my thoughts.

At my mention of alchemy Lang's gleaming eye gleamed more darkly still, and while I expatiated on the subject he held me fixed with a keen, unblinking gaze, nodding rapidly and humming under his breath in what seemed a sympathetic accord, as if he, too, were a tireless plunger into the luminous abyss of beneficent magic.

He was leaning towards me more intently than ever now, his slender fingers still clasped before himself, as he hummed and nodded, nodded and hummed. The very air in the room seemed to quiver with the force of his interest and approval.

After a while, a silence fell, and I glanced aside, somewhat uneasily, into the palely smoking fire. Why had I allowed myself to gabble on at such length? Why had I revealed so much of myself? If this was the confessional, I had none of the shriven penitent's sense of relief and happy cleansedness.

I thought of the queer thing Lang had said when he had first turned to me with that actorly pretence of startlement.

What had he meant, addressing me as *Herr Doktor* and welcoming me as having *come amongst us at last*?

As if he had read my thoughts, the Chamberlain said now: 'Yes, we had been expecting you, although we did not know'—here there was the flash of another winning smile—'quite what you would be.'

He stood up from his chair in a sort of twisting leap and began to pace rapidly the narrow confines of the room, with short busy birdlike steps, rubbing his hands together. In time I would become accustomed to the man's abrupt, quick manner of movement.

'I should tell you,' he said, 'that His Majesty had a dream in which a spirit announced to him that a star would come from the west, a star sent by Christ Our Saviour himself. It would be a great good omen to the throne and, amongst many other fortunate tidings, a token of victory over the Turk.'

He spoke, it seemed to me, in a strange, declamatory fashion, over-loudly and with what seemed unnatural point and force. Sitting there while he paced and discoursed, I had the feeling of being the sole spectator, an audience of one, at a not particularly subtle piece of playacting.

Now he stopped by my chair and smiled down at me, his wide mouth stretching into a scarlet crescent, and said: 'From your name—Christian Stern—it seems that you must be that God-sent star, for how else should we interpret such a happy confluence, hmm?'

I gazed up at him in wonderment and alarm, at a loss as to how I should respond to such an extravagant, indeed such an absurd, notion.

Christian Stern: the star sent by Christ! Now I understood why Wenzel the High Steward had treated me with such suspicion and distrust, accusing me of lying about my name and where I had come from, as if I were claiming to be the new Messiah.

Lang remained on his feet for a moment, smiling down at me. He was amused, it was clear, by my wondering and bewildered look. Then, to my further astonishment, he winked—yes, winked, almost gaily—before briskly resuming his seat.

At that moment I seemed to feel the tapestry behind me stir and sway, as if it had been disturbed by a momentary breeze, a breeze of which I thought I heard the passing. Or perhaps it was not a breeze but a breath, a sort of falling sigh.

'Wenzel,' the Chamberlain said, leaning forward again, his smile giving way to a frown, 'Wenzel the High Steward should not have imprisoned you.' He had lowered his voice to a whisper, arching his eyebrows into two devilish points and nodding portentously. 'His Majesty'—this he didn't speak at all but mouthed mutely, stretching his vivid lips around the shapes of the words—'is displeased.'

My mind by now was in turmoil. What a little while ago, in that prison cell, in the depths of darkness, had seemed a waking nightmare of menace, pain and likely death, now in daylight had all at once become transformed into an enchanted fantasy, a fairy tale, it might be, in which I was as the lowly lad to whom the Emperor's emissary magically comes, amid the sound of bugles, bearing tidings of royal favour and the promise of limitless good fortune. What could it mean?

I was being tricked, I was sure of it. Lang and Wenzel had joined in a conspiracy against me, whereby Wenzel would bluster and threaten while Lang would charm and cajole. But to what end? What did they suspect me of? To what enormity did they imagine I might be persuaded to confess?

Lang rose again and went to the table and took up from it the pile of books, of which there were at least half a dozen. He came back with them and sat down in front of me as before. Setting the books on his lap, he laid his hands on them and fixed on me a long and, as it seemed to me, speculative look, although what it was he might be speculating on I could not guess. I had again that sense of being a spectator at a performance, of watching a playlet put on specially for me, the plot of which I could make no sense of.

The Chamberlain now began to pass the books to me one by one. Among them were *The Archidoxes of Magic*, by Philip von Hohenheim—better known as the sublime Dr Paracelsus—and a rare manuscript copy of Cornelius Agrippa's *De Occulta Philosophia*. There was the *Atalanta Fugiens* of Michael Maier; one of Galen's countless treatises on medicine; and last but most certainly not least, the Englishman John Dee's renowned *Monas Hieroglyphica*, in that fine first edition printed at Antwerp by Willem Silvius, a copy of which in the Gottfried library at the university in Würzburg I had for so long and sorely coveted.

As he handed over each volume, Lang put to me a set of questions concerning its contents and its author, aimed, obviously, at discovering if I was truly as well-read in alchemy and natural philosophy as I claimed to be. Fortunately I was familiar with all these works, save the Galen, but that was no more than a physician's handbook, commonplace and of little significance. I suspected that he had included it only as a decoy, hoping to lure me into overreaching myself by giving it an undue weight.

The Chamberlain himself was no expert on these

volumes or their authors, as was clear from the mechanical manner in which he had rattled off his list of rote-learned questions, and also the relief that was evident in his smile when the examination was concluded.

He took back the books and set them on the floor beside his chair, complimenting me on the breadth of my reading and my profound knowledge of a multitude of arcane matters. His left eyelid fluttered. Surely, I thought, I must be mistaken. Surely the man had not winked at me again.

'Such a show of learning is remarkable,' he said loudly and, again, with a forced and heavy emphasis, 'even in a scholar from—Würzburg, did you say?'

If this last was intended as a sally, I mean his pretence at having grandly forgotten the city's humble name, then it fell flat, and he frowned and sighed. His fingers were linked together again in front of him, so tightly that the knuckles had turned white; his smile, too, showed distinct signs of strain along its edges.

Now he unclasped his hands and shot up a finger, making a show of suddenly having remembered something. He reached inside his black robe and brought out a large circular gold object strung on a gold chain. 'You recognise this?' he asked.

Certainly I recognised it, and with a shock. It was the medallion I had seen the night before, attached to that same chain around the neck of Dr Kroll's murdered daughter.

'There is,' Lang said, 'a mechanism: see?' With his thumb he pressed a hidden spring and the Medusa's head, or the face of Phoebus Apollo, whichever it was meant to be, sprang open on a hinge, revealing a compartment filled to the brim with a paste of some kind, very fine and smooth and of a pinkish-brown tint.

Was this, I asked myself, yet another test, another insidious attempt to trip me up and make me reveal—what?

And how had he got hold of the medallion?

I was tired; my brain ached. What did this man, what did all these people, want from me? I felt as if I had been caught up in the workings of some terrible machine from which I would never be released.

Lang, gazing down at the medallion, was rocking himself back and forth in his chair, nodding again and making that humming sound, or more a sort of buzzing, at the back of his throat. 'This is a curious stuff,' he said, touching a fingertip lightly to the surface of the paste and leaving there a tiny, moistly gleaming hollow. 'It has been analysed in His Majesty's laboratories. The entire night was given over to the task.' He glanced up at me from under his brows, smiling his jester's thin-lipped, crimson smile. 'You know His Majesty keeps many scores of adepts here,' he said. 'They are constantly at work—alchemists, astrologers, doctors of medicine, natural philosophers such as yourself. He has a great faith in the chymical arts.'

He compressed his smiling lips yet more tightly and widened his eyes in what seemed a sort of mischievous merriment. 'It is a sorcerer's balsam,' he pronounced, pointing to the paste, 'compounded, if I recall the formula rightly, of red and white arsenic, dittany root, dried frog, a pinch of pearl and a flake of coral, a few grains of amber, all pounded together and mixed with gum tragacanth and dissolved in some rare oil. Oh, and there is also a dash of woman's menstruum'—once more he let his voice sink to the featheriest whisper—'perhaps that of young Mistress Kroll herself.'

He offered up the medallion on the palm of his hand. I leaned down and sniffed the paste; it had a flat, stale, yet slightly sweetish odour, rather like the smell of dead-flower water.

In other circumstances I would have laughed. I knew very well that what Lang had said was nonsense, that no matter how diligent or subtle the Emperor's chemists might be, they could not have dismantled into its constituent parts so intricate a mixture as Lang had claimed this one to be. It was, I guessed, nothing more than a simple paste made up of some element, alum or the like, finely ground, with an admixture of attar of roses, that old standby, with a few common spices thrown in—in other words, the kind of harmless potion that a girl anxious to win over her lover could get for half a groat from a village apothecary.

I sat back on the chair, frowning at my hands. What was I to say—that the Emperor's chemists had gulled him with their talk of pearl and coral, of dittany and dried frog and all the rest?

'Likely it's a prophylactic of some kind,' Lang said, 'a nostrum against the plague, or the pox, or'—this again he mouthed almost silently—'an unlooked-for conception.'

'Yes,' I said slowly, 'it's possible, yes. Yet I wonder—I wonder if the Emperor's chemists have not . . . well, if they have not exaggerated, somewhat.'

Lang's eyes widened and he put a finger quickly to his lips. 'Ssh!' he said softly, and then assumed again his former loud, assertive tone. 'Oh, I think not,' he almost shouted. 'I'm sure their analysis is correct.'

'Yet I must say I doubt it,' I persisted. 'It seems to me it is no more than—'

'Ahem!' the Chamberlain exclaimed, giving me a hard, admonishing stare. He clicked the medallion shut and stowed it away inside his habit. 'Let us say no more of it.'

Picking up the stack of books from the floor, he rose and crossed the room and set them back on the table. Then he stopped, and stood quite still, with his eyes cast upwards and moving his lips silently.

Again at my back there was that breath of something, that faint, lapsing sigh, and again the tapestry seemed to sway.

Lang turned quickly then, his black robe swishing. Fixing on me with his dark stare he declaimed: 'You are requested to do the Emperor the honour of abandoning your plan to travel on to Dresden—it was Dresden you said you were bound for, yes?—and instead to remain here in Prague, at His Majesty's pleasure. You shall have accommodation, of course, and an allowance from the privy purse—the details we shall look to later. So: what do you say? I emphasise'—his tone grew heavier and more hortatory still—'that it is His Majesty's express wish to have you remain and bide here amongst us, Herr Doktor Christian Stern.'

A moment passed. Lang, posing by the table, his head lifted and his nostrils flared, was staring at me expectantly. Tongue-tied and floundering, I looked back at him, and said nothing. What could I say? My mind was aswirl.

In the fireplace a smouldering log emitted a thin derisory piping note.

Lang abruptly abandoned his histrionic pose and came and loomed over me. In exasperated dumbshow he urged me, as it seemed, to say something, rolling his eyes and making scooping gestures with his hands, as if to draw the words up out of me. But what words?

I tried to rise from my chair but he prevented me, pressing two fingers on my shoulder. 'Speak!' he commanded.

I ran my tongue over my lips, which had gone dry as paper. 'If,' I said, hesitantly, 'if it is His Majesty's wish, then of course I cannot but stay.'

'Good!' Lang cried, with a fierce, false smile and giving his head a great upwards toss. 'Good, good, good.'

Another silence followed. We remained as we were, in a kind of tableau, I seated and the Chamberlain leaning over me with a sort of devilish, exalted smile, his eyebrows arched. Could I really believe that the Emperor had expressed the wish that I should stay in Prague, on the strength merely of a wisp of a dream? And what of the murdered young woman, with whose death the Chamberlain seemed so little concerned?

I heard a sound then: it was distinctly the sound of a door opening and softly closing.

I twisted about on the chair and stared at the tapestry behind me. It was not, I realised, hanging against a wall, as I had thought, but was suspended from what seemed the middle of the ceiling. It was there to act as a curtain, separating off another part of the room and making a secret chamber of it, where someone, some third person, had been in hiding all this time, hiding and listening.

The Chamberlain, having heard the sound, too, puffed out his cheeks and blew through comically flapping lips a long sigh of wearied relief. He was all at once a different man; he had stepped down from the stage.

'Well well, Herr Doktor,' he said, with a new expression now, one of glinting, spiteful disdain. 'I hope you are gratified to have gained so easily'—he gestured towards the tapestry—'the Emperor's ear.'

5

And so, amid such drama, tumult and outlandish pantomime, began my sojourn in the Capital of Magic. Sometimes I wonder if when I was there I was among human beings at all, or if what I took for men were only their simulacra, a host of speaking and breathing automata, conjured up at his command by Rudolf's sorcerers, fantastically humanised versions of the manikins and marionettes that danced and twitched in darkened booths on every street corner at festivals and on market days, in that city of masks and make-believe. When I look back on those days, it seems to me I might have imagined it all. Yet how readily at the time I took for granted my great good fortune, saying to myself that Fate had surely smiled on me. Had not the very thing I had aimed for in coming to Prague—the favour of the Emperor Rudolf and an entry into his court—had it not been granted to me, overnight, in the winking, as it might be, of His Majesty's Chamberlain's eye? True, this wonderful stroke of good fortune had come about not through any action on my own part, but solely by the chance of my name being what it was. But what is chance, I ask, and what do we know of how the heavens may direct our lives?

In Rudolf's Prague I was to encounter all manner of signs and portents of impending wonders. The first and not the least of these, I considered, was that I was to live in, of all places, Golden Lane.

Yes, Golden Lane! It was there, at the end of that baffling

inquisition played out by Chamberlain Lang, that I found myself once more, in daylight this time, being conducted to a little house, one of a row, with two square windows on either side of a narrow front door. Here it was that, at the Chamberlain's direction, I was to be lodged. A walk of but ten paces along the lane would bring me to the spot where, the night before, I had stumbled on the corpse of Magdalena Kroll. Was I to believe it was mere happenstance that had brought me back there, to the very place where all these remarkable happenings had their beginning, and that I shouldn't take it for an omen, and a favourable one, at that?

But for all that my fortunes had been so magically reversed, I was bewildered still. My mind was a compass: on one side of the dial there was Felix Wenzel, on the other Chamberlain Lang, though the needle, for all its fluttering, would point in one direction only, towards the phantom presence hiding in its little closed-off chamber behind that deceptive tapestry, in front of which I had, that momentous morning, so innocently and all unknowingly sat.

Could it really be, I asked myself again, that His Majesty had dreamed of me, or of some prevision of me, as Lang assured me he had, and taken the dream for a portent of good fortune? It seemed too fanciful, even for one so famously fanciful as the Emperor Rudolf. But maybe it was true: after all, what spark of light from the celestial sphere might not have struck through a window chink and lit upon the royal brow and ignited there the notion of the imminent coming of a Christ-sent star? And who was to say that I, Christian Stern, was not indeed the starry messenger whom Rudolf had foreseen in his sleep? I have always considered the appearance of things to be no more than a gauzy veil behind which a truer reality is covertly and marvellously at work.

My house in Golden Lane was a house in name only, consisting as it did of a single, not very large, low-sized room, with a sleeping-couch in one corner, two chairs, a tiled stove and a fireplace, and a table to work at. There was a cramped scullery off to one side, and an alcove with a hanging piece of unbleached canvas, behind which stood a wood-framed cackstool with a china pot set into the seat of it. The place was all frontage, since it was backed up against the ramparts of the castle. With the walls being white-washed, or better say grey-washed, and with those windows like eye sockets and the door for a mouth, I felt as if I had been set down inside a hollowed-out death's-head.

But of course I did not mind any of this—what matter the conditions of my habitation?—for I was on fire with excitement and eager anticipation. Such things I would do here, of whatever sort they might be, such marvels I would achieve, in this bone-coloured cell! For surely it was true—you see how quickly my doubts were quelled?—surely I was indeed the Emperor's chosen one, the brightest star shining in the imperial firmament. So what if Rudolf was half cracked and given to the wildest delusions? Let him be as mad as the man in the moon, for all I cared.

Prague! Yes, I was in Prague, and the Holy Roman Emperor himself had prophesied my coming.

The cat was another portent. One day I opened my door and he walked in, swiping his flank against my leg in a cursory caress. He was a big black tom with a malignant green gaze. He had a deep scar on his forehead, and the tip of his tail was missing. I could see by the look of him, as he nosed about the room in that fastidious way cats have, that he meant to stay. I called him Plato. He was a good mouser, but lazy. He liked nothing better than to see me at work and would crouch on the corner of my desk with his paws tucked in, purring like a soft engine, studying me intently as I laboured over my books.

The chief agitation I was prey to, now that the first frights and fanfares were past, was a hardly governable impatience. Once already I had been within touching distance of the Emperor—twice, if I were to believe that it was the face of Rudolf himself, and not a fantastical vision of him, that I had seen looming over me as I lay in a drugged stupor in that prison cell. And I had no doubt at all that it was indeed Rudolf who had been listening behind the tapestry, as Philipp Lang had given me to understand at the end of his extravagant performance. The inevitable consequence of all this, I was certain, could be nothing other than an imminent direct audience with His Imperial Majesty.

This expected encounter I rehearsed in my mind, over and over, throughout those first hours, there in my unexpectedly acquired quarters, that sudden place of shelter and calm, in Golden Lane. Yet when it came, that meeting face to face with the Emperor, the circumstances were such that I could not have anticipated.

I had paid the potboy to cart my things from the Blue Elephant, and since I was famished now, with nothing in my belly save the painfully persistent memory of the mouldy lump of bread I had consumed in my gaol cell in the dawn hours, I took out my purse and gave him another coin from my father the Bishop's bounty and sent him back to the inn to fetch something hot for me to eat.

I paced and paced. How hard it is to think calmly of kings!

Presently the boy returned, bringing a dish of mutton stew covered with a muslin cloth, along with a flask of wine. He also brought a message from the innkeeper, saying that since I had not paid for my room, and since I had been the object and cause of a violent disturbance in the night that had led the other guests to complain, he would keep my horse in lieu of recompense. I was not much upset by this, for it would save me the cost of livery, and the poor brute was half dead anyway.

For the boy's final task before he left I had him light the stove, or attempt to light it, since it was no easy thing, the tinder being damp and the flint resistant. In the end, after two or three failed attempts, he succeeded in getting a half-hearted flame going, but he had no sooner departed, jingling my money in his pocket and mounted on that old forfeited jade of mine, than it sputtered out, leaving me to shiver in the cold again.

I sat down at the table to eat, taking a chair in front of one of the two low windows that gave onto the lane. The stew had cooled by now, and the meat, as I soon discovered, was rancid. I poured a mug of the purple wine, and so fuddled and weary was I that the first few mouthfuls of the drink made me feel thoroughly light-headed.

The muslin napkin that the bowl had been covered with, a dainty thing, I took as a subtle token of remembrance from the innkeeper's wife. Thinking of her and her come-hither eye, and of her unspoken offer, which I had rashly spurned, I could not prevent myself falling into a melancholy reverie.

Again there came to my mind, try as I would to fend it off, the image of the fat sentry strung up on the gibbet like a boar's carcass in a sack.

What had the fellow done to merit summary execution? Was it only that he had seen the dead young woman in the snow? Had the mere fact of having been a witness to her slaughtered state been enough to get him hanged? If so, there was no doubt I would have shared the gallows with him, had it not been for the Emperor's prophetic dream.

That my neck had been saved by a night-time fantasy was, I acknowledged, either miracle or madness, and most likely the latter. Whichever it was, I had no reason to think the royal dreamer might not come to his senses at any moment and hang me, too, if for no other reason than that of my being an impostor. The wine forced me to look at my circumstances without seeking to delude myself: pretend though I might, I knew, in the depths of my heart, that I was no Christ-sent star.

These gloomy ruminations, along with the bad mutton, robbed me of my appetite, and I pushed the dish of stew away uneaten. Globules of congealing fat floated on the surface of the tepid gravy, and by a tenuous association they brought back to me another memory, of Chamberlain Lang touching his fingertip to the sickly-smelling paste inside Magdalena Kroll's gold medallion and making a little indentation there, a little smooth hollow, like a baby's navel. Somehow the tiny gesture seemed to me another portent, a portent not of good fortune this time but, on the contrary, of some unforeseeable, dire eventuality.

At that moment I looked to the window and, with a jolt, saw there a man's large, pale face looming in the glass, no more than an arm's length away from me. He was regarding me with an intent and candid gaze. He had a queer expression, sceptical, it might be, or outright disdainful, although he was smiling, his pale lips pursed and twisted up at one side. He wore a conical black hat with a broad, circular brim.

I couldn't understand how it was that we were at eye level, this fellow and I, since I was sitting down and the window was low. Was he kneeling on the cobbles, or crouching by the window ledge in some awkward fashion, in order to have a better view of me and what I was about?

In a flurry of indignation I jumped up and crossed quickly to the door. I stepped into the lane, thinking to challenge the brazen fellow and send him off about his business with a cuff and a kick.

He turned and greeted me quite calmly, with a show of courtly grace, sweeping off his elaborate black hat and making a low bow. 'Good day to you, sir,' he said.

He was a dwarf.

I returned his greeting uncertainly, looking him up and down. He bore my scrutiny in a tolerant and even prideful manner, with that same cold, twisted-up smile.

'I am sent by His Majesty,' he said.

'Oh,' I said. 'I see.'

He was a singular creature indeed, and an unlikely imperial emissary. From crown to waist he looked a normal man—in fact, he was impressively burly, with broad shoulders and a fine stout chest—but below that he was all contorted and gnarled, with stunted legs, thick-thighed above and tapered below, like the nether parts of a mandrake root. He had a well-shaped head, and his shiny black hair was drawn smoothly back over his skull, like a helmet moulded out of pitch. His eyes were as green as glass.

We stood regarding each other, I at the door and he still by the window. Flakes of snow fluttered about us, falling and rising like mayflies. The dwarf's look had turned to one of cold amusement and faint but unconcealed contempt; it was as if it were not he but the world that was deformed.

'It is cold, sir, is it not?' he said pointedly.

'Forgive me,' I stammered hastily. 'Please, step inside.'

'Why, thank you,' he said, with sarcasm, and bowed again, holding his hat aside in one hand and making with the fingers of his other that elaborate twirling and tumbling gesture from chin to breast that courtiers do. The whole performance had about it, to my eye, a deliberate show of mockery.

He came forward, I stood aside, and he stepped past me. I would say he swaggered, except that his way of walking was so awkward, and so painful to behold, as he lurched and swayed, leaning heavily on an ebony cane with a gold knob for a handle.

His name, he announced, was Jeppe Schenckel.

Once we were inside, and I had shut the door on the swirling snow, he paused for a moment to look about, making no attempt to hide his curiosity. He seemed at once to take note of everything—or, rather, I should say, of how little of everything there was, for the only indication that I was in residence was an untidy mound of my things, clothes and books and the like, where the potboy had deposited them unceremoniously on the low bed.

'I must say,' Jeppe Schenckel remarked with a sniff, 'it is not much warmer in here than it was outside.'

I told him how the stove had been lit but then had gone out, and to my amazement he put down his hat and went at once to the hearth. He squatted and busied himself with flint and steel, and in a matter of moments he had the flames going again, vigorously this time.

Having been at first disconcerted by the fellow's lordly

manner, I watched him now in thorough bemusement as he squatted there at the stove on his haunches. I would not despise or mock a man for his deformities—after all, even the most comely of mortals is far short of godlike—but as I contemplated this malformed creature I could not but marvel at mankind's inexhaustible variousness. The Gnostics held that the world was created by a demiurge, a sort of imp, whose mischievous delight it is to twist men's destinies out of true, and often I find myself thinking that they were right.

Satisfied that the tinder had taken, the dwarf laid a log of limewood on the flames. He shut the door of the stove and, brushing motes of ash from his hands, came to the table and clambered onto a chair, cocking one stubby leg over the other. I said that I regretted having nothing to offer him—the stew by now had grown a cold grey skin all over its surface—and when I held up the flask he shook his head, saying with a prim frown that he did not drink wine and never had.

He sat there before me, displaying a marked daintiness of manner and elegance of gesture, despite his ill-shaped form. He was very pale, with skin of a waxen transparency, against which his eyebrows darkly gleamed. He was dressed in costly fashion, in a suit of black velvet, with silvery lace at wrists and throat. In the crepuscular light of the already dimmening afternoon, I felt myself at once drawn to and repelled by this finical and strangely self-assured, misshapen manling.

Could it really be that he had been sent by the Emperor? And if he had been, what was his mission? I longed to ask for enlightenment, but the calm collectedness with which he comported himself prevented me.

Snowflakes were crowding greyly against the window-panes. I filled my mug again from the flask, which, to my vague surprise, I noticed was almost empty. I was weary still after the turbulence of the night, and the wine was putting me half in a daze, and before I knew it I had launched again, with a thick tongue this time and much effortful blinking, upon the rambling story of myself and my origins and all my lofty achievements.

Why I was so ready to repeat it all I don't know. Perhaps I wished to affirm something of myself against the puzzles and uncertainties I had been stumbling among since my arrival in the city; or, more likely, I was just nervous. The dwarf took it all in with quick little nods and a faintly weary, faintly impatient smile, as if none of it were new to him. That was his way, as I would discover: it pleased him, in the intensity of his defiant vanity, to give the impression that no one could tell him anything he did not know already, that everything he heard was merely a confirmation of facts he had already in his possession, and which anyway he considered of little interest or value, to him, at least.

Afterwards, when I sobered up and came to myself again, I bitterly regretted having indulged in so much wine-tainted tattle and braggadocio. I had the feeling that I had parted with something I would have been well advised to safeguard and withhold—not merely the legend of my life so far, which was no great marvel, but, more importantly, some part of my essential self. And Jeppe Schenckel—perched there before me, sardonic and majestically at ease, with his big hands folded on the knob of his cane—had plucked it up deftly and stowed it away, neatly folded, in an inner recess of his elegant velvet jerkin.

'So,' he said now, 'you are the new star over Prague.'

I was shocked by such a blunt and knowing reference to the Emperor's dream of my coming. Perhaps the fellow had not been sent by Rudolf at all; perhaps he was an agent of Chamberlain Lang or, worse, of Felix Wenzel, set to spy on me and report back to whichever of the two was his master. Or perhaps he was the agent of some other persons unknown, whom I had not encountered yet but who knew of me and were eager to know more. It seemed to me that I was in a hall of mirrors, turning this way and that and seeing myself from unexpected, unlooked-for and alarming angles.

The dwarf glanced about the room again, smiling in that crooked way of his and nodding a little, like one revisiting scenes familiar to him from of old. 'I trust, sir,' he said, 'that you're aware of what an honour it is to have been housed here.'

'An honour?' I said, turning a doubtful eye upon the cramped and bare little room.

The dwarf drew back his head and lifted his eyebrows in a show of exaggerated surprise. 'Did they not tell you,' he said, 'that this was where the English magus Dr John Dee was housed when he first came to Prague?' He smiled thinly, gratified by what was no doubt my expression of frank astonishment. 'Yes,' he went on, 'the great Dr Dee lodged here while awaiting the arrival of his family and before moving on to grander accommodation in the Old Town. What wondrous works these walls must have witnessed, eh, what rare spells they must have heard intoned, even in the short time the illustrious magus was here.'

A chill dampness had sprung up on my forehead and on my upper lip. It was truly as if a spirit had appeared before me in the room, a luminous apparition, majestic and awe-inspiring. Although his reputation nowadays is somewhat tarnished, John Dee in his great days was one of the world's most renowned men of learning, an expert in natural philosophy, a master alchemist, mathematician and astronomer. He was the foremost authority on the teachings of the ancient Egyptian high priest Hermes Trismegistus and was steeped in the mysteries of the Cabala; he spoke regularly with angels; he had been for many years the Queen of England's most trusted and valued magician. That he had dwelled in this place, in this modest little house, I took as yet another augury of the momentous future that lay ahead of me there in Prague.

John Dee—why, I thought, he might have sat upon the very chair where I was seated now! The thought made my young self tremble inwardly for awe.

The dwarf was regarding me with the same queer, speculative and loftily amused expression that he had worn when I had first looked up and seen the creature peering in at me through the window. Had he known John Dee? If so, there were a thousand questions I would dearly have wished to put to him.

By now he had moved on to another matter. 'Do you know who she was,' he asked, 'that person whose cold corpse you found here in the lane last night?'

That gave me a further start of surprise. Yes, I thought, sweating the harder, yes, for sure, he must be an agent of Wenzel or of Philipp Lang. 'I know that her name was Magdalena Kroll,' I said, feeling like a man making his way carefully forward over a sheet of ice of doubtful firmness. 'I also know, because I was told so, that she was the daughter of Dr Ulrich Kroll, the Emperor's physician.'

Even as I was saying this, the dwarf was nodding his big smooth head with impatient dismissiveness.

'Yes yes,' he said, 'but are you aware of *what* she was?'

God knows why, but on the instant I clearly saw before my mind's eye an image of the medallion the dead young woman had worn around her neck, and that Chamberlain Lang had now in his possession; I saw, too, the lozenge of smooth paste it contained, and the little gleaming dent that the Chamberlain's fingertip had made in it. The mind has its own motives, and hides them from us.

'No,' Jeppe Schenckel said, with a smug twinkle, 'I see that you do not know.' He uncrossed his thumb-like little legs. 'But I can tell you: before she was anything else at all, she was the Emperor's mistress.'

6

Despite the general fuzziness induced in me by the wine, as well as the adventures I had endured since coming to Prague, I had now the sensation of something loosening and then sharply settling, as if the mechanism of my understanding, like the oiled tumblers inside a lock, had relaxed and suddenly disengaged. Now I knew why the soldiers had been sent to the Blue Elephant to apprehend me; why Wenzel had questioned me so relentlessly; why Chamberlain Lang had smiled at me with what had seemed such peculiar intent, arching his dark eyebrows in that cautioning way. Now I knew what had so alarmed the sentry when he recognised the corpse sprawled in the snow, and probably, too, why the poor wretch had been so summarily dragged to the gibbet.

The Emperor's mistress had been murdered, and the world had been taken hold of and turned upon its head.

The dwarf, I could see, was silently laughing at me, savouring spitefully my renewed look of reeling surprise and shock.

'Yes,' he said. 'His Majesty's latest little plaything, cruelly dispatched.'

After scrambling down from the chair, he asked to be shown the place where I had discovered the corpse. I rose and put on my beaver coat and my old fur hat and led the way out into the lane. The snow had stopped again, leaving in its wake a vast, hollow hush. We turned to the left and walked along until we reached the patch of ground that by now had taken on for me the aspect of a profane shrine—a place of execution, of ritual sacrifice.

We stopped, and the dwarf stood leaning on his stick, gazing at the spot I pointed out to him, and nodding slowly with his lips pursed.

Small fragments of frozen blood, like shards of rubious glass, were scattered about, and there were scraps of velvet ripped from the young woman's gown that had been stuck fast to the cobbles when she was plucked up roughly by the night watch and carted away.

'Well, she's not the first wench to die in Golden Lane,' the dwarf said, in his offhand fashion, 'and likely she will not be the last.' I told him how her throat had been all torn as if by an animal, and he nodded again. 'He must have been playing with her,' he said, with a strange, strained frown.

He turned away and set off along the lane, heading in the direction of the castle. I hurried after him.

'Master Schenckel,' I said, 'you tell me that you are from the Emperor. May I ask if he sent you to me personally, and if so, to what purpose?'

This he ignored, as if I had not spoken. In the time I spent at Rudolf's court I came to recognise a trait common to all courtiers, which was the distracted way they had of seeming always to be trying to overhear something that was being said just out of earshot. For the most part what they couldn't quite hear was being said only in their over-heated imaginations; nevertheless they seemed unable to rid themselves of the conviction that somewhere, and probably somewhere quite close by, people were whispering to each other secrets of immense significance and import.

They were all the same, all infected with a wandering attention, Felix Wenzel and Philipp Lang and their like, and even this poor cripple, stumping along on his stick. Their interest was always in part elsewhere, and these were the signs: when you were speaking to them they would hold their faces somewhat averted, their heads slightly inclined, until you managed to say or do something that suddenly drew their full attention. Then they would rotate their heads slowly, dragging themselves unwillingly away from the conspiratorial hubbub they could not quite hear, and peer at you in a dazed and puzzled sort of way, blinking like tortoises.

This careless and disdainful affectation made me at first indignant, but then it came to be only amusing. Sometimes I almost felt sorry for them, the distracted ones, thinking how exhausting for them such constant, anxious vigilance must be. A time would come, of course, when I would be forced ruefully to acknowledge that they were wise where I was foolish, for if I had attended more carefully to what was going on and what was being said around me, in quiet corners and behind half-closed doors, I might have saved myself a great deal of trouble and pain. But, then, most things in life are learned too late, and wisdom, if it comes at all, comes tardily.

So we walked on in silence, the dwarf and I.

There had been a slight thaw earlier but now it was freezing again, and wisps of snow were strewn among the cobbles, like tatters of soiled white ribbon. I feared that the dwarf might miss his footing and take a tumble on the icy ground, but despite the unhandiness of his gait he was as loosely agile as an ape. What a strange thing he looked, in his coat of dark velvet and his broad-brimmed pointed

64

black hat and those short thick twisted limbs on which he lurched and lumbered. If man and the macrocosm are mirrored in each other, as the mystical Platonists assert, what sort of a world would it be that Jeppe Schenckel represented?

As we went along, he related how the Emperor had set his eye on Dr Kroll's handsome young daughter one night at a banquet at the castle, and had taken her straightway to his bed. 'She was already betrothed,' he said, 'but of course that counted for nothing. The young man in question, Jan Madek by name, an impetuous and foolish fellow, set up a great cry of protest when he heard that his girl had been snatched from him, and went about the town complaining bitterly of His Imperial Majesty. In the end he made off, taking with him a hoard of valuables belonging to the girl's father—among them an iron strongbox in which were locked away a sheaf of magical texts, so it's said, which the Emperor had sorely wished to have for himself. Meantime Mistress Caterina Sardo, His Majesty's concubine and mother of his ill-gotten brood of bastards, is compelled to turn a blind eye. Or was so compelled, I should say, since the Kroll girl is now conveniently dead, and all is well.'

We went on some paces, and then the dwarf chuckled. 'They whisper at court that it was La Sardo who cut her rival's throat,' he said. 'But why would she do the deed herself when she had executioners at hand to call upon?' He gave me a sly glance and again laughed softly. 'It is a dark world you have ventured into, Master Stern. You will need a strong light to guide you through it.'

Was he offering himself, I wondered, as the one to go before me holding the lantern aloft? But if he was to be my guide, he could begin at least by saying where he was leading me.

We gained the top of Hradčany Hill, and went round by the towering walls of the cathedral and crossed the broad paved way in front of the Royal Palace. In its pomp and splendour the palace seemed to me magnificent beyond any such edifice I had ever beheld, even at Würzburg. I had often tried to imagine Prague and its glories, but the reality of it was grander and more gracious than anything I could have dreamed of.

Past the castle, we stopped on the height there to look out over the city. The sky was white and the air was draped with a freezing mist, pierced by many spires, all of them appearing black in that pervasive icy miasma. Despite the wintry murk, I could see the river and its bridges and, beyond, the clock tower in the Old Town Square.

'Ah, Prague, Prague, look at you!' the dwarf said, shaking his head and sighing. He might have been gazing upon an erstwhile lover who had once been young and fair but had by now grown old and feeble. 'The centre of the world!' At this he chuckled again.

We walked down into the narrow streets of Kleinseite, and the dwarf again spoke of the magus John Dee, and of Dee's partner in magic, the rascally crystal-gazer Edward Kelley, an Irishman and a notorious fraud. Schenckel had many curious incidents and escapades to recount of this ill-matched pair. He told of the scandalous pact that Kelley had forced on the deluded and unfortunate Dee whereby—supposedly on the urgings of an angel-spirit, Madimi by name, whom Dee himself had conjured—the two men were to share between them everything they possessed.

'This included, of course, their spouses,' the dwarf said,

'for Dee's wife was young, and charming to look at, and Kelley lusted after her. Foolishly the doctor agreed to the pact, with the result that Kelley sired a son on Mistress Dee, a child that her husband, to save face, was obliged to bring up as his own.'

I could not fail to note how the dwarf savoured these juicy titbits, lingering over them with relish, while yet keeping up a tone of pious reprehension, pursing his blood-less lips at one side and sniffing in sham disapproval. Despite myself I could not but be entertained and amused by the fellow's sharp tongue and spiteful humour.

'They were necromancers, of course, the pair of them,' he said, with another sniff, 'and practisers of the black arts, however much they denied it. Dee, besides, was sending back secret dispatches to the English Queen and Walsing-ham, her master of spies—oh, yes, indeed, I know it for a fact—and is lucky to have kept his head on his shoulders. The Emperor thought much of him for a time, but soon saw through his wiles and his sinister ways.'

Jeppe Schenckel, it was plain, had been no admirer of the venerable Dr Dee. I, of course, could hardly believe my ears to hear this legendary scholar spoken of with such dis-respectful, sardonic amusement.

'As for Kelley,' the dwarf went on, 'the fellow rose high only to suffer a plunge all the deeper. And plunge he did: you know His Majesty had him imprisoned twice, and twice he attempted escape and twice fell down from the high window of his prison cell and broke a leg? A different leg each time, unfortunately—or fortunately, depending on how one looks at the matter.' He laughed softly, rolling his big shoulders in happy enjoyment at the thought of the mountebank's misfortunes.

'Yet still he lives on, seemingly unkillable, locked away in a dungeon high on the wall of Castle Hněvín at Most, which is far enough away from Prague but not so far that he cannot be kept an eye on. They say he's engaged in writing a voluminous treatise on the Philosopher's Stone, which he intends to dedicate to the Emperor and in that way worm his way back into the royal favour and secure his release.' Again that soft, malicious laugh. 'If he does hope for mercy, I fear he will be disappointed. Once His Majesty is done with you, you are done with. Which is a thing, young master'—he gave me another sly glance—'that you would do well to keep in mind.'

A dog all skin and bone appeared out of an alleyway and approached us, leering and pitifully cringing, but the dwarf brandished his stick and drove it away. 'Prague is a city of dogs,' he said, with a scowl. 'I would have them all destroyed, except that the Emperor thinks them possessed of magical powers and protects them.'

We walked on. I must say, I reprehend and distrust any man who would needlessly mistreat an animal: the one who kicks a dog would as soon kick me.

'You know that Kelley has no ears?' Schenckel said. 'They were clipped off him long ago, in England, for being a counterfeiter of coin. Now he wears his hair long enough to cover the scars. What a rogue he is. He would still be a spy, had he the freedom for it. He connives even yet with all sorts of conspirators, according to the Chamberlain'— he smirked at me—'Herr Lang, your friend and patron, that is. They say young Madek, too, had secret dealings with him.'

Here was yet another mention of Jan Madek, whom Magdalena Kroll had spurned in favour of the Emperor and whom High Steward Wenzel had dubbed a renegade. I wished to know more of him, but when I enquired, the dwarf, as I expected, pretended not to hear. He was an inveterate pretender, as I would come to learn. He liked to give one to believe that he carried a store of secret knowledge, to which he alone was privy, though at first I thought it all a show.

Now he stopped to glance in at the window of an inn; evidently he was quite the looker-in at windows, this strange, maimed little man.

'Dr Kroll travelled out to Most and questioned Kelley,' he went on, squinting in an effort to see through the thick bottle-glass panes. 'It seems His Majesty suspects that Kelley somehow came into possession of that strongbox with all Kroll's accumulated magic in it. A lot of foolishness, needless to say—Kelley is a spent force.'

Schenckel's mention of Dr Kroll prompted me to press him to elaborate on the Emperor's infatuation with the good doctor's daughter, thinking I might by that means learn more of Madek and why the High Steward Wenzel had been so interested in him. The only response I got, however, was a remote and faintly irritated stare, as if I were standing annoyingly in the way of someone or something of far more consequence.

Having come down now to the lowest level of Kleinseite, the dwarf and I set off across the Stone Bridge. I enquired again as to where it was we were going, but again was ignored. No doubt I should have persisted, perhaps should even have turned on my heel and left him to go on alone to wherever it was he was bent. But curiosity will win out over indignation every time, or at least that is certainly the case with me.

A frozen river, I always think, is an uncanny phenomenon, a violation somehow of the laws of nature. As I looked down from the bridge at the scarred and splintered surface of the Vltava, I imagined the titanic struggle that had gone on, since the onset of winter, between the surging flow of water and the irresistible frost, a struggle the end of which was this broad expanse of ice stretching from bank to bank and up and down for as far as the eye could see. It seemed to me now, as I gazed upon it, the very emblem of death and of dying. I thought of Magdalena Kroll, after her throat had been torn open and she had been let drop from the assassin's grasp, lying there in the snow, her consciousness quieted for ever but her body still straining, creaking, her very flesh inwardly groaning, fighting with all its failing strength against the encroaching cold, until at last it could fight no more and her life's quickness ceased and all went rigid.

I shivered. The mist was filling my chest with a wet, icy heaviness.

By now the effects of the wine that the potboy had brought to me had worn off—how much I drank in those first days in Prague, I who up to then had been, of necessity if not by inclination, so moderate in everything!—and I was again impatient to know where we were going. For it was clear we were not strolling idly, as it might have seemed at first: we were bound, in however roundabout and lackadaisical a fashion, towards some definite destination, of that I was sure. My heart sank. What new challenge might await me, what further baffling interrogation might even now be in preparation? Jeppe Schenckel still would reveal nothing, and when I asked for the third time, with a marked sharpness, where it was he was leading me, he turned aside yet again in a pretence of bland distraction.

We had reached the other side of the bridge, and there we entered the Old Town. Once more I was filled with wonder at the handsome aspect of the buildings and the broad sweep of the many streets leading into that vast and noble central square. I stopped to gaze up at the bristling spires of the Týn church vanishing on high into the mist, while at my back the clock in the bell tower of the Old Town Hall began sounding the hour, the chimes rolling across the square, like enormous slow bronze hoops.

It was market day, and the place was thronged with towns-folk, and there was a medleyed clamour of merchants crying their wares and customers haggling, and animals lowing and the squeals and squeaks of a bagpipe band, while over all, in the tremulous air, there floated a trans-parent, dun-coloured cloud composed of dung smoke and the breath of human beings and animals and the steam from their warm flesh. I thought, What a thing a great city is! and I shivered again a little, this time not from cold but in wonderment yet again at the fact of being where I was, here, in Prague, at the centre not merely of the world, as the dwarf had sneeringly said, but of the universe itself, or so it seemed to me.

When at length I left off gaping slack-jawed at the impos-ing and busy scenes around me, and looked to find what had become of the dwarf, I could see him nowhere.

I was glad, at first, to think myself rid of him. Then I spied him wheeling into one of the little cobbled streets that meander away behind the Týn Kirche, an unmistak-able black figure dragging itself along, like a bat with a broken wing. I hesitated. Why should I not let the fellow go—what was he to me? But of course my interest had been too sharply piqued already, and the next moment I

71

found myself elbowing my way through the crowd and hurrying down the narrow street where I had seen him disappear.

I soon caught up with him, and was not surprised when he barely graced me with a glance. On he went, with me in his wake, telling myself what a fool I was to be trailing him obediently like this and yet unable to make myself fall back. Skitters of snow were dancing zigzag through the sombre air, and the daylight was so dim by now that lamps were being lit already in the windows of the taverns.

I overtook him again as we passed under the balcony of one of the houses, where a woman in a soiled petticoat leaned out and called down to him. He pretended not to hear her, and she gave a raucous laugh, and spat after him. How must it be to be him? I wondered. His broad pale face showed only blank indifference. I pictured him young, a little boy littler than all the rest. I saw him wheeled around by a ring of screaming children twice his size, like a bear cub baited by a pack of slavering hounds, with no way of escape, weeping tears of rage and shame and already plotting his revenge upon the world. Is it only hindsight that gives such a glare of significance to that first venture of mine down from the castle heights into the dark heart of the city, following blindly in the wake of that ill-favoured creature? Or did I know, by some access of insight, by some grim premonition, how large this little man would loom in my life?

Now he stopped again abruptly—he was a great one for stops and starts, for veerings and vanishings and sudden reappearings, like a conjurer's monkey—and I stopped with him.

We had come to the tall door of a fine broad high-built

house. The windows were heavily barred, which gave to the place a sequestered, brooding air. The dwarf reached up and twitched a rope beside the door. Faintly, from far within, I heard the bell jangling.

'What house is this?' I asked.

I expected no reply, and got none.

The snow was coming on heavily again. I confess I was eager to be out of it and welcomed the prospect of shelter, no matter what starts or surprises might await me behind the high, black door. I had been in the city hardly one full day and already I had been apprehended and accused of murder, threatened with the rack, thrown into gaol, then suddenly released and set up in a house of my own, without my even asking for it. What new thing now, however outlandish, could possibly surprise me?

At length there was the sound from within of bolts being drawn, and the door was slowly pulled open on its protesting hinges. Peering out from the gloom of the hallway was a diminutive aged creature of indeterminate gender. It had eyes like recently opened oysters, and it was bald, save for a few strands of darkened silver hair drawn across a leathery skull. It spoke, though, with a woman's voice, feathery and thin.

'Ah, Master Schenckel,' she said to the dwarf, with a chuckle so soft it was hardly more than a succession of faint quick breaths. 'Good day to Your Worship.'

The dwarf offered no greeting in return, but pushed past the strange little creature and made his way into the hall. He said not a word to me, either, nor gave me any indication of what I was to do, whether to follow him or draw back. It was only by the old woman's not unkindly nod that I knew I was to enter also.

73

I stepped over the threshold and bowed to the little woman, who, however shrivelled and worn, was endowed, I could see, with a certain grace and even an air of authority. Inside the wide, ill-lit hallway the walls were hung with numerous large, time-blackened portraits of hardly distinguishable gentlemen and ladies in antique dress.

'Come, sir,' the woman said, in her whispery voice, inviting me onwards with an outstretched, clawlike hand. 'Come along.'

The dwarf was already at the far end of the hall, and now he dodged out of sight under a dim archway. I hurried to catch up with him, and the three of us proceeded in single file—Schenckel leading, with me after him, and the servant some way behind—through a series of chilly, anonymous rooms. We came at last to an equally anonymous doorway. The dwarf tapped lightly, glancing up at me sideways with that crookedly peculiar smile of his, at once amused and sour.

We waited, but there was no response. Then the old servant came up, and she tapped too, more loudly than the dwarf had, and after a moment, still receiving no reply, she put her face close to the wood of the door and spoke some words, in the faintest murmur, as if she were reciting a magical invocation. This time a step sounded within, the door was opened, and the dwarf slipped quickly inside. Once again the old woman gave me an encouraging nod, and after a moment's hesitation—what or who awaited me here?—I followed the dwarf's example and stepped through the doorway.

Directly opposite me, on the far side of the room, a fire of logs was blazing in the hearth, towards which Dr Kroll was slowly striding. Whenever in later years I thought of that man, I always saw him with the glow of firelight playing on his mournful, ravaged features. The scene was so closely reminiscent of the one I had been thrust into that morning at the castle that I instinctively glanced off to the side, half expecting to see Felix Wenzel there too, standing in the shadows.

The fireplace was flanked by a pair of arched windows with stained-glass panes that shed a feeble and somewhat lurid radiance into the room, creating a gloomily ecclesiastical effect.

Kroll turned. 'You're welcome to my home, young man,' he said gravely. 'Will you take some wine?'

Jeppe Schenckel had made off into the gloomy reaches of the room, although I could sense his sharp little eyes fixed on me.

The servant woman went to a table and poured the wine into a crystal goblet and brought it to me, bearing it in both hands, as if it were a chalice. More wine! As I took the glass from her, my fingers brushed against hers, and with a sort of shiver I felt the brittle, warm texture of her old woman's skin and the twig-like frailty of the bones beneath it.

I smiled my thanks, and she nodded, smiling too.

How vivid everything suddenly seemed, vivid and almost painfully immediate—the heat of the fire, the wine's strong, harsh savour, the dim light in the windows, the servant's papery flesh. Indeed, it often seems to me that I was never so keenly alive, to myself and to the world, as I was in those earliest, turbulent days in Prague, city of flame and shadows.

The servant woman withdrew, closing the door behind her soundlessly. I was sorry to see her go. To a motherless son, all women, no matter who or what they are, bring back a formless recollection of maternal warmth.

Jeppe Schenckel, off in his far corner of the room, had climbed onto a couch and was perched there, leaning back against a brocade cushion. Dr Kroll had turned once more to the fire and was gazing pensively into the flames. I took another deep draught of wine; as I did, I noticed a tremor in my hand, a tiny, rapid quaking. There was a general sense of some large, impending event: it was like the moment in a playhouse when the performance is about to begin, the audience all eagerness and the players waiting in the wings, ready to stride out upon the stage and set in motion the machinery of the drama.

Perhaps, I thought, perhaps Chamberlain Lang would make another entrance, and launch into another theatrical show.

But it was not Lang who appeared. Instead, a door opened to the right of the fireplace, and a short, fat man in a rich robe trimmed with ermine stepped into the room.

7

I recognised him at once. Here was the face that had appeared above me in the prison cell, the face of the Emperor Rudolf—now at last I could be certain that the vision of him I'd seen had been no drug-induced dream.

His Imperial Majesty was a good head shorter than I, a soft, somewhat flabby figure, with notably small and shapely hands and delicate, dainty little feet. He had over-all the air of an anxious voluptuary. His forehead was high, and he had a good strong nose, the effect of which was off-set, however, by a weak, pinkly moist lower lip protruding under a flowing moustache of a dark auburn hue. His abundant beard could not hide the pendulous Habsburg jaw; his eyes, above heavy, sagging lower lids, were large, dark blue and keen of gaze, expressing equal hints of curi-osity, suspicion and, most unexpectedly, humour. Under his cape he wore a coat of thick, jet-black velvet braided with gold and silver thread, a ruff of stiffly pointed lace, and a high black felt hat adorned with a pale grey swan's-down feather and studded around the brim with a variety of precious stones set in silver.

I said just now that he had stepped into the room, but sidled would be a better word. Rudolf's mode of forward motion had as much of retreat in it as advance, so that even as he came towards me he seemed at the same time to be shying away.

I fell to one knee before him, bowing my head, and for a

moment saw myself as a knight of old, swearing fealty to some legendary monarch in an old saga. Behind me I heard the dwarf snicker softly.

'Your Majesty,' I began, 'allow me to offer my humblest—'

'Yes yes yes yes,' Rudolf said impatiently, 'yes, good, perfect. But stand up, now, stand up.'

I rose and faced him. I felt that my lower lip might be quivering, and quite likely it was, I being so nervous.

He gazed up at me for a long moment, during which I did not dare even to blink. 'Christian Stern,' he said. 'That is truly your name, yes?'

'Yes, Your Majesty,' I said. 'Christian Stern, I am he.'

He nodded, frowning a little, thinking. 'We have been expecting you,' he said. 'You know that?'

'Indeed, sir, Chamberlain Lang said something of the sort.'

'Oh, Chamberlain Lang!' he exclaimed, waggling his head in an almost comical fashion. 'Chamberlain Lang says many things.' He came forward, and grasped me by the upper arms and made me lean down close to him. 'We had a dream of you,' he whispered. 'The star that would come from the west, the star sent by Our Saviour as a sign to us.'

I heard myself swallow.

'Come,' he said, drawing back from me and leading me aside, 'come and talk to us about yourself and your alchemical studies, for as you will surely be aware we have a warm interest in the subject, yes, indeed.'

He had a hushed, hoarse manner of speaking, with much heaviness of breathing—I suspect he was afflicted with the dropsy, among numerous other ailments, which had aged him prematurely—so that everything he said seemed imparted in confidence and not meant to be overheard by the common ear.

78

He was walking ahead of me into the dim corner where the couch was. When he spotted the dwarf perched at the end of it he gave a great loud laugh.

'Ho there!' he called, peering. 'Is that our stunted knave? Schenckel, you grow littler by the day—soon we shall be able to stow you in our codpiece. What do you say? Up, rogue!'

The dwarf climbed down from the couch, one shoulder crookedly raised as if in expectation of a blow. 'You say true, Majesty,' he replied, in his soft, lisping way. 'And should it be, your piece would be filled out well, for the first in a long time.'

Rudolf laughed again and cuffed the little man on the side of his large head, then grasped a handful of the flesh under his jaw and tweaked it hard. 'Animal!' he said merrily. 'Apish abomination!' He turned to me. 'This fellow, who is supposed to be our fool, plays us for a fool instead. Some day we shall have him hanged for his disdaining jests. Go, sir!' he shouted at the dwarf. 'Go you, with Dr Kroll, and leave us in peace alone with our bright new star.'

Dr Kroll, still by the fireplace, turned and made a low bow, and without a word moved backwards respectfully to the door, which the dwarf, with that surprising agility of his, reached first and drew open. The two, one so tall and the other so short, exited together.

'Now, Christian Stern,' Rudolf said, 'sit down here by us.'

And so it was that I found myself sequestered in close company with the ruler of the world, the Dominus Mundi, as the fire crackled and the winter's day waned and outside the silent snow fell heavily.

What did we speak of? Many things, but mainly matters magical, inevitably. I was required to give a detailed

79

account of what subjects I had studied and what I knew, and what work in the art of alchemy I had accomplished. I am afraid I pretended to be a more committed adept of this art than I really was: my true calling was natural philosophy, which, although it gives cognisance to certain manifestations of the craft of magic, concerns itself with investigating the visible, graspable world in all its varied aspects and phenomena.

Rudolf put numerous questions to me but could manage to show no more than a passing interest in my answers; after all, he had already heard me boasting about myself and my accomplishments from his hiding place behind the scene of poor Actaeon's slaughter while I was undergoing Chamberlain Lang's inquisition. And, of course, like so many men in positions of great power, he was in general a less than good listener. When spoken to, he had a way of remaining quite motionless, gazing fixedly at the speaker's lips, as if he were hanging on every word that was being said to him, whereas in fact, as I soon discovered, he was only waiting for the one who was addressing him to pause for breath, at which moment he would resume at once his own discourse at exactly the place where he had left off when the other had begun to speak. For Rudolf, to be spoken to at all was to be interrupted. He prized above all the sound of his own voice, and plainly much enjoyed hearing himself expound on his views of the world and its infinitely curious ways. And why would he not? He was Emperor, after all.

At the time, in my youthful pride, and as a graduate of the respected seat of learning that was Würzburg, I was disdainful of all amateur scholars, yet despite myself I was surprised and impressed by the extent of Rudolf's knowledge of a range of arcane subjects. Certainly he was acquainted intimately with a large number and variety of the ancient texts. In the course of that first conversation between us, if I may describe as conversation so one-sided an exchange, he spoke of how Plato in the *Timaeus* had conceived of the world as itself a living being, a doctrine which, as he—needlessly—reminded me, the new Platonists of the previous century, particularly those under the patronage of the great Florentine lord Lorenzo de' Medici, had revived and developed. He mentioned a number of the central Hermetic texts, such as the *Corpus Hermeticum* and the *Asclepius*, and the works of Marsilio Ficino and Pico della Mirandola, for the latter of whom, as he approvingly noted, man was the measure of all things, the *magnum miraculum*. He spoke with enthusiasm also of the Cabala, the deep and secret doctrine of the Jews, and even touched on the *gematria*, that ancient magical art based on the calculated attribution of numbers to the letters of the Hebrew alphabet.

For Rudolf, as also, I should repeat, for me, the tangible world represented an infinitely intricate code by which the countless parts of creation were connected, all to one and one to all, in a living, harmonious continuum. The secret nature of the world was to be apprehended first and foremost through the portals of natural philosophy, in which alchemy and astrology played a part—not so great a part as His Majesty believed, I considered, although I did not say so.

The old servant came to tend the fire, taking no notice of us, where we were seated side by side on the couch. In the doorway behind her an enormous deerhound appeared, a mighty beast that, standing on its four legs, would come up to the height of a tall man's waist. It paused on the threshold for a moment, peering into the dimness of the room.

'Ah, Schnorr,' the Emperor murmured, 'dear old Schnorr.' The dog pricked up its ears and came padding forward, and lay down at the monarch's feet with a rattle of bony limbs and a soft, contented sigh.

'You are aware this is a house of mourning,' Rudolf said to me in a quiet voice, glancing in the direction of the servant where she knelt at the fireplace with her back turned towards us. 'Old Fricka there, she nursed Dr Kroll's daughter when she was a babe.' Now, like the dog, he too heaved a sigh, and wiped his dampened eyes with his fingertips. 'Poor Magdalena,' he said softly, 'our darling Magda.'

That the Emperor Rudolf was a reluctant monarch is a fact known to all, and he has been much criticised for it. There are some who contend he sacrificed the empire itself to his mania for magic and magicians, and left all Europe to flounder into this war without end that today is tearing whole nations asunder. Be that as it may—I am no historian, nor pretend to be—for my part I held him in the highest regard, although I did not blind myself to the undoubted flaws and fissures in his character. Yet a king who doubted his very right to rule with absolute power over his fellow creatures could not but win the admiration and respect of the ardent young man I was then and, indeed, I still am, somehow, somewhere, deep down in the musty reaches of my by now so aged and decrepit self.

The years he had spent as a youth under the chilly fostership of his uncle King Philip of Spain—how could I, a foster-child myself, be other than sympathetic?—had left a deep mark upon Rudolf. Life at the palace of El Escorial was an endless round of prayer and penance, while the manners he was required to observe at court were stiff, austere and cold. All this had dulled—more, had damaged—the

82

sensitivity of his soul, and his only defence was to fashion for himself a mask of imperious pride that he could present to the world.

Yet he was, as I can attest, an enlightened prince, one whose mind was ever open to the endless variety of people and things. He knew well the evil that fanaticism wreaks, and on more than one occasion told me, with a shudder, of the day King Philip insisted on taking him to witness an *auto-da-fé* in Toledo, when a band of Lutheran heretics were herded to the stake and burned alive. Never would he forget, he assured me, the stench of human flesh being consumed in those flames.

The daylight was steadily fading as the dusk came on. Billows of snow blundered softly against the stained-glass windowpanes. The house all round was still and silent. The old woman struggled to her feet, with a weary groan, and shuffled out. The fire crackled and spat. The hound, which was old and infirm, could not stay awake and soon dropped its great head to the floor with a thud. Its pelt gave off a brownish, biscuity odour, warm and not unpleasant; it seemed to me, I am not sure why, the very smell of childhood itself. The Emperor touched the animal's back with the toe of one of his black calfskin slippers. The beast lifted its head from the floor and looked at him, then laid it down again, with another soft thump.

'The Englishman Dee,' Rudolf said, 'could change himself into the form of a dog—did you know that? Oh, yes. Many a night he was seen in that wise, racing through the streets of the Old Town, when he first came to Prague and lodged with our former physician Dr Hájek. Much magic was done there, at the House of the Green Mound.'

He laughed quietly, shaking his head. 'What a saucy

83

rogue he was,' he said, 'that Johannes Dee. When we first summoned him he arrived before us an hour late, and instead of begging our pardon, he fell straight off to rebuking us for our sins! God had pledged to him, he said, that if we renounced our wicked ways—our wicked ways!—our power would be the greatest the earth has ever known, and that we should make the Devil our prisoner, which Devil he did conjecture to be the Great Turk. Ha.'

He was silent for a moment, still shaking his head, still wryly amused. I was greatly taken by his antiquated mode of speaking, and the slight trace of a Castilian accent. The dog, asleep already, twitched and moaned, dreaming no doubt of the days of glory when it brought countless antlered behemoths tumbling in their blood to the dust. I have always been curious about the inner life of animals, and meant to make a study of it, in fact, but the years caught up with me. So many things left undone, my investigation of the animal brain the least of them.

'We did not know,' the Emperor said, 'whether to have the fellow flogged for his insolence or set him up as our chief wizard, as Elizabeth of England had done. He claimed to converse with angels, one of them a young girl who spoke to him in his own tongue and also in Greek and bade him write down the things she said. Also he had a shewstone, a black, polished round he claimed was given to him by the archangel Uriel, in which his assistant Kelley, that benighted creature, did his crystal-gazing for him.' Suddenly he turned his head and peered closely into my face. 'Tell us, young sir, have you ever conversed with an angel?'

'No, my lord,' I said, 'I have not.'

It was at once obvious I had answered too swiftly and with too much candour, for something dimmed in Rudolf's eyes, and he sat back on the couch, and although he was nodding his head it seemed rather that he was shaking it, in sad disappointment. I cursed myself for my rashness: I might as easily have assured him I was in frequent communication with whole choirs of angels. Always tell the great ones what they want to hear, that's another of my mottoes, though at that time I had not yet formulated it, if for no other reason than that I had as yet encountered no one I could count great, except, now, amazingly, this one, the greatest of all.

After a moment or two I was relieved to see the Emperor's darkened mood passing, for he smiled again, and even, to my surprise and no little consternation, laid a hand against my cheek, with such sudden intimacy and seeming fondness that I had a hard job of it not to flinch away from his touch. His palm was soft and plump and warm and slightly moist. I may say that had any other man dared to caress me in such a fashion I would have slapped him for a fawning man-girl.

'Ah, well, you are young,' he said, 'and no doubt you will grow rapidly into much new knowledge of matters both angelic and mundane. I was your age when I inherited the empire.' He smiled, and patted my cheek, lightly, with that soft, silky palm. 'For now, you shall be our talisman, our charm, our new-risen star!'

The touch of his hand had made me tense, and I sat as still as a statue, hardly daring to breathe. Rudolf now slumped again into despondency, lowering his great chin until it crushed the lace ruff and sank down into the velvet material of his coat.

When he spoke, his voice was faint, yet plangent with a sudden onrush of anguish. 'Oh, young man, young man,'

85

he said. 'I know that I am dead and damned, for my spirit is possessed by Evil.'

This sudden strange outburst filled me with alarm and dismay. What was the cause of such a blurted, horrified confession? And what was it he was confessing to?

On the floor the dog whined and panted in its sleep, surely dreaming again of the hunt.

'I don't understand you, my lord,' I said. 'Why should you be damned? What is this evil that you think possesses you?'

He looked at me with stricken, starting eyes, and for a moment I saw him clearly as he must once have been, long ago: frightened, lonely and lost in the vast, hushed and sunless palace of the Spanish King.

'I have done terrible things,' he said, his voice shaking. 'I have plunged myself into the darkest of the dark arts, into goety and black magic and the worst of witchcraft. Listen'—here he leaned forward urgently, coming so close that I felt his breath on my face—'I employed the *Picatrix*, that magic handbook of the Arabians, to cast a spell on my brother Matthias, whom I hate. I had Dee and his man Kelley call up spirits out of the deep who would aid me in my pursuit of the Philosopher's Stone. Once I saw the Evil One himself, face to face, as you and I are now. Oh, yes.'

He turned his tormented gaze to the fire and its flames, and it was as if he were seeing devils dancing there.

'A child was born, somewhere in Styria,' he said, speaking in the lowest, most horrified whisper now, 'and news of it was carried to the castle, a boy-child that came out of its mother's womb with a golden tooth already fully grown. I sent for the creature to be brought to me that I might inspect it, but the captain of the guard, a hapless dolt, misunderstood his orders and carried back to me instead the infant's severed head. It had no gold tooth.'

He stopped, and sat trembling, fingering agitatedly the stuff of his cape. I could hear him breathing, taking in slow deep draughts of air and sounding for all the world like a dying man entering upon his last agony. The dog, sensing distress, woke from sleep and lifted its great carven head and looked up sombrely again at the suffering man.

'My lord,' I said earnestly, 'you must remember, God is willing to forgive all sin, even the blackest.'

Rudolf continued silent for a moment, but then drew himself suddenly upright, lifting that bearded, pendulous chin, his nostrils dilating and his moist lip thrusting itself out. His expression had turned in an instant to one of haughty disdain. 'We do not believe in God,' he said, in a new voice, strong, full, deep and solemn. 'Neither in Man nor in God have we the slightest speck of faith. The world is all wickedness and folly, and Heaven and Hell a lie told to soothe or frighten us.'

He rose from where he was seated and paced to the hearth. He had a heavy woman's way of walking, slouching from side to side, letting his weight fall on one hip and then the other. Still his gaze was fixed on the flames, seeing there again perhaps a presentiment of the Abyss but seeming, this time, to scorn it and its attendant demons.

'We have a task for you,' he said, without turning.

I, too, rose from the couch and crossed to the fireplace and stood next to him. In that moment I felt as protective towards him as if I were his son. He did not look at me.

I said that whatever task he might think to entrust me with, I would fulfil it with the greatest diligence and care.

Now he did turn; now he did meet my eye.

'There is no one we can trust,' he said. 'We are surrounded by schemers and knaves. Our courtiers prey upon us like leeches, sucking our life-blood.' He shuffled a step forward and stood again close up before me, gazing searchingly into my face.

'But now you have come to us, Christian Stern,' he said. 'You have come to us out of a dream. Tell me, are you a phantom, or are you real?'

'I am real, my lord,' I said, 'as real as this floor we stand on, as real as those flames.'

He went on peering at me, now stroking his fat lower lip between a finger and a thumb.

'Shall we trust you, our visitor from beyond the crystal spheres?' he said, more to himself, it seemed, than to me.

'You may trust me in all things, sir,' I answered, in a strong, steady voice that I judged suitable to the weight of the moment. 'I am ready to swear an oath of loyalty if you should—'

'Nonsense!' Rudolf snapped, but without anger, so it appeared, and almost, to my amazement, laughing. 'We have oaths sworn to us by the dozen every day, and to what end? We are everywhere scorned, tricked, traduced. Listen, listen'—he took me by the arm and led me to the couch and made me sit at his side again—'tell us what you think of my officials, those you have so far encountered. What of Wenzel, our High Steward, what have you to say of him? The fool imprisoned you and we might not have known you had come had not the gaoler thought to report your presence to the Chamberlain. What do you say of *him*, our Chamberlain, Master Lang?'

I hesitated. How was I to answer these questions? What further new test was this?

'I think, my lord,' I said slowly and with care, 'I think that both the men you mention acted as they believed would serve Your Majesty's best interests. There was great agitation everywhere, panic, alarms. The unfortunate lady, Dr Kroll's daughter—'

'Yes yes,' Rudolf said again, impatiently, 'we know all that. But our best interests are *their* best interests first—*that* they know.'

He let go of my arm, which since we had sat down he had been holding with an urgent grip. He peered about the room with narrowed eyes, as if there might be others there, secret listeners, lurking in the shadows.

'Wenzel,' he murmured, 'yes, Wenzel. He is too much of the Protestant party, while Lang lives in the ear of the Vatican. Lang and the Nuncio from Rome, Malaspina, are a pair of Machiavels and conspire together, we know that well. They are all conspirators, all of them!'

He stopped, and said nothing more for some moments, but making a strange sound under his breath, a kind of droning, wordless mutter. The dog, sitting up now and watching him with grave attentiveness, shifted its mighty haunches, its nails clattering on the wooden floor.

The last of the afternoon's light was shrinking fast in the windows. The fire sizzled.

Suddenly Rudolf seized my arm again. 'You, Christian Stern,' he said, the flames reflected in his eyes, 'you are the one we shall put our trust in. You are the one who will act for us against all the plotters and the spies with whom we are trammelled about. We ask of you what we would ask of no other.'

I waited, trembling a little before those eyes, which burned into mine with such fierce entreaty. 'I am ready, my lord,' I said, 'to do whatever you ask of me.'

Still he kept me fixed with that burning stare, while his fingers dug themselves deeper into the flesh of my arm. He drew me near to him and again made me lean down, so that he could put his face close up to the side of mine, with his lips almost against my ear. I smelt again the faintly foetid odour of his breath.

'Find,' he whispered hoarsely, 'find who it was that so cruelly destroyed the Lady Magdalena. She was dear to us, she was our beloved, precious one. Discover her destroyer. That will be your task.'

There was a long silence, save for the hissing of the fire and the snow's faint whispering against the window. Then all at once the hound lifted high its great head and opened its jaws and delivered itself of a slow, soft, drawn-out howl.

'Ah, Schnorr,' the Emperor said, laying a hand fondly on the creature's head. He turned to me again. 'You see? Schnorr knows—*he* knows.'

8

After that momentous, hardly to be credited, yet ambiguous and troubling encounter, there followed an irksome interval of empty days before I was to find myself again in His Majesty's presence. Yet if I was impatient, I had to admit I was thankful, too, for this period of respite. The task His Majesty had set me, to discover the murderer of Magdalena Kroll, was a heavy weight on my thoughts and a heavier burden on my heart. The lightning-flash frights I had suffered in the immediate wake of my discovery of her corpse had left me in a state of unshakeable fear that affected me like an ague, darkening my days and haunting my dreams at night. I had made my way to Prague determined to find a place in Rudolf's favour, and had succeeded beyond my most fantastical hopes, but if ever proof were needed of the old warning to beware the getting of what you wish for, I was assuredly it.

I had not the least notion how to go about the business of tracking down the girl's killer. Where should I begin? What matters should I look into? Whom was I to question? I was a scholar of natural philosophy, not an investigator of crimes. Barely arrived in Prague, I knew next to nothing of the city's secrets and intrigues. All the same, I was convinced that the causes of the young woman's death lay deep in the tangled affairs of court.

Her corpse had been examined by Dr Kroll himself—what a task that must have been!—who had established that she had not been ravished before being so brutally put to death. Nor had she been robbed of any of her possessions: the gold medallion and some gold coins of no little value that she had in a purse in a pocket of her gown had not been touched.

No rape, no theft—what, then, had been the motive for her murder?

Behind these questions, and pressing upon me as urgently as any of them, was the matter of what would happen if I failed in the commission that had been laid upon my inexperienced shoulders. Yet again I was assailed by the memory of the fat sentry, that poor harmless fellow, strung up in the castle yard, his dangling limbs, his empurpled visage, that awful apple-like thing wedged in the gaping round of his mouth. They could hang me, too, and just as briskly, should my capricious royal patron change his mind and decide that I was, after all, of no more significance in his firmament than a shooting star.

Needing to begin somewhere, I sought out the cadaverous guard who had appeared out of the snowy darkness that night to relieve his soon-to-be-hanged counterpart. I was told, however, that he had fled the city, which, if true, was surely the wisest thing he could have done.

Next I requested a meeting with the Emperor's High Steward, Felix Wenzel. What I might say to him I did not know, but I confess it would have been gratifying to flaunt myself before him in my suddenly reversed role of royal confidant. However, he did not even respond to my request. This, I managed to persuade myself, was not so much a mark of his contempt for me as a sign of his alarm: it was he, after all, who had so impetuously imprisoned His Imperial Majesty's God-sent star.

I also dispatched a note to Chamberlain Lang, asking if he would speak to me and answer some queries. Unlike Wenzel, he replied immediately, in fulsome terms, saying he would be only too eager to offer me every possible help—except that he had business to attend to on behalf of the Emperor, which would take him away from the city for some days.

I knew above all that the person I should question was Jan Madek, the young man to whom Magdalena Kroll had been betrothed before she was snatched from him by the Emperor. But Madek, as I knew, had vanished, and no one could say where he might be found.

The only distraction I had from my worries was the funny little house in Golden Lane. The task of settling myself there was greatly if mysteriously eased when straight off I began to be supplied, as if by magic, with all the necessities of life: a store of victuals, a keg of wine, warm bedding, linen, firewood and the like. Obviously the directive had been handed down by someone—Chamberlain Lang, so I assumed—that I was a person of consequence and was to be treated accordingly.

But here is the odd thing: I was never in the house, not once, when those supplies were deposited there. I would come back from one of my long, exploratory rambles about the city—the foul weather persisted, but I was becoming accustomed to the freezing mist in the air and the frozen snow underfoot—to find a baked chicken, say, still warm, in a covered dish on the table, or a bale of faggots beside the hearth, or a fine new silver drinking cup hanging by its handle from a nail above the stove. Yet I found nothing to show how they had come to be there, or who had left them. It was as if a secret sentinel had been set to keep watch on my comings and goings, who, when he saw me leaving the house, would flash a signal to a likewise hidden band of carriers that they might hurriedly enter the house and make their clandestine deliveries and be gone as tracelessly as they had come. But who were they, and how had they gained entry? They must have had a key to my front door—who would have given it to them, and what was the purpose of such secrecy?

This was to be another of Prague's many mysteries that I would not succeed in solving, and I mention it only by way of an example of the general strangeness of life in that city on the Vltava. Everyone did everything, even the most commonplace tasks, in so much stealth and secrecy that they seemed to live their lives engaged in a vast, compulsory and endless conspiracy. Magická Praha, the Praguers call their city, but it is a mundane magic they practise.

Welcome as these services and deliveries were, they, and the clandestine manner in which they were carried, increased my anxious state. I was like a shepherd who feels the eye of the unseen wolf fixed on him, and my unease was of a piece with the deepening sense I had of being at the centre of an intricately devised, immensely subtle and cruelly malicious game. There in Prague I felt as if I had been blindfolded and led into the middle of a vast room and spun about by the shoulders and released to grope my way here and there dizzily, with arms outstretched—rather as I had done when I was first thrust into that dark dungeon in the tower on the wall—while all round me unseen gamesters, hands clasped to mouths to stifle their mirth, pranced and skipped adroitly out of my path.

Yes, it's true, in all my time in that city I never lost the sense of being used for a plaything, of being the butt of an elaborate, malicious jest. There were many jesters, and they came in many forms.

I am thinking of that hazy, snow-lit morning when I looked out of my window and saw a closed carriage outside, stopped in front of my door. I had not heard it arrive, and wondered how long it had been waiting there—for it was in wait of a passenger, that much was plain, and who could that passenger be but me?

The carriage, or coach, I should say, was a grand affair, painted gleaming black, with much gold ornamentation and gilded wheel rims. I saw with a little shock of excitement that on the door was emblazoned the Emperor's coat of arms, with its double-headed eagle rampant. Two black geldings stood steaming in the traces with nostrils flared, stamping a hoof now and then and agitatedly tossing a plumed head. Thinking I was to be taken to the castle, I donned my coat and cap and hurried outside. It was a cold and misty day, though the sky was the brightest it had been since my arrival in the city.

The coachman was huddled high up on his box, sunk in a black greatcoat and wearing a leather helmet with a visor that obscured much of the upper part of his face, including his eyes, so that it was a wonder he could see his way at all. I spoke to him but the fellow gave no reply, indeed made no acknowledgement at all of having heard me or of being even aware of me; the only indication that he was a living creature and not a golem got up in human garb was the smoky plume of his breath, which mingled with the steam rising from the horses' gleaming flanks. Now, still without so much as glancing at me or saying a word, he reached down sideways and, with the handle of his whip, deftly flipped open the carriage door. I had hardly climbed inside

95

and taken my seat when there came the loud crack of the whip and, with a violent lurch, we rumbled away at a rolling pace up the lane, the horses' hoofs sliding and thudding on the snow-clad cobbles.

We turned a corner, and then another, and I began to feel a downward tilt. When I pulled back the curtain at the window I saw that indeed we were not headed upwards in the direction of the castle and the Emperor, as I had expected, but were instead descending the hill towards the river.

Soon we crossed the Stone Bridge and entered the Old Town. I sat forward on the edge of the upholstered seat, looking keenly out of the window and noting the aspect of the streets we were passing through; I recognised none from my previous venture into this part of the city with Jeppe Schenckel. By now I had begun to feel apprehensive. What new and mystifying encounter awaited me this time? To ease my mind, I decided to believe that, since it was the imperial coach I was travelling in, and I was again in the Old Town, I must be on my way for a second visit to the house of Dr Kroll, there to engage in another confidential parley with His Majesty.

Yet it soon became apparent that we were not going in the direction of Dr Kroll's house, either. We continued on, into the deepest depths of the Old Town, and at last the coach came to a skidding halt at the steps of an ancient church. I sat quietly in the creaking stillness, waiting for some indication of what I was to do. But no one came, and at length I pushed open the door impatiently and stepped down into the snow.

The street in both directions was narrow and winding. Few people were about, and those few were heavily shawled and hatted against the cold. The air here was saturated with a particularly dense, milky fog, and a muffled silence reigned. One of the horses turned its head and rolled back at me a great dark eye, burnished and gleaming like black glass.

I tried the driver again, calling up to him, but he sat huddled as before, unmoving and silent. 'Damn it, man,' I cried, 'what place is this, and why am I here?' At this he stirred himself, and pointed with the whip towards the church door. 'Thank you!' I snapped, intending not the least note of gratitude.

I climbed the steps and entered the church. Again I saw myself as the blindfolded one at the centre of a malicious game, stumbling helplessly forward, pulled and plucked at by misguiding phantom hands.

Inside the church it seemed colder than it had been outside. At the sound of my step, a pigeon that had been perched in the embrasure of a small rose window high up under the cross-hatched stone arches of the ceiling took flight and circled about with a noisy clatter of wings before alighting on a granite buttress and releasing a single feather, which see-sawed down through the frigid, grainy air.

I looked about in the gloom, peering everywhere, but there was not a soul to be seen. I sat down in one of the pews in front of the altar and drew myself deep into my coat for warmth, but even the thickness of the beavers' fur could not keep out the chill.

I was not then, and would not ever be, a man of faith. I believed in God, more or less—more, it shames me to say, in times of peril or need, and less when times were easy and I was not in danger and had money in my purse. But whatever respect I might have had for the Church, either that of Rome or Luther's reformed version, had been thoroughly knocked out of me by my foster-parents, for whose brand of hypocritical piety I had had from my earliest days the deepest loathing and contempt. I did not hope to be forgiven my sins in this vale of tears; nor did I look for redemption when the time should come for me to be interred in its clayey depths. The world, in my estimation, was all we could ever hope to have—was more, indeed: was everything. I would enter death as a shadow enters darkness, and that would be the end of me; this I believed then, and I believe it still. Yet as I sat there in that cold nave, under the unblinking eye of the sanctuary lamp, I seemed to feel something brush against me, seemed to sense the touch of some ancient tragic suffering presence. Let us say it was the spirit of the place, whether benign or otherwise I know not, and it caused a numinous shiver to run all along my nerves.

A door slammed somewhere, the sound of which sent echoes skittering among the pews and up into the dome of the ceiling, disturbing that pigeon again. A moment later a figure came bustling out of the sanctuary in a flurry of dark robes. He crossed the altar, almost forgetting to genuflect, and waddled rapidly forward to greet me, sketching a rapid blessing on the air as he approached. Stopping before me, he grasped me by both my arms and examined me keenly, shutting one eye and drawing his head far back and cocking it to the side.

'Greetings to you, *professore*,' he said, 'you are very welcome to my little church.' He spoke Latin in a light and airy manner, ending his words with a breathy little falling dip, attaching to each one a sort of phantom vowel. 'I am Malaspina, Bishop of San Severo and the Holy Father's Nuncio to the Emperor Rudolf. Are you hungry?'

98

I must say that, from the start, I was greatly taken with this worldly prelate, not least for the fact that he was so very unlike that other Bishop, my unholy father.

Girolamo Malaspina was a man of force, of character and, most notably, of weight, which is not to speak figuratively, but of actual physical bulk: he was of truly remarkable proportions. I have never encountered a human being who gave the impression of being so nearly a perfect sphere—or two spheres, I should say, for with a round head set atop a seemingly neckless, squat, round body, he resembled nothing so much as one of those absurd diagrams of planetary motion that Ptolemy devised to account for anomalies in the orbits of the heavenly bodies, in which a little circle is superimposed on the circumference of a much larger one. He had very short arms and very short legs, and such was the size of his belly, an enormous round, that it seemed he must at any moment topple over and roll helplessly this way and that about the floor, his little limbs bristling like a beetle's. His face might have been fashioned from handfuls of sallow dough slapped together into a ball, so fat was it that the features were almost entirely sunken in the flesh, like specks of fruit stuck into a yeast loaf fully risen and ready for the oven. His eyes in particular, tiny, dark and gleaming with merriment, might have been a couple of raisins poked by a child's thumb into the pale wad of flab below his forehead.

He wore a black robe with a hood, and a velvet jerkin with a thick fur collar, and a hat of black felt that sat close upon his globular head like a large poultice, quite covering his ears.

Now he turned me about and, putting a hand into the small of my back, swept me ahead of him out into the street, where the moribund coachman and his haughty pair of steeds awaited us.

'So kind of His Majesty to lend me his coach,' Malaspina said, 'for my own has a broken—a broken—what do you call it?' He pointed.

'Axle?' I said.

'The axle, *sì sì sì!* Such a strange word.'

It took time, effort and ingenuity for the Nuncio, with my assistance, to manoeuvre his vast bulk into the coach. At one stage in the procedure I had to put my shoulder to the broad, black-clad episcopal posterior and give it a mighty shove, which elicited from the holy man first a squeak of protest and then a helpless, wobbly laugh.

We set off and trundled round a corner into another, even narrower street. No sooner had we entered it than the Nuncio thumped a fist on the wooden roof above our heads to signal to the coachman to stop, which he did, on the spot, with a bone-shaking lurch. I put out my head at the window and looked back. It was such a short distance we had travelled that even the Nuncio in all his rotundity could surely have walked it and saved us the effort of getting him into the coach in the first place, an effort that now had to be repeated in reverse in getting him out of it again. None of these awkwardnesses seemed to embarrass this irrepressible churchman or blunt his good humour.

We had been delivered at what turned out to be the nunciature. This was a tall, narrow house squeezed between a church on the right side and a pie shop on the left, which, given the fat man's calling and his tremendous girth, I could not but think a nicely apt arrangement.

Entering the building, we proceeded to a fine high chamber, where two fires burned, at opposite ends of the room. There was a long table of pink-veined marble, at the midway point of which two places were set, also opposite each other, with pewter dishes dully agleam, knives and spoons of old silver, and goblets of Bohemian crystal that sparkled and flashed in the light from the twin fires. The Nuncio stood for a moment to survey these splendours, then gave a sigh of deep satisfaction, happily patting the ample upper slope of his belly with his little plump paws.

'*Ecco, signore,*' he said. 'Now we shall feast!'

9

And feast we did. That was the day I underwent a Dama-
scene conversion and became the trencherman I have been
ever since. All young men should hasten to train themselves in the delights of the table, for these delights outlast
all others, even those of the bed, a thing you can take my
word for.

The meal that was set before us was opulent, rare and
bewilderingly varied. To start there were slices of pigeons'
livers on toasted flatbread and a rounded loaf of minced
pork studded with globs of glassy fat. Next came a plump,
sweet carp swimming in a clear sauce fragrant with herbs,
after which we cleansed our palates with quince-flavoured
water ices. At the pinnacle of the repast there was borne in
on a silver platter a spit-roasted capon stuffed with truffles;
ah, how my mouth waters even now at the far-off memory
of that noble bird! To follow, there was fruit compôte slath-
ered with clotted cream, an almond cake drenched in
honey and, to close, rocky lumps of a fine old crumbly Par-
migiano cheese—the first such I had ever tasted.

As for wine, the rarest vintages were poured in abun-
dance. We had a vigorous and fruity Württemberg Riesling
the colour of straw, then a glorious red all the way from the
Tuscan hills, blood-warm and thick, and, when all that had
been drunk to the dregs, a cold clear aqua vitae from Friuli
distilled from wine leavings that made an icy tinkling in
my mouth yet ran like liquid fire along my veins. There

were little thimble-sized cups of a bitter brew, much favoured by the Turks, so the Nuncio informed me, which I had not encountered before, and which was so strong a stimulant that presently my heart was palpitating and my hands were trembling, so much so that I felt as if I had been struck by a bolt of lightning.

The food was served by a trio of novices. Two of them were big-boned country girls, pink and jolly, but the third, with a heart-shaped face and delicate little hands, was as slight and darkly voluptuous as one of the countless sinuous nymphs that Bartholomeus Spranger used to paint in those days for the Emperor Rudolf's insatiable delectation. She kept her eyes cast demurely down; the other two giggled helplessly when the Nuncio pinched their backsides, which he did repeatedly and with progressive shamelessness as the dishes came and went and the wine freely flowed.

The Nuncio expounded volubly on various topics—the food, the wine, the weather and suchlike—though he said nothing about the reason for my being there. I assumed, since I had been fetched hither by the imperial carriage, that His Grace had something from the Emperor to convey to me, some communication to be delivered as discreetly as if we were in the confessional, and I was content to eat and sup and bask in the warmth of the twin fires, confident that I should eventually be enlightened.

Perhaps it was the wine that made my eye stray with ever more interest to the paintings crowding round me on the four walls. Most were deftly made, and one or two I thought very fine indeed, although I was, and am, no connoisseur of such things. All of them, in subject matter and in execution, were of a passionate voluptuousness verging, and more than verging, on the openly indecent.

One of these works, hanging on the wall directly opposite to where I sat, I kept returning to, with a guilty inward hotness. It was a tall, narrow canvas and depicted what I took to be Venus, the goddess of love, posed under an apple tree heavily laden with fruit. She was naked, save for a braided gold necklace and an elaborate circular hat of clustered white feathers as wide as a small cartwheel—the hat was shaded in with particular delicacy and niceness of detail, as if the painter had sought to tease the viewer by distracting him away from the goddess's frankly displayed charms. By her side stood Cupid, a tiny, fat fellow with a shrivelled pizzle and a miniature pair of swan's wings. He was being set upon by bees, and was looking up at his mother in angry distress and proffering to her a honeycomb that he must a moment past have wrenched out of a mossy cleft in the trunk of the apple tree behind him.

What was most striking in the scene, and the thing that at once stirred my blood and troubled my conscience—though only a little, to be sure—was the manner in which the goddess, her head tilted to the left, looked out at the viewer—at me, that is—with a slyly inviting, shameless simper that was to occupy my nocturnal fancies for many a night to come.

The Nuncio saw how my glance roved back repeatedly to the pale-limbed lady—although it was obvious she was no lady, and no goddess, either, for that matter. His little dark deep-set eyes glittered with lubricious merriment. 'You have a taste for pictures, I see,' he said. 'Mine is a fine collection, do you not think? There is a nice balance of quaintness and'—he hesitated, searching for the word— '*salacità*. Eh? What do you say? They are salty—salacious— enough for your taste, yes? The Emperor himself covets not a few of them, in particular that one'—he turned fully about on his chair to glance up at the Venus and Cupid behind him—'to which you seem to be especially drawn.'

I cleared my throat and said in a somewhat thickened voice that I thought the paintings very fine, very—here I, too, sought the apt word, but stumblingly—very pictur-esque. The Nuncio chuckled, his adipose jowls trembling.

He seemed altogether a disreputable old rogue, but with my legs fixed comfortably under his generous table I felt more warmly towards him than ever. I was of that age when the smallest kindness seemed a token of eternal friendship.

When the novices had cleared the table, the Nuncio and I moved with our glasses of liquor to the hotter of the two fires and seated ourselves in deep, soft chairs on either side of the hearth. My brain felt heavy and dulled after so much food and drink, and I was having distinct difficulty keep-ing my eyes fully focused. But Malaspina, although he had drunk fully as much as I had, seemed as sharp as he had been at the start of the meal. He sat opposite me in his broad armchair, his robes draped over his enormous mid-riff, and fixed me with a mischievous and fondly mocking eye. 'So now, young man,' he said, 'you must tell me all you have seen and done since you came to this sinful city.'

Which, of course, having been made loquacious by the wine, I was only too happy to do. I told how I had arrived from Regensburg at close of day and lodged in the Blue Elephant—I mentioned the lice and the dying diamond merchant, but not the innkeeper's wife—and how the old soldier and I had blundered in our cups out into the night, and how I had found Magdalena Kroll, dead in the snow with her throat torn out. I recounted too, with a quaver of self-pity, how in the middle of the night the soldiers had broken into my room at the inn and hauled me off to be questioned by High Steward Wenzel.

How distant it all seemed, to my half-drunk mind's eye.

At the mention of Wenzel's name, the Nuncio's little eyes glittered all the more brightly, but he made no comment, only signalled for me to continue.

I described being thrown into that cell in the tower by the castle wall, and how I had allowed myself to sink into despair, until Chamberlain Lang rescued me and directed that I be set up in my house in Golden Lane.

'Ah, yes,' the Nuncio said, nodding. 'The Chamberlain is a clever man, clever indeed. But'—he tapped a finger to the side of his little knob of a nose—'dangerous, too. *Sì, sì, molto pericoloso.*'

Then I told how Jeppe Schenckel had come to Golden Lane and fetched me away for an audience with the Emperor at the house of Dr Kroll. The Nuncio sat forward in his chair with a grunt of surprise. 'His Majesty himself was there?' he said.

'Yes,' I answered. 'He knew me already, for he had dreamed of my coming.'

'*Vi aveva sognato?*' he exclaimed, falling again into his native tongue. 'He dreamed of you?'

'He did,' I said, not without a note of boastfulness. 'He dreamed of a star from the west, sent by Christ, which he took to be a dream of me, because of my name.'

Here I paused, frowning and blinking, once more struck by the fearful fact that my neck had been saved from the noose by the simple chance that one half of my name had 'Christ' in it and the other half had 'star'.

Malaspina shook his head—no easy thing, given the

almost entire lack of a neck upon which to shake it. 'Yes, His Majesty is much swayed by such deceptive portents,' he said. 'He surrounds himself with sorcerers who fill his ears with all manner of wicked nonsense.' He looked at me narrowly. 'Have a care,' he said, 'that he does not seize on you to be one of them.'

I was about to declare indignantly that I was no sorcerer but had discretion enough to say nothing, given that it was exactly my ambition to be numbered high among the Emperor's squadron of savants.

Having mentioned the dark arts, the Nuncio then launched into a lively polemic against John Dee and his henchman Kelley, describing them as arch-wizards whose maleficent influence at court had been for so long a cause of deep alarm to the Vatican and to the Holy Father himself.

'I summoned them here to the nunciature,' he said, 'those two *mascalzoni*, at the direction of His Holiness and with the Emperor's blessing, and held them under guard for many days, questioning them closely. I put it to them that they were spies for that harlot Elizabeth of England, and were dedicated to promoting the Protestant cause in Bohemia.'

He nodded slowly, remembering, his eyes aglitter. 'Dee was cautious and kept a guard on his tongue,' he said, 'but Kelley, that *cacochymicus*, although claiming to have renounced Lutheranism and to have pledged himself to Rome, spoke openly of his contempt for the Pope and his ministers and denounced Mother Church for her supposed corruption. *Dio mio, che coppia di furfanti!*'

He rose with an effort from the armchair and waddled to the fireplace. Taking up a fire iron, he prodded vexedly at the burning logs.

'At my urging, His Majesty banished the wicked pair,' he said, 'allowing them no more than a week in which to quit the city. They fled into the German lands, but soon crept back and sought sanctuary with the great lord Vilém Rožmberk at his castle at Krumlov in the Bohemian southlands. At last Dee returned to England, but Kelley, whose sins the Emperor had made himself forget, was summoned back to Prague to take up again his godless and abominable alchemical labours.'

He threw down the fire iron angrily and let himself flop back into the large chair, which yet was hardly wide enough to accommodate his enormous bulk.

'Kelley at first had a great success,' he said darkly, panting a little, his fat face taking on a livid hue. 'His Majesty granted him a patent of nobility, gave him the title Golden Knight, so-called, and set him up as court alchemist! So great was his fame that Elizabeth herself, *quella strega*, sent agents here to Prague with instructions to entice the sorcerer back to England by whatever means.'

He brooded for some moments, but then grew calm, and folded his hands once more over the mighty mound of his stomach; after a pause, he chuckled. 'But he was still a charlatan,' he said, 'and a fool. He let himself be led into a dispute with an officer of the Crown, and in a duel ran the fellow through the heart. After that there was nothing for him but imprisonment again, for good, this time, although the Emperor, it's said, still pines for his favourite magician.'

Despite the effects of the wine, I forced myself to listen to all of this with as much attention as I could muster, not because I had not known the facts already—the misadventures of Dr Dee and his companion Kelley made up one of the many scandalous epics Praguers loved to tell over and over—but because I seemed to hear behind it a caution aimed at me directly. What was it this cunning old cleric was urging me to guard against? Did he see me, too, the Emperor's man, one day disgraced and exiled?

I felt a tiny sharp chill, as if a drop of icy water had trickled down my spine. Suddenly the fires seemed to give off less warmth, while the food I had eaten seemed to turn over in my belly, a heavy parcel of hot and greasy mush.

Presently the three novices appeared again, bearing musical instruments, two viols and a lute, and sat down and entertained us with some jigs and galliards and, to close, a slow and stately pavane. The two who played at the viols might as well have been sawing wood or shearing sheep, but the little dark one, bent over her lute with her oval face inclined, performed the pavane with such grave passion and drew out such sweetness from the notes that tears prickled at my eyelids. I have always had a weakness for a melancholy tune, especially after drinking.

When they had finished their performance and retired, I lay back in my chair, lulled and drowsy, and sank into a sort of dream, in which an earless giant in golden robes stood outside a tall window and harangued me, though nothing of what he was saying penetrated the thick and misted squares of glass that separated us. How comical he looked, out there in the snow, that gilded monstrosity, comical and at the same time terrifying, mouthing at me in violent silence.

I dozed. I dreamed. The fire warmed my shins.

It was the dark young novice who woke me. I opened my eyes with a start to find her leaning over me and gently shaking me by the shoulder. I had sunk so far down in the chair that I was almost reclining in it full length, but now I straightened hurriedly, blinking and coughing.

Opposite me, Malaspina's chair was empty.

The novice had such lovely almond-shaped eyes, dark and shining; I wanted to reach up and take her in my arms.

Seeing that she had succeeded in rousing me, she stepped back, smiling. I knew it must be afternoon by now, and asked her what the hour was, thick-tongued and mumbling. She shook her head and pointed mutely to her lips. She had brought me another small cup of the dark and fragrant Turkish brew. I drank it off in two quick draughts, though it was hot enough to scorch my tongue. My skull seemed filled with thick white heavy smoke.

I tried to stand, only to slump back helplessly into the chair. Still the girl stood before me, with her arms folded and her hands hidden in the sleeves of her habit. In my muddled state I thought her enchantingly beautiful, a heavenly vision, almost, like that Beatrice of whom the poet of the *Paradiso* sang so ardently.

At last she took the empty cup from me and went away. I sat for a while gazing blearily into the grey ash, all that was left of the fire. I shivered. I felt chilled suddenly. Where was my coat?

In a while I came back to myself sufficiently to be able to struggle to my feet and go off in search of the Nuncio. Eventually I found him in an alcove off the main hall of the house, seated before a lectern on which was propped a sumptuously illuminated book of hours.

I apologised for my ill manners in having fallen asleep, but he waved a fat hand dismissively.

'*Eravate stanco,*' he said, smiling. 'You were weary, you have had many trials.'

The gorgeous book before him was open at a page depicting a mounted knight in silver armour dispatching with a long and slender spear a fancifully curlicued dragon with bright green wings and scarlet claws, while a dark-eyed, slender lady stood by, watching dispassionately as the dying monster spewed up its heart's blood. The lady, in her dark gown and elaborate headdress, reminded me of the silent girl who had lately woken me from my sodden sleep.

'The young one, the dark one,' I said, 'she doesn't speak. Has she taken a vow of silence?'

The Nuncio shook his head. 'Serafina, that is her name. She has no tongue. It was cut out by her brother.' He glanced up at me. 'Yes,' he said, 'her brother. He had taken her maidenhood from her by force, and thought to make it so that she would not be able to betray him. A foolish fellow—he forgot that even a tongueless girl can point. His father hanged the son with his own hands.' He smiled and shrugged, and laid a finger lightly on the page before him. 'So, you see, it is not only in the old tales that terrible things happen.'

He drew himself up out of the chair, like a cork from a bottle, swaying and panting. 'That reminds me: I received the news this morning that another corpse has been discovered, this one in the Stag Moat.'

I looked at the dragon writhing in stylised agony.

'They say it is Madek, *quel povero giovane*,' the Nuncio said. 'Do you know the name? Jan Madek? Yes, I see you do.'

That was when I began to discover the limits of my powers as the Emperor's man. Prompted no doubt by a desperate whim—there are those who will say he ruled his empire entirely by whim—Rudolf had charged me with the task of finding out the murderer of Magdalena Kroll and I had, as I quickly discovered, not a shred of official authority upon which to conduct my investigation. No one thought to consult me or keep me informed of developments relating to the girl's murder, and had it not been for the Nuncio I would most likely not have known of the death of Jan Madek until after he was waked and buried. That death and its ramifications, of course, lay behind the wily Bishop's decision to send the imperial coach to fetch me to the nunciature: he wanted to appraise my character and judge if I was to be taken seriously as one who might be capable of nosing out a murderer.

I think he was not much impressed by what he saw; even so, at his urging I borrowed his carriage, directed his coachman to take me to the castle, and then hurried on foot down to the Stag Moat. I arrived there just before sunset and saw that Madek's bloated corpse had still not been removed from the water; apparently most of the day had been lost while waiting for Wenzel the High Steward, who had insisted on coming down in person to view the body. He had just left, in fact, and now a soldier with a net began working it around the sluggishly bobbing bundle. Finally the fellow hauled it out, the frozen surface of the water breaking around the cadaver with tiny musical tinklings, and laid it on the bank. It seemed not a human form at all, but some pulpy crawling thing that had been dragged up by accident from the ocean floor. The face was the colour of a fish's belly, and was swollen to bursting and all bruised and cut. Where the eyes had been there were only two puckered and blackened hollows.

I could find no one who knew how long Madek had been there. I did learn that early that morning he had been found—a grossly swollen carcass trussed in a goatskin jerkin and ripped hose—floating face-down in a deep part of the stream that in those days still ran through the moat. Those who had seen him had taken his humped form for that of some animal, a deer, maybe, or a wild boar, that had ventured onto the ice and broken through and perished in the freezing water. Eventually one of the Imperial Guard, grown curious, had made his way down the steep bank and poked at the thing with his halberd. At once it flopped over and emitted a great belch of gas so foul it sent the shocked soldier scrambling backwards on his behind up the grassy slope, spluttering and retching.

By now a horse cart had been ordered, and while waiting for its arrival, I had to argue with the sergeant in command to be allowed to examine the thing before it was taken away. The sergeant was a decent fellow, but Wenzel had instructed him that no one was to be let near the corpse. I had to invoke the Emperor's authority and claim that I was a medical doctor sent to ascertain the exact cause of death. My bluff must have been persuasive, for at last the sergeant relented.

When the Nuncio had first told me of the discovery of

the body, I had thought it must have been Madek who had cut Magdalena Kroll's throat, in a fit of jealousy and rage; afterwards he had fled down here and, tormented by remorse, must have drowned himself. Now, however, squatting on one knee beside what was left of the young man, I saw the burn marks on the flesh, and the print of the rope on his wrists, and realised that his eyes had not been taken by fish or water rats, as I had originally assumed, but had been gouged out before he died. Jan Madek had been cruelly tortured and then strangled, as the leather cord buried deep in a groove around his neck attested.

I had not one murder to investigate, but two.

The cart came then, and as Madek's body was being laid upon the rough-hewn boards, the horse turned and regarded it with what seemed a stoically sympathetic eye. What things animals know, things deeper than we are privy to.

I climbed the bank of the moat, slipping more than once on the frost-laden grass and almost falling. A coldness had seized me that was not the afternoon's cold. Fear, too, spreads an icy air.

In the preceding days I had talked to anyone I could find who had known Jan Madek, yet I had been able to discover precious little about him that I did not already know. He had been an apprentice physician under the tutelage of Dr Kroll, living in rented quarters on one of the upper floors of the doctor's house; his father was a rich surgeon in Augsburg who had paid handsomely for his son to come to Prague and study with the world-renowned Ulrich Kroll; and Madek had hardly settled in Kroll's house before he had succumbed to the spell of the doctor's bewitching and, as everyone agreed, clever and calculating daughter.

Magdalena Kroll, I was told, was as ambitious as she was fair, and while it amused her to dally with the handsome young Augsburger, she had dropped him from her favour without hesitation the night she caught the Emperor's eye in the banquet hall at the Royal Palace.

Madek was young, and he took hard the loss of the fair Magdalena. She had become betrothed to him in a light-hearted moment one evening when the two of them danced together at a gathering of students in a beer hall in Klein-seite. I tracked down an acquaintance of Madek's, one Krister Kristensen, a big fair-haired Dane with glossy pink cheeks and invisible eyelashes, one of the astronomer Tycho Brahe's assistants, who had been present on the occasion. 'Oh, yes,' Kristensen boomed, in his comical accent, laughing and showing his big square teeth, 'he was mad for her, the wench, but she thought it all a joke.'

After Rudolf had taken his beloved from him, the young man had at once begun neglecting his studies. He had fallen to drinking, and often in the alehouses he was heard to abuse the Emperor's name and curse him for a whore-master. Matters became so bad with him that in the end Dr Kroll turned him out of the house. Later it became known that when he left he had taken with him an iron box—the strongbox Jeppe Schenckel had spoken of that day when he was leading me to Dr Kroll's house to meet the Emperor— that was said to contain a cache of precious papers on alchemy and natural magic the doctor had assembled over many years. For a week and more, the young man was not seen or heard of in the city. Dr Kroll posted a notice for information on his whereabouts, but in vain. The rumour went round that the renegade had abandoned Prague alto-gether and returned home to Augsburg.

But he had not gone home. Instead, he had been seized, and tortured, and then throttled and thrown into the Stag Moat. He had been not yet twenty years old. 'Damned foolish fellow,' Krister Kristensen said jovially, wiping his blond moustaches with the side of a thumb.

I returned to the nunciature, where I was told the Bishop had retired for the evening. All the same, I was shown to his bedchamber, which was not much larger than a cubbyhole, and almost entirely filled by an enormous four-poster bed overhung with a baldachin of scarlet brocade. A fire was blazing there, of course, and the air hummed with its heat. 'I am from the south,' the Nuncio said, pressing a hand to his breast. 'I cannot bear the northern cold!' He was propped against a mound of cushions, still wearing his black felt hat, as well as a voluminous woollen robe the same shade of scarlet as the canopy above him.

I told him of Jan Madek, of the burns on his body, of his gouged-out eyes. He nodded sombrely.

'Yes,' he said, 'it is as I had expected. It does not do to speak, in public, as he spoke.' He bent on me a keen look out of those dark, sharp little eyes of his. 'And you, *dottore*, you must go carefully.' He smiled. 'Perhaps you need an *angelo custode*—a guardian angel.'

And so, when some short time later I departed the house, I was accompanied, on the Nuncio's instructions, by the angelic young novice Serafina. The imperial carriage was waiting outside; I expected to see the driver frozen into a figure of ice, but he was animate still, though as silent and unresponsive as ever.

We rumbled and rattled our way across the Stone Bridge and again ascended the long hill towards the castle. The girl sat close by me, a tender presence, like some shy creature of the wild that had settled at my side for warmth. When I looked out of the window I saw a clear patch of sky above the castle, a wash of densest blue, with a single star, dagger-shaped and faintly atremble, shining out into the gathering darkness, and its blade seemed to pierce my heart to the core.

I fell to watching the girl, covertly, not turning my head but only swivelling my eyes sideways. She was beautiful, in her delicate way, and when she caught me peeping at her she smiled, and blushed, and no doubt I did, too. She had changed out of her habit and wore a plain grey gown under a heavy sheepskin coat. Her hair, which before had been hidden under a stiff hood, hung loose now, black and lustrous. She had a southern duskiness, and when she smiled, her teeth glistened like damp pearls.

At the house in Golden Lane the stove had gone out, but Serafina soon had it blazing again. It was bitterly cold, and we had not taken off our coats. I sat down at the table and rubbed my eyes. I was weary, in the aftermath of the wine and my dealings with the mutilated corpse of young Jan Madek, and thought was not easy, though I had many things to think on.

I believe I dozed again for a little while. When I woke, the stove was warming nicely and had taken the chill off the air.

Now I looked up, and Serafina was standing beside me. I rose to my feet. She was so much the littler of the two of us, bright-eyed as a blackbird.

I had tried to get her to understand me, speaking both in German and in Latin, but she had only smiled at me, shaking her head slowly and sadly. Perhaps she understood only Italian, a language of which I had no more than a word or two. I mimed my gratitude—the stove was blazing strongly now—but she shook her head again. There was to be, it seemed, no communicating with her, not by way of words, at any rate. She looked about, searching for something to write on, and, finding nothing, leaned forward across the table and in the mist on one of the windowpanes drew with a fingertip a rough figure of a man, and beside it that of a girl, kneeling, with bowed head. I turned to her in puzzlement. Smiling and biting her lip she lowered her head, like the figure on the windowpane, and joined her hands before herself.

It took some time, with more signs and smiles and encouraging nods, before I understood her meaning. She was telling me that she was happy to be there, and that while she was there I had only to indicate to her what I wished her to do and she would do it. Her innocence touched me, but made me shiver, too. I thought of Jan Madek, eyeless on the bank of the frozen stream: he, too, had been young; he, too, had thought the world a simpler and a gentler place than ever it was, is, or will be.

The first task Serafina undertook—without my asking, need I say—was to clean my hair, for my stay at the Blue Elephant, short though it was, had left me with a healthy and ever-burgeoning infestation of lice.

I was doubtful about this procedure—I am one of those who does not care to be touched overmuch—but Serafina heated a kettle of water on the stove, and had me sit on the side of the bed and lean over a dish she had placed between my feet, and poured the water over my hair and scrubbed a solution of oil and lye into it with her fingers, which were surprisingly strong. Next she brought a chair to the stove and had me sit there while she plied a fine comb, crooning

118

softly to herself. I smiled to see her hold the comb up to her eyes and peer at the harvest of squirming creatures she had collected from my scalp, frowning and shaking her head and making a deprecating sound with her lips. Afterwards, when she had done with my hair, she leaned close over me—she had a sweet warm fragrance—and with a tiny pair of copper calipers plucked the last of the lice out of my eyebrows, although I had not even known they were there.

She made herself very busy that first day. I noticed that she seemed familiar with the little house and the things in it, but I did not give that much consideration at the time. She made my bed and swept the floor, and folded my clothes and put them away in a cupboard by the stove. She took up the bowl of stew the potboy had fetched from the Blue Elephant, which I had left standing on the table and forgotten about. She carried it outside, wrinkling her nose at the stink of the rotten meat, and emptied it into the drain.

She had taken off her coat while she was working, and now she put it on again, and touched my arm as a sign that she was leaving. I took her hand, however, and led her to the table and made her sit. The night was fast deepening and I had lit my oil lamp. I wished very much to hear her say something, though I knew it was impossible.

What did I want from her? Love-making, the vigour and comfort and pleasure of her young body? I think not, not really. Instead, I was overcome by a sense of sweet melancholy. Serafina's presence there in the little house had made me realise how lonely I had been, for a long time; I fear I had, in those young days, a lamentable tendency towards self-pity. Being motherless, I had always a craving for the company of women. But I was wary of them, too.

A woman had been the main cause of my precipitate departure from Würzburg. A young lady of the town had developed a passion for me, a passion I had been foolhardy enough to reciprocate, or pretend to. Mathilde, she was called, Mathilde Westhof. Her father, Matthias Westhof, was a powerful figure, being the college chancellor. There had been a scare when for some weeks Mathilde thought herself with child. Although in the end it proved not to be the case—she was a fanciful girl—I judged it wise to bring the affair to an end and absent myself from the city, using the deaths of my foster-parents and the mortal illness of my father the Bishop as an excuse for flight.

For all that, I still missed my Mathilde, who was sweet-natured, though somewhat too clinging for my taste. Had I married her it would no doubt have pleased her father, but I'm sure that in the end it would have frustrated my ambitions and hindered me in my work as a scholar. Do not judge me too harshly: I was young, and callous, and single-minded—I saw myself as a second Erasmus in the making—and now I am old and soft and sit daydreaming by the fire, up here on the frozen shores of the Baltic.

Serafina was nothing like the buxom Fräulein Westhof, yet her presence had brought the lost and distant dear one sweetly to my mind, and now we sat there, the mute girl and I, gazing at each other helplessly in the flickering lamp-light, two sad souls lost in wordless need.

At last she rose and touched my face lightly with two fingers—it seemed a blessing, or even a sort of kiss—and went to the door and was gone.

The coach, I realised too late, had not waited for her, otherwise I would have heard the sound of it departing. She would have to walk all that way down the hill and across the bridge and into the tangled heart of the Old Town. I pictured her hurrying along through the wintry gloom, alone and defenceless, and cursed myself for a careless scoundrel.

I sat down again at the table. The figures she had drawn on the windowpane were still faintly visible, two vague shadows, somewhat together, in the twilight.

II

The next day I sought, and was granted, an audience with His Majesty. I had spent a sleepless night, writhing and sighing on my couch in the corner, preyed upon by all manner of fancies and fears, as the red eye of the stove dimmed and the darkness closed me about entirely. Strange to relate, the sight of Jan Madek's bloated corpse had affected me more strongly than had the discovery of his beloved Magda Kroll lying dead in the snow. The girl had been a stranger, unknown and by now for ever unknowable, but somehow the young man seemed—not familiar, that's not the word I want, but plausible, yes, frighteningly plausible. By which I suppose I mean that I could easily have been as he was, a parcel of whey-like flesh dumped on a riverbank with a knotted leather cord biting into my swollen neck.

When I arrived at the castle I was conducted to the Great Hall, where I found the Emperor standing alone before one of the big square leaded windows, looking down at the city. He wore a heavy, dark cloak and a tall hat studded with jewels. Under the great dome of the ceiling a vast stillness reigned, and my footsteps echoed loudly as I walked with a solemnly slow, respectful tread towards him down the length of the hall; I had learned to be careful always to approach him as if for the first time, so capricious was he and so unpredictable his temper.

He had heard me, I knew, yet he kept his back turned to me. I stopped. The silence about us seemed to vibrate. A faint mist pervaded the furthest corners of the enormous room. So large a space was it that markets were set up there at Shrovetide and Christmas, and sometimes even tourneys were held, the mounted knights pounding up and down the straw-strewn floor with lances bared, while spectators on either side cheered and waved their caps.

'Your Majesty,' I said, 'the young man who was found yesterday, the drowned young man, Jan Madek: you know he was . . .' I hesitated '. . . you know that he was acquainted with Fräulein Kroll.'

He nodded slowly, still not allowing himself to turn from the window, as if he could not bring himself to face me, as if he could not bear to take more cognisance of me than the little he had taken so far.

There was a long silence. I cleared my throat. Should I speak again? I wondered. But before I could, he did.

'Look at them,' he said, 'our subjects, so many strangers.'

I waited. Still he did not turn, but remained facing the window, stoop-shouldered, gazing down upon the city, like a child studying an ant hill.

'I suspect, Your Majesty,' I said, speaking very slowly and softly, 'that the young man is the one who murdered Fräulein Kroll. I think he killed her out of jealousy, and then was killed himself—by whom, I do not know. This is what I believe.'

How did I expect him to respond? I wished that he would turn, so that I might see his expression and perhaps guess what he was thinking. He had directed me to find the girl's killer, and now I was confident I had done so, although the mystery of Madek's own death remained. Could he not say something? Anything?

He sighed, his shoulders drooping deeper. 'I used to go

among them,' he said. 'I would put on commoner's apparel and have myself brought down in a plain carriage to the Old Town, where I would walk about, disguised. Strange, to be noticed by no one, like that. I might have been a ghost, the ghost of myself. I felt happy and at the same time afraid—of what, I don't know. Perhaps I thought I would lose myself, and never return. Yet it might have been a joyful release, to be gone, simply.'

He stopped. The stillness shimmered; I seemed to see it, like an undulation in the air about us.

'Your Majesty,' I began, determined to have something from him, some acknowledgement of what I had said so far. At that moment he turned with such abruptness, his cape swishing, that I retreated a startled step, convinced he meant to strike me. Indeed, in my mind's eye I saw him draw back his arm in a rage and slash his hand across my face.

But on the contrary, and to my great astonishment, I realised that he was smiling.

'Come,' he said, with sudden boyish eagerness, extending a hand and taking me lightly by the arm. 'Come, we shall show you our wonder rooms.'

He led me out of the palace and across the snowy courtyard. I could hardly match the swiftness of his pace, as he trotted along on his little stout legs, his cloak trailing behind him and his tall hat askew. After passing under an archway, we climbed a broad stone staircase to an upper floor of the Long Corridor, which connected the royal living quarters to the northern ramparts, where the building of the Spanish Hall had lately been completed.

'Now you shall see,' he muttered eagerly. '*Now* you shall see!'

Much has been spoken and much written of Rudolf's fabled collection of objects rich and strange. Yet anyone who has not walked through those magnificent, cluttered rooms cannot begin to comprehend the majestic madness that lay behind the amassing of so many treasures and so much trash. In four successive great chambers were gathered countless of the world's rarest artefacts, along with the most tawdry of curios, all jumbled up together. Cabinets reaching halfway to the ceilings contained drawer upon drawer of precious stones and ancient coins, quaint figurines moulded in gold or carved from ivory, jasper, jade. There were bezoars—gallstones, that is—plucked from the innards of animals and men, said to be a guard against poison and the plague; there were skeletons, dried foetuses, fossils, feathers of gaudiest shades; there was a unicorn's horn as long as a man's arm, and the jawbone of a siren, polished and delicate as a seashell; there was a life-sized statue, worked by an intricate hydraulic mechanism within it, that moved its limbs and sang a strange, droning song.

Each room revealed things increasingly rare and wondrous: I was shown a nail from Noah's ark, and a grain of the earth from which God had fashioned Adam, the first man. Pictures stood against the walls—dozens upon dozens of them propped one on top of another and even suspended across the ceiling—by his court painters Spranger and Sadeler, by Dürer and many other masters, including Arcimboldo, whose fantastical portrait of Rudolf as Vertumnus, the Roman god of the seasons, in the form of vegetables, fruits and flowers of many varieties, was displayed most prominently. There were shelves of precious books, Copernicus's *De Revolutionibus*, the *Geographia* of

Ptolemy, the great *Codex Argenteus*, containing Bishop Ul-filas's ancient Gothic translation of the Bible, a priceless volume, which Rudolf had borrowed from the abbey of Werden in the Rhineland and had never returned.

The Emperor was fascinated by the fluctuating line that separates animate and inanimate, human and beast, flesh and mineral. In one of the rooms were kept all manner of mechanical apparatuses, lifelike figures and clockwork dummies, a wax figurine that would weep when exposed to the sun, the mummified corpse of a hermaphrodite child, a pair of Barbary apes that His Majesty insisted could count up to a hundred by beating their fists on the floor of their cage. By the time we reached the fourth room, in which was stored a trove of the most ingenious and ex-quisitely crafted astronomical instruments, my head was spinning.

There had been time for me to examine no more than a fraction of this vast and bewildering collection when Rudolf, who at first had been full of childish eagerness and glee, suddenly lost interest in showing off his treasures. With an impatient gesture he turned on his heel and made his way back as we had come. I imagined he wished to speak with me further about the death of Jan Madek, but all thought of Madek, and even of Magdalena Kroll, had seemingly been banished from the royal consciousness. That was how it was with Rudolf: his gaze so often was directed away from the main prospect and fixed upon things at the side, the inessentials.

We were passing again through the second room, which housed his lesser collection of pictures, when I happened to glance aloft. High up on one wall I spotted what struck me as a particularly lifelike portrait. It was a head-and-shoulders study of a woman: she was pale, with a broad brow and sharp chin and somewhat protuberant eyes, and her reddish-gold hair was gathered into a long and fashionably untidy plait. The bodice of her gown was low, showing off her long, slender neck and the smooth, creamy upper slopes of her bosom. Her lips, dark pink and voluptuous, were turned upwards at their outer corners in a faint and, as it seemed, a knowingly penetrating smile. She was looking down-wards, so that her gaze seemed to meet mine directly, and indeed as I walked on, still glancing back and up, her eyes followed me in a most uncannily realistic fashion.

At the doorway I paused, letting Rudolf go ahead of me, and turned back to snatch a last glimpse of the woman's strange and striking image. But, to my consternation, I saw that the portrait's frame was empty.

Of the many amazing things I had witnessed today, that surely was the most astonishing of all—a picture that could make itself go blank, in the twinkling of an eye! What powerful magic could there be that would work such a wonder?

I peered up at the wall more keenly, and now realised I had not been looking at a picture after all. It was a window, small and square and edged with an ornamental stucco frame, giving onto the return of a staircase, where a woman, a real one, of flesh and blood, had paused to look down at me with that faint and coolly quizzical smile, before passing on, out of the frame.

12

When I had got over what for ever afterwards I thought of as the Wonderment of the Window and followed Rudolf out through the doorway, I found that he was nowhere to be seen. I went down the stone staircase and passed under the archway into the great courtyard, but still there was no sign of him. I felt a prickling sensation at the back of my neck. Had the wizards in his employ discovered a spell whereby he could disappear himself, as thoroughly and abruptly as the woman had vanished just now from that little high-up window?

I stood in vague perplexity, looking about and asking myself what I should do. I was still uncertain of court etiquette—but, then, was I ever to be certain of it?—and was conscious that His Majesty had given me no opportunity to take my leave of him; did that mean I was free to quit the castle precincts, or must I wait, in case he should reappear, as suddenly as he had vanished, and, finding me gone, think me careless, if not downright insolent? I had a vision of another squad of soldiers coming for me, this time to the little house in Golden Lane, and marching me back to that gaol cell in the tower on the wall and leaving me there to rot.

I heard a light step behind me and turned, greatly relieved, expecting to find the Emperor there. It was not His Majesty, however, but a young woman, a servant, with a little pink-tipped snub nose and her hair in thick braids wound in spirals at either side of her head.

'If you please, sir,' she said, with what I strongly suspected was a smirk, 'my mistress wishes you to come to her.'

'Your mistress?' I said.

'Yes, sir. Please, this way.'

She turned, and I followed her back under the archway and up the stone steps.

At the top of the staircase we passed the door to the wonder rooms, then walked along a short corridor and up another, steeper, flight of stairs. On the return, half-way up, there it was, as I had expected, the window giving onto the room below where the Emperor's pictures were stored, the little window through which I had glimpsed the woman regarding me. Looking down, I in turn saw standing there, in exactly the spot where a little while ago I had stood, a person, a stranger, looking up at me, just as I had looked up at the woman. I glimpsed him only briefly, in the second or two while I paused at the window, yet I had an intense impression of him, of his assured stance and bold stare. But what a creature he was. I could not have said if he was man or boy. He had a boy's stature, delicate and slight, but his face—ah, that queer, ageless face! He had shiny black lifeless hair cut short, and small, dull eyes out of which he considered me coolly and, so it seemed to me, in a peculiar fashion, somehow at once penetrating and indifferent.

The young woman ahead of me had stopped and was waiting for me, with an enquiring expression.

'The person there,' I said, hastening after her and gesturing back over my shoulder towards the window, 'did you see him?'

'Yes,' she said. 'That was Don Giulio, my mistress's son.'

Her mistress? Who was her mistress? I put that question

aside for the present. 'But is he,' I said, 'is he a boy, a man? What is he?'

This she chose to ignore, and turned and walked on.

I continued to follow her, feeling strangely shaken.

We went down another, longer, corridor, and presently entered a small, bright chamber in which three women were seated upon ornate Italian chairs. One of them I recognised. It was the woman I had seen at the window.

Now that I knew she was real, I thought her even more striking than she had seemed when I mistook her for a painted image. She was not young, yet her face and hair had a palely luminous quality, a kind of limpid sheen, as if she had lived all her life under moonlight. In one hand she was holding an embroidery hoop, and with the other was drawing a needle and a long scarlet thread through the stretched cloth. As I watched, she pulled the thread tight and leaned down and severed it neatly with her small, gleaming white teeth.

I made my usual clumsy attempt at a bow, my boot heels scraping on the wooden floor. She returned an acknowledging nod.

'Has His Portliness been requiring you to admire his gewgaws?' she asked.

This caused the two young women, seated one on either side of her, to quiver faintly, like a pair of swans ruffling their feathers. One of them tittered.

'Why, madam,' I said, groping for words, 'if such things are gewgaws, I'm sure I've never seen the like for preciousness and interest.'

'Yes,' the woman said, drawing out the word, as if it were one of those many long lengths of silk that were twisted into skeins in a rosewood box on the floor beside her chair. 'Yes, I suppose that must be how they seem, at first sight.'

The young woman who had conducted me there stepped past me, seated herself in a fourth chair, and took up a piece of embroidery of her own. I could see I was to be an entertainment, and the atmosphere of the room was giddy with amused expectancy. I felt twice as tall as I was and ten times as clumsy.

'You know who I am, I presume?' the woman said.

I had taken off my hat and was turning its worn edges round and round nervously in my fingers. I recognised that she was Italian, for she spoke in the same manner as Bishop Malaspina did, with a breathy drop at the end of each word.

'I would think,' I said, 'that you must be Mistress Caterina Sardo.'

'Oh, yes,' she answered, with a little toss of her head, 'mistress I must be, certainly mistress—*da sempre e per sempre.*'

Her three handmaids glanced at each other, eyes wide in fearful delight, rustling their plumage again, then quickly recomposing themselves. The one on the right had a mandolin in her lap; the other was holding closed a slim bound volume, with a finger inserted in it to mark her place. The third leaned over her embroidery in a show of earnest industry. They looked as if they had posed themselves consciously, after some set-piece from a painting.

The room had a faint but heavy musky smell; I have always savoured the flesh-and-violets fragrance of women.

Caterina Sardo rose to her feet, tossing the wooden ring with its cloth and threads behind her onto the chair. She came forward and placed herself directly in front of me, looking into my eyes. She was impressively tall: in height I had no more than the width of a couple of fingers on her.

'And you are the miraculous star from the west,' she said. She let her gaze wander over my face, and then all the way down to my feet and back up again. 'I grant, you have something of a starry aspect.' She smiled with a mischievous compression of the lips. 'But are you a good Christian, I wonder? We are all Christians here at court, you know. Very pious.'

Despite her lambent look, there was a sense about her of overuse, as of something faintly soiled; it lay upon her almost palpably, like a skim of sweat. This tainted aura did not offend or repulse me—no, on the contrary, it stirred me deeply, indeed alarmingly. She seemed a woman who had done much, and would do more: a woman who would do anything.

Now she drew herself nearer to me, still thinly smiling. She narrowed her eyes and seemed to look straight into me, into my very thoughts. My forehead was burning.

'Leave us,' she said sharply, without taking her eyes off me. At once her trio of handmaids rose meekly, putting aside their things, and with their heads down filed past us one by one to the door, which the last one closed softly behind her.

A silence swelled in the room, settling about the woman and me, like a soft, weightless gauze.

'It was you who found the trollop with her throat cut, yes?' she said. Her tone was husky and almost caressing, belying the callousness of her words. 'All her prettiness marred, her lovely flesh all hacked and bloodied.' She clicked her tongue in mock regret and shook her head from side to side slowly and mechanically, reminding me of one of her husband's cunningly articulated statues. 'Such a waste.' Then she smiled again. 'Come,' she said, 'come sit and tell me things. In this place no one talks to anyone else except to meddle and conspire.'

We sat. There was a blue-tiled stove in the corner; the air, with its womanly aroma, was warm and dense.

I feared being required yet again to embark on an account of myself and my antecedents, but it turned out there was little she did not know about me already. Anyway, as I would discover, she found herself far too fascinating to waste time being much interested in others.

Abruptly she put on a show of recollecting herself and said, 'Oh, but I haven't offered you refreshment. You'll be in need of something, after your dusty hour among the royal treasures.' She lifted an eyebrow. 'You were impressed, you say, by his bibelots and baboons?' She gave a brief little laugh. 'Everyone always is—except me.'

'Such a collection is surely one of the wonders of the world,' I exclaimed.

That lifted eyebrow fluttered when she laughed.

'Oh, surely, yes,' she said dismissively. 'Did you see his pictures? They were collected for him by my father, who was his agent and curator. This is how I come to be here, so far from my Tuscan homeland—' she sighed '—here, where one does not see the sun for six months of the year.'

She took up a little bell from a small table beside her and twitched it, producing a muted tinkle. A moment later the door opened and there entered again the snub-nosed girl who had first fetched me there.

'This is Petra,' Caterina Sardo said. 'She is the maid of my chamber, the rock upon which I depend. She knows all my secrets—don't you, Petra? *Tutti i miei segreti.*' She turned to me again. 'Isn't she pretty? Except for the nose, that is; there is nothing to be done about the nose. But you should see her unclothed—perhaps you shall, one day. We often cuddle up together of a night, she and I, under the blankets, and tell each other stories.'

The girl was blushing and biting her lip, but behind this show of prudery I detected something else, a shiver, as it seemed, of the memory of secret pleasures, of forbidden doings.

'Bring some Tokay for our guest,' Caterina Sardo said. 'And a plate of those sweetmeats that we so much like, the ones with almonds and cherries.'

Petra, still biting a corner of her lip between uneven little teeth, made a curtsy and withdrew.

'Do I shock you by my talk?' Caterina Sardo asked, watching me with amusement.

'You must forgive me, madam,' I said. 'I am not used to court life—I have not learned its manners sufficiently yet.'

'Ah. You think me lewd.'

'Not at all—'

'But you do. I see it in your look. Well, no doubt you're right. Court life, as you call it, conduces to indecency. It's all we have to stave off the tedium, the monotony, the boredom of it all.'

There was a light tap at the door and young Petra came back, carrying a pewter tray on which were a flask of tawny wine and two little goblets of carved Bohemian glass hardly bigger than thimbles.

'Thank you, Petra,' Caterina Sardo said. 'Put it here, please, on the table between us. And, yes, you may pour.' She watched the girl's face as she filled the glasses. 'The Herr Professor thinks me a shameless doxy,' she said, still regarding the girl. I began to protest, but she laid a hand on mine to silence me. 'He denies it, but he thinks me wanton. What do you say, Petra?'

The girl glanced sideways at her mistress and then at me. Her look was a mixture of calculation and amused malice. 'Madam likes to tease,' she said, 'but it's all in jest.'

Caterina Sardo turned to me with her palms outspread. 'You see?' she said. 'You see how it is? Even the maids of the chamber mock me.' She smiled up at the girl with narrowed eyes. 'You are a minx, and too saucy by far. I shall have to think of a suitable punishment for you later. Now be gone.'

It was plain the girl was well used to her mistress's suggestively teasing ways, and she poured the wine unhurriedly and handed us each a glass. 'There are no cakes,' she said.

'What?' Caterina Sardo cried. 'No cakes? Pray, why not?'

'The baker forgot to make them.'

'Forgot! I shall have him hanged by his thumbs—remind me to order it.'

The girl glanced at me again with a wry little smile—there was indeed something lewdly knowing in her look—then made a mocking sketch of a curtsy and left the room, shutting the door behind her with a muffled but pointedly insolent bang.

I sipped the deep-toned, honey-sweet wine, and thought with no little wonder how in a matter of a few days my life had been so strangely and alarmingly transformed. What if, in that moment, I had known how much more there was to come—how, for instance, on a day not far off, the winter sun shining snow-bright in a high window and the great cathedral bell shaking the air above the rooftops, I would find myself on my knees between this woman's thighs, there to lap a drop of this very wine from the tiny, whorled vessel of her navel, preliminary to moving southwards and imbibing a different ichor elsewhere? What if, indeed.

'You knew that she was with child, the Kroll girl?' Caterina Sardo suddenly said.

I stared at her. She had been gazing pensively at the stove beside us, and now she turned her head slowly and looked at me. 'You didn't? Ah, Professor, for such a learned man you seem to know so little.'

And you, madam, I thought, *could tell me so much*.

She leaned back in the chair, hunching her shoulders forward and settling into herself with a satisfied sigh, smiling up at me from under her lashes. Her mouth, I should say, was truly a delightful shape, the upper lip a perfect Cupid's bow resting lightly upon the lower, and tapering at the corners into a notch in the soft, full flesh of her cheek.

'Yes,' she said, taking a delicate sip of her wine, like a cat lapping its milk, 'the venerable doctor's spotless daughter was carrying in her belly a little surprise.' She gave a breathy laugh. 'Everyone would have thought they knew whose it was,' she said, 'but as I might have told them, His Lowness could never have hoisted himself high enough to get a hearty girl like her with child.' She held out her glass. 'Pour me some more Tokay, if you please, Herr Professor.'

'Then it was Madek's child?' I said. 'Jan Madek, her betrothed?'

She shrugged, laughing softly in gleeful malice. 'Oh, yes, Madek, perhaps,' she said, 'or some other. Mistress Magdalena, so meek and mild, in truth liked nothing better than the bit between her teeth. They could have kept her at a staging post and hitched her up as often as they liked and as she wished, a mount ripe and ready for all comers.' She

136

stopped, and turned to me, her eyes wide and a hand to her mouth. 'Oh, *Dio mio*, but I have shocked you again, I see. How terrible I am—there's no controlling this tongue of mine.' And she smiled, and showed it, the tip of that tongue of hers, sharp and pink and glistening.

I stood up, to do what I don't know. I felt a great constriction suddenly, as if something that had been wrapping itself stealthily around me had all at once drawn tight its coils. I looked at the glass I was holding. The wine on my tongue seemed a thick and glutinous humour; my innards heaved at the taste of it.

And yet, for all this, my blood was fairly on fire. I had never heard a woman talk so freely, with all of a man's crude carelessness, and I was hotly, horribly, excited.

Caterina Sardo looked up at me now in feigned alarm.

'Why, sir,' she said, putting a hand to her breast, like a maiden in a fable, 'but you are impetuous. Why do you jump up? Do I affect you so? I would not wish—' another low and throaty laugh '—to discompose or frighten you.'

Through a window above the stove I could see a little patch of blue sky, like the one I had glimpsed through the carriage window the previous day after crossing the Stone Bridge with Serafina by my side. This time, however, I might have been in some altogether other, distant realm of the universe, peeping down at our world through the wrong end of one of Galileo's magnifying spyglasses.

'Sit,' Caterina Sardo said, in a drawling voice, 'do please sit, and we shall be calm and speak of milder things.' I sat, but not with any ease, for I still had the fidgets and my collar felt tight enough to choke me. Again she put a hand on mine. 'Tell me what you make of His Majesty,' she said. 'Do you think him entirely mad?'

Under the pretext of setting the empty glass on the table I freed my hand from hers, not because I disliked her touch—quite, quite the opposite was the case—but I was frightened of it, and of myself. I could feel my brow all flushed and damp.

'I think you mock me, madam,' I said, making myself smile.

She laughed softly, leaning her head back and showing me the soft pale slender column of her throat. At the same time she reached up a hand to touch the tendrils of hair where they strayed from the thick, loose plait that hung down her back.

'Oh, but that is my way,' she said. 'I provoke everyone, I am famous for it. But you must understand, I only bother with people who interest me, and they are few . . .' here she lowered her voice to a husky whisper, and leaned forward and put her face close to mine '. . . very few.'

I coughed and frowned and busied myself pouring out two more thimblefuls of the heavy, sweet wine. I could feel her watching me, in my discomposure, with rich enjoyment.

'You know,' she said, accepting the wine from my hand, 'you know it was that pander Felix Wenzel who put the girl in his way?'

'Fräulein Kroll?' I said.

She made a grimace. 'Of course Fräulein Kroll—who else? And when I say Wenzel put her in his way, I do not mean Madek, that helpless poor milksop.'

She took a sip from her glass, smiling at me slyly over the rim. 'Yes,' she said, 'it was Wenzel who coached her in all the intricacies of poor Rudi's tastes and preferences. Although, of course, he could not make her into a boy—that was beyond even his powers.' She laughed with bitter mirth. 'Why, I believe it was Wenzel who chose the very gown she wore that night, and at the banquet pushed her forward himself, with her father's consent and encouragement, into His Greediness's path. The fat old fool would have fallen over her had she not stopped him with her brilliant smile, and her even more brilliant bosom, which was so brazenly on show that he might have got that sharp nose of his wedged in its cleft.'

She drank again, and mused in silence for a while, looking up at the window and that patch of sky and nodding a little to herself. 'Wenzel,' she said then, with disgust, seeming to spit the name. Then she turned again to me with almost an angry look. 'You know him, of course—it was he who had you hauled off to the tower and clapped in irons, yes? That's his weakness—he always overreaches himself. It will be his downfall, one day.'

Her attention wandered again and she brooded for some moments. Then she tapped me on the knee sharply with a hard little knuckle. 'You should speak to Rudolf about him,' she said, 'put in a bad word for him. Rudi is greatly taken with you, you know—he truly thinks you have been sent to him from Heaven. But be warned: his favour is a fickle thing, and soon wavers. Strike now, before his passion for you cools.'

Afterwards I would brood for long hours on that first encounter with Caterina Sardo in her sewing room, turning it this way and that, as if it were a globe of bevelled glass, studying the flashes of light it threw off, flashes that did not illuminate but only dazzled the eye.

She had turned away from me again, and her thoughts, I could see, had drifted elsewhere. I put down my glass and once more rose to my feet.

'I hope you will excuse me, madam,' I said. 'I should leave now and return home, before the snow comes on again.'

'Home?' she said, looking up at me vaguely. 'Where is home?'

'In Golden Lane,' I said.

She nodded. 'Oh, yes, yes, I knew that, and had forgotten. Our friend the Chamberlain put you in a house there. Is it to your taste? Does it suit you? I should come there and visit you.' Something sparked in her eyes again, and she smiled darkly, giving me a sportive look from under lowered brows. 'Would you like that, Herr Professor? Would you like me to come and see you in your little house?'

'Of course, madam,' I said stiffly. 'You are welcome to call on me whenever you care to. Although—'

She put her head coquettishly to one side. 'Although?'

'The place is hardly—how shall I say?—palatial.'

'Oh, I did not always live in palaces. And, besides, I have not been outside these quarters for—oh, I don't know how long.' She rose up and approached me slowly, swaying her hips a little and smiling. 'Yes, expect it,' she said. 'Petra and I shall descend on you one day, out of the sky, like a pair of benignant harpies.'

I bowed, and began backing cautiously away from her, cap in hand, making for the door.

She had picked up my glass, in which a drop of wine remained, and now she handed me her own, which was still nearly half full.

'Drink,' she said. I stared at her. 'Go on,' she said, more softly, 'drink where I have drunk.'

I hesitated, not knowing what she meant or intended, then put the glass obediently to my lips. She watched me as I drank the wine, flaring her nostrils and nodding. In her turn she raised my glass, and inserted into it that sharp tongue tip of hers, reaching all the way to the bottom and licking out the last drop.

Then she stepped forward and kissed me, softly, swiftly, her lips barely brushing against mine, light as a butterfly's wings and moist from the wine. As she did so I could feel her smiling.

'Now our pact is sealed,' she whispered. 'Our secret pact.' She lifted a finger and put the tip of it first to my lips, and then to her own. 'For we shall be great friends, yes, Herr Professor? Oh, yes, great friends, I am sure of it.'

13

The Stag Moat was a deep ravine that ran along the northern flank of the castle. In earlier and more turbulent times it had been a broad line of defence against attack, but Rudolf had fenced it off as a breeding place for deer, which grazed freely on its steep grassy banks. Today the winter grass was white with hoarfrost, and it crackled like cinders as I walked over it. I had come down from Caterina Sardo's sewing room bemused and atremble—what pact was it she imagined we had sealed? I felt excited, expectant, fearful, all at once. These were murky waters I was wading in, and there were creatures in the deeps that could drag me down with them to their dark grottoes.

After crossing the courtyard, I went out by the Powder Tower and walked down the slope through the snow-laden trees. I was hardly conscious of where my steps were taking me, and it was with some surprise that presently I came to the place where Jan Madek's corpse had been found floating. A stretch of the thin stream at the bottom of the ravine had been sealed off with sandbags, and soldiers in leather jerkins were cutting channels to drain away the icy, sluggish water.

Felix Wenzel, his head drawn deep down into the collar of a big bearskin coat, stood on the bank of the stream, watching the men at work.

When I greeted him, he did not so much as glance in my direction. Nevertheless I tarried there beside him, as the

142

soldiers continued their delving. Their task was not easy, for the ground was frozen and hard to break and they could hardly keep their footing in the gelid mud. The day was perfectly still, under a clear, china-blue sky, and the men's spades as they struck the earth made a medleyed, iron ringing in the diaphanous air.

At last Wenzel spoke. 'I should have hanged you when I had the chance.' He turned his head and looked at me with cold contempt. 'What business have you here?'

His eyes, which I had thought black when I saw them first by firelight, were a shade of darkish blue, and they glittered like splinters of lapis lazuli.

'I have a commission from His Majesty,' I said, 'to discover who it was that murdered Magdalena Kroll.'

My words were no sooner uttered than I regretted them. That was always my weakness, to blurt and boast.

Something moved in the depths of Wenzel's eyes. Was it surprise, resentment, anger—alarm, even? He was silent for a moment.

'Even a monarch sometimes oversteps his powers,' he said. 'I am High Steward of this realm, and if there is an investigation to be carried out, I and my officers shall be the ones to do it.'

I said nothing to this. It's a rare thing in life, I was thinking, that a man should stand out and show himself, in so stark and unequivocal a fashion, to be one's unremitting enemy. In that way at least the High Steward had done me a service. Yet it puzzled me that he should harbour such a deep antipathy against me. Had he really believed I was the one who murdered Magdalena Kroll, when he sent his men to seize me that night at the Blue Elephant? It seemed unlikely that a man as shrewd as he should have allowed himself to make such a blunder, yet here he was, still talking of hangings, and warning me not to trespass on his privileges. The difference now was that I was no longer afraid of him, having more menacing things to fear. Or not as much afraid as I had been.

'This'—he gestured grimly with his chin in the direction of the labouring soldiers—'is Chamberlain Lang's work.'

'What is it they're searching for?' I asked.

He shrugged. 'That's a question for the Chamberlain.' He glanced at me sidelong with a sort of smile. 'Why not enquire of him, since he has made himself your patron and protector?'

I gave no response, which in itself was a response. After a while he spoke again, with a bitter smile. 'So, tell me,' he said. 'Have you an idea as to who murdered the girl?'

Now I, too, gestured towards the soldiers delving and dragging in the mud. 'I believe the Imperial Guard found the culprit here. Jan Madek was heard to speak violence against her for her betrayal of him.'

He gazed at me for a long moment then, thoughtfully fingering the sharp point of his beard. 'Yes, that is plausible,' he said. 'He was a hothead, certainly. We can be grateful he did not do worse. Had he harmed, or even tried to harm, a certain imperial personage, it would have shaken the state. The Catholics are itching for the chance to put one of their party on the throne.' He nodded slowly, still stroking his beard. 'Tell me, Stern, which side are you on?'

'I don't know that I know what sides there are,' I said.

He scoffed at that. 'Oh, come, man!' he said. 'You know there's Rome, and there is us.'

'Us?'

'The party of reform, and of stability.'

'The Protestants, you mean?'

Still he held my eye. 'I ask again,' he said. 'On which side of the line do you stand?'

One of the soldiers straightened from his work and shouted something to his fellows. Wenzel went down to the dwindling water's edge and called across to him. It was only some buried implement the fellow had found, a mattock by the look of it. Wenzel shook his head and climbed back up the bank, and we stood as before, beside each other but not together.

'My father was a bishop,' I said. 'He held to the faith of Rome.'

He laughed. 'A bishop's bastard, eh? That's no surprise.' He looked me up and down. 'And as to faith, what are you?'

'A philosopher of nature. God is in all things.'

He nodded, though not out of accord, and the look in his narrowed eyes was one of mockery. 'In all things, yes?' he said. 'In the canker that killed my father at the age of thirty? In the lump of iron that dolt just dug out of the mud? In the knife that slit Magdalena Kroll's young throat? Are my farts a divine afflatus? The God of all things is the God of none.'

'I would not have taken you for a theologian, my lord steward,' I said drily.

'And I would not have taken you for a fool,' he replied.

He began to move away, then turned back and faced me again. 'Will you allow yourself to be advised?' he asked. 'When there are sides, and there are always sides, you either choose, or the choice is made for you.' He paused, tipping his head back and looking narrowly at me along his nose, in that way he had. 'You were with Mistress Sardo just now. Oh, yes: there's nothing that happens here at court without my knowing of it.' He came a step closer to me, smiling now. 'Have a care,' he said softly. 'Your head hangs by a thread, and she has to give but one tug for you to lose it.'

He walked away along the riverbank. I watched him go, and then, hearing a whirring high up behind me, I turned. Looking up, I saw a crane flying above the trees. God knows why, but it sent a shiver through me to see that sublime bird, the magnificent stretch of it, straining through the clear blue icy air.

It was curious. Wenzel had asked me who I thought had killed the girl, yet he had made no mention of who might have killed her killer.

Presently I climbed back up the slope and passed into Golden Lane by way of the White Tower. I wondered if that was the tower where I had been imprisoned for, strange to say, I could not remember where I had been held that first night—or perhaps it is not strange, for the mind has a peculiar power to suppress those things it considers better not recalled. I tried to put that facility to use now, and banish from my thoughts Wenzel's warning about Caterina Sardo and the gleaming thread by which, according to him, my life was suspended.

Serafina was in the house, scrubbing the deal table with soap and water. The sight of her cheered me, as she worked there with her sleeves rolled up. Something in the way she leaned and stretched—the way her hand held the wet rag sweeping in broad loops over the pale wood—made me think of the crane rising above the snowy trees; suddenly, almost magically, it ceased to seem a bird of ill omen and

146

became, in this new manifestation, an image of life's lightness, of its soaring possibilities. How sprightly is the spirit's power to lift itself up from the depths, even on the darkest days.

Plato the cat greeted me in his accustomed fashion, weaving himself around my ankles and making a rattly purr deep in his chest.

Spelt cakes were cooking on top of the stove, and the air in the little room smelt sweetly of them. There was a marrowbone broth, too, and eggs and butter and honey that Serafina had brought in a basket from the nunciature, along with a little pail of mulled wine spiced with cloves and cinnamon. The fragrance of the drink brought back to me a piercing memory of my father the Bishop's palace in Regensburg, and the few visits I was allowed to make there as a boy; the Bishop liked his grog, and there was always a pot of it simmering down in the kitchens.

Serafina dried her hands and poured me a mug of the warmed wine. I reached for one of the cakes, which looked to be done, but she slapped my hand away and shook a finger at me, sternly smiling. She made signs to warn me that the cakes were not ready yet, and that anyway they would burn my mouth if I ate them straight from the stove.

It was surprising how quickly I had learned off the rudiments of her lexicon of signs. Already we had begun to communicate with some ease, and the range of our exchanges was remarkably broad, for all that when she was not there I could never recall exactly how we had managed to make ourselves understood to each other.

She had, I think, dear Serafina, the sweetest nature of any woman I have ever known. I say woman, but she was hardly more than a girl—she was, as I was shocked to realise, probably of the same age that Magdalena Kroll had been when her short life was so brutally quenched.

And yet how dissimilar they were, Magdalena Kroll and my Serafina—whole lives apart. At certain fixed hours of the day, Serafina would interrupt whatever task she was about and would go off into a corner and kneel there and pray silently for some minutes, her head bowed and eyes closed and her hands joined in a steeple before her, the tips of her fingers touching her silently moving lips. As for Magdalena Kroll, although I had not known her alive, I thought it unlikely, remembering how Caterina Sardo had spoken of her, that she would have been given to kneeling regularly on cold stone in devout communion with her Father in Heaven.

I filled my mug again from the pail of warm wine, and sitting myself down in the warmth of the stove, I plunged at once, irresistibly, into thoughts and speculations on all the day's events: the tour of the wonder rooms; the encounter, in equal measure bewitching and alarming, with Caterina Sardo; the confrontation in the Stag Moat with the vengeful High Steward. I thought of Madek too, of his scorched flesh, his empty eye sockets, of the cord about his neck. There were, I was convinced, two modes of murder here, two separate sorts of savagery. The doctor's daughter had been slain in an extremity of passion and madness, but the young man who loved her had been tortured and put to death by judicial process—that leather cord alone was the executioner's mark. But who had directed him in his grim task? That was the question that gnawed at me now.

As I mused on these matters, it came to me, not for the first time, that just as the universe is a vast and intricate code, some fragment of the meaning of which we seem somehow on occasion dimly to apprehend, through the force of the intellect, through magic and natural philosophy, but also in other, more mundane ways—most notably, and I suppose surprisingly, in the throes and ecstasies of profane love—so too behind the closer world, the one in which we lead our little lives and accomplish our worldly deeds, there is an altogether deeper, secret realm, where the puppet masters rule, pulling at the strings that control and direct us in what we imagine is the freedom of our actions. Of them too, the hidden masters, we are allowed to catch a glimpse now and then, when in all their dark sovereignty they choose to show themselves in order to cow and coerce us.

Wenzel had said I was a fool, and no doubt I was, by his standards. But I knew enough to understand that I had been right not to let him trap me into declaring which side I stood on in the matter of religion. Even then, before the century had turned, the world was buckling on its armour and picking up its sword in preparation for this terrible thirty-year-long war that has torn Europe asunder in a squabble over whose version of God should have ascendancy. A pox on priests, I say, and if my curse should condemn me, then I'll frolic with the suffering souls in Hell and not hanker after a Heaven that is none of mine.

I drank my drink, and huddled closer to the glowing stove. But the coldness in my bones was the coldness of dread, and no warm blaze could dispel it.

And the day was not done yet, not by a long way.

It was somewhat later, and I was sitting with Serafina at the table, the wood of which was still damp from her washing of it. We were finishing up the dish of broth and a platter of spelt cakes when a closed carriage came rumbling down the lane and stopped outside the door. I thought with a sinking heart that it would be Jeppe the dwarf, come to fetch me off to yet another undesignated rendezvous, and I was relieved, if startled as well, when I peeped out of the window to see Dr Kroll step down from the carriage and stand for a moment surveying the unimposing front of my little house.

Coming in at the door, he had to stoop—in these confines he loomed even larger than he had on the previous occasions when I had been in a position to take the measure of him. I greeted him with as much composure as I could manage: I felt a chafing awkwardness before his imposing presence, which made my abode and all the things within it, including, especially, myself, seem diminished. He pressed upon the place, this large unsmiling grieving man, like the shadow of a cloud on a summer's day, dimming the light suddenly and making everything seem to shrivel and shrink.

He looked at Serafina with a quizzical frown; at once she rose and took up her basket and put on her cloak and was gone, slipping out at the door as silent and quick as a cat.

'That is one of Malaspina's females, yes?' he said, leaning down to peer through the window at her hurriedly departing form. 'How is it she was here?'

'The Nuncio lends her to me, as a housekeeper,' I pointed to the table and the food Serafina had prepared for me, 'as you see.'

He shrugged this aside. 'Do you lie with her?' he asked. He waited. I let him wait. 'All right,' he said, 'don't answer. It's nothing to me whether you do or don't. I've no doubt there are greater sins you'll be damned for. But beware Malaspina: he is well named, for he is a poisoned thorn indeed.' He looked about disparagingly. 'Is this the best Lang could do for you?'

'Doctor,' I said, 'will you sit and take a mug of wine with me?' He looked at me hard, seeming to nibble on some small speck between his teeth, a muscle in his jaw working. 'Come, sir,' I said, and dared to lay a hand on his arm. 'Sit, you are in pain.'

He sat, and stared unseeing before him, his cheek still twitching. I poured a measure of the mulled wine into a mug and set it before him. He did not touch it, however, and seemed not even to notice it.

'This morning I buried my daughter,' he said. 'She lies beside her mother, in the Josefov cemetery, the Beth Chaim.' He glanced at me. 'Yes, my wife was a Jew. Does that surprise you?'

'I have the greatest respect for the Jews,' I said.

He gave a sort of laugh, and turned to the window again. 'I did not ask you for a testimony,' he said. 'I have no interest in what you think of the Jews, or anyone else. I'm not interested in anything about you, except that you were the one who found my daughter dead.' He was silent for a moment, then gave his head an angry shake, like a horse tormented by flies. 'I thank God my Rahel did not live to see our child so foully slaughtered. I wish I had not lived to see it myself.'

The winter sun had almost set, and the lane outside was momentarily aglow with a thin, honeyed radiance.

I said, 'The Emperor is set on knowing who it was that took her life.'

He laughed again, more darkly. 'And how is he to go about discovering that?'

I was preparing to answer when he stood up abruptly,

accidentally knocking over the mug of wine I had offered him. He paused there and watched the purplish stain spread across the recently scrubbed wood. Then he turned towards the door. 'Come,' he said, 'come walk with me.' He glanced again about the little room. 'In Prague even the walls are listening.'

I donned my coat and cap, and opened the door. We stepped out into the last of the winter twilight's golden dust.

We walked up the lane in silence, and then along by the wall as far as the Powder Tower and across to the cathedral and entered there through the high bronze double doors.

Under the immense, net-vaulted ceiling, the hallowed space was deserted. Our breath smoked in the chill air. We went forward and stood before the high altar, bathed in the crepuscular multi-tinted radiance falling down upon us from the towering stained-glass windows. Tall candles burned in silver sconces.

'I'm told it is you whom His Majesty has tasked with finding the killer of my daughter,' he said. 'Is that so?'

'That is so, yes,' I answered.

Wenzel: it would have been Wenzel who had told him; again I cursed myself for having spoken so intemperately to that man.

'And what have you discovered?' the doctor asked.

'It seems plain,' I said, 'that the young man Madek did the deed, in a transport of jealous rage.'

'That is what you think, is it? That is your finding?'

I felt a stirring of uncertainty. 'Yes, Doctor,' I said. 'Have you cause to doubt it?'

He was gazing up now at the silver crucifix set high above the altar. 'Have you ever thought,' he said, 'how strange a thing it is that the Christian faith should be founded on an atrocity? The Son of God, nailed to a wooden post.' He turned to me; his grieving eyes were hooded. 'I carried out an examination of the young man's corpse,' he said. 'He was dead while my daughter was alive.'

At first I could not take it in.

'But how could that be?' I asked. 'It was he—it was he that murdered her, surely. And he was caught, and tortured, and put to death.'

'That's what you may believe.'

'Yes, yes,' I said. 'I thought—' I broke off. By now I was not sure what I thought.

He shook his head. He was looking up again at the crucifix. 'Listen to me,' he said, in his slow deep weary way. 'He died before she did, killed by whom I know not. You shall have to look elsewhere for the killer of my daughter.'

14

After quitting the cathedral, I returned to Golden Lane wrapped in confusion and prey to a host of troubled speculations. The midwinter darkness had fallen swiftly, and there was a vast sky of glistening stars, just as there had been that other night when I had stumbled on the body of the doctor's daughter under the castle wall. I had no choice now but to believe that it could not have been Madek who had murdered her—'I know a week-old corpse when I see it,' Dr Kroll had said, and there was no doubting him. Two killers, then, for two corpses. I would have to tell the Emperor. That was not an interview I looked forward to with anything but dread.

Everything I had believed about this bloodstained business had been put at naught. I dearly wished I had not been charged with solving the riddle of the young woman's death. Indeed, I wished I had never come to Prague, and so desperate were my thoughts that night that I considered gathering up my belongings and fleeing the city at once under the shroud of darkness. Death had attended me since my arrival there: would it not be wise to leave now, lest I, too, should be caught up in the Dark One's web?

But how could I go, and where should I go to? Flight would be futile: they would find me, they would hunt me down, wherever I went.

Whoever *they* might be.

I felt I was half a dead man already.

Then I bethought myself, and chided myself for my weakness of spirit. Was I a child, mewling in fear of the dark and its imaginary monsters? Had I learned nothing from all my years of study at Würzburg? The world is a world of men, not devils, however devilishly men may act. That I could not yet see the faces of those who had murdered Magdalena Kroll and dispatched her forlorn lover did not mean they were faceless. Somewhere in the city, now, at this moment, those killers were going about their lives just as I was; they were just as vulnerable as I, just as prone to blundering mistakes, even as baffled, for all I knew. The Emperor had put his trust in me, in *me*, against the likes of his High Steward and his Chamberlain—against the whole world, I was his chosen man. I would not, could not, fail him.

The embers in the stove had redness in them still. I stoked them to life, and heated the last of the marrowbone broth and ate it with spelt cake crumbled into it, and drank also the last of the mulled wine, not caring that it was cold by now. Then I trimmed the wick of my oil lamp and got myself into bed, still in my clothes, to read some pages of Pliny the Elder, who was a favourite author of mine in those days, and still is.

Life's little rituals—how should we survive without them?

I am not sure how much time had passed before I heard a sound outside that woke me from the doze I had dropped into, but the lamp had burned low, so it must have been a matter of some hours. The book was still open in my hands but my chin had sunk onto my chest; my eyelids felt hot and were as heavy as flakes of lead.

The sound seemed to be a sort of panting, or harsh

gasping, as if some creature were in the lane outside, nosing at the lower part of my front door. Had I been in a hut in the woods, instead of in the centre of a great city, I would have said it was a wild boar scavenging after scraps, for the sounds were very like a sort of swinish snuffling. I listened intently, thinking it might be my imagination playing a trick on me.

But no: something, or someone, was out there.

Plato, who had been asleep in my lap, had woken too, and stood up now on all four paws and arched his back, his fur bristling.

I rose soundlessly from the bed and crept to the door and wrenched it open.

It was black night outside, for the sky had clouded over, and either the lamplighter had not come on his rounds yet or the lamp at the far end of the lane had been doused. The result was that at first I could see nothing—I had left my own light at the bedside—but I heard a quick scuffle and then the rapid patter of feet, or paws, as it might be. Stepping over the threshold, I peered in the direction where the sounds were retreating and seemed to see a low, bent shape hopping and scampering along at a rapid pace. I thought of Jeppe the dwarf, but I knew it was not he. I could not be sure it was even a human shape. I had the impression, I could not say why, of a large and general gleefulness, as if the night itself had joined with the fleeing creature to make savage fun of me.

I called out a challenge, only the thing by now had disappeared into the darkness. I went back inside the house and tried to strike a little warmth from the stove, but in vain, for all that remained were ashes. The air was bitingly cold.

It might have been an animal, I thought, some half-wild

thing that had escaped from the royal menagerie, in which were kept all manner of exotic creatures, including apes—perhaps it was one of those that had climbed out of its cage to go wandering about in the night. But I didn't think so, not really. I was convinced it had been a human form, though no bigger than a large child; however, the impression it had left behind, of dark and malignant mockery, was far from childish.

I lay awake for a long time, listening to the sounds of the night, afraid that whatever the thing had been might return. I kept the lamp lit beside me; its flickering flame threw hunched and undulating shadow-shapes upon the walls and ceiling. Dawn was coming up when I fell at last into a kind of sleep, and dreamed of walking along a riverbank. Seeing something resembling a swollen grey sack bobbing in the shallows, I waded out and grabbed it and turned it over, only to find a drowned girl, eyeless and without a mouth and wound tightly all round with leather cords.

I woke, gratefully, to the sound of Serafina raking out the stove.

Soon she had a pot of water heating for my morning shave, and soon, too, a warm brown fragrance began to suffuse the air, from a pot of that Turkish coffee drink I had first tasted after my lunch with the Nuncio. It was wonderfully stimulating, and already I had developed almost a craving for it, especially at morning time. Handing me my cup, Serafina put a finger to her lips and shook her head, swearing me to secrecy, for she had pinched a bag of the precious beans from the larder at the nunciature and ground them in a clever little machine that she had brought with her.

The sky was clear again, and an angled spike of early sunlight came in through the window.

I sat down at the table and read some more pages of Pliny while Serafina heated up the remains of yesterday's spelt cakes, which added their own sweet savour to the air. My cup was already empty, and she came and poured out another dose of the hot black brew, her breath warm against my ear. Then she sat down beside me, with Plato the cat in her lap—they played together endlessly, those two. She smiled at me; she had such a sweet, shy smile, I see it even now, as if she were here before me.

Just then, however, in the midst of the morning's homely contentments, I experienced a stab of foreboding as sharp as the shaft of sunlight in the window. I felt no concern for myself; I feared for Serafina. I had accepted her services as though they were my natural due, yet now it seemed to me that in some way, a way I could not name, I was leading her inexorably into peril.

A moment later she stood and turned away from where I sat. As she did, I took her hand and looked up at her earnestly, as if somehow to communicate—what? A warning? Yes, a warning, though of what kind I could not have said. At first she smiled, but then, seeing the anxiety in my look, she frowned and drew away from me, and went to the stove. She stood there with a hand to her mouth, glancing back at me over her shoulder.

I wished I could tell her what the matter was, but how could I, since I myself did not understand the nature of the chill draught that had caused me such an inward shiver? And what should I have said, had I been able to speak? Just this: that the world bides, crouched in cover, waiting to spring, and that there are moments when all unexpectedly we feel upon our cheek a waft of its ravenous breath.

Ah, my poor Serafina, my poor lost girl.

On impulse I rose from the table and went to the cup-board where I kept hidden the purse of money my father the Bishop had sent to me from his deathbed, and from it I took the gold ring that I believed had belonged to my mother. I caught hold of Serafina's hand again—she tried to resist but I would not let her go—and slipped the ring onto her finger. She stared at it, and then at me.

'It was my mother's,' I said, my voice shaking, 'do you understand? It belonged to my mother.' She shook her head almost angrily, frustrated by her own incomprehension. I put a hand to my breast, and lifted up her hand and pointed to the ring on her finger. '*Mia madre*,' I said. 'It was hers, yes? *Mia madre*.'

Now she smiled at last—it seemed like the sun coming out—and nodded rapidly. She was blushing, and there were tears in her eyes. She turned away from me to hide her face. I put a hand on her shoulder, and thus we stood, for a long time, she with her back to me, and I touching her, feeling how she trembled.

At last she stirred and looked towards the window, where something had caught her attention. Almost before I knew it, just as she had done yesterday when Dr Kroll had come, she took up her coat and, without a glance in my direction, opened the door and was gone.

I moved to follow her, and reached the doorway just as a carriage was stopping outside.

'I see we have frightened away your little pet mouse,' Caterina Sardo said, putting out her head at the carriage window. 'Look how she scurries! Will you be very cross with me now?'

She withdrew her head and opened the door. Giving me

her soft hand, she stepped down to the cobbles, where she paused and leaned her head to one side with a look of pouting reproof. 'What?' she said. 'Not even a greeting?'

'Forgive me, madam,' I answered. 'It's early, and you find me at something of a disadvantage.'

'I gave you warning that we should descend on you,' she said mischievously. 'I am always as good as my word; that's something you must learn.'

Behind her, Petra was getting down from the carriage, with her cheekily mocking eye and wound-up thick plaits and her pink little button of a nose. 'Well, then, you're welcome, ladies,' I said. 'Will you come inside?'

Caterina Sardo turned to the maid and widened her eyes in feigned shock. 'Why, Petra,' she said, 'hear how he makes a lady of you! We shall have bowing and scraping and kissing of hands next.'

I stood aside for them to enter through the doorway, then followed after. As we came in, Plato the cat ran out, darting swiftly past me in the doorway. He had a keener nose for trouble than I did.

Caterina Sardo wore an elegant gown of heavy black silk and a starched ruff with pointed lacing all round its edge. The sleeves of her gown were puffed, which made her small pale delicate hands seem smaller and more delicate still.

She looked about the room and wrinkled her nose. 'Oh, you drink that vile stuff the Mussulmans so love,' she said. 'I can smell the stench of it, like burning hair.'

'I'm sorry, madam, that it offends you,' I said. 'I find it enlivening.'

She cast a laughing look at me. 'Do you, now.' She turned back to the maid. 'Petra, don't stare so at the Herr Professor's things! Don't you know how rude it is? Anyway, you may go. Come back and fetch me in . . .' she glanced at me with an eyebrow arched '. . . an hour, say? The *gentile professore* will divert me for that long with wonderful facts and fancies. Won't you?'

Petra was biting her lip and trying not to smirk. 'Yes'm,' she said, and having made a flouncing curtsy, she turned to go. Passing me she paused, however, and whispered, 'Sir, will you tell me what that object is?'

She was pointing to a little brass astrolabe that I had set on the windowsill. It was one of my most prized possessions— I have it yet—fashioned according to my specifications and at much expense by that master craftsman Isaiah Ortelius of Nuremberg. I took it up and laid it on the girl's palm. 'It is an instrument,' I said, 'for predicting the positions of the sun and the moon, the planets, and even of the fixed stars. A very ingenious contrivance.'

She gazed at the gleaming thing in silence for a moment, then thrust it back into my hands and departed as speedily as Serafina before her.

'You frightened her,' Caterina Sardo said, with a shrug. 'She thinks such devices the work of the Devil.' She came and stood before me, very close, smiling into my face. 'But perhaps you are a devil, Christian Stern. A minor one.'

In my confusion I could think of no reply. Why was she here, at this early hour of the morning, dressed as if for a state occasion? That the obvious answer did not at once occur to me is an indication not so much of the purity of my mind but of my cognisance of the fact that she was the Emperor's mistress and the mother of his children. Besides, she was older even than the innkeeper's wife at the Blue Elephant; it seemed unlikely, to say the least, that such a personage would present herself on a winter morning at a hovel in Golden Lane with the aim of seducing a penniless young scholar. And yet I had not forgotten that kiss she had given me in her sewing room—how could I forget it, light and brief though it had been?

'You must excuse me,' I said, 'but I have no refreshment to offer you, since you don't like the Turkish brew.'

'Why, sir—do I seem in need of refreshing?'

'I merely meant—'

'Oh, fie! Must you be so grave? I shall not eat you—' she gave a little silvery laugh '—unless you should wish me to. Dr Kepler, the stargazer, who knows everything, or claims to, tells me the female spider devours the male once the mating business is done with. What a world we live in—can you believe such a thing?'

Before I could answer—and what would I have answered anyway?—she turned aside with a sort of cheerful flounce. It struck me that in her bustled black gown and puffed sleeves she did somewhat resemble a large and sinisterly lovely spider.

Now she walked about the room, picking up this or that of my things to look at and then toss carelessly aside. She put her head into the scullery, and after that drew back the curtain that hid the cackstool.

'My my,' she said. 'Surely Chamberlain Lang could have done somewhat better for you than this. I shall speak to him.' She took up the astrolabe. 'Did you mean to slight me by ignoring me while you entertained my maid's silly curiosity about this thing?'

She did not look at me.

'No indeed, madam,' I said, with a certain stiffness, 'but I am a scholar and a teacher, and it is my habit to reply when my knowledge is appealed to.'

'Please don't do it again,' she said, but mildly. 'I can be very cross when I am crossed.'

She sat down suddenly at the table, and with a gesture invited me to join her. I took the other chair. She folded her pale hands in her lap.

'Do you like my gown?' she asked. 'It's new—this is my first wearing of it.'

'It's very handsome,' I said. 'It becomes you well.'

'Do you not think it a little too close-fitting at the bosom?' She looked down at herself, frowning. 'I seem so flat.'

She glanced up at me again and laughed. I have never been so much laughed at, without minding, as I was by Caterina Sardo.

'Did you study medicine?' she asked. 'At—where was it?'

'Würzburg. Yes, I did. A little.'

'Then you can advise me. I think there is something the matter with my heart. I have consulted Dr Kroll, but he says there is nothing amiss, although between you and me, I think he is a humbug and knows nothing. Will you measure my pulse? They say the pulse tells all about the heart's condition.'

She held out to me a white wrist traced with fine blue veins. I pressed my thumb to it. Her skin was cool, and delicately brittle, like paper.

'It seems usual to me,' I said. 'I can detect no trace of fever or the like.'

'But I can,' she said, with another sulky pout. 'I am quite feverish, I'm sure of it. Here, feel.' She took my hand and put it to her breast. 'Don't you think the beat is much too swift?'

'It's not easy to tell, madam,' I said.

She gazed into my face. I'm sure I was blushing—yes, yes, I know, I blush like a girl; it has always been one of my afflictions. Cautiously I withdrew my hand.

'Wait, you must try again,' she said. She unhooked the top part of her gown, and took my hand again and slipped it into the opening. She wore no chemise, and my palm encountered her bare flesh, curved and warm, and the hard little tip of her breast. 'Do you feel it now, how fast it runs, my poor heart?'

'Madam,' I said, my voice thickening, 'I am not so qualified as you may think. I'm sure that Dr Kroll—'

'Oh, a fig for Kroll! I tell you, he knows nothing.'

I gave my hand a gentle tug, but she held me fast by the wrist.

'Do you find me pretty?' she asked, peering closely into my face.

'Certainly, madam,' I answered.

I glanced towards the window and the pallid wintry day outside. I thought of Jeppe the dwarf, how he had stopped there and peered in. What if someone were to do the same now, and spy me fondling the bosom of the Emperor's mistress?

'I'm not so much as I once was—pretty, I mean,' she said. 'But I am shapely still, do you not think? Infants are a wearisome burden, but I gave all of mine out to wet nurses, as I'm sure you can tell.' She had taken on a feline stillness, her gaze at once piercing and softly remote. 'You're trembling,' she said. 'I can feel it. Do I disquiet you? Are you afraid of me?'

'I worry, madam, that someone in the street might—'

'Might see us? Might see *you*, with your hand in my bodice? You must not worry. His Majesty doesn't care, you know, what I do, or whom I do it with. He has his toys, his games, his naughty pictures that his court painters make for him. And his girls, of course, and boys, he has them, too, by the score.'

There was a vein throbbing in the flesh of her breast; it was as if I held some plump warm living creature in my hand.

'How much of the hour has elapsed, I wonder?' She looked about vaguely. 'You have no clock. Rudi has hundreds—did he show them to you? Such a clamour when they chime! When it does not give me the megrims it makes me laugh, which makes him cross. He's such a booby.'

She stood up suddenly, freeing my hand and letting it fall to my lap. She did up the hooks of her gown.

'So I shall not die, you say, and old Kroll is right.' She shrugged. 'Oh, well. I rather liked the notion of myself a corpse, all pale and still and at peace. Do you ever wish to be released from this bad world?'

'To die, you mean?' I asked. I was looking up at her. My own heart now was making a sort of agitated booming in my breast.

'Yes, to die,' she said. 'I do, often. My life is nothing but tedium; I cannot value it.'

Her tone so belied her words that I had to smile. She laid her fingers against my cheek, and then sat down again. 'Ask me something,' she said.

'Ask you what?'

'Anything. Anything in the world.'

I did not hesitate, although no doubt I should have. 'Why will His Majesty not marry you?' I said.

She stared at me blankly for a moment, then drew back her head and laughed. I had a vivid picture of myself taking her by the shoulders and fastening my lips to her tender throat, yet at the same time I was in a sweat of terror—anyone might look in at that window, at any moment.

'Well,' she said, still laughing, 'I did say you might ask anything.' She put a fingertip to her chin and pursed her lips and turned her gaze upwards, considering. 'Let me see.' She crossed one knee on the other and jiggled her foot. 'He never wished to marry, I believe. His mother, that hag, persuaded Philip of Spain to engage his daughter the Infanta Isabella to him when the girl was five, but nothing came of it. Later on Maria de' Medici was offered to him as a bride, but he eluded her, too. He can be very clever and cunning, when he wants, you know. Of course, he could never marry me, even if he wished to—the court would not have it.'

'And are you not more persuasive than the court?'

'Ah, I fear not,' she said, with wistful amusement, shaking her head. 'Anyway, why do you think I would want the old goat to marry me? I'm happy as I am. Behind my back they call me the Invisible Mistress, to mock me, not realising that is exactly what I wish to be, and to remain—invisible.'

She took my hand again, but this time only to hold it between both of hers in a way that was hardly more than amicable, as if we were two children, playing at being grown-ups.

'And now it's my turn to ask you something,' she said.

'Of course, madam.'

She gave my hand a reproving little shake. 'You must call me Caterina, or Cate. That is how my friends address me, if I have any friends—though you are going to be one of them, of course.'

I look back to that day and try to see myself as I was then—that is, I try to recall what I was thinking—but in vain. I was swept up in a mindless transport of mingled wonderment, fright, and confused desire. That such a woman, set so high in the great world, even if her position was unacknowledged, should be sitting there before me, confiding in me as if I were already her lover, seemed at once outlandish and peculiarly fitting.

Her hands holding my hand were soft and cool. I could feel the smooth yet slightly brittle stuff of her gown against my fingers and, under the gown, the warmth of her lap. Her hair today was coiled in two plaits above her forehead on either side; her lips glistened pinkly. I could feel yet in my palm the imprint of her bare breast that she had led me to caress, so tenderly, so teasingly.

'What is it you wish to ask me, madam? Cate, I mean.'

'Just this,' she said. 'Did the Chamberlain's men find what it was he set them to search for in the moat?'

This was not at all a question I could have expected, and it sent a chill into me. I took away my hand once more, though she strove playfully to keep it captive.

'I don't know what they found,' I said, 'if they found anything.'

'And what do you think they were looking for?'

'A blade, perhaps,' I said, 'the one they thought Jan Madek used on Magdalena Kroll. But the effort was wasted.'

'Oh? How so?'

'Madek did not kill the girl. He was dead before she died.'

She frowned. 'Before?' she said.

'Yes. Her father examined Madek's corpse. The young man was already dead when Magdalena Kroll was murdered. And he did not drown himself, as I at first imagined he must have done.'

167

'Then what killed him?' she asked.

'First he was tortured and his eyes were put out; then he was strangled with a cord.'

I had meant my words to shock, which only shows how little I knew this lady yet.

'Ah, I see,' was all she said. She frowned again, thinking. 'I thought it was something else.'

'Something else?'

'That the Chamberlain was searching for. He pretends to be my confidant, but there are things he does not tell me. A strongbox—did he mention anything like that?'

'No,' I said. 'But I have heard talk of it before.'

At this she fairly pounced. 'From whom?'

'From Schenckel, the dwarf.'

She made a grimace. 'That toad,' she said, but distractedly, for she was still deep in thought.

'And what would have been in this locked box?' I asked. 'Something of value, something precious, surely?'

She nodded, looking away, her brows drawn together in the shape of a chevron. 'Oh, yes,' she said, 'very precious, I think.'

There was a tap at the window then, and she looked up with what I thought was, despite all her brave talk, a flicker of alarm. It passed when she realised who was there.

'But see,' she said, 'here is Petra, ever prompt.'

She gathered her skirts close about herself and stood up. She was a changed woman now, flirtatious no longer, though not because of the maid's sudden appearance; I guessed she was still brooding on that missing strongbox.

I wanted to press her to tell me what exactly was in it—for I was sure she knew—but I did not dare. Sometimes even the mildest enquiry gives off an alerting flash.

Petra was in the doorway. Caterina proffered me her hand, which I took lightly in mine, and bowed.

'Good day, *professore*,' she said, all coolness now.

'Good day, madam,' I replied, my manner formal too.

She went to the doorway and out into the street. Petra, behind her, turned to me with a fleeting, brazen grin. Then they climbed into the carriage and it rolled away.

I waited all afternoon for Serafina to return, but there was no sign of her. At evening I went down and took my dinner at the Blue Elephant, despite the memory of that execrable dish of mutton stew. The innkeeper's wife was not to be seen, which I was glad of—there had been enough of women about me for one day.

The day, however, still had its night to come.

Having finished my dinner, such as it was, I took up my mug of ale and went and sat in the inglenook, by the fire, as I had sat with the old soldier on a night that seemed so long ago now as to have been in another time, in another life. I fancied I could detect Caterina Sardo's fragrance on my fingers yet. Why, really, had she come to me today? I was not so besotted, or so simple-minded, as to think it had been purely for the pleasure of having me put my hand on her heart. Why had she asked those questions about Chamberlain Lang and what he might have been hoping to find sunk in the mud of the Stag Moat? I had by now heard more mentions of the strongbox than I could count: what was Caterina's interest in it? Once again I saw myself as a lost traveller starting awake at nightfall in a place I did not recognise, with only darkness before me, darkness and danger.

I had returned to Golden Lane and was asleep in my bed, with the lamp doused, when a sound wakened me. I looked to see a dim figure in the room, shimmering towards me. I sprang up with a cry, thinking to be attacked—I was remembering the sinister visitant of the night before—but a hand reached out and touched me.

It was Serafina.

Naked under her flimsy shift, she slipped into the bed beside me. Her delicate hands were chill, and mine must have been too, for she shivered at my touch. When she kissed me I led her gently to open her mouth, for, although it shames me to say so, since the day when Bishop Malaspina told me of her disfigurement, I had been eager to explore inside that poor damaged hollow, where only the stump of a tongue remained.

She clung to me and wept. I touched her face, the buds of her breasts, the soft, warm scrap of fleece at her lap. Yes, we kissed and touched, but all the same, though I know I will not be believed, fondling was as far as it went, throughout that long night. It surprises me to think myself so chivalrous. Or was it that I had been too distracted by recollections of another's breast, another's warm and warmly promising lap?

I I

January 1600

15

Surely there could be no better blazon to lift the heart on a clear crisp winter morning than the brassy blare of a bugle. That day, in the first month of a new year and a new century, even Rudolf the Melancholy smiled to hear those raucous notes. He hurried to the nearest window, his pale feminine hands clasped at his breast in excited anticipation, and peered down into the broad courtyard below. A multitude of townsfolk was massed there, filling the entire square. Through it a squad of halberdiers was clearing the way for the royal bugler; following after him, four sturdy young men bore between them on their shoulders a wooden pole from which was suspended by thick leather bands a very large, flat packing case wrapped securely in canvas.

I was among the band of courtiers gathered under the magnificently vaulted ceiling of the Great Hall of the Royal Palace, and counted myself the equal of any there, even Felix Wenzel—even, for that matter, the all-powerful Chamberlain Lang. You shall judge the great transformation that had come about in my fortunes when I describe the outfit in which I disported myself that day.

I wore a shirt of finest linen with a soft lace collar and matching lace ringlets at the wrists; a doublet of dark blue velvet boned to make a narrowing to the waist; wine-red trunk hose, paned, complete with a stiffened codpiece; silk nether stockings; and shoes of Spanish leather with silver buckles. I was, it pains me to confess, particularly vain of my hat, which was of soft velvet like the doublet, gathered into a high crown and decorated with a jewelled band and a jaunty white cockade at the left side. Over the weeks I had grown the beginnings of a pencil beard, which today was oiled and neatly pointed, and complemented by a fine stiff moustache; the beard and whiskers, to my pleased surprise, had come out a softly reddish hue. My hair was cut short and brushed well back—the Blue Elephant's lice were the merest memory now—with a woven lovelock trailing gallantly over my right shoulder.

I wore a ruby ring, too, a gift from the Emperor himself. It was not so large or ostentatious as the one Chamberlain Lang liked to display, but to my eye it was more tasteful by far.

So, as you see, I had undergone a marvellous transfiguration, overseen and financed by a great lady. I was, in short, quite the gentleman.

'Come,' His Majesty said, 'come, let us go down.' He scurried to the door, with the rest of us behind him in a rush.

In the courtyard the four young men had halted, looking very solemn and self-conscious. They had come on an immense journey, by foot, all the way over the Alps from Venice, bearing their precious cargo.

Rudolf thanked them, one by one, and presented to each of them a gold Joachimsthaler, specially minted for the occasion, while the crowd, held well back by the halberdiers, elbowed and jostled, craning for a rare view of the people's reclusive sovereign.

He directed that the package, which when seen close to was indeed a mighty thing, should be brought up to the

Long Corridor. So the four carriers, a pair in front and a pair behind, shouldered the two ends of the wooden pole again and tramped up the stone stairway, with us courtiers in their wake. Rudolf skipped ahead of them, glancing back anxiously, as if he feared that, after lugging their precious cargo safely over the mountain passes in the depths of winter, the quartet of bearers might still come to disaster in this last short stage of the journey.

Jeppe Schenckel, climbing the stairs beside me, snickered. 'Look at him,' he murmured, gesturing after the Emperor. 'Like a virgin on her wedding night, worrying for her maidenhead.'

In the picture room the package was set down on the floor and stripped first of its canvas covering, then of layer upon layer of soft carpet cushioned on cotton wadding, until at last, to a general and deliberately exaggerated sigh of wonder and admiration, the gorgeous treasure was revealed, aglow in its heavy gilt frame.

It was *The Feast of the Rosary*—how clearly I can bring it to my mind's eye, even yet—a scene commissioned a century past from the master painter Albrecht Dürer by the banker Jakob Fugger and a guild of businessmen in Nuremberg, Meister Dürer's birthplace. Since its completion, the picture had stood as a panel above the altar in the Church of San Bartolomeo in Venice, a favourite place of worship for the numerous German residents of that seaborne city.

For years Rudolf had been lusting after this masterpiece, in which not only his ancestor the Emperor Maximilian I is depicted, but also, in the background, the painter himself, peering out at us with a curiously uncertain eye. At last the painting was in his possession, and now he stood gazing at it, where it leaned in its glory against the wall, the packaging strewn at its base, like the jumble of a lady's petticoats that she had let fall at her feet.

Without taking his greedy gaze from the picture, Rudolf flapped a hand at the courtiers crowding behind him, dismissing us from his presence.

In silence we shuffled out of the room, leaving him to his pleasure.

On the morrow there would be a banquet to celebrate the acquisition of His Majesty's heart's desire—his agents had paid nine hundred ducats for the painting—but for now he wished to savour it in solitude, as if indeed it were his bride and he must be left alone with her.

At the foot of the staircase I was accosted by the Englishman Sir Henry Wotton, diplomatist and, as everyone knew, master spy, who plucked at my sleeve and drew me to one side. 'How pleasant to see His Majesty so pleased,' he said genially, 'eh, Dr Stern?'

He was a clever fellow, this Sir Henry, and handsome enough, in his way, clad in purple silk, with a beard fuller than mine, and a humorous though ever-watchful eye. I have an instinctive wariness of these silky-smooth Englishmen. But this one's Latin was faultless and elegant, and I always would forgive a man much for a well-turned phrase.

'Yes, Sir Henry,' I said. 'His Majesty does love a picture.'

'And this one in particular, it seems.'

'It's a masterly thing, and he is a connoisseur.'

'Indeed, indeed.'

He had an unctuous way of bowing, lowering his head but a little way and softly closing his eyes for the space of a moment.

We walked out into the square, on the far side of which the great dark brown masses of the cathedral loomed

sombrely in the pale winter sunlight. The crowd had not dispersed and there was an air almost of carnival. After long
weeks of bruised grey skies, a little early sunshine worked
a remarkable effect in this ice-bound, land-locked city.

'I am told, sir,' Wotton said, glancing carefully about
him, 'that you have close access to the royal ear.'

I wondered who would have told him so, but then
bethought myself that he would not have needed telling,
since after all my standing with the Emperor was by now a
broadly known fact. 'His Majesty is well disposed towards
me, yes,' I said, putting a certain stiffness into it so that he
should know there was no intimacy on offer here.

He nodded again, smoothly smiling. 'You are almost, I
hear, a member of the royal household.'

I knew well what this was a sly allusion to, and gave him
a cold stare. 'You seem to be talked to by many people, sir,'
I said.

He gave again a slight bow, still smiling his bland diplo-
matic smile. 'It's true, I'm keen of hearing, and catch at
things in flight—it's what I was trained for, to listen well.'

It was a question at court as to why Sir Henry was in
Prague at all. He gave it out, to anyone crass enough to
enquire, that he was bound for Italy, to process some business at the Vatican on behalf of James of Scotland—but
Prague was hardly a way-station on the road to Rome. His
chief patron, the Earl of Essex, had earned the displeasure
of Queen Elizabeth after a disastrous campaign in which
he was supposed to have quelled the unruly Irish but had
failed. I speculated that perhaps the wily envoy had thought
it prudent to quit his native land and take himself off for a
while to a distant and safer place, until the royal lady's
choler had cooled and his aristocratic master was out of

danger. It was said that Essex in a rage had half drawn his sword on the Queen: 'He lost his head yet kept his head,' as Chamberlain Lang had put it to me, with a wink.

But for all the polish of Wotton's manner, I could see from a glint of urgency in his eye that there was something he hoped to have of me.

'Do you know the countryside round about?' he asked, in a mild, conversational tone. 'I imagine it's very fair, especially in springtime.'

'No doubt,' I said. 'But I've seen little of it myself—Regensburg is my place of birth, and I've not travelled much here in Bohemia.'

We had skirted the cathedral and were walking down the cobbled incline past St George's Basilica. The Englishman seemed deeply preoccupied.

'Are you familiar with the town of Most?' he asked.

Aha, I thought, now I have your drift. 'I have not been there, no,' I said.

'How far away from Prague is it, do you know?'

'Some five and twenty leagues, I believe. May I ask why do you ask?'

Oh, how innocent I made myself sound!

I noticed to my surprise that we had come to Golden Lane—that street seemed to work magnetic powers on me, although it was weeks since I had moved from there to far grander quarters up here on Hradčany Hill.

'That's where I lodged,' I said, pointing to the familiar door, 'when I first came to Prague.'

'And when was that?' Sir Henry enquired, without, it was obvious, the least interest in knowing the answer.

'Not very long ago,' I said. 'I arrived last month from Würzburg, where I had been a scholar.'

We had stopped before the little house which used to be mine, and which I gazed upon now with some emotion, thinking of poor mute Serafina.

'You have been in Prague only since then?' Sir Henry exclaimed, in exaggerated wonder. 'So short a time in which to have risen so far!'

I could see from his quick frown that he regretted having spoken so unguardedly; I imagine wincing is what a diplomat most often finds himself doing. But, after all, he was right. The swiftness of my ascent was a source of constant surprise to me, as well as constant, secret misgiving: the loftier the perch, the further there would be to fall.

'So, Most,' Sir Henry said, with the air of one hurrying to change the subject. 'Most is quite far off—five and twenty leagues, you say?'

'I believe so, yes,' I answered.

'Hmm. But there is perhaps a good road?'

'Are you intending to travel there?' I asked.

He hesitated again. 'I should require a permit, I imagine?'

'Yes, most likely.'

'And who would issue it?'

We had come to the end of the lane. A scudding cloud covered the sun; it was as if a lamp had been blown out.

'If you wish, Sir Henry,' I said, 'I can enquire of His Majesty's Chamberlain.'

'Oh, no no no no no no no,' he said hurriedly, lifting his hands in soft protestation. 'I'm sure His Excellency Herr Lang has matters of far greater importance to attend to—I would not dream of troubling him with such a trifle.'

We stood in the cloud's shadow, the Englishman frowning and absently fingering a scrap of ribbon on the front of his doublet. I knew now why he had come to Prague, and why he wished to travel to Most. That was where the sorcerer and spy Edward Kelley was held captive, at the Emperor's behest, in a prison cell set high on the wall of Castle Hněvín. But why should such a lofty gentleman as Sir Henry Wotton wish to talk to the likes of Kelley, disgraced and locked away as he was?

Up on the hill, the cathedral bell began to chime.

'Ah, is that the hour?' Sir Henry said. 'I must leave you, Herr Doktor, for I have a pressing appointment at the castle.' He lifted his hat and bowed, with an oily smile, and hurried away.

I walked back to my former abode and tried the door, but it was locked, and I had long ago misplaced the key. With my hands at either side of my face, I peered in at the cobwebbed window, as once Jeppe Schenckel had peered in at me. Inside, it seemed as empty as it had been on the morning I moved out.

It was Caterina Sardo who had effected my transfer to new and, as she said, more suitable quarters at the castle.

'This will not do!' she had exclaimed one day, as she was putting back on her gown. 'There's not even a proper place for me to do pee-pee!'

And so the next morning, after I had quitted the house, with Plato the cat tucked under my arm, the Chamberlain's men came back, as covertly as before, and took my things and transported them up to the castle, to a room in the Northern Wing, hard by the Foundry there, a room with tall windows that looked out over the Stag Moat and the spot where Jan Madek's corpse had been found in the frozen stream. There was an ornate desk for me to work at, a table with carved legs for me to eat my supper on, and a canopied bed for me to sleep in, that bed where, on lazy, love-drunk afternoons, Caterina Sardo would join me in secret.

This love of mine was mad, of course, but oh, so sweet. Or no, not sweet, for Caterina had a bitter taste. For me our passion was as a deep draught of some dark and instantly intoxicating liquor. And drunk I was, my state of mind a constant, terrified euphoria. I was like a condemned man on the gallows, looking all around at a fair and sunlit prospect, forgetful of the noose about my neck, a silken noose so soft I could hardly feel it, the noose that, when the terrible moment should come, would snap tight and quench me for ever.

Caterina ridiculed me for my fears. 'Oh, Rudi is too much engrossed in his toys. He won't find us out,' she would say. 'And even if he does, he will not care. He loves you more than he loves me—more even than he loves our children, the ones he deigns to acknowledge.'

She made a joke of the gap in age between us. She would say I must think her a hag, then lie back and smile to hear my earnest assurances that she was the freshest, loveliest, altogether the most captivating creature it was my miraculous good fortune ever to have held in my arms. In truth, to me her flesh had a slightly tarnished texture, but, however unnatural it may seem, this tarnishing was the very quality in her that most excited and enthralled me. She would lie languidly in my arms like a large pale soft-skinned doll that had been toyed with overmuch. Then at other times she would seem to retreat from me into a feline stillness, and turn her back on me, inert and indifferent.

I itched to break through the carapace of her amused disdain. She never said she loved me without laughing.

It delighted her to provoke me. 'Go on,' she would say,

'strike me—I won't feel it. And if I do, I shall like it anyway.'

It was she who had chosen and paid for my new clothing, who had directed me to cut my hair and grow my boyish beard, and plaited with her own fingers the lovelock that hung over my shoulder. At times I felt like a doll myself, a manikin for her to play with, to dress and undress, to tease and scold, to fondle and, at the end of it all, put hotly to bed.

Of those offspring of hers, hers and the Emperor's—Philipp Lang once said to me, with a grim laugh, 'She has not children, but wolf cubs'—she would not speak, and kept them from me. It angered her if I so much as mentioned them, not that I often did; I was reticent especially in the case of the uncanny man-boy Don Giulio, whom I had first glimpsed that day when, on the way to my initial encounter with his mother, I looked down from the little window on the return of the stairs and saw him in the picture room, looking up at me as earlier I had looked up at his mother.

Caterina's rages were always a sudden incandescence. She would shriek and spit and kick, cursing me in Italian; then a minute later she would fall to her knees before me and implore forgiveness, raking her nails down my chest and cursing herself for a fool, a madwoman, a strumpet—'Oh, I am a bad, bad girl!'

She made me tell her of every woman I had ever known and loved. I was unwilling at first—not least, if truth be told, because there had been so few—until I saw how it stoked her passion to hear of my loves in precise, in dirtiest, detail. She would watch me avidly as I spoke, her eyes glittering, her lips moist and slightly parted, each breath flowing from her more as a slow, silent moan.

From Rudolf's well-stocked library she would bring books, coarse and obscene texts by Aretino and his like, which she would have me read aloud to her while she lay beside me with her skirts around her waist, lazily pleasuring herself.

She was a priestess of passion, to which she gave herself with narrow-eyed concentration and cold delight. On one of the first occasions when we lay together in the house in Golden Lane—I'm sure if I were required to, I could recall and recount in perfectly framed images every single such occasion—she stood up naked from my sleeping couch and turned to say something to me, and for a moment the wintry sun in the window made a radiant soft wheel of light about her head. It was then that I saw how closely she resembled the painted Venus who had stirred me to secret desire that day in Bishop Malaspina's house. I believe that inside every man there is hung a stylised portrait of the ideal woman, a model against which to measure this or that flesh-and-blood mortal he holds in his arms. Caterina Sardo was no vision of perfect loveliness—her skin had a slightly sallow cast, her breasts and belly were no longer those of a young woman, her legs were thin and touched each other at the knees—yet to me she seemed the being towards whom I had been yearning all my life and at last had found, my tainted sweetling, my darling succubus.

It was to her I went after my encounter with Sir Henry Wotton; it was to her I always went when I was troubled or in need of advice. I did not realise it at the time, and probably should not admit it now, but of course one of the springs of my love for her was the fact that, with only a little adjustment, she might have been my mother.

She was in her sewing room that day with, as always, Petra and her two other young ladies-in-waiting—I thought of them as the Happy Harpies. When I entered she dismissed them, and they went off tittering and simpering as usual. *Dear Christ*, I would often think on those occasions, my heart clenching in fright like a fist, *what if one of them should have a mind to betray their mistress and me?*

She patted the cushions beside her and bade me sit. 'The Englishman?' she said, nodding. 'Ah.' When she was thinking hard, her lips would become pale and thin and her eyes would narrow. 'We must tell the Chamberlain of this. It's a thing he will wish to know.'

'Would he allow Sir Henry to travel to Most?' I asked.

She laughed softly, this time shaking her head. 'Certainly not,' she said, amused at my simple-mindedness. 'Wotton is the most watched man in Prague—after you, that is.'

'I?' I said, with a rush of alarm. 'Am I watched? By whom?'

Again she laughed. 'By everyone, my dear and darling fool!' she exclaimed. 'No one has been known to rise so swiftly in favour here since—why, since the days when Kelley's master, the magician Dee, so captivated poor Rudolf and made a dunce of him.'

I walked to the window, thinking hard myself, now.

For all my newfound foppery, within myself I was as uncertain and as fearful as ever. I had made not the slightest advance towards discovering who had murdered Magdalena Kroll, and each way I turned I found myself facing blankness and confusion. I received only vague or plainly evasive answers from everyone I spoke to who might have been expected to know where the girl had been and what she had been doing in the hours before her death. By some she had been seen that evening in the vicinity of the

Emperor's private quarters; others swore they had glimpsed her in a carriage travelling towards her father's house in the Old Town. But Rudolf assured me she had not been with him that day, while her father insisted he had not seen or spoken to her at all in the week before she died. Yet she must have been somewhere, she must have been doing something, before she was seized upon and slaughtered.

As to Madek, I had early on come to the conclusion that his death had been ordered by the Emperor himself. Had the young man not gone about the city abusing Rudolf, calling him a tyrant and a monster and even muttering threats against the throne? What king would countenance such behaviour in a wild young man whose beloved girl that same king had cavalierly taken from him?

Then, over the days devoted to the celebration of Christ's birth, Rudolf appeared to lose all interest in the affair, and ceased even to mention the name of Magdalena Kroll. However, I was by now familiar enough with him and his ways to know that his attention was like a river that plunges underground and disappears only to gush forth again at some other place. The day would come when I would be called before him and required to account for myself and say what progress I had made in solving the mystery of the girl's death. And how then should I reply? That I had failed, and failed again, to discover the merest clue as to who had murdered her, and why.

One morning I was summoned urgently to the Throne Room. There I found my master pacing the floor agitatedly and waving a sheet of paper in his hand. It was a letter he had received from Madek's father, begging His Imperial Majesty to deliver justice to his son by finding and punishing his destroyer.

'What shall we answer him?' Rudolf softly wailed. 'What shall we *say*?'

I took the letter, telling him I would answer it, which, I'm compelled to confess, I had no intention of doing—what should *I* say, any more than Rudolf?

Nevertheless, he was glad to be relieved of the burden of writing to the bereaved man, as I had known he would be.

These days, he had other matters to concern and, I hoped, to distract him, not only at court but in the detested wider world. The rivalry of his brother Matthias, for instance, who coveted the throne, and the constant agitations fomented by his young cousin Ferdinand of Austria, scourge of the Protestants, were a never-ending source of anxiety and torment to him. He cared nothing for their plans and ambitions; he wished only that they would leave him in peace, with his ivories and enamels, his basilisks and bezoars, his myriad clocks as they steadily ticked away the dragging hours of his jaded life.

I, too, had other tasks to occupy me. Rudolf, in his whimsical way, had one day decided to charge me with overseeing the labours of the royal alchemists in the numerous laboratories and workshops housed in the Powder Tower. Also I had, again at the Emperor's instigation and insistence, embarked on an ambitious text devoted to a detailed interpretation of certain passages on the transmutation of metals in the work of Albertus Magnus, that dubious savant who was one of Rudolf's obsessions at the time. These tasks I found irksome in the extreme: the Powder Tower turned out to be a nest of schemers and scoundrels, while Albertus Magnus was as dry as dust.

As will be apparent, much of the shine had worn off my initial captivation with Prague and all I had taken it to represent. Rudolf was a demanding taskmaster, as capricious in private affairs as in public ones. He would work up an enthusiasm for this or that topic or author, maintain it passionately, then pass on restlessly to some new source of wonder, some new promise of revelation and final enlightenment.

As for myself, I had grown secretly to disregard many of the things His Majesty held most dear. Towards alchemy in particular I nursed a deep and incurable scepticism; now that I had ample opportunity to observe it in operation and was forced to deal with its operators, I came to the conclusion that half of them were mad and the other half rank fraudsters. And all of them were swollen on self-interest and quaking in fear of being found out.

Do not mistake me: I still held fast to my conviction of the hidden order of the world and the interconnectedness of all things. Only I no longer believed that the great code could be uncovered by the likes of that collection of crackbrains pent up in the Powder Tower, who passed their days like spellbound goblins, feverishly immolating metals and producing by their labours nothing more than little piles of smoking black dust. They were a tormented lot, and sometimes I almost pitied them. Their world was a mass of potential transformations, in which nothing was stable and nothing could be controlled. It was, for them, as a handful of mercury, and everything they thought to grasp slipped through their hapless fingers.

Of course, I allowed myself to show no sign of these doubts and disillusionments to Rudolf, who was as gullible as he was haunted, and whose innocent faith in his wizards I would not have dreamed of destroying, even if I had possessed the power to do so. Yes, I had rapidly learned to dissimulate as subtly and as skilfully as any of the courtiers around me, whom in my deceitful heart I despised.

Yet I never felt safe. The thought was always in my mind that one day, sooner or later, Rudolf would tire of me, when some newer star rose in his firmament. And if he banished me, would I be banished also from his mistress's bed? In thrall to her though I was, I had no illusions as to the fastness of Caterina Sardo's attachment to me, for in her way she was every bit as capricious as Rudolf himself.

When I dwelled on these things I would feel that noose of silk about my neck draw another notch tighter.

'You must talk to the Chamberlain,' Caterina said, behind me now, drawing me out of my reverie. 'You must alert him that Wotton aims to meddle. You will not be thanked if you don't speak and the Englishman is allowed to work his wiles.'

I turned to her, meaning to say something, but she silenced me by taking my hand and guiding it to her breast.

'Now touch me,' she said, in her huskiest whisper. 'Touch me here—yes. And here. And now here. Ah!'

Her moist lips were parted, her eyelids fluttering.

And below the scaffold whereon I stood, the invisible crowd waited, holding its collective breath in eager anticipation of my fall.

Later that evening, when Caterina had at last released me from what amused her to term the duties of the bedchamber, I walked in the gathering dusk down to Golden Lane, where again I peered in at the windows of my former house. No one was there, and nothing was to be seen, and yet I lingered. What had drawn me back was not nostalgia— although Serafina naturally was in my thoughts—but the conviction, based on I knew not what, that there was hidden here some part of the puzzle I had been set to solve, and that I should find, if only I could hit upon the right place to look.

The narrow street was deserted, and all was silent in the winter twilight. I turned away from the house and paced the little distance to the spot where the girl's corpse had lain. No trace of her remained, except, for me, an echo, a resonance, of terror and pain. They say life is cheap, but I think it dear, very dear. Why had Magdalena Kroll been murdered? That was one of the questions I went on asking myself, for I knew that only when I had the answer could I begin in earnest to search out who had done the deed. The other question, however, that of motive, seemed to me by far the most pressing. Was this not strange? Yet I believed, again for no reason I could think of, that the killing of the girl, the murder itself, had been an incidental event, an isolated patch of flame on the periphery of a far greater conflagration.

There was a sound behind me, a movement, a scuffle and a scuttle, I was sure of it. I whirled about, peering this way and that into the descending darkness. The street in both directions was empty and still.

16

I followed my mistress's advice—all her advisings were commands—and next morning found myself once again in that little room with the prie-dieu and the deceptive, freely hanging tapestry. Very different, however, were the circumstances of my coming there this time. Far from being marched thither by guards or soldiers, I was preceded by a page in yellow stockings and a cocked hat. He was a gawky young fellow with hair crookedly cropped and an unsightly cluster of pustules on the back of his neck—but a page is a page and greatly to be preferred to an armed guard any day.

As I crossed the courtyard and passed in front of the Royal Palace I was smugly pleased, young coxcomb that I had turned into, by the sound of my Spanish boot heels ringing importantly on the flagstones, and the feel of my short cape, edged with fox fur, flaring behind me on the breeze.

Chamberlain Lang was in his black habit, as always. He had left me waiting, also as always, and then he entered the room hurriedly with that curious, quick-stepping, gliding gait—he really had the look of a tall black busy waterbird—his fingers clasped before him in a parody of piety, smiling his broad, sly smile.

'So Wotton has been whispering sedition in your ear, has he?' he said merrily.

'I should not say that,' I answered, 'not sedition, no. He asked only if it might be possible for him to travel to Most.'

'Aye, and to visit Castle Hněvín and confabulate there with that treacherous Irishman Kelley, I'll wager. Did he mention him?'

'He mentioned no one,' I said. 'But I took it Kelley would be the object of his travelling to Most.'

'I have no doubt you took it aright.' He pursed his lips thoughtfully. 'To what purpose, I wonder, would he wish to see and speak to that scoundrelly fellow? Hmm?'

He was watching me sideways, with his thin and devilish smile and one dark eyebrow arched.

I said I could not think what he might want with Kelley; keeping one's thoughts to oneself, I had come to realise, was in general the best policy at Rudolf's conspiratorial court.

There had developed between Chamberlain Lang and myself a wary regard, which it pleased him to pretend was a warm and open relation, if not a friendship, even. But I distrusted him, and he knew it; as to what his true estimation of or feeling towards me was I could not begin to guess, so mercurial and enigmatic a creature was he.

I knew, as who at court did not, that he and Felix Wenzel were locked in a relentless and entangled struggle for dominance. Wisdom, what little of it I had, told me I should throw in my lot with the stronger of the two, which undoubtedly was Lang. Yet I hung back, prizing my independence, or what I imagined to be my independence. I was therefore caught between these two clever, cold and dangerous men, a not so very hard nut that neither could crack, at least not as long as Rudolf continued to smile upon me and keep me close to his side.

There was also, worryingly, the question of what the Chamberlain was to Caterina Sardo, and what she was to him. When I thought about this, the suspicion would insert itself into my mind, like the thinnest of thin, sharp blades, that he might once have been to her what I was to her now. For I was not so blinded by my passion for the woman that I imagined she had not set her eye—and more than her eye—on another man of position and power at court.

I was in a maze, making my way forward cautiously, turn by turn, but whether I was going towards the exit or the centre, I could not tell. A day would come, I felt dreadfully sure of it, when I should have to turn and run, perhaps for my very life. With that eventuality in mind, I saved carefully every other piece of gold or silver I had from the Emperor. This escape money I stored in the leather pouch my father the Bishop had dispatched to me from his deathbed. By now my money bag was reassuringly full, and getting fuller by the day, and was a much-needed comfort to me.

The Chamberlain, still with his hands clasped before him, paced up and down the cramped space of the little room, humming softly, which he always did when he was busy scheming.

'This is what we shall do,' he said at last. 'Instead of allowing Wotton to travel to Most . . .' he stopped, and placed himself close in front of me, his voice sinking to a conspiratorial murmur '. . . and I do not think he should be allowed, do you?'

This was one of his favourite ploys, to pause dramatically, as if he had been halted in his tracks by a doubt, and plead earnestly for reassurance, for which of course he had no need or desire, since never was there a man more certain of his own certainty than Philipp Lang.

He set to pacing again, his crow-black robe rustling around him.

'No,' he said, 'we shall keep a watch on Wotton, and instead of allowing him to go to Most, we'll fetch Kelley and bring him here. Perhaps that way we shall discover what it is the Englishman wants of the rascal.' He stopped again, by the hearth, and glanced back at me over his shoulder with his mischief-maker's grin. 'What do you say, Herr Doktor Stern? Is this not a sound plan?'

It was not a question; indeed, questions from the Chamberlain were for the most part nothing more than teasing provocations.

He came now and put a friendly arm about my shoulders. 'We'll meet at the banquet this evening,' he said. 'Mistress Sardo tells me you are to be there. You have become something of her knight, I think, sporting her pennant on your lance.'

He winked the way a lizard blinks, effortlessly dropping one eyelid like a tiny silk flange. His hand squeezed my shoulder.

My mouth had gone instantly dry.

It was a part of my foolishness to have convinced myself that I could conduct a passionate liaison with the Emperor's mistress, the mother of his children, and no one would know, not even Philipp Lang, from whom nothing that went on at court could be hidden, as I was well aware. But such is youth, with its delusions and insatiable blind desires. And then how easily, at whatever age, we hold off from our minds the things that frighten us most.

Yet there were times when that facility failed me. Often now I start awake in the hour before dawn, the wolf hour, aghast and sweating, like a traveller in the mountains who in a momentary break in the fog finds himself teetering on the brink of a frightful precipice. Fear at first rose as a kind of fog, a general miasma that constricted my throat and forced my teeth to clench; then it cleared and showed me the specific forms of which I should be most afraid. Chief of these was my failure to do as the Emperor had commanded me and find out the killer of Mistress Kroll, and on the heels of that would come the baleful realisation of the peril I was putting myself in by indulging my passion for Caterina Sardo. In the midst of all this there would appear before me yet again the vision of the hanged sentry, who in my feverish fancy had become a stylised figure, an image from the tarot, foretelling terrors to come.

The banquet that night took place in the Spanish Hall, which had been lately built to house the rarest treasures of Rudolf's priceless collection of paintings. In pride of place, propped on a gilded table, was *The Feast of the Rosary*, which His Majesty in solitude had sated himself upon all afternoon and now had grudgingly released to general view.

Not that there were many at the table who paid it the slightest regard. One of the disillusioning discoveries I had made since entering the royal household was how uncourtly court life so often was. Dinners such as this one were especially disorderly occasions, the diners a gorgeously bedizened rabble—all that silk and satin, all those fabulous furs!—who hooted and howled like a pack of hunting dogs, and threw gnawed bones and crusts of bread at each other. It was not unusual for bouts of fisticuffs to break out, sometimes of such ferocity that the Imperial Guard had to be called in to restore a modicum of order. At one such repast I saw a lady of high rank shamelessly performing an act of frottage on her neighbour, one of Rudolf's drunken generals, the livid eye of his cock and her busy hand plainly visible to anyone who cared to cast a glance below the level of the table.

The Emperor this night was in one of his darkest moods, and sat slumped with his fat chin sunk in his ruff and his sable cap askew, watching through hooded eyes the graceless antics taking place around him. How to guess what tormented thoughts were turning themselves over behind that sombre brow?

Opposite him, but at the other end of the table, was seated Caterina Sardo, his mistress and also, amazingly, mine. She did not look at me, not once, or I at her; it afforded me an intense, peculiar pleasure, this mutual ignoring, our secret suspended in the air between us, a shimmering crystal sphere, invisible to all save the two of us.

Seated on the Emperor's left was a frail-looking creature of indeterminate age. It was not until halfway through the evening that I recognised him as Don Giulio. He, too, remembered me, as I saw from the way he stared at me with his curiously dead yet piercing eye, smiling his blank, secret smile. He was Rudolf's and Caterina's eldest son, so I had been told, though it was not, I should say, his mother who had told me. Once I enquired of her about him, just once, but immediately she blazed up in fury and called me a meddler, and did not come to my bed that night.

Don Giulio's presence at his father's side caused me a wounding pang of jealousy. It was not that I would have wished Caterina to bear a child of mine, for I wanted nothing from her except herself, her flesh, the touch of her hand, her cool and tantalising smile. But I could not bear the thought of Rudolf, that fat frog, lowering the great bloodless soft sack of himself down upon my slender Venus and inflicting upon her tender innards the makings of this sickly-looking mooncalf.

I closed my eyes and pressed my fingertips hard upon the lids. Madness! Madness, desire and dread delight: that was my predicament. I was as a man trapped on an upper floor of his burning house who cannot think what to save from the flames, himself or the things he treasures.

Chamberlain Lang was there, and Felix Wenzel too. Lang was all talk and smiles for a dark-eyed lady at his side—he was a tireless seducer, of woman, man, maid or boy, it seemed to be all one to him—while Wenzel, seated opposite, kept a narrow watch on him. Poor Wenzel, there were times when I felt sorry for him: he could not mask his passions even if it were to save his life. His hatred of Lang was as intense in its way as my love for Caterina Sardo, the signs of love and hatred being strangely similar, as I came to learn.

And in the midst of all sat Bishop Malaspina, a round black puffball, taking in everything with his merry little eyes, missing nothing, not even, I'm sure, the flush of jealousy in my cheeks.

While the main course was being served—it was slices of spit-roasted wild boar with a glaze of honey and wine—Kepler the astronomer came and sat by me in friendly fashion. He had travelled recently to Prague, at the invitation of Tycho Brahe the Dane, and we had no sooner met than a warm mutual regard was forged between us. I it was who took him on his first tour of the workshops in the Powder Tower, where the air smelt perpetually of scorched metal and wormwood, a scent I can still summon up as if I were there again in that place of crazed dreams and the bitter ash of deluded hopes. I could see by the astronomer's ill-suppressed sardonic smirk that he had no more regard than I for those poor desperate labourers hunched over their crucibles and retorts.

Kepler tonight was already on the way to being drunk, as was evident from the glassy look of his eyes—although those eyes were not good at the best of times, having been damaged by a childhood bout of smallpox, which had left him double-visioned. He used to make a joke of this, asking who had ever heard of a cockeyed astronomer? He was a skimpy little fellow with a narrow face and a short, coarse black beard. He was generally of an amiable disposition, although quick to take offence, especially in matters pertaining to his work and his reputation. His aim was to succeed to the high position of Imperial Mathematician, displacing the present incumbent, Tycho Brahe, who sat opposite us now at the far side of the table, planted between the wide arms of his chair, massive, majestic and remote. Although Brahe was a dedicated and famous astronomer, he regarded his science with aristocratic disdain, and had once confided to Kepler, so the latter told me, his conviction that no true gentleman should stoop so low as to publish a book.

Abruptly the Emperor rose and turned to depart, and at once my Caterina rose too and went forward and took his arm, while Jeppe Schenckel, who as usual had been seated on a low stool at his master's feet, scrambled up and followed after. I watched them go. Caterina still refrained from looking my way, though she must have felt the heat of my yearning gaze, for these were the young days of our passionate entanglement, and I was besotted.

The company, which had struggled unsteadily to its feet,

maintained silence while His Majesty progressed to the door, but when he had gone it was bedlam once again.

'Come, my friend,' Kepler said, 'let us take ourselves away from this gilded squalor.'

Outside, the January night was cold and clear under a vast velvet sky studded with stars. We went together through the Stag Moat, where I expected to meet the ghost of Jan Madek stepping out of the shadows under every tree, and thence down to Nový Svět, to an inn Kepler knew there. It was a cramped, low-ceilinged place, but clean, and decently run. The innkeeper, a saturnine fellow with a cadaverous grin, served us the best of Pilsen beer and slices of cold venison, tender and sweet. What a gourmand I had become, what a smacker of lips and patter of the belly, and all in a matter of weeks! Had I gone on as I was going, I would have ended up a second Malaspina.

I must declare that at the time I had not a full appreciation of Kepler's greatness, and regarded him as no more than a wandering scholar struggling to make his mark on the world, much like myself. I prized his company, however, and his lively conversation.

We sat by the window of the inn, with a wedge of the pinpricked sky visible above the rooftops opposite. Kepler, deep in his cups by now, talked freely and with bitter wit of his colleague and rival, Brahe the Dane—it was the topic around which he perpetually orbited. This fabled nobleman had in his student days engaged in a duel in which he had lost the bridge of his nose, and wore now a false bridge made of an alloy of silver and gold, held in place with a resin gum. Under the patronage of the Swedish King, he had built a mighty observatory on the island of Hven in the Øresund strait off Denmark, and there had amassed over the space of twenty years a great portfolio of star sightings, which Kepler was beadily determined to get his hands on.

After a falling out with King Christian, Brahe had sought a new patron, which he conveniently found in Rudolf. At the Emperor's invitation, Brahe haughtily removed himself and his household from Hven and set off for Prague in an immense caravan of coaches and horse carts piled high with everything from battered saucepans to the most precious astronomical instruments.

The chief disaster of that long and surely wearisome journey southwards was the death of Brahe's beloved tame elk, which at a castle where the entourage was lodging for the night made its way to an upper floor and there drank a dish of beer, and in a drunken stupor fell down the stone stairway and broke its neck. Brahe was inconsolable; even now, all this time later, he would speak tearfully of his lost pet to anyone willing to listen.

'He is a fine astronomer, in his mechanical way,' Kepler said, dipping his nose into his beer mug, 'but also petty and vain. He fears I might outstrip him, which of course I shall.'

He narrowed those botched eyes of his and considered me closely for a moment.

'Can you keep a secret, Stern?' he asked, to which I said of course I could. 'Then listen,' he said. 'A day will come when I shall reveal the secret of the cosmic harmony and show the very inner workings of the universe itself.' He sat back, keeping his narrowed gaze fixed on me and portentously nodding.

It was not the first time I had heard this kind of talk among the many aspirants to greatness whom Rudolf had gathered from all corners of the empire, and it would not be the last. What I could not have known was that, unlike all those others, Kepler's boast would one day be proved to have been no less than the truth. His *Harmonices Mundi*, published some twenty years later, in which among many daring hypotheses he put forward the theory that the planets in their orbits move not in circles but ellipses, would cause a revolution in astronomy as significant as the one Copernicus brought about by setting the sun at the centre of the planetary system.

We were both well drunk by now, although of the two of us, he was in a worse way than I.

'Listen, Stern,' he said. 'I hear the Emperor set you the task of finding out who it was that murdered his mistress—what was her name? Kroll, yes, that's right. So have you solved it yet?' I told him I had not, and he ruminated in silence for a while, shaking his head slowly from side to side. 'I heard tell the culprit was some young fellow who had a mind for her himself—is that not so?'

'No,' I answered, 'it is not. Jan Madek was his name. He died too.'

Kepler brooded again for a while.

'A bad business,' he said. Then he fixed me with a narrowed eye. 'You'll do well to come out of it with your own gizzard intact.'

This was not a thing I wished to hear, and I hastened to divert him to other matters. I asked him what he knew of Edward Kelley.

'Dr Dee's famous familiar?' he said, laughing. 'A foolish fellow, and a rogue. He promised Rudolf the Philosopher's Stone and delivered him fool's gold. Kelley—pah!'

The secret contempt that Kepler and I shared for that pack of alchemists toiling ceaselessly in the Powder Tower had forged a pact of amity between us. I found in Kepler a like soul to mine, for we both considered a great part of the magic Rudolf believed in to be no more than an elaborate nonsense got up by charlatans to bedazzle and bamboozle him. In particular we agreed that the great aim of transmuting base metal into gold, the alchemists' Holy Grail, was a fruitless and vulgar fantasy. We never said as much to each other, I think, not in so many words—in Prague you had to keep a guard on your tongue, as I had early come to learn—but each knew that the other knew it, and the knowledge afforded us mild gratification and shared amusement. Yes, he was a great man, was Kepler, and a generous spirit: I miss him still. He died in Regensburg, of all places, where he lies in an unmarked grave. *I measured the heavens*, he wrote in his self-composed epitaph, *now the shadows I measure*.

A fiddler seated by the fireside struck up a tune, and Kepler, who was a wild fellow when he had drink in him, grabbed the innkeeper's daughter, a little jolly thing, and whirled her about in a crazy dance, stamping his heels and hooting and hallooing like a happy demon. The innkeeper leaned on his arms on the counter and watched the capering pair with a doubtful yet indulgent eye; it was clear that Kepler was a regular customer whose antics were tolerated.

At last Kepler came reeling back to the table and flopped down onto a stool, wiping his brow and panting. He called for buttered ale, and we clanked tankards in a toast to Terpsichore, the muse of song and dance, and after that made another toast, this time to the innkeeper's girl, who, flushed and damp and dizzy, had gone to hide behind her lanky father.

'My wife will not dance,' Kepler said dolefully, 'and calls

me a clown when I do, saying I demean myself.' He brooded blearily, gnawing at the inside of his cheek. 'Barbara, she is called—I think you haven't met her? I confess she is a trial to me at times, though she's a good mother to our babes, I'll say that for her.' He turned to me with a crooked grin. 'And you, sir, you have no wife?'

'I have not,' I said.

He laughed, making a phlegmy rattle. 'But you don't lack for a warm bed, so I hear.'

'Oh, yes?' I said, and an arrow of terror came whirring straight through the fog of alcohol and buried itself in my breast. 'And where do you hear that, may I ask?'

He drove an elbow merrily into my ribs and near knocked the wind out of me. 'My friend,' he said, 'do you imagine there are any secrets at this court?' He chuckled. 'By God, sir, but you do take risks!'

Again I saw the scaffold rearing up against a blue sky, and me standing on it, plumed and garlanded in Caterina Sardo's colours, and about to dance a final jig.

Kepler was attending to the fiddler again, tapping a toe in time with his tune. 'Music,' he said, 'ah, music. You know the planets move according to its rules? Yes, indeed, there is a music of the spheres, though not as the old Greeks had it. In my great book, with which I shall one day astound the world, I shall show that the laws of musical consonance are to be found not in numbers but in geometrical ratios. The Lord, as I can prove, is a geometer.'

He went on then, in rambling and confused mumblings, to relate to me how, according to his theory, the mechanism of the solar system, of which our world is a moving part, was designed by God according to the laws that the divine Euclid had long ago discovered, and that the orbits of the six planets circling the sun were fixed upon a kind of geometric grid consisting of the five perfect Platonic solids, from the four-sided tetrahedron to the icosahedron of twenty sides—and so on.

I thought it all a drunken fantasy, and was too drunk myself, and too ignorant as well, to appreciate the exquisite simplicity of his system.

I must have fallen into an ale-induced reverie of my own then and stopped listening to him, for presently, with a start, I came to, in the way that one does at such times, sharply and suddenly. He was speaking of music again, though of the earthly and not the celestial kind.

'It is called,' Kepler said, putting his face up close to mine and jabbing my knee with a bony finger for emphasis, 'it is called *a wolf on a string*. Listen.' He pointed to the fiddler. 'Do you hear that fearful buzzing he makes now and then—there, just then, did you hear it? Do you know what it is? No, of course you don't. It occurs, my friend—are you listening?—when a particular note played on a particular string matches some resonating frequency in the wood of the instrument, producing a cacophonous howl, not unlike that of the wolf. Isn't that a strange thing, that two parts of the same instrument, instead of making delightful music together, should be so disharmoniously at odds?'

I said dully that, yes, yes, I did understand. What puzzled me was the portentous tone he had adopted, gazing into my face and nodding. What had this wolfish business to do with me, and why was he telling me of it as if it were a cautionary parable? Ah, if only I had been a better listener in those days, what a deal of trouble I should have saved myself.

'Do you wonder,' he said, 'if the string and the wood are

aware of the harsh discord they make together, or is it only others that hear it—eh?'

He nodded again, solemnly, and, so it seemed, again in a warning way, tapping a finger to the side of his nose.

Now he rose, meaning to cut another caper, but the innkeeper's daughter, seeing his intent, fled from him into the back part of the premises, laughing, and slammed the door behind her. The innkeeper came from the counter and put a firm but not unfriendly hand on Kepler's shoulder and guided him to the door and bade him a curt and unceremonious good night.

I followed, and together the two of us staggered up the narrow cobbled street, which seemed now as steeply treacherous as the side of a mountain, holding on to each other for support, though it was a question which of us was the drunker. Kepler tried to sing a bawdy song but could manage only the first verse, which he repeated a few times, doggedly, and then gave up.

We stopped to relieve ourselves against the wall of a house, and an old dame in a mob-cap put out her head at an upstairs window and shrieked abuse at us. At that moment I saw, with the sudden access of clarity drink sometimes affords, how like to my own present circumstances was the city itself, in which the grandeur and opulence of a great metropolis, the very centre of the world, sat atop a stew of squalor, vice and violence.

Stumbling on again, we came to another inn, and there Kepler stopped, saying he must drink a thimbleful of schnapps, to counter the buttered ale and settle his gut, to the unruliness of which, he confided, he had been a martyr all his life. He begged me to stay with him, but I was feeling sick myself by now, and could think of nothing but my bed. We embraced clumsily, though he complained still of my abandoning of him, and I went off, my mind a jumble of geometric figures and whirling stars.

Behind me I heard Kepler fumbling at the door of the inn, which I think must have been shut. Then he made another attempt at remembering the rest of his dirty ditty, but again in vain.

'Stern!' he shouted after me, with a cackle of bawdy laughter. 'Stern von Stern, I admonish you. Remember, remember what I say: wolf on a string. That's what you are, you whoreson. Ha!'

17

I was surprised, and disagreeably so, to discover that I was to be the one who would travel to Most and fetch the sorcerer Kelley back to Prague. Chamberlain Lang mentioned it to me airily, in passing—'It will be but a matter of two days or three'—as if the journey to Most were a short amble beyond the city gates. I thought to protest, but then thought better of it. The Chamberlain's directives were couched always in such a way as to make them seem the politest and most tentative of suggestions, but there was no mistaking within them the steely cord of command.

When the Emperor heard of my mission, he grew greatly agitated—Lang by this stage of his grand career was so sure of his position that he often made decisions without bothering to inform his imperial master—and he drew me with him into the most private of his private chambers and sat down with me in a window seat on the shadowed side of the room. About us were displayed some of his most precious possessions, the ones he kept exclusively for his own pleasure. These included a great bowl carved from natural crystal in which supposedly there was embedded the name of Christ—though all I could see was an indecipherable swirl of tints, lapis blue, acid green, the tawniest copper—which he believed to be the Holy Grail itself. There were also pictures by Spranger, the court painter, that would have been too lewd to show in public. And there was a singular item that caught my eye at once: a sort of mechanical bronze salt cellar by an Italian master, on the double lid of which were set facing each other a naked man and woman who, when the cellar was operated, would engage in vigorous copulation.

'Tell us,' Rudolf whispered in his breathy way, 'why does the Chamberlain require the presence of Kelley here? Does he forget it was by our specific order that the fellow should be banished to Most?'

Lately, when he was in a state like this of agitation and alarm, it was his habit to grasp me by the hand and pull me close to him, gazing deep into my eyes like a querulous child. At first such gestures of enforced intimacy had startled and discomfited me, but I had got used to them, as I had got used to so many of his more peculiar ways.

I told him all I knew, which was that Sir Henry Wotton had enquired of me as to whether I thought he would be permitted to travel to Most, and that when I spoke of this to the Chamberlain he had at once become suspicious, and decided to bring Kelley to Prague and question him.

'Yes yes yes,' Rudolf said, 'but to question him about what?'

'That, sir, I regret to say, I do not know.'

He looked away, making that buzzing sound at the back of his throat that he did when he was distracted, his glance darting here and there about the room but seeming to see nothing save the demons crowding in his mind. A moment later he turned and fixed on me with sudden sharpness, his eyes aglitter—it was one of the most disconcerting aspects of the man, how he would switch from seeming a helpless dodderer and in an instant become the shrewd and mindful monarch that he was, the ruler of the world.

'And what of our dear girl,' he said, 'poor Mistress Kroll, what have you discovered of her killing?'

I swallowed hard, and assured him that my investigations were continuing, that I was proceeding in certain clear directions, following up certain clues, assembling an account of the girl's last hours—a shameless lie—questioning this person and that, examining the thing minutely from every angle.

A silence fell. I cleared my throat, avoiding his eye. He sighed. The back of my neck had grown hot.

'And now you are to go to Most,' he murmured, almost sadly, 'at our Chamberlain's behest.' Then he frowned, and shook his head. 'They scheme and scheme, the lot of them,' he said. He fixed on me again, with a hard glint of suspicion. 'Does the Chamberlain send messages by you?'

'Messages, Your Majesty?'

'Dispatches, I mean—reports, plans.' He tightened his moist grip on my hand.

'No, sir,' I said. 'I am not his courier.'

'Hmm.' He was peering into my eyes, reminding me of Jeppe the dwarf looking in at my window, avid and searching. 'He has never sent you to our cousin Ferdinand of Styria, for instance?'

I felt, when he held me in his grip like this, that we were a pair of skaters halted motionless upon the thinnest of ice, our skates about to buckle beneath us, or the ice to crack, or one of us to fall and bring the other down with him.

'Forgive me, sir,' I said, 'but I know nothing of your cousin, except his reputation.'

'Oh, yes? And what is that? What is his reputation?'

'That he is a champion of the Catholic cause,' I said. 'To the point,' I added, amazed at my temerity, 'to the point, according to some, of being a fanatic.'

Rudolf had given up peering at me and his glance was

skittering about the room again. 'A fanatic, yes,' he said, 'and ambitious, young though he is. I fear him. I fear him as much as I fear my brother Matthias—more, even. When I think of Ferdinand I hear the pyre crackling, and the martyr's cries.' He nodded, his eyes fixed now, gazing again into his own inner abyss. 'It is only a matter of time before one of them, my brother or Ferdinand, unseats us and steals our crown.'

'Come, sir,' I said, 'this is your imagining. No monarch could be more firmly set upon the throne than you are.'

He smiled then, strangely, wistfully, and drew my hand to his breast and pressed it there. 'Ah, Christian,' he said, 'how young you are, with all of youth's certainty. I am old, older than my years. I feel broken, broken upon the wheel of my tormented self.' He released my hand. 'Go,' he said, 'go to Most, and bring Kelley back to us. We have a soft place in our heart for him, rogue though he be. His boasting amused us, his subterfuges and outrageous claims. You know he stole John Dee's young wife and got a son by her whom Dee had to adopt? Yes, everyone knows that story. Poor Dee. He was an innocent, in his way. We hear he has fallen on hard times, at home in England, though it's said the Queen favours him still, and will not see him starve. The mob plundered his house at Mortlake and burned his library, after someone had told them he was a necromancer. Ah, yes, poor Dee.'

He went silent and remained so for several minutes. I rose quietly and walked away, leaving him to his musings. I do not think he noticed my going, lost as he was in his fears, his memories, his madness.

When I told Caterina Sardo of the Chamberlain's command, she was at once amused and vexed.

'Why should he send you?' she cried. 'What is he up to, the sly brute?' She twisted a button on my jerkin, as she liked to do, and fixed her smoky gaze upon me. 'What shall I do, when you are gone?' she murmured. 'Who will there be for me to play with? Perhaps I shall take another lover, someone handsome and noble, and not rough-hewn as you are. Kiss me now, kiss me, my starry Christian. *Baciami, baciami, mio caro.*'

We were in the corridor outside her sewing room, in broad daylight. I looked about fearfully, expecting to see her handmaids peeping through chinks at us, giggling and shoving each other for the best view.

Caterina laughed. 'What a nervous lover you are,' she said, smiling into my face. 'Do you fear that Rudi's guards will come and seize you and take you to the torture rooms? I should like to see you upon the rack, sweating and weeping and crying for your mama. They say'—she pressed herself against me—'they say a man stands up stiff when he is stretched like that. Have you heard tell of such a thing? I would hoist up my petticoats and plant myself astride you, and none would know whether your groans were of pleasure or of pain. Would you like that, my fearful darling? Would you?'

The threads of the button broke where she had been twisting them, and now she slipped the button into her mouth, and kissed me, and I felt the hard round wafer of bone, wet with her spit, sliding from her lips and passing between mine.

She leaned her head back a little way, still with her body folded hotly into mine.

'Swallow it,' she said. 'Think that it is the host, the holy host, and this is our Black Mass.' I swallowed, gagging a little, though the button was not large. She kissed me again, the merest peck this time. '*Ah, mio eroe*. Now let's to your room, and consecrate there our sacred ritual!'

Ritual it was, sacred it was not, and may God forgive my blasphemous soul.

Caterina Sardo went at love-making with all the passion and single-mindedness of a votaress at a shrine. She was endlessly inventive, and devised for the two of us dark pleasures the like of which I could not have imagined in my most heated fantasies. Thinking of her, even now I feel a lick or two of the flames of those days and nights, and glimpse again the hellish glow they shed. In her arms I seemed to myself to be dwelling in a paradisal Hell.

That afternoon we had just dismounted from the two-backed beast we had been vigorously making and were lying side by side on my bed, sweating and panting, when there came a sound from outside the door that stopped my breath and set me starting up in fright. It was the same scratching and snuffling I had heard that night outside my house in Golden Lane, as if some animal were rootling about out there. At once I drew on my shirt and was rising from the bed, intending to sneak to the door and wrench it open and surprise whatever it was that was there, but Caterina put a hand on my arm and held me back.

'Stay,' she said softly. 'Stay, my dear.'

'But there's something out there,' I whispered. 'I must see what it is.'

'No,' she said, in that same soothing fashion, as if to calm an anxious child. 'Don't fret yourself, it's nothing. Come, lie down here and hold me in your arms.'

'Did you not hear—' I began, but she put a finger to my lips and silenced me.

'I heard nothing,' she said. 'No one is there. Shush now, shush, and hold me, so. That's right. Now put your hand here, and feel the wetness, yours and mine.' She hummed a tune in my ear, a tender little lullaby. 'What sweet music we make together, you and I, yes?' She giggled, and squeezed her thighs tight around my hand that was trapped there, and turned onto her side and pressed her cool damp bosom against my chest. 'Don't you hear it—' she giggled again '—the music of the spheres?'

I moved aside from her, freeing my hand from her steamy lap. There were swaths of shadow under the ceiling, and a sliver of winter sunlight burned whitely in a crack in the shutters.

Wolf on a string, I thought, wolf on a string.

And a little later, when she had dressed herself and was leaving, I opened the door for her and, looking down, saw with a spasm of fright the corpse of my poor cat, my dear old Plato, stretched out at the threshold, with his throat sliced open and his blood spread all about him in a gleaming crimson pool.

My mistress gave him no more than a glance—she had never liked him—and lifted the hem of her skirts as she stepped over his lifeless form.

'Good riddance,' she said. She gave me a cold stare and was gone.

I gathered up what remained of the creature and wrapped it in a piece of rag: how insubstantial it was, hardly more than a scrap of fur and a few lengths of stringy sinew. I carried it down to the Stag Moat, half blinded by tears—a soft heart was always one of my weaknesses—and interred it under a big round stone beneath a myrtle tree.

I was making my way up the steep bank when I saw a

figure sitting on the cold, hard crest above me, watching me approach.

It was Don Giulio, Caterina's uncanny son.

He greeted me in his grave, elderly way, and I stopped and sat down beside him. He had his legs drawn up and his arms folded about his bony knees. He was wizened and thin-limbed, with a sunken chest; his hands, however, were man-sized and greatly disproportionate to the rest of his frail person. I could see nothing in him of his father, and little of my mistress, his mother, except a way he had of holding his head slightly to one side, as she did, as if listening to something far-off and faint. He wore a black jerkin and black hose and narrow black shoes with pointed, upturned toes; his close-cut, dead-seeming yet shiny hair looked like a cap of fusty black satin pulled down tight upon his skull.

His eyes—have I mentioned his eyes? They were small, deep-set, pale and somewhat glassy. They always seemed to me not to belong to him, somehow: to be in fact the eyes of some other, even stranger, creature than himself that was hiding crouched inside him, spying out upon the world through two pale-lashed, pink-rimmed sockets neatly cut into the clay-white mask that was his face. His gaze had an unnervingly fixed quality, and when he blinked, which he did infrequently, it seemed more a sort of start, as if he were registering involuntarily some small internal shock.

He asked what I had been doing, and I told him, and he nodded.

'They say that cats have nine lives,' he said. 'That was not so of this one, it would seem.'

'He was a stray,' I said, 'and attached himself to me. Who knows how many lives, and deaths, he had before this one?'

He thought on this for some time, with a solemn frown.

Even looking at him up close, I would not have ventured an estimate of his likely age. He could have been a young man but seemed not to be; nor was he a boy. Indeed, what he appeared most like was a child who had remained a child and yet at the same time had grown old and frail and feeble. His hands, I noticed, those enormous hands of his that looked anything but frail, had a queer faint tremor; in fact, he seemed to tremble in every part of him, as if he were quaking ceaselessly within.

'I am sorry for your cat,' he said. 'I mean, I am sorry for you, to have lost it.'

I thanked him for his consideration. He had turned away and was looking at the sky.

'Clouds are peculiar, don't you think?' he said. 'Like so much cannon smoke.' He blinked, and twitched, and then went on: 'I have been studying the Battle of Lepanto. Did you know the Turks poured oil on the sea and set it alight, so that those sailors who threw themselves overboard from burning ships were boiled to death?'

'No,' I said, 'I did not know that.'

He gave a low laugh, not much more than a sort of wheeze. 'Few do know it, I find,' he said. 'I know a lot of things like that. I remember things. I have a good memory.'

He unwound his arms from about his knees and stood up. 'Does it seem strange to you, a name such as yours?' he asked.

'I don't believe so,' I said. 'I've never found it strange. But, then, I am well accustomed to it.'

He was above me now on the bank, and I was looking up at him, shading my eyes against the hard blueness of the winter sky. Standing there, the young-old creature seemed no more substantial than the slow floatings of the luminous clouds behind him, and I felt, for an instant, as if something cold and sharp had touched me, the tip of some pointed, shimmering thing, a needle, or a narrow blade that punctured me with infinite delicacy, causing no pain and leaving only an invisible mark.

'I must go now,' Don Giulio said.

And he walked away, with his light, quick, almost hopping gait.

18

The next morning early, Chamberlain Lang sent a closed carriage to call for me. I went down in the dawn light and there it was, waiting in the courtyard. There is always something sinister about a stopped carriage, I find: a presentiment, no doubt, of the final journey. Neither did I like the look of the brace of piebald nags that would pull it—they might have been rescued from the shambles—and I wondered if they were up to the journey. I am a city man, and the thought of being stranded in the middle of some awful plain, amid wild nature, chilled my blood.

I had expected to travel alone, but when I climbed into the carriage I discovered there the pustular page boy with the yellow stockings, his cocked hat in his lap, and beside him a melancholy-seeming old scarecrow of a fellow with a yellowed moustache and a rheumy eye. The page, called Norbert, was to act as my valet, while the other, a knight by the name of Kaspar von Kratz, in scuffed boots and a fur-lined leather coat that reached to his ankles, was meant to be—well, the truth is I never found out exactly what he was meant to be, but since he was armed with a flintlock and a sword I supposed that I must think of him as my bodyguard.

They had brought with them provisions of bread and cheese and cold sausage, on which they were now breakfasting. The cheese was ripe, and the smell of it, at such an early hour, made my stomach heave.

'You look poorly, sir,' the old knight said. He rooted about in a bag on the floor between his feet and came up with a flagon of wine, and offered it to me. 'Here, restore yourself with a swallow or two of Bull's Blood.'

I looked at the neck of the flagon and the old boy's moist and sagging lips and said my thanks and pushed the vessel aside. This, for some reason, caused Norbert the page to give a spluttered guffaw, which resulted in him spraying my sleeve with a scattering of spit-soaked breadcrumbs.

It would be a trying journey; that much was clear.

Nor was our complement yet complete. We were going out by the castle gate when the carriage drew to a sudden stop. I looked out at the window and there was Jeppe the dwarf, in a heavy black cape and buckled shoes and his witch's conical black hat. Another spy! He saw the surprise in my look and was amused. 'Good morning, Herr Professor,' he said, and swept off his hat and bowed.

No one but Jeppe Schenckel could address me as 'Professor' and put into the word so pointed a note of mockery and wry disdain.

The driver, a fat and surly fellow, got down from his high seat with many sighs and muttered oaths and put his hands under the dwarf's elbows and lifted him up and bundled him into the carriage, and we went on again.

The dwarf took his place beside me, squirming and flouncing. He inspected our two companions with a deprecating frown.

'Ah, I see we are four,' he said. 'Where shall we put Kelley? On the roof?'

Sir Kaspar had greeted him with a shaky salute, which he had ignored. Young Norbert, his mouth full of bread and sausage, was gazing at him in fascination, with bulging eyes, and prudently I drew back my sleeve for fear of another spattering of sticky dough.

Of all the people who might have been sent to accompany me on this mission, Jeppe Schenckel was the last one I would have expected. Why was he here, and on whose orders? He looked aslant at me now, working again that eerie gift he had of reading my thoughts.

'I am lent to you by His Majesty,' he said, adding, with a straight face, 'He thought you might lack for companionship. Although as it is'—he eyed again the motley pair opposite—'you are amply provided for in the way of company. My my, but the Chamberlain thinks of everything.'

So Rudolf had sent his man to keep a watch on me. It was hardly surprising, since Rudolf trusted no one. But should I believe it? Nothing in Prague was simple; nothing was ever as it seemed. It was to Dr Kroll's house that the dwarf had led me that first day. Was he Kroll's creature, too—was he Wenzel's? It could have been any one of these—Rudolf, the doctor, the High Steward—who had deputed him to accompany me. And to what purpose? My mission was to go to Most and bring back Edward Kelley to Prague. What danger could there be in that, to necessitate my being spied upon and guarded?

All that long day we made our way northwards, following the western bank of the Vltava. It was upland country, desolate mostly but with glades and passages of frost-laden beauty that made me think of my Bavarian homeland.

The roads were middling good, but our horses were old, and the going was slow and difficult. The dwarf hardly spoke, only sat beside me in his finery—his ruff, his lace cuffs, his silver buckles—like one of those lifelike manikins in

Rudolf's wonder rooms. I believe he had the gift of sleeping with his eyes open.

As the day wore on I was aware of old Sir Kaspar's gaze wandering in my direction now and then, with a sharpness in it I had not thought him capable of. Was he yet another spy, and if so, what was his mission? What momentous matter awaited me at Most that I should need such watching?

Fear rose in me like black bile, a burning bubble in my breast.

At noon we stopped at a dirty inn where I knew better than to touch the pike-perch pie we were offered—I had already smelt it before we entered through the low door. The wine at least was drinkable, dark ruby in colour and peppery on the tongue. I like the wines of Bohemia: what they lack in subtlety they make up for in robustness. I wish I had some here, in this cold northern refuge where I have come to a sort of rest at last.

Jeppe Schenckel had not bothered to get down with us from the carriage, but remained sitting there by the window, his gaze fixed calmly before him. I envied his composure, unnatural though it was. But, then, was there anything natural about that man?

Soon we were on our way again, in the direction of Mělník, where the Vltava and the Elbe merge. The old knight and the page boy played an endless and to me incomprehensible game involving a wooden board with holes in it and small wooden pegs that they moved here and there with great speed and dexterity. They kept trying to cheat each other, amid much hilarity, the boy spluttering and the old man rumbling and coughing and wiping his eyes with his fists. Their merriment grated on my nerves; I tapped my foot impatiently, crossed and uncrossed my arms, and loudly sighed, all of which signs of my annoyance they ignored, or perhaps did not even notice.

Between bouts of uneasy sleep, I passed the tedious hours by trying to gather together in my mind the disparate strands of the mystery at the centre of which I was floundering. I knew I must somehow solve it; increasingly I was convinced that in the end no less than my life would depend on it. For Rudolf I had at the outset been the miraculous star come to his Bethlehem, a harbinger of wonders. But in the weeks since my advent I had proved less than a wonder worker, as I had anxiously to acknowledge. How far would His Majesty's patience stretch, how long could I hope for his tolerance to endure?

The task I had been assigned, onerous though it was, at first had seemed straightforward. Rudolf had taken to himself a new young mistress, and the young man who loved her had set up a protest so clamorous that it had cost him his life—so, at least, I had reasoned. Then the young man's beloved in her turn had died, at whose behest and by what hand I still knew not. There was a court full of candidates for me to choose from—any of Rudolf's intimates, as likely a friend as an enemy, could have ordered the girl's death. Chamberlain Lang, for one, might well have sent the assassin forth that December night. Caterina Sardo had revealed to me how Felix Wenzel had as good as pushed the girl into the Emperor's arms. Why else would he do so except to set a spy in the seraglio? And if that was the case, and Magdalena Kroll was indeed Wenzel's informant, I felt certain that Chamberlain Lang, had he learned of the ploy, would not have hesitated to be rid of her. As for Caterina Sardo herself, what was there to prevent me thinking she might have murdered her usurper, except that she had me so helplessly entranced?

I thought and thought again, and gradually, as we rattled and lurched along those frozen roads, a new notion formed itself in my mind. In the beginning I had taken it that Jan Madek had cut the throat of his faithless girl; then I had discovered that Madek had been the first to die. That had puzzled me, but still it had not occurred to me to doubt that the two deaths were directly linked. But what, I asked myself now, what if there was no connection between them at all? Perhaps my philosophical belief in the hidden unity of all things had deceived me in this case—perhaps I had not given randomness its due.

If I had been baffled at the start, so had others been. I recalled Wenzel questioning me that night after I had been dragged from my bed at the Blue Elephant. I could see even then that he did not know, any more than I did, who had killed Magdalena Kroll. And then there was Dr Kroll's strange start of surprise, or so it had seemed, when he heard Wenzel demand of me if I knew the whereabouts of Jan Madek. Had the doctor an inkling that Madek was already dead?

If Magda Kroll was no part of Madek's death, then why had he died? What had he known that had had to be tortured out of him? What had he seen that in consequence his eyes had been put out?

Late that afternoon, as the carriage made its way towards Most and my thoughts churned, my eyes met those of Sir Kaspar. From the opposite corner of the coach he was watching me now with a hooded gaze, a gnarled hand gripping the hilt of his sword. Another thought came to me, as alarming as anything that had gone before. What if the knight was not a spy at all, but something far more sinister? Maybe I was not meant to return from Most; maybe my travelling companion was also my executioner.

We were still some way short of Mělník when our driver turned the carriage sharply westwards, and soon we reached the Ohře and followed it as far as Louny. We lodged for the night outside the town, at a staging post the condition of which I forbear to describe, except to remark that this time it was not lice I had to contend with, but a squadron of fleas.

Jeppe Schenckel took one look at the place and declared he would sleep in the coach. That creature could sleep on a bed of nails if nothing better was on offer.

The next morning, hitched up to a new pair of horses not much less decrepit than the old ones, we crossed the river by a wooden bridge that creaked and cracked in such loud protest I feared it would give way under our weight. I was amazed that in the end it held.

It was late afternoon when we arrived at Most, a handsome little town at the foot of a wooded hill, its clustered rust-red roofs glowing in the last of the day's pale sunlight. The narrow streets were busy, and I was glad to be among such bustle and cheerful sounds after two long, weary days on that desolate road.

We made our way through the town and out at the other side, and hauled our way up Hněvín Hill, atop which sat the castle, an unimpressive pile with a vile-smelling moat and a single blackened tower set on the southern wall. As we entered by the main gate chickens ran squawking from under our horses' hoofs, and a pig lying in a patch of sunlight gave us a disdainful stare out of its little pink eyes before heaving itself up and trotting out of our path.

When we had pulled up in the courtyard, our driver went in search of an ostler, and we four passengers got down and stretched our legs.

By now even Jeppe Schenckel was looking travel-worn and dusty, and there was a dent in his conical hat. Leaning on his ebony cane, he glanced about the shabby square, sniffed, and then pronounced the place a dismal hole.

Sir Kaspar walked a little way off from us and let go a tremendous fart, about as loud as the firing of a small cannon. Grinning, he gave himself a doggy shake. The page boy scratched his pustules.

By now my mind was a little more at ease; this place seemed altogether too mundane to die in.

There appeared then a brisk young lady about my own age. She was severe of aspect, with a sharp little face and large dark eyes. This was Elizabeth Jane Weston, Kelley's stepdaughter. She wore a long white apron, her sleeves were rolled up, and her hair was covered with a white linen cap. She had been churning butter—'We are abandoned here to fend for ourselves as best we can,' she informed us—and was in no mood to be hospitable.

'Have you come to release my stepfather?' she demanded. 'It is about time.' I told her he was not to be released, but that Chamberlain Lang had sent us to fetch him back to Prague. 'To Prague?' she snapped. 'For what reason?'

'The Chamberlain has questions he wishes to put to him,' I answered.

At this she pressed her lips tightly together and glared at me from under her black, heavy brows. 'Dr Kelley cannot travel,' she said. 'He is crippled and sick.'

'The Chamberlain will not be balked, madam,' I said.

'The Chamberlain, the Chamberlain! Already we have

223

had that fellow Kroll and his men, who threatened and mistreated my stepfather, and now there is you. I shall write to His Majesty. He knows me, he knows who I am. I shall entreat him, and lay a complaint against you.'

'There will not be time for that, madam. We leave for Prague in the morning.'

She glared again, and then without another word she turned and strode away.

Kelley was held in the black tower. The turnkey, a slow and solemn fellow with a suspicious eye, unlocked the door and led the dwarf and me up a winding cold stone stairway, which brought back to me a sharp and shiver-making reminder of that night in Prague when I myself was incarcerated in a tower not unlike this one.

I had expected Kelley to be a greybeard and was surprised on entering his cell to find him a man not much above forty, though he was obviously ill and in pain. He was lean and bony, with drooping whiskers and a shovel-shaped beard that had gone prematurely white. To hide the lack of his ears, his hair was indeed long at the sides. His left leg was heavily bandaged and rested on a cushion set upon a low stool.

He was seated by the window at a table laden with books and manuscripts. He wore a black skullcap and a fur-lined coat, and a black shawl was draped over his shoulders. It was clear to me that he had heard of our coming and had set himself up in a scholarly pose with the aim of impressing us.

He looked at us both with a keen, searching eye, then fixed on me. 'You must be this Christian Stern of whom there has been so much talk,' he said. 'Even out here, in this godforsaken wilderness, we have heard tell of you.'

'Good day to you, Doctor,' I said. 'Yes, I am Christian Stern.'

He turned a sour look upon the dwarf. 'Schenckel,' he said, 'you I did not expect. Does His Majesty still keep you for a lapdog and feed you bones under the table?'

'You are out of sorts, I see, Doctor,' the dwarf said, 'but your tongue is as sharp as ever.' He smiled sardonically. 'We have come to take you back to Prague—that will be a treat for you and put you in better spirits, eh?'

Kelley looked to me again. 'Who wants me in Prague?' he asked. 'Is it Wenzel? He already sent his man Kroll to quiz and torment me on all sorts of nonsensical matters.'

'No,' I said, 'it was not the High Steward who sent us, but Chamberlain Lang.'

'Ah, Lang,' Kelley said, nodding grimly—it seemed to me he had paled a little at the name—and added, after a pause: 'What of these killings we hear of, Kroll's daughter and young Madek? Is that why you've come for me? If so, your journey was wasted.'

'What do you know about these deaths?' I asked.

He shrugged. 'Only what little news comes to us here—tittle-tattle and gossip, most of it.' His gaze darkened and grew sharper still. 'Who was it murdered them?'

'It's not known,' I said. 'It is a mystery.'

'A mystery!' He snorted. 'I trust Philipp Lang does not imagine I know who the culprit is. Perhaps he thinks I crept into Prague and butchered those two myself.' He pointed to his bandaged leg. 'I am so fleet-footed, as you see.'

Jeppe Schenckel went forward, past the desk, and looked out of the window at the twilit landscape of hill and wood and town. 'You have a fair prospect from here,' he said. 'There are worse prisons in the world.' He turned back to

Kelley. 'Madek came out here, so I'm told. Was it an inter-esting visit? Was it profitable?'

Kelley brushed the question aside with a contemptuous sweep of his hand. 'I know nothing of Madek,' he said, and made a show of rummaging absently among the papers before him. I could see from his manner that he was lying. 'I never met the fellow.'

The dwarf laughed. 'You see how it is with him?' he said to me. 'He lies for sport, to keep in practice.' And then to Kelley again: 'Madek was here. The fact is known. Why did he come?'

Kelley looked him up and down, smiling a little. 'Ho, weasel!' he said. 'Did His Grace the Chamberlain give you leave to open the questioning on his behalf?'

Schenckel, too, was smiling now. 'As you know well, sir,' he said softly, 'I am not the Chamberlain's man.'

Kelley turned to me. 'But you are, yes? I hope you keep a long spoon by you, to sup with that particular devil.'

I sighed, for my patience had by now worn thin. I was tired after the journey; my head and bones ached from the bucking of the carriage. I was hungry and dispirited, and in no mood to suffer this man's taunts. 'Sir,' I said, 'we shall leave at first light. Be good enough to have your-self ready for the road. It's not an easy journey, as no doubt you know.'

He shook his head. 'I cannot walk. My right leg was bro-ken and is half mended, while this one'—he indicated his bandages again—'refuses to heal, and I fear may rot. Come closer and get a whiff of it, if you like.'

'We'll find some arrangement,' I said. 'But be ready when we come for you.'

He put his head back a little way and gazed at me almost

merrily. 'Why, sir, you are haughty! The Emperor's favourite, indeed. I wish you well of the heady height you've scrambled up to—it will be a long way down.'

I looked to Schenckel, and he nodded. Without another word we went out together and down the stairs—what a thing it was to see the dwarf negotiate those steep and treacherous steps!—and had the turnkey let us out.

'It seems hardly worth locking him in,' I said to the fellow, 'given the poor state your prisoner is in.'

'Oh, he do hobble well enough, when he wants,' was the reply I got. 'But I'll say this for him: I've never known the like of him to bear up under pain.'

'You see how Kelley does it,' the dwarf said to me as we crossed the courtyard, where dusk was giving way to night, 'how he wins round simple souls?'

'Aye,' I said, 'and ones that are not so simple.'

He laughed, nodding. 'God bless His Majesty,' he said. 'The world does take him for a dupe. What would he be without the likes of you to save him from his follies, not to mention the Edward Kelleys of this world?'

'You take risks, dwarf,' I said.

'Do I?' he enquired, assuming a look of large surprise.

'I don't care to hear His Majesty spoken of in this way, as a dupe or a dunce.'

'Ah, but you would not betray me, would you?' the dwarf said, smiling. Then his look changed, turning malignant. 'I may take risks,' he said, 'but you have a greater disadvantage—you cannot cure yourself of an innocent heart. It will do for you yet.'

A wave of anger rose in me—who was this fellow to lecture me? But I let the wave go past without breaking: I was too weary to resist it. And, anyway, was he not right?

19

For my dinner, so-called, I was given thin gruel and the leathery leg of a roast chicken. There was no salt, the oaten biscuits were hard, and I was offered only water to drink. The dining hall was vast and draughty, with walls of undressed rough stone and a high, black-beamed ceiling.

I ate alone. Jeppe Schenckel, who seemed to survive on air, had waved away the gruel and the blackened fowl and then called for a servant to show him to his bed. Sir Kaspar and the page boy ventured down to the town in search of an alehouse—by now the two had become fast friends, however ill-matched a pair they might have been. My volume of old faithful Pliny was with me, but this evening I was not in the mood for his placid wisdom. I left the book unopened beside me on the table.

Presently Elizabeth Weston appeared and sat down opposite me. She had taken off her apron and her cap. She was not beautiful, but she had an air of intelligence and self-possession that I found appealing, despite her simmering anger and the sourness of her manner. She watched me as I ate. Her silence bristled with indignation.

'You shouldn't think I mean your father harm,' I said at last.

'Oh, of course,' she snapped back, with blunt sarcasm. 'You are only the one who will take him to Prague and deliver him to the torture chamber, and then discreetly withdraw.' She looked aside angrily. 'He is my stepfather, anyway, not my father. My own father died when I was little; I don't remember him at all.'

'Yes, of course,' I said, 'I had forgotten. Forgive me.'

She turned back and gazed at me stonily for some moments. 'Don't imagine I have a great affection for the man up in that tower,' she said. 'He's a schemer and a cheat. Because of him I am washed up here, in this back end of the world. In his great days, after Dr Dee had returned to England and Rudolf made him his court alchemist, he possessed vast properties here—land, estates, villages entire. He had a brewery, a mill, nine houses—nine!—in Jílové, where the gold mines are, and two great mansions on Charles Square. I was a girl then and took all this as our due. Then the Catholics raised a conspiracy against him, and Rudolf, frightened of the Pope, banished him, and me along with him. And yet'—she put a hand wearily to her brow—'I would not see him suffer.' She paused. 'What does the Chamberlain want of him?'

I debated with myself if I should tell her how Sir Henry Wotton's clumsy intervention had roused Lang's suspicions. The Catholics, I mused, were not the only ones given to conspiracy. Elizabeth of England had her interests here in Bohemia, and Wotton was only one among many who acted as her eyes and ears at Rudolf's court. The Queen was right to be wary: Rudolf was a religious waverer and, besides, he was a Habsburg and a nephew of Elizabeth's arch-enemy, Philip of Spain. And what was this other Elizabeth, sitting here opposite me now? And what, for that matter, was I? Chaff, both of us, before the wind of the world's great affairs.

'I am only the Chamberlain's agent,' I said. 'I am not privy to his thoughts or aims.'

At this she made a kind of sneer. 'Come, sir,' she said. 'You may be here about Lang's business, but my stepfather tells me you are the Emperor's favoured aide and confidant.'

'Madam,' I said, pushing away the bowl of gruel, 'there are matters afoot at court too densely tangled even for me to penetrate them, no matter how much in favour you imagine me to be.'

And how favoured was I, anyway? I had no position, no office, no title; I had requested the Emperor to appoint me to the Privy Council, but he had hemmed and havered and in the end done nothing. I knew well how tenuously I stood. I was a tall tree clinging to a rock, with only thin and sickly roots to hold me upright.

'You must know what Lang wants of my stepfather,' Elizabeth Weston said. 'I can't believe you don't.'

'A valuable thing was taken,' I said. 'A young man and his betrothed were murdered. Dark deeds.'

Yes yes, I thought suddenly, the strongbox: was that, and the theft of it, the true cause of Madek's death? The thing had been mentioned so often I had come to disregard it. But perhaps it was of the utmost significance.

'And what has my stepfather to do with these "dark deeds"?' the young woman asked.

'Jan Madek, the man who died, was here,' I said. 'He must have come for some purpose.'

She was silent, watching me. A draught from somewhere made the candles on the table dip their flames, and shadows pranced momentarily on the wall beside us.

'What is this thing that was taken?' she asked.

'A strongbox, containing documents, of what exact nature I can't say.'

'You can't say or you won't say—or you don't know?'

I made no reply. She looked to the side again, nodding, thinking.

'Kroll when he was here asked about the same thing,' she said. 'He and his men threatened my stepfather and made him suffer—I heard his cries, up in the tower. He is a sick man; he should not be treated so.'

'It's thought,' I said, 'that Madek took the box and hid it somewhere.'

She was still gazing away, and I was not sure if she had been listening to me or was lost entirely in her own thoughts.

'Your stepfather denies that the young man was here,' I said, 'but I know he is lying.'

She gave a low laugh, and then a bitter sigh. 'You should never ask him a question direct—he will always reply with a falsehood. It's his way.'

'So I am told.'

Again the breeze bent the candle flames, again the shadows pranced. Elizabeth Weston rose and went to a tall wooden cupboard in a far corner and came back with an earthenware flask and two small crystal glasses. She poured out a drink for both of us and handed a glass to me. 'Plum brandy,' she said. 'I make it myself—like everything else we have, since His Gracious Majesty will allow us nothing, not even a stipend to live on.'

The drink was sweet and somewhat cloying stuff, but it had a warming effect that I was glad of. The wind outside was steadily rising, and somewhere off in the depths of the castle a door that someone had left open banged and banged.

The young lady before me, her anger abating a little, sipped her drink and said nothing for a while. Then she laid a cheek on her fist and regarded me with a speculative eye.

'Where do you come from?' she asked. 'I mean, where is your birthplace?'

'Regensburg,' I said. 'And you?'

'England, in the county of Oxford.'

'Your German is admirable.'

'I also speak Czech, Italian and Latin.'

'Of course, I have read your Latin verse,' I said.

She smiled wryly. 'I see you are a liar, too, like my stepfather.'

No doubt I coloured. She was right: I had not read her poetry, and had only meant to flatter her. I knew her reputation, although it was slight at the time. Afterwards, with Kelley dead, when she was allowed to settle again in Prague, she made a famous name for herself, penning ponderously ornate odes to Rudolf, to Prague, and Bohemia, to herself and her circle of admirers. She was a remarkable woman—that is, she became one, by becoming famous. I cannot speak for the quality of her verse, except to say it was not to my taste.

She took up the flask and refilled my glass and her own. 'Do you think my stepfather mad?' she asked.

'Mad?' I said. 'He does not seem so to me. He was John Dee's first man, and a master of the scryer's art, so it's said.'

'Oh, all that stuff and nonsense!' She gave me a mocking look. 'Only men could take it seriously. Do *you* believe in it?'

I had to smile, despite myself.

'Dear me, madam,' I said, 'you do ask a hard question.' I paused for a moment. That door was still banging in the wind. 'I think,' I said, 'that the world is a great cipher set for us to solve. I have no doubt there are certain men born with the gift of seeing deep into the essence of things, who have a secret knowledge of the true nature of matter and its potentials.'

She was looking distractedly into her glass. A gust of wind struck the walls and windows with a great soft crash. 'He claims to talk with angels, as did Dr Dee,' she said. 'I came upon him once squatting on the ground and keening like a wolf. He stands sometimes atop the tower, too, at night, with arms outstretched, shouting blasphemy at the heavens and summoning up spirits. At times like those, I'm not sure whether to laugh or to be frightened of him. I sometimes think perhaps he *is* sick in his mind—'

'Often people with occult powers do seem so, to the rest of us.'

'—but then I see how cunning and calculating he is, and I think otherwise.' She tilted her glass and rolled the base of it like a hoop this way and that upon the tabletop. 'Do you dabble in these things—alchemy, the transmutation of metals, all that?'

'I studied it for many years,' I said, 'and credited much of it. But I was young then, and believed all sorts of things.'

She smiled at me almost warmly. 'You are hardly old now,' she said.

'I put my faith in natural philosophy, of course,' I went on, 'to that science of things that can be proved and disproved in the visible world. But for the rest, I have grave doubts.'

'You don't believe in magic, then?'

I shrugged. 'There are phenomena that cannot be accounted for by reason alone,' I said, 'that much I'll grant. But many of the wonders your stepfather and Dr Dee claimed to be capable of I believe to be no better than—well, than humbug.'

233

I could see that this time she had indeed stopped listening. She was looking about the room and frowning.

'It's hard for me to live here,' she said. 'I'm lonely and afraid. The guards—' She stopped; I waited.

She shook her head. 'I see how they look at me, I hear the things they say. This is an uncouth place, wild and forsaken. I wasn't meant for here, and cannot be at peace.'

Now came a sudden lashing of rain outside. The wind took on a new intensity, and two of the four candles on the table were abruptly extinguished.

'Have you no one else in the world?' I asked.

She was busy relighting the candles. 'Oh, yes, there is my mother, and my brother, John, but they are in Prague— they live there in secret, unknown to the Emperor, while I am left in banishment.'

She poured us another drink. The storm howled about the castle, a huge fury of air and rain and hail. I thought of the man in the tower, at his desk, muttering incantations to himself and to the night.

A great flash of lightning lit the whole hall for an instant; then came the peal of thunder. Elizabeth Weston, I saw, had turned white, and her lip trembled.

'I'm afraid,' she said. 'I'm afraid of the world.' She looked at me anxiously. 'Do you think he conjured it?'

'The storm?'

'Yes. To show you his power.'

I leaned back in my chair and gazed at her. 'You said he was a fraud. And even if he weren't, no mortal has the power to command the elements, whatever Dr Dee and his like may say.' I reached across the table and touched her hand. 'Do not be afraid.'

I thought she would shrink from my touch, but she did not. Her hand was warm.

Another flash, another crash.

'Please, don't be afraid,' I said again, more softly.

She looked at me; she looked at my hand. 'Will you take me to Prague?' she asked, curling her fingers around mine so tightly it seemed she meant to break them. 'Take me there,' she said fiercely, watching me. 'Take me with you.'

20

Her bedchamber was another vast, cold stone hall furnished with large, dark items of furniture of uncertain purpose. In contrast to these outsized, over-ornamented chests and commodes and mighty cupboards was her cedarwood box bed, as tall and broad and deep and plain as a wardrobe, sequestered in a far corner, as if it had fled there in fright of so much useless immensity all round. Into this bed, which was enclosed behind a pair of wide doors, we had climbed, the two of us shivering from the cold and she apologising for the unlit stove. She shut the doors behind us, enveloping us in darkness. The feather-bed mattress was high and soft.

Outside, beyond the room's rough walls, the storm raged on, like a maddened giant, beating its fists against the house and hurling shafts of lightning in at the windows.

'Hold me,' the young woman whispered, trembling in my arms. 'Oh, hold me!'

After that first urgently whispered plea to be held and sheltered, she said not a word, but went at our love-making with wordless vehemence, panting through gritted teeth, writhing under me and pummelling me with her fists. She struggled violently, as if she were being ravished—not by me, however, but by herself. It angered her, I could feel it, that she had given in to her own fear and need and desire.

I was a little frightened of her, and, obscurely, of myself, too.

When we had spent ourselves and the bout was over,

we lay in the darkness side by side, I fitting myself as best I could to the confined space. The bed was short, for it was meant to be slept in half sitting up, and I kept banging my feet against the end wall of the box and my elbows against the doors.

Guilt had settled itself square upon me, like Prometheus's eagle. It would do no good to tell myself that she had given me the bounty of her body calculatedly, like a parcel of precious goods, having first placed the invoice in my hand with her own warm fingers. Now I would have no choice but to take her back with me to Prague. That was the price of my pleasure, and it would serve me right if I suffered for it. I pictured Caterina Sardo fixing her eye upon the young woman and knowing at once exactly what had gone on here tonight, in this shut-in cramped little bed, as the storm raged and that loose door in the distance swung to and fro on its hinges.

We fell asleep, the two of us, she with her back to me and I with my arms around her. I don't know for how long we slept, but when we woke, we woke together, with a violent start.

'Was that a cry?' she whispered, reaching out for me blindly in the dark and taking hold of my wrist.

'A cry?' I said. I had heard nothing—or had I? 'What kind of cry?'

'Outside somewhere, out in the night.'

'It was likely Sir Kaspar and the boy, returning drunk from town.'

'No, it wasn't a drunkard's cry.' She scrabbled about on the bed for her clothes.

'What are you doing?' I said. 'You can't go out in such a tempest.'

The thunder had moved some way off, but the wind was still strong and the rain as heavy as ever. I put my arms around her again and made her lie down. I could feel the rapid beating of her heart. She began to weep, angrily at first, then sinking into sorrow.

'Why did you have to come here?' she said, sobbing. 'Was it not enough that we should be banished and abandoned here? Have we not suffered enough? Now you'll take him to Prague and they'll send him to the dungeons and torment him.'

She sat up quickly. 'Listen to me,' she said. I could barely make out her form above me in the dark. 'What if I were to tell you what the Chamberlain and the others want to know? Would you go back then, back to Prague, and leave my stepfather in peace?'

'How do you know what they want to know?' I asked.

I could hear her putting on her shift. She had dried her tears; suddenly she was all urgency and determination. It was as if she had forgotten our passionate struggle earlier, or as if it had not taken place at all.

She had seen what to do; she had seen a way out.

She clambered over me, bathing me in her woman's rich aromas, and opened the doors and stepped out onto the stone floor. I too began to pull on my things, and made to follow her.

'No no, stay,' she said. 'It's too cold out here; I am only fetching the lamp.'

I sat down again on the untidy bed with my legs crossed and my back against the wooden wall behind me. She brought the lamp and set it on a little table in front of the open doors, and climbed again into the tall deep box and settled herself beside me.

'What have you to tell me?' I asked.

She took my hand. 'I think you are a good man, Christian Stern,' she said. 'Am I right to think so?'

'I don't know,' I said. I had not yet addressed her by her name, not once. 'I don't think any man is good or bad entirely. We are all mixed, and act according to the circumstances we find ourselves in.'

But again her attention had lapsed, and she was not listening.

'I want to trust you,' she said, and pressed my hand. 'I have to trust someone.' She was silent for a time; I could feel her thinking, thinking. In the distance, the thunder rumbled on.

'The High Steward, Felix Wenzel,' she said finally, 'he used to send letters here.'

For a moment I was at a loss. Of the things I could have expected her to say, this was not one.

'Letters?' I said. 'You mean, to your stepfather?'

'Yes, but not directed to him.'

'To whom, then?'

'To—to someone else. Wenzel used my stepfather as a channel, a channel between himself and . . .'

'And?' I urged.

She bit her lip and squeezed her eyes tight shut.

'The Queen,' she whispered, in so low a voice I barely caught the word.

'The Queen?' I said. 'What queen?'

'Our Queen—Elizabeth.'

'Elizabeth? Elizabeth of England?'

For a second my chest felt like an empty hollow. I seemed to have no breath at all, as if the force of the sulphurous stormy air had sucked it out of me on the spot.

The young woman shivered. 'Dear Lord Christ,' she murmured. 'What have I said?'

That far-off door was banging more frequently now, and with quickening force, like something becoming more and more enraged.

I could not think what to think. Was she lying? But, if so, to what purpose? Was it a trick she was playing on me, perhaps, to save her stepfather, to save herself? But what trick might it be, and how would it work?

'What did they write about,' I asked, 'Wenzel and the Queen?'

'I don't know what they wrote about,' she said impatiently. 'Secrets, I suppose, plans and strategies. Plots—the kind of things such people deal in.'

'But how do you know about the letters? Did you see them? Did your stepfather show them to you?'

She tried to pull away from me. 'Stop it!' she cried. 'You're hurting me!'

I let go of her hand; I had not realised I had been gripping it so fiercely. 'I'm sorry,' I said. 'But you have to tell me. I have to know.'

'I saw one letter. He had been careless and left it on his table. It was from Wenzel, I think.'

'What did it say?'

'I couldn't make it out. It was written in code.'

'What kind of code?'

'One he devised.'

'Your stepfather?'

'Yes. I made him explain it to me. He had drawn up two codes, one for Elizabeth's use, the other for Wenzel's. He alone had the keys to both. The letters would come by secret couriers, from Prague, from London. He would

240

translate them, from one code into the other, and send them on, Wenzel's to the Queen, the Queen's to Wenzel. That was what they used him for. He was their—their go-between.'

'Why did he do it? What return did he get?'

'Wenzel had promised that when he came to power he would allow my stepfather to return to Prague, that he would set him up again in one of those grand mansions he used to own on Charles Square—that he would be a great man again.'

'When he came to power?' I said. 'Wenzel?'

'Yes. When he had brought down Lang, and the Emperor along with him, and put his brother on the throne instead.'

'The Emperor's brother? Matthias?'

'Yes, yes, I suppose so. I don't know.' She had begun to cry again, distractedly, almost absentmindedly; her tears glittered in the lamplight. 'Oh, God, oh, God,' she mumbled, pressing her fingers to her mouth. Then she grew calm, and dropped her hands, and sat back, as if all her energy had suddenly deserted her. 'What have I done?' she asked herself, so simply and calmly it was as if she had expected an answer. 'I should never have spoken.'

I leaned back against the wooden wall of the bed behind me and closed my eyes. I, too, felt weary. It was as if I had been bearing a great weight for a long time without realising it, and only now had I registered it, a thing heavy enough to break my back that yet I had not known was there.

'I don't understand,' I said, and could not keep my voice from shaking. 'The box, the strongbox that Madek stole from Kroll—'

'He brought it here,' Elizabeth Weston said.

She, too, was leaning against the wall behind us; she, too, sounded as if all her strength were lost to her.

'What was in it, this box?' I asked.

'Magic papers, documents, spells, suchlike—things that Kroll had collected over many years, and that the Emperor was jealous of and desired for himself.'

So what Jeppe Schenckel had said was true: there had been precious papers, and Madek had stolen them.

'He offered them to my stepfather,' she went on, 'that he in turn might offer them to Rudolf, and thereby secure an end to his exile and be allowed to return to Prague.' She sighed. 'Poor Madek—he was determined to be revenged on Wenzel, and on Kroll. He wanted his Magdalena back, and for her father and the High Steward to suffer for allowing her to be taken from him. He was half mad with jealousy and rage.'

'So he gave your stepfather the strongbox,' I said.

'Yes.' Her voice was very small now.

'And what did he ask for, in return?' I knew the answer to that question, of course; how would I not?

'The letters,' she said. 'My stepfather was supposed to have destroyed the originals, after turning them into code, but instead he had kept them, in secret.'

'And did he give them to Madek?'

She gazed before her into the light of the little lamp on the table outside, nodding. 'Yes. He knew Wenzel had deceived him, that all his promises were false. He knew he would not be brought back to Prague in triumph. He had been waiting too long, and had despaired. Now he wanted his revenge, wanted to see Wenzel destroyed, and Kroll along with him. So he removed the papers, Kroll's papers, from the strongbox, and put into it instead the Queen's and

Wenzel's letters, and locked it, and gave it to Madek. "Take them to Prague," he said. "Destroy Wenzel, as you want to do. Bring the pillars of the temple down."'

Again we were silent.

'And the papers that had been in the strongbox, Kroll's papers, which the Emperor wanted—what did your step-father do with them?'

She gave a little low laugh. 'He put them in the fireplace and burned them,' she said. She paused, and then went on: 'They had betrayed him, you see, all of them—Wenzel, Ulrich Kroll, the Emperor himself. And now, through this vengeful young man, he would have his revenge on them.'

I put my head back and rolled it slowly to and fro against the bed's wooden wall. Yes, yes, yes, I saw it all. Kelley had come to understand that he had been tricked, that Wenzel had no intention of restoring him to his former position of power and influence; nor would the Emperor release him from exile here at Most. The days of grandeur were gone for ever: it was the end, the sorcerer robbed of his powers. There was nothing left to him except vengeance.

'I do not know what happened when Madek went to Prague,' Elizabeth Weston said, in a calm, slow voice that seemed to come from far off. 'I suppose he told Wenzel he had the letters, and threatened him with them, and Wenzel seized him.'

'They tortured him,' I said. 'They put out his eyes. Then they strangled him with a cord and threw his corpse into the Stag Moat.' I paused, struggling to gather my thoughts, to make some order of them. 'But what became of the strongbox?' I asked, of myself rather than of her. 'He would have told them where it was. He could not have held out and stayed silent under the torments they inflicted on him.'

She shook her head.

'He didn't give it to them. Whatever he did with it, he didn't surrender it. That was why Kroll came, with his men, looking for it here. They tortured my stepfather, too. In the end they would have put him to death, as they put Jan Madek to death, except I suppose they feared the Emperor might one day change his mind and ask again for his old wizard and want him back.'

'And did your stepfather tell Kroll he had given the letters to Madek?' I asked.

Again she shook her head. 'I don't know. All I know is that Kroll left in a fury, threatening to return. Yes, he was very angry, but he was afraid, too, I could see it, afraid of Wenzel, afraid of the Emperor, afraid of all these plans and plots he had allowed himself to become entangled in. And then his daughter died.'

'Yes,' I said, 'she was murdered, cruelly murdered. Do you know by whom?'

'What?' She gazed at me vague-eyed.

'Do you know who it was that killed her, the doctor's daughter?'

She made an impatient gesture. 'No,' she said shortly, 'no, of course not. Do you?'

We live upon the conviction that we are safe, that the ice will not shatter beneath us, that the lightning will not strike the tree under which we shelter from the storm, that the door will not burst open and the soldiers come tramping up the stairs to seize us in our bed. Yet deep down we know it is all a delusion, although one that we must cling to, if fear is not to overwhelm and consume us, like the deadly crab that grows inside a man and eats his innards. And indeed that night, sitting there on that cramped bed,

244

side by side with that frightened woman, I seemed to feel inside me a saw-edged claw stealthily opening.

Elizabeth Weston turned to me. 'But why have you come?' she asked. 'Why did Lang send you—why now?'

I hesitated.

'Sir Henry Wotton,' I said, 'do you know of him, who he is?'

'I know he is the Queen's man, her representative, her ambassador. He used to come to our house, long ago, in the great days.'

'He asked for leave to travel to Most,' I said. 'It raised the Chamberlain's suspicions.'

I might have added that it was I who had gone to the Chamberlain with word of Sir Henry's request, but I kept silent; I kept silent.

The wind keened in the chimney; the lamplight wavered. The thunder had ceased at last.

'So that's all there was,' Elizabeth Weston said, in a tone of weary wonderment. 'Wotton's asking, and the Chamberlain's suspicions? That's all there was, to cause all this?'

'Yes,' I said.

I said it and, saying it, felt something turn in my gut, the creature's jagged claw again. I was not innocent here; I was complicit. I was the Chamberlain's man, just as Jeppe Schenckel was the Emperor's, as Kroll was Wenzel's. Is there anyone who is not owned by someone?

'And yet Lang will not let him off,' Elizabeth Weston said, 'now that Wotton has put a doubt into his head.'

In the toils of our love-making earlier the pins had come out of her hair, and gleaming strands of it hung down now about her shoulders. The bodice she had pulled on was unlaced, and I could see in the opening the smooth slope of a breast. Yet our moment of love-making seemed far off now, a stylised scene, like the mythical subject of a painting, which the painter has placed at a far distance, somewhere down in the lower corner of a vast landscape of tree and stream and dream-blue mountains.

'What will they do to him, in Prague?' the young woman asked.

We were both gazing dully before us, as we sat there in the lamplight, side by side.

'As I have said, he will be questioned.'

'Questioned? That is a pretty way of putting it. They'll torture him, won't they? It's what they always do—they call in the one in the black hood, with his pincers and his burning irons.'

I was silent. She nodded slowly, gazing before her. For a long time she did not speak, and then she said: 'It was a cry I heard. It *was*.'

21

She was right; she had heard a cry. In the morning, Kelley was discovered at the foot of the black tower, from the top of which he had fallen or more likely cast himself to his death on the stone flags below. It was his stepdaughter who found him. When I arrived she was kneeling in the mud, cradling his broken, bloodied head in her lap. She looked up at me without expression, except that her mouth was twisted strangely at each corner, as if in a mad sort of smile. I could think of nothing to say to her.

Jeppe the dwarf appeared, stepping carefully in his fancy shoes through the mire the storm had churned up.

'What's this?' he said. 'The sorcerer soars too close to the sun and melts his wings?'

'Go and find our coachman,' I said to him. 'Tell him we leave in an hour.'

I went myself in search of Sir Kaspar and the page boy. They had returned at midnight, drunk and drenched by the storm, and finding no one to show them the way to a bed, they had slept in a barn outside the castle wall. When I came upon them they were sprawled in the straw like a pair of corpses. I kicked them on the soles of their boots to wake them. The boy mewled piteously and would not open his eyes until I got him by the scruff and jerked him to his feet, and even then he hung from my grip like a stringless puppet. In his wet garb he smelt like a sheep, and the front of his jerkin was caked with dried puke. Also he had a black eye and a split lip.

'Got into a dispute with the night watch, he did,' Sir Kaspar said huskily, sitting up and yawning.

'Damn it, man,' I said, 'you could have taken better care of him.'

At this the knight gave me a large and wounded look. After rising quakingly to his feet, he shook himself, then hawked and spat. His tousled aspect resembled that of the morning itself—the storm had passed, but the sky was surly still, with racing, smoke-coloured clouds through which a watery sun dodged and danced.

'Dr Kelley is dead,' I said.

The old man stared. 'Slain, was he?'

'He fell from the tower, some time in the night.'

'Christ in Heaven,' the knight said, and gave a delighted, wheezing laugh, shaking his head. 'The Chamberlain will have your hide for this!'

'Yours too, I don't doubt,' I said. 'The dwarf has gone to rouse our driver. You go too, and get ready to depart.'

I could see him weighing whether to defy me—he was a knight, after all, even if a dusty one, and what was I but a sophister and a scribbler?—but in the end he shrugged his bony shoulders and went away muttering.

Still Norbert, the horrible boy, hung in my grip; I let go of him, and delivered him a kick and sent him off to forage for something for me to eat for my breakfast. I walked back to the high cold hall where I had dined last evening but found no sign of a servant, and no fire had been lit. After wandering about for a while, through other rooms, I had still encountered no one—the castle seemed deserted.

Finally I chanced upon a little stone chapel and spied

Kelley's corpse lying on a bier with lighted candles surrounding it. The blood had been washed from his skull, and he was got up in a black robe and a silk ruff, and his jaw was bound with a white rag to keep it from lolling. His hands were joined upon his breast. He might have been a statue of himself, with skin as pale as marble and his mouth sternly set. Curious, the little kindnesses that death affords us, the balm of dignity it effects. In life the sorcerer had not looked half so noble and serene as he did now.

I went on, passing through another series of bare and dingy rooms. I was in search of Elizabeth Weston, though I hardly imagined she would be in any mood to speak to me. I had no doubt that she, no less than the Chamberlain, would regard me as responsible for her stepfather's death.

I was in a quandary as to what was to be done. It seemed imperative that I should transport Kelley's remains back to Prague. He had been a great man in that city once, and the Emperor, I felt sure, would wish that he should be given due respect and have his funeral and be buried there. But what about Elizabeth Weston—what was I to do with her? Her term of banishment would be at an end, now that her stepfather was dead, but had I the authority to allow her to accompany his corpse to the city, despite the rash promise I had made her last night in the heat of desire and after too many glasses of plum brandy? And when she got to Prague, what then? Her mother and her brother might take her in, but since they were living there in secrecy they would be loath to draw attention to themselves, even for the sake of a daughter and a sister. And then again, there was the question of Caterina Sardo. What would she say and, more importantly, what would she do, when she saw me with a girl in tow? Diligent dissembler though I was, I knew my Caterina, she of the sharp eye, and sharper claw.

I had returned to the dining hall, and was sitting at the bare table there—where was that boy with my breakfast?—grappling with these delicate questions, when Sir Kaspar came in, gaunt and crapulous still. He seemed in something of an uncertain state himself, and went about the room fiddling at things—raking the cold embers in the fireplace, pouring out a mug of water, stopping at the doorway to stare out into the courtyard, all the while whistling faintly, tunelessly, to himself. In the end I lost patience.

'For God's sake leave off foostering, Sir Knight!' I snapped. 'If you have something you wish to say to me, then say it.'

He came and sat down at the table, not looking at me but letting his bloodhound's mournful gaze wander here and there.

'It's the runt,' he said—'what's his name?'

'You mean the dwarf, Schenckel?'

'Aye, the dwarf.' He picked at the grain of the table with a horny thumbnail. 'I went up to the doctor's room, to his cell, you know, just to have a look about—'

'Why?' I said. He peered at me, frowning. I kept my patience, and asked again: 'Why did you go to his cell?'

He shrugged, lifting one shoulder high, and once more let his gaze wander. 'Just to see that everything was—that everything was in order, and so on. Anyway, the dwarf was there before me.'

'Oh, yes?' I straightened on my chair, laying my hands flat on the table. 'And what was he about?'

He leaned forward with a confiding squint. 'He had been searching.'

'Searching?'

'Through the doctor's things, you know—his papers, and that.' He paused. 'I reckon he had already found something, for as soon as he saw me he turned aside, fussing at his doublet, and then turned back to me and put on a haughty look and asked why I was there and what I thought I was doing.'

'And what did you say?'

'I said you had sent me, to tidy things up and see that all was in order.'

'And did he believe you?'

He grinned, which, with his long head and his great discoloured teeth, gave him for a moment a remarkable resemblance to a horse. 'What matter if he did or didn't?' he said. 'What is he but the Emperor's buffoon?'

'Did you challenge him on whatever it was he had taken?'

Again he grinned. 'I thought I'd leave that to you, Herr Doktor,' he said.

Norbert the page boy, who looked to be recovered somewhat from the night's excesses—though his swollen eye, all purple and yellow, was a thing hard to look at—came to announce that he could find not a scrap of food anywhere in the castle. The servants, having heard of the doctor's death, had apparently fled and gone into hiding in the town.

I swore, and turned to Sir Kaspar. 'What about the carriage?' I asked. 'Are we set to leave?'

'The carriage is prepared,' he said, 'but the ostler left the horses unfed, and I doubt they'll consent to travel without their grub.'

'Christ God!' I exclaimed. 'What a country this is!'

The old knight nodded sagely. 'You're in the right of it there,' he said. 'Not the place at all, for us folk from the German lands.'

After another search I came upon Jeppe Schenckel in the muddy courtyard, leaning on his cane beside the coach, putting on the air of one who has been kept waiting long and is impatient to be off. The sun was higher now, glinting strongly amid the scudding clouds, throwing down splashes of pale radiance and then withdrawing into shade again. Our driver had hitched up the horses, which had their muzzles deep in nosebags of feed the fellow had managed to find somewhere.

The dwarf kept up his bland look and would not meet my eye.

'What did you take from Kelley's cell?' I demanded. 'And don't say you took nothing, because you were seen.'

He glanced narrowly in Sir Kaspar's direction, then looked back at me. It was clear he intended to brazen it out.

'I know not what you are talking about,' he said. 'What thing am I supposed to have taken?'

The page boy, lounging in the doorway, looked on with an expression of lively anticipation: there was a promise of trouble in the air. Even the fat coach driver had paused in his tightening of the horses' belts and buckles to give us his attention.

'I ask again,' I said, 'what did you take?'

'Pish, sir!' the dwarf answered. 'Who am I to stand here and be interrogated by the likes of you?'

Behind him, Sir Kaspar, with unhurried deliberation, drew his broadsword—it was a fearsome weapon—and turning the blade flatwise struck the dwarf a ringing smack athwart his shoulder blades. The dwarf, letting go of his cane, threw up his arms and with a grunt dropped heavily onto his crooked knees, his face twisted in pain. He knelt there, swaying, until Sir Kaspar, with a terrible grin, stepped forward and put a foot into the small of his back. Crying out, 'Down, dog!' he pushed him over, and the little man collapsed onto his face in the mud.

Behind us, Norbert the page boy gave a shout of laughter.

The old knight lifted his foot again and jammed his sole down on the back of the dwarf's neck, pinning him in the mire, and turned to me merrily. 'What say, sir, I slice off a bit of him?' he asked eagerly.

'Enough!' I said, holding up a hand. 'Enough, now.'

It gives me no pleasure to see a man squirming on the ground with another man's foot on his neck, whoever he is or whatever ill he has done. Besides, if it was some document Jeppe had filched from Kelley's cell, and it was inside his doublet, the mud would soon be getting at it.

The old knight, plainly disappointed that there was to be no more fun, reached down and, saying, 'Upsy-daisy!' hauled the dwarf upright and set him on his feet.

Schenckel's face was a mask of mud, through which his eyes shone with a murderous fury.

I held out my hand. 'Give it to me,' I said. 'Whatever it was you took from the doctor's desk, give it to me, now.'

22

It was noon before we managed to get going at last, in a ragged caravan consisting of our coach, with Sir Kaspar, Norbert the page boy, and the dwarf inside, and me sitting aloft next to the driver to act as lookout—and, if I am honest, so as to be out of sight of the dwarf in his humiliated and vengeful state—while behind us came a cart drawn by a moth-eaten mule, with Dr Kelley's corpse placed upon it, wrapped in a canvas shroud. I had urged Elizabeth Weston to take my seat in the coach and let young Norbert have charge of the cart, but she had insisted that she must be the one to drive her stepfather on his last journey. Turning from me with a face set in stone, she had stepped up to the driver's seat, spurning the hand I put out to assist her, and cracked the cart's reins as if they were a pair of whips. Her things were packed in a leather bag at her feet.

The dwarf was indeed a sorry spectacle, all soiled and bruised and smarting with pain. Taking pity on him before we left, Elizabeth Weston had led him into the castle and cleaned him up as best she could. Yet he remained a wretched sight, and I felt a little sorry for him myself, and somewhat ashamed, too, at having let him be so harshly treated. But, after all, he had sought to deceive and betray me.

What he had removed from among Dr Kelley's papers—all of which, I know, I should immediately have secured as soon as I had heard the doctor was dead—was a clutch of some dozen thin and yellowed sheets of parchment, with holes punched along the left side and bound loosely together with cord into a sort of untidy chapbook. The pages were covered all over, in minuscule script, with a strange hieroglyphic of letters and symbols that I could make nothing of. When I pressed the dwarf to tell me what the thing was, and why, out of all the mass of documents on Kelley's worktable, he had taken it alone, he refused to answer, and turned away from me with a face fully as cold and unyielding as Elizabeth Weston's.

Now, as we set off on our slow way towards Prague, I took the pages from my satchel and pored over them closely once more. The writing, in two separate columns, seemed to be some kind of cipher, made up of Roman, Greek and Hebrew letters all jumbled together with numbers and many strange symbols that I could not identify.

Had this document, I wondered, been among Dr Kroll's trove of precious papers? Had Kelley overlooked it and failed to destroy it when he burned all the others? Surely that was what Jeppe Schenckel had taken the document to be.

After an hour of fruitless wrestling with the puzzle, I suddenly understood. It was only when I laughed that I realised how little cause or opportunity I had for laughter in those days.

The thing was not a code at all, but the key to a code—*two* codes, Elizabeth's and Wenzel's. I laughed again, bitterly this time. So that was Kelley's final, cruel joke: he had given the coded letters to Madek, but not the keys to break the codes. That was what Kroll had come here to find, but he had failed—he could not have been much of a torturer that Kelley could hold out against him.

If the journey up to Most had been hard, the return was ten times worse. Along with the bad roads and the mud left by the storm, our broken-down horses, and the vile way-stations we were forced to stop at, there was for me the constant consciousness of that cart trundling along behind us, with its grim, shrouded cargo, and the unforgiving young woman driving it.

Also the weather had worsened, and for many leagues we endured driving showers of snow and icy rain that stung my face and numbed my hands. Beside me the fat coachman, swathed in a filthy and evil-smelling fur cape, ignored me and complained to himself endlessly in a low, sing-song mumble.

The Ohře, when we came to it, was in spate, and this time I thought we must surely perish as we crossed the rickety bridge. We were just past midway when I heard from behind me a terrible cracking sound. Turning, I saw the left wheel of the funeral cart on the point of sinking back into a jagged rent it had made in the boards of the bridge. But Elizabeth Weston was a woman of spirit, and with a shout and another whipcrack of the reins across the mule's haunches, she drove the animal to a greater effort, and the moment was saved.

We stopped again at Louny, but this time found better quarters within the town walls. We passed a tolerable night there, although Elizabeth Weston still kept her face turned against me, while the dwarf, poorly and in pain though he was, again refused to get down and instead elected to sleep in the coach with his cape wrapped round him, as he had done on the way up.

I made sure that Elizabeth Weston had a clean and comfortable room, and bade her good night. The only reply I got was the sound of her door slamming in my face.

I knew well why she was angry with me—how would

I not know?—and I even sympathised with her, to a degree, and felt the guilt of it to a greater degree. But I was not the cause of her stepfather's death. True, it was my task to bring him back to Prague to face the Chamberlain's questioning, and likely more than questioning—the rack stands always ready and serves all masters equally. Yet I believed it was not the Chamberlain whom Kelley had feared most, but his own former ally and fellow conspirator, Felix Wenzel. For it was Wenzel whom Kelley had betrayed by putting into Jan Madek's hands the means with which to menace the High Steward—with which, indeed, to destroy him, if he chose.

In the end all Kelley's stratagems had come to dust. He had served Wenzel faithfully, had diligently acted as his go-between with the English Queen. He had guarded his secrets, aided his cause, supported his interests. But he had known in his heart that Wenzel one day would betray him, and cheat him of all he had been promised.

The next morning in Louny, I commissioned a pair of saddled horses and sent Sir Kaspar and the page boy ahead of us to Prague, to carry the news of Kelley's death to Chamberlain Lang. I thought it prudent that he be forewarned of the ill tidings being borne towards him, trussed up in a canvas shroud.

Yet still my chief concern was what I should do with Elizabeth Weston when we reached the city. I had hoped she might be able to join her family, her mother and her brother, wherever it was they were living in secret in the city. But this, she gave me to understand, she had no intention of doing—evidently there was no love lost between her and her relatives. As to what she did intend to do, that she would not say either.

We were a league or so short of the city when, realising I could put it off no longer, I called our little caravan to a halt and got down and went back to speak to her where she sat on the driving seat of the cart, red-eyed and shivering.

'Mistress Weston,' I said, 'Elizabeth—you must tell me what you plan to do in Prague, how you intend to live, and where.'

Silence.

There had been more rain but it had passed, and the twilight was windy. Behind her the sky was a blaze of cold yellow light low in the west.

I tried again. 'My dear'—that brought an outraged glare—'I cannot arrive at the castle with you and your stepfather's corpse on this cart. I don't know what manner of welcome we are to expect, but I can guess it will not be warm. I wouldn't wish you to suffer by association with me. I was charged with transporting Dr Kelley back to Prague to be questioned, instead of which all I can produce is his lifeless body. Let me lodge you somewhere safe, until I have had time to fix the matter, as best I can. These are dangerous times, and Prague is a dangerous place.'

Silence again, and that stony frontwards stare.

I lingered, yet not knowing what else to say to her. She sat motionless, hunched and white-faced, with the reins loose in her hands. It grieved me that she would give not the least acknowledgement of what we had been to each other, albeit briefly, while the gale raged about us and she reared and writhed in my arms, caught up in her own tempestuous throes. I might have reminded her of how fiercely she had clung to me, of the passionate kisses we had exchanged, of the tears that had suddenly burst from her at the crest of our embracing, and of the sighing languor in which she had lain beside me, afterwards. There were a hundred things I could have spoken of, feelingly, tenderly, but that rigid face and the cold rejection in her stare silenced me.

I returned to the coach and ordered the driver to drive on. In the end I realised there was but one place I could take her, and even there I was not sure what sort of reception might await her.

Soon the city gates came in sight. The winter day was fading fast.

The Nuncio was at his dinner and would not be disturbed; so said the ruddy-faced novice who opened the door to me at the nunciature. I was in no mood to observe the niceties, however; pushing her to one side, I strode into the hall and set off in the direction of the dining room. In the street I had left a corpse on a cart, attended by a drenched and despairing young woman who, to my alarm, was beginning to show signs of fever. No, I was in no mood to be hindered or refused.

The novice, Sister Maria, trotted after me, twittering anxiously. I paid her no heed.

Malaspina was seated at the long marble table, in front of a platter of roast goose, with a goblet of wine the size of a ciborium at his elbow. He showed no surprise when I pushed open the door and appeared before him.

'*Buona sera, signor Stern!*' he said, smiling fatly, and gestured with his knife for me to be seated. I remained standing.

The two fires facing each other were lit, and the air throbbed with their heat.

'I have come from Most,' I said. 'Dr Kelley is dead.'

'Is he now?' the Nuncio said. 'Did you kill him?'

'I believe he took his own life.'

'*Dio mio!*' He made a sign of the cross on the air. 'I shall pray for him, although self-murder is a grave sin.' He smiled again. 'Do be seated, Doctor. I hate to be stood over—*mi rende nervoso*—and you are so tall. You will take some wine, some food, perhaps?'

'I want nothing,' I said. 'Nothing for myself, that is. The doctor's corpse is on a cart outside your door, and his step-daughter is with him.'

'His stepdaughter?'

'Elizabeth Jane Weston.'

'*Ah, sì, l'inglese—la poetessa.*'

'She needs shelter, she requires care—the journey was hard, and I think she has the fever. Will you take her in?'

At this his smile faltered a little. '*La febbre?*' he said. 'The fever, that is bad.' But he quickly recovered himself and waved his knife. '*Prego, signore*—please sit.'

I walked to the fireplace, the one to the left, the one where he and I had sat after our mighty feast that day when the Emperor's borrowed coach had carried me here. I held out my hands, red and mottled from the cold, to the warmth of the crackling flames.

'So, Bishop,' I said, 'will you offer her sanctuary?'

I heard him sigh. He set down his knife and fork. 'Tell me what happened,' he said. 'Tell me why you were at Most.'

I was gazing into the white-hot heart of the fire. The world has such extremes, of fire and ice, of space and depth, of adamantine hardness and gossamer insubstantiality—how is it we are not terrified every moment of our lives?

'Chamberlain Lang sent me there,' I said. 'I was to trans-port Dr Kelley back to Prague.'

'Oh, yes? For what purpose?'

'The Chamberlain wished to question him.'

'I see.'

I had stood with my back resolutely turned to him while he spoke, but now I went and took up my place opposite him, on the other side of the table. Still I would not sit.

Nothing I had said had surprised him. Had he known already of Kelley's death? Most likely news of it was all over the city by now—it was evening, and Sir Kaspar would have arrived not much after midday.

'Let me bring Mistress Weston in,' I said, 'if only to warm herself here at the fire.'

He lifted his shoulders and held out his soft little hands, showing me his palms, as if to say, *Of course—I have no choice!*

Outside, a cold rain was falling again, so fine it was hardly more than a whisper in the air yet sharp as a shower of needles tipped with ice. When we had arrived, Elizabeth Weston had not wanted to be parted from the corpse of her stepfather and had attempted to remain on the cart; but I would brook no resistance, and took her firmly by the arm and put her into the shelter of the coach. Earlier, as we'd reached the Stone Bridge, the dwarf had left us and hobbled off without a word into the twilight.

Now in the coach the young woman was sitting slumped against the frame of the window. Her eyes were closed, and I could hear her rapid breathing.

'Elizabeth,' I said. 'Come, here's a place for you to stay.'

I touched her hand; her skin was on fire. She looked at me and seemed not to know who I was.

The Nuncio had come to the door of the coach and greeted her with unctuous courtesy.

'You are welcome, *signora*,' he said. 'Sister Maria will look after you. We shall put you into a good room on the *secondo piano*, where you will be warm and safe.'

She turned to me, though still she refused to look me in the face. 'My stepfather,' she said weakly, in a sudden agitation, 'what of him?'

'Do not worry, *poverina*,' the Nuncio assured her, 'the good sisters of the Church of St Peter, which is close by, will take charge of him. They will wash him and lay him out, with candles and flowers, and they will pray for his eternal salvation. Come, now, come inside.'

She tried to hold back, but she had not the strength to resist any longer and at last allowed me to help her down from the coach. She stepped weakly into the hallway, where the plump nun took her by the arm and led her away. She did not look back.

'And you, *dottore*,' Malaspina said to me, 'what shall you do, now?'

'I must go to the castle,' I said, 'to deal with Chamberlain Lang, taking my long spoon with me.'

He frowned quizzically. '*Il tuo lungo cucchiaio—che cos'è?*'

'It's a saying,' I said. 'Dr Kelley reminded me of it. "To dine with the devil you must use a long spoon."'

'*Ah, sì, certo.*'

He smiled, his little dark eyes almost disappearing into the folds of flesh surrounding them. '*Dio ti benedica*,' he said, 'God bless you,' and he made the sign of the cross again, though not without a touch of irony.

'God *help* me, rather,' I said.

The driver was asleep, slumped in his stinking cape, and swore when I woke him. He cracked his whip. We moved on, leaving the cart behind; the canvas, wet from the rain, had moulded itself to the shape of the corpse that was wrapped in it.

As we turned the corner, I looked back. Malaspina was still in the doorway; he lifted a hand in farewell.

I had forgotten to enquire after Serafina.

So many things I had not done.

23

A vast and brooding silence reigned throughout the castle. It was as if everything—the furniture, the tapestries, all the piled-up treasure in the wonder rooms, even the very walls—were suspended in an anxious hush, not daring to make a murmur. All this was due to the Emperor, who was sunk deep in one of his darker melancholic moods and had not been seen since I had left for Most. He had sequestered himself in the innermost of his private chambers; not once had he come out, even to dine. At morning and evening, trays of food and drink were left at his door. Some he took inside, others he left untouched, and of the ones he did take in, he ate little of what was on them.

In the Royal Palace I walked through vast echoing halls; it never ceased to puzzle me that a place that housed so many people could so often seem so empty. At my approach, lurking servants scuttled away into the shadows, quick and soundless as silverfish. I was in search of the Chamberlain, and at the same time wishing I might not find him. No doubt he, too, like Elizabeth Weston, would hold me responsible for the death of Edward Kelley. In the Chamberlain's conception of things, there must always be someone to blame; culpability—the culpability of others, that is—seemed, for him, to maintain a necessary equilibrium, like the weights in a scale or the pendulum of a clock. It was a stratagem aimed, no doubt, at staving off the prospect of the inevitable day when he himself should be called to account.

Tonight even the Great Hall, always such a busy centre of gossip and intrigue, seemed deserted. Halfway along that majestic space, however, I spied Jeppe Schenckel perched on the stone bench in one of the window embrasures, looking down upon the lights of the city, his hands folded one over the other on the knob of his cane and his misshapen, stout little legs drawn up under him.

He was as changed as could be from the last time I had seen him, kneeling in the mud at Castle Hněvín and looking every inch a troglodyte. Now his hair gleamed like a cap of grooved pitch and his jaw was shaved to a shine as bright as that of his shoes. He wore black hose and a jacket of scarlet silk, complete with a ruff and starched lace cuffs. He was entirely his accustomed smooth and polished self again. But I could sense his anger: it made the air seem to vibrate around him.

Looking back now, I think I was always afraid of Jeppe Schenckel. Or is that the word for it—afraid? I am not sure. He was, for me, the very emblem, the very figure of Prague itself, gaudy, sinister and deformed. I knew that in his heart he harboured an evil intent against me, one that had sprung up long before that moment at Most when Sir Kaspar's sword blow knocked him sprawling at my feet—oh, long before. It had been there from the start, from that first day when he was dispatched to escort me to meet the Emperor at the house of Dr Kroll.

But what was it that he hated in me? It is true, he loathed everyone—he loathed the world itself, in which he was condemned to be a freak. But for me he reserved an especial animus, and I felt the force of it always like a harsh hot wind against my face. I had in a manner usurped him, although this notion, when it first occurred to me, caused me puzzlement and dismay. When I thought upon it, though, I saw that it was true. What was I for Rudolf but another diversion, another amusement, another jester?—another freak.

I stopped. I knew he had heard my step, but he did not turn.

'Have you come to return that thing you took from me?' he asked, keeping his gaze fixed upon the lights far below, flickering and flaring in the darkness. I said nothing, and went on saying nothing, until at last he stirred himself, but only to cast a sidelong glance contemptuously in the direction of my knees. 'I suppose you mean to give it to His Majesty yourself,' he said, 'to prove anew your loyalty and devotion.'

'It is not the thing you thought it to be,' I said. 'You were mistaken.'

He turned about fully to face me now, untangling his legs from under himself and letting them dangle halfway down the stone front of the bench.

'It *is* the thing,' he said, 'or at least one of the things that His Majesty charged me with finding, and bringing back to him. Charged *me*, mark, not you.'

I laughed, which made him frown.

'I tell you,' I said, 'you were mistaken—you are mistaken. You thought those pages were part of Dr Kroll's great collection of magical nostrums, which His Majesty coveted. They were not. They are not.'

The dwarf's large, pale face was flushed with anger. 'How wise you think you are,' he said. 'But you know nothing.'

'Some things I know, many things I do not,' I said. 'But in this one thing I am right. Kelley burned Kroll's papers, all of them.' I took the bound sheets from inside my doublet and held them aloft. 'There is no magic here,' I said.

He looked at the pages, his eyes aglow. Then he smiled, with cold malice. 'You are lying,' he said.

'I am not lying,' I responded. I folded the parchment sheets and put them back into the deep pocket I had taken them from. 'I say again—this is not magic.'

'Then what is it?'

'It's better, I think,' I said, 'that you should not know.'

He watched me out of his cold, glass-green eyes. I could see him thinking, judging, calculating.

'Things are happening,' he said softly. 'Matters are coming to a head.'

'Matters?' I asked. 'What matters?'

He was smiling again.

'I tell you,' he said, very softly now, 'I tell you, you know nothing. You think you do, but you do not.' He paused. 'Kroll's dog was slaughtered—did you hear?'

'His dog?'

'Yes, old Schnorr—you remember him? His throat was cut, just like Mistress Kroll's. They say the creature's head was nearly severed from the trunk.' He rolled his eyes in mock horror. 'There is a fiend abroad,' he whispered.

I was about to speak again, but stopped. For some reason there had come into my mind the image of Serafina, in her heavy coat, seated beside me in the coach that first day when Malaspina sent her with me to the house in Golden Lane. Perhaps the dwarf was right: perhaps I knew nothing, and all the nothings I knew might be the end of me.

I could lose everything—in the blink of an eye, everything could be gone.

I heard footsteps behind me, and turned to see Chamberlain Lang approaching with that strange quick-stepping, gliding walk of his, like a wading bird rapidly treading through the shallows.

'Ah, here you are, Herr Doktor,' he said, beaming at me and rubbing his hands, as so often. He glanced at the dwarf and in a different tone said shortly: 'You, creature, be gone.'

Schenckel dropped down from the bench. Bowing and simpering in a parody of obsequiousness, he poled himself away on his ebony cane, casting back at me a last malignantly mocking glance.

'Look at the brute,' Lang said to me. 'Were he not His Majesty's pet fool, I should have him weighted with a stone and sunk in a cesspit.'

We moved to the window and stood side by side, looking out. It was fully night now. A scant flurry of snow swirled against the glass.

'So, tell me, Herr Doktor,' the Chamberlain said, 'tell me what happened—' he gave a shudder of feigned horror '— in all its awfulness.'

'We arrived at Most,' I said, 'where I informed Kelley that you had sent me to fetch him back to Prague, that there were questions you wished to put to him.'

He chuckled. 'Why, then,' he said, 'you must have spoken to him very harshly, for him to do as he did and make away with himself. Or was he testing to see if he could fly?'

'He believed he would be tortured, sir, if he returned here.'

'Oh, did he, now.'

'I think he would have died anyway, before long. There was black rot in one of his legs, and the other one was grievously damaged too.'

The Chamberlain waggled his head in comical dismissiveness. 'Yes, the fellow was forever falling down,' he said. He drummed two fingers against his lower lip, frowning.

'And you, where have you been, all this time? I hear you arrived in Prague many hours ago.'

'I would have come to you sooner,' I said, 'except there were matters I had to attend to.'

'Oh, I'm sure, I'm sure,' he said smoothly. 'We all know what a busy fellow you are.' He put an arm around my shoulders in that exaggeratedly fraternal way of his. 'Come and sup with me,' he said, 'will you? You must be in need of refreshment, after your long journey.'

'Sir,' I said, 'tarry a moment.'

He paused, and took his arm from around my shoulders. Grasping me by the sleeve, he held me a little way away from himself, fixing me with a quizzing eye. 'That is a serious look,' he said. 'I think I like it not. What further things have you to tell me?'

I brought out the folded sheets of parchment and handed them to him.

'What's this?' he asked, flicking through the pages and frowning.

'It was among Kelley's papers.'

'Oh, yes?' he said absently, scanning the columns of numbers and letters. 'But what manner of thing is it? I can make no sense of it.'

I hesitated. 'Jeppe Schenckel had got hold of it, but I took it from him.'

'The dwarf?' he said, glancing towards the door where Schenckel had gone out. 'Why would he take it? What's it to him?' Again he tapped his fingers against his lips. 'But, of course, he is Wenzel's pet ape, and trained to do his master's bidding.'

'He claimed to have seized it on His Majesty's behalf.'

At this the Chamberlain leaned back his head and gave a

hoot of laughter. 'His Majesty is far from such matters at the moment. This seems to be one of his deeper bouts of heartsickness. He calls it his wolf, did you know that? *My wolf has his fangs in me*, he says, and shivers and shakes. His wolf—ha!'

'Wolf on a string,' I murmured.

He threw me a keen glance. 'What's that?'

'Nothing,' I said. 'Wolf on a string—a musical term. It came into my head.'

'Ah. Right.'

His mind was elsewhere. He examined the parchment chapbook again, holding it so close to his face that it almost touched the sharp tip of his nose. 'It is written in a code of some kind, is it?'

'I suspect, sir,' I said, 'that it is, rather, the keys to a set of codes.'

He looked up and gazed at me, though without seeming to see me, the cogs of his mind turning and turning.

'The keys to a set of codes,' he said, 'and Wenzel's man snatched it up. But what codes does it solve? Perhaps it's the dwarf we should subject to a little light torturing. Who knows what nasty wriggling secrets might spill out of him?'

He moved closer to the window, and looked again at the muffled lights of the city. Snow was still falling, but at random, half-heartedly. Time passed. The hall in which we stood seemed to me a vast lung, silently breathing. I thought of Elizabeth Weston. I thought of her stepfather's corpse wrapped tight in its drenched canvas shroud.

When there are sides, Felix Wenzel had said, down in the Stag Moat that day, *you either choose, or the choice is made for you*.

I had known, all along, without knowing I knew, that sooner or later this moment would arrive, when I should have to place myself alongside either Lang the Chamberlain or Wenzel the High Steward. The choice should have been easy. Wenzel it was who had seized me, who had accused me of murder, who had threatened me with the rack, while who had it been but Philipp Lang who had plucked me from his clutches?

For all the dissimilarities between us, I had always believed that essentially we were not unalike, the Chamberlain and I. Just as he did, I saw the world as a place of possibilities, of opportunities; like him, I considered Fate not a fixed but a malleable force. Wenzel was a fanatic, one of God's self-appointed merciless avengers. He was that most dangerous of the types of men, both a lover and a hater of himself.

Yes, between these two it should have been an easy choice, but it was not. All the same, I made it; I could do no other.

'Sir,' I said, 'there is a thing you should know.'

Lang swivelled about on his heel and fixed me with his full attention, his head lifted and held to one side. 'Oh, yes? And what thing is that?'

'There was a strongbox,' I said. 'It belonged to Dr Kroll, but Jan Madek took it. Originally in this box were kept alchemical papers, secret formulae, magic ciphers, things the doctor had collected over many years.'

Lang was watching me more closely than ever now, his eyes narrowed. 'This is the box His Majesty wished to have for himself, yes?' he said. 'He talked of it often. I confess I paid scant attention—it seemed but another of his mad obsessions, and a minor one.'

'Yes,' I said, 'the same box. Madek got hold of it, some-how, and brought it out to Most, and gave it to Dr Kelley.'

'Did he? Hmm. And what did Kelley do with it?'

'He burned the papers that were in it—'

271

'Ha!' the Chamberlain exclaimed. 'His Majesty will not be best pleased to hear that.'

'He burned the papers,' I went on, 'and replaced them with others.'

'What others? Come, man, you're making my head ache, with these enigmas.'

Yet still I hesitated. Sometimes, asleep at night, one seems to miss a step and start awake in terror; I have always believed that the step we seem to stumble on is the buried recollection of a moment in our lives when we have taken some perilous but unavoidable decision. Standing there in the Great Hall now, I experienced just such a sense of stumbling, or not stumbling but a kind of helpless falling, a kind of slow pitching forward, from one darkness into another. The step I had taken was onto the level of the Chamberlain, and from that level there would be no descending.

We paced together the length of the long, dully gleaming floor and back again. The Chamberlain's arm was once more round my shoulders. He listened to me with the closest attention, saying not a word until I had finished telling him what I had to tell, of Wenzel and the English Queen, of their conspiracies, of their correspondence, and Kelley's encoding of it. Then he released me and turned away, nodding, and took a long deep slow breath, as if he were drawing some fine and precious fragrance from the air.

'Ah, yes,' he breathed. 'Yes.'

He was smiling now—oh, that carnival-mask smile of his, the eyes shining, the mouth a crimson crescent, the nose seeming as if it might curve all the way down and touch the tip of his chin. He gazed about the enormous, barrel-vaulted room.

'You know,' he said, 'I have always disliked this place,

this so-called Great Hall. It is supposed to express the grandeur of empire, the overarching magnificence of sovereignty, the all-embracing enclosure of the body politic. All I see is show and bombast.' He paused, humming to himself, then held up the pages of parchment. 'And these,' he said, 'these pages, they are Kelley's codebook?'

'So I believe.'

He frowned, touching the tips of his fingers to his lower lip yet again, thinking it out.

'Yes, of course,' he murmured, 'of course. Kelley, safely out there at Most, was the perfect go-between. Of course.' He looked at me sharply. 'And the originals, the original letters, between Wenzel and the Queen—what of them?'

'Kelley was meant to destroy them, once he had translated them into code and dispatched the coded versions to Elizabeth in London and to Wenzel here.'

'And did he?'

I said nothing.

The Chamberlain put his head far back and looked at me long, and then smiled. 'Ah,' he said, 'he did *not* destroy them—that's what you've come to tell me. He kept them, and kept them safe.'

'He put them in the strongbox that Madek had brought, and gave them to him.'

'He gave the letters, those precious documents, to *Madek*?' he exclaimed. 'To that young hothead?'

'He did,' I said. 'But he did not give him'—I pointed to the papers in his hand—'the codebook.'

The Chamberlain softly laughed. 'Ah, yes, that would be Kelley—treacherous to the end. And where'—he fairly pounced—'where is this famous box, with the letters in it—where is it to be found?'

'I do not know.'

We were silent, gazing at each other. Then he nodded rapidly, and this time linked his arm in mine, and led me to the window. How vast the city seemed, down below us in the darkness there, how vast and far and strange.

'You don't know, you say,' he said. 'Am I to believe this? What did Madek do with the box? What did he do with the letters?'

'I believe he brought them back here to Prague, to use against the High Steward.'

'Against him? To what end?'

I shook my head, and said nothing. He let go of my arm. I felt only an odd sort of emptiness, as if I had been hollowed out, so that all that was left inside me was a cold dark echoing space. I thought again of Elizabeth Weston, I thought of her saying, *What have I done? What have I done?* Now I asked myself the same question.

'You know,' Lang said, 'you know I can do nothing, unless I have those letters.'

'Yes,' I said. 'I know.'

He put out a hand and drew me with him to the window again, where again we stood side by side, facing the night. The snow had stopped.

'And this,' he said, looking down at the wad of parchment in his hand, 'this is the vital tool, yes?' He turned and gazed at me, his eyes alight. 'You must find them,' he said.

I began to speak, but he put up a hand to stop me. 'No,' he said. 'No excuses. Find them. Find them, Christian Stern, and when you have found them, and given them to me, I shall do what Madek could not—I shall destroy Felix Wenzel.' He sighed happily. 'Oh yes, I shall destroy him.'

24

Just then, while the Chamberlain and I stood there by the window, the great doors off at the far end of the hall swung open and a body of soldiers came marching in. My first, fearfully thrilling, notion was that Prague had been over-run by an invading army, and that this was the advance party sent to secure the castle. My second impression was of a heroic painting suddenly come to life, there were so many plumed, silken warriors bristling with lances, swords and halberds, moving resolutely towards us in close forma-tion, shoulder to shoulder. The Chamberlain hastily thrust the codebook into a pocket of his black habit.

At the head of this troop was a tall man with a long face, a Spanish beard and a wide, waxed moustache, and a sharp, distrusting eye. He wore a feathered hat, a somewhat tired-seeming ruff, and an armoured black leather jerkin crossed by a broad silk sash. His Spanish breeches were the colour of terracotta, and his high boots were polished to a glossy shine.

I recognised him at once as the Archduke Matthias, Rudolf's younger brother, whom Rudolf feared and detested.

The Archduke stopped before us with a rattle and a clank.

'Ah, Lang,' he said to the Chamberlain. 'You still here? They haven't found you out yet and sent you to the block?'

'No indeed, Your Royal Highness.' The Chamberlain

touched a finger to his throat. 'The head is still attached, as you see.' He bowed, with deliberate, stiff insolence. 'We did not expect you until the morrow.'

The nobleman grinned, showing a fearsome set of long, yellowed teeth with gaps between them.

'Surprised you, did we?' he said. 'You don't like surprises.' He turned a cold glance in my direction. 'And this long streak of piss, in his furs and furbelows—what's he?'

Lang did not miss a beat. 'This is Herr Doktor Stern,' he said smoothly, 'His Majesty your brother's Chamberlain.'

I glanced at Lang, struggling to hide my surprise. Matthias glared at him, though all he got back was the blandest of bland smiles.

'Chamberlain?' Matthias said. 'I thought you were that.'

'Strictly speaking, sire, I am High Chamberlain.'

Matthias grinned again, again showing off his awful teeth. 'So he's your fetcher and carrier,' he said, eyeing me a second time. 'He looks the part.'

At this Lang once more bowed and made an elaborately obsequious gesture with his arms, sweeping them low and wide before himself as if he were spreading out a cloth of silk before the Archduke's feet.

'Your Highness's wit is as sharp as ever,' he said. 'Doktor Stern is a star very close to His Majesty's heart.'

Matthias yet again looked me up and down, curling his lip. 'Bum-boy, are you?' he snapped.

Abruptly he turned away from me, with the air of one letting something unpleasant drop from between a finger and a thumb. Behind him his escort stood gaping vacantly and faintly creaking; they appeared bored and weary and out of temper, as all soldiers do when they are not fighting or pillaging.

'Where is my brother?' Matthias demanded.

'His Majesty is—meditating,' the Chamberlain said.

'Meditating? Ha! Hugger-muggering with his wizards as usual, I dare say, casting spells and calling up demons? He was always a gullible donkey.' He looked about. 'Food,' he said shortly. 'My men are hungry, and so am I. We have had a long and trying march from Vienna. Damned foul Bohemian weather.'

The Chamberlain rubbed his hands about each other in a washing motion. I saw that, despite his ill-concealed contempt, he feared the Archduke: it showed in the fixed, brittle quality of his smile.

'You know it is the Emperor's official birthday tomorrow—' he began.

Matthias snorted. 'Of course I know, damn it! Why else do you think I'm here?'

'There is to be a great banquet—'

This time the Archduke stamped a boot heel hard on the floor. He had the look of a man who had been born swaddled already in a uniform; I imagined that when he took off his armour there would persist a tiny military tinkling, a faint warlike rattle.

'It's not a banquet I'm asking for, man!' he bellowed. 'Good plain food—meat, bread, a barrel of ale.'

This caused a flurry among the armed gathering at his back, a sort of wistful sway from side to side. It must indeed have been a long journey they had come on, and a hungry one.

The Chamberlain began to reply, but again the doors at the end of the hall were thrown open, and Felix Wenzel came hurrying in. Seeing the figures assembled by the window, he skidded to a halt—he had been running full-tilt—and put one hand agitatedly to his ruff and with the other smoothed forward his close-cropped hair.

'Ho, Wenzel!' Matthias called out jovially. 'Here's my man!'

The squad of soldiers rapidly parted to make a path for their commander, who strode down the length of the room and took the High Steward's right hand in both of his and pumped it vigorously.

'Your Highness,' Wenzel said, panting, 'I was not told of your arrival, I—'

'Yes, I caught everyone off guard,' Matthias said cheerfully, glancing over his shoulder and smirking at the Chamberlain. He turned back to Wenzel. 'We're in need of feeding and watering, my men and I, but there would appear to be nothing on offer.'

'But of course, sir!' Wenzel burbled, summoning up one of his wintry smiles, which he seemed to assemble out of a number of small, disparate parts. 'I shall send word to the kitchens straight away.'

'Right!' Matthias called, with a wave of his arm to his men. 'Nosebags await.'

And with another great clatter, as of numerous heavy pots and pans being kicked across the floor, they were gone, with the Archduke and Wenzel in the lead.

The doors banged shut behind them.

I turned to Lang. ' "Chamberlain"?' I said.

He chuckled. 'Yes—congratulations. Oh, don't look so anxious. I had to say you were someone; I had to account for you. And, besides, by raising you up, I raise myself. If Wenzel can be High Steward, why should I not be High Chamberlain?'

'But what will His Majesty—'

'I shall remind him that he has so far forgotten to grant you a title. If he bothers to ask, that is.'

'I feel like Caligula's horse,' I said, 'that he made into a senator.'

The Chamberlain laughed again. 'And a fine steed you are!' he said, clapping me on the shoulder. 'Now, let's off and have our supper—the Archduke and his squad of blunderbusses are not the only hungry ones, eh?'

I thanked him, but begged that he would allow me a half-hour to change out of my travelling clothes. He was silent for a moment, regarding me with narrowed eyes and the trace of a quizzical smile.

'There will be a mighty to-do,' he said, 'now that Matthias is here. And have you heard that His Majesty's cousin Ferdinand arrives tomorrow? There will be many calls upon your loyalty, Herr Doktor. You will remember where it lies, won't you, yes? And you will remember what you have to do? Those letters are somewhere here in Prague. It is for you to discover their whereabouts, and seize them, and bring them here—to me.'

I stood and looked at him stolidly. We both knew he did not have to remind me of these things; he had my soul in his fist. He laughed again, and tapped a knuckle lightly on my breastbone, winked once, and turned away.

I set off for my quarters in a deep confusion of thought. I felt the urgent need to speak to the Emperor, if only to have the comfort of hearing from him that I was still in his favour, but I doubted he would see me in his present state of desolation. Would he appear tomorrow, for the birthday banquet? Surely he would not miss one of the most important days in the imperial calendar—it would not be allowed.

I was walking down a stone corridor, debating with

myself if I should go to His Majesty's private rooms and cajole or, if all else failed, make my way in by force. Turning a corner, I entered a stretch of darkness where two successive wall lamps had been extinguished, by a breeze, as I must suppose. Suddenly, with a violent rushing, something, some black-winged thing—I thought at first it was winged—came flying at me. Ducking aside, I cried out in fear and put up my arms to protect myself. It lasted but an instant, this frightful onslaught, and then the thing was gone, past me, off into the darkness.

I crouched there, with my arms in front of my face, unable to stir for terror. The thing, whatever it had been, had not touched me but had sped past, like a night bird sweeping out of the darkness and disappearing into it again. Only it had not been a bird: I had caught its human smell.

Recovering myself, I ran back to the corner, where the creature must have gone, but when I got there and looked along the lit corridor, there was nothing to be seen. I felt a sharp pain in my right shoulder, and for a moment I thought I might have been stabbed, until I remembered that in flinching aside I had staggered and crashed against the wall, where I must have struck some sharp protrusion.

I stood and listened. At first there was nothing, but then I heard, faintly, beyond the harsh rise and fall of my own breathing, a familiar scrabbling, snuffly sound, receding into the distance, into the far depths of the castle. It was the same sound I had heard at my door in Golden Lane, the same one I had heard outside my chamber that day when Caterina Sardo and I lay on my bed spent and exhausted, and she would not let me get up to go and find out what was there.

Now it came to me, for the first time, that what I had

heard was not a scrabbling or a snuffling, as of some animal rooting and clawing, which it had seemed. It was laughter.

Yes, laughter: a rasping, throaty sort of sniggering.

Moaning in distress, I dashed again back through that patch of darkness to the sanctuary of my chamber.

Opening the door, I had another fright. The room was brightly lit, with many candles and lamps burning. I was given only a moment to register this before I suffered a second assault, although this time I recognised my assailant straight off.

'*Te la sei scopata!*' Caterina Sardo shrieked.

'I what? I—'

'You *fucked* her!'

Her right hand was lifted, and in it she was grasping a dagger—I saw distinctly a tiny jewel of light flash upon its tip. My back was pressed to the door. She was almost upon me when I put a hand against her breast and gave her a sharp shove that sent her flailing backwards as far as the foot of the bed. She stopped for a moment, breathing hard, and then with a peculiar, catlike cry she flew at me once more, the knife raised. This time I stepped forward and grasped her by both wrists; she was strong, with all the force of her fury, and there we stood, swaying and grunting, like a pair of well-matched wrestlers.

'What are you talking about?' I panted.

'*Quel troia di merda!*' she hissed. 'That English cow—who else? You slept with her!'

I had never seen her like this, flushed and sweating, her face contorted and her eyes on fire and her teeth bared and flecked with foam. Her voice, too, was hardly recognisable; it seemed to come, swollen and thick, from deep inside her, and each word as she forced it out was immediately swallowed again, making her almost choke.

'Caterina, listen—'

'*Vaffanculo, maiale!* You did, you slept with her, I know you did!'

She jerked her right hand, the one that held the knife, trying to surprise me into freeing it. Instead I bore down with all my strength on her wrist until I felt the bones inside it grate against each other. She gasped in pain, squeezing up her eyes, and let fall the blade at last. I kicked it away, and it spun across the floor and disappeared under the bed.

Still we strained together there, teetering and swaying, her wrists in my hands, her fingers bent into claws.

'Stop, Caterina,' I begged her. 'Please, stop!'

Her only answer was to try to kick me, which she would have succeeded in doing had not her heavy skirts prevented it.

My arms were aching; I knew I could not fend her off any longer—her strength was frightening. I took a quick side-step and with a gasp flung her from me. She stumbled, and fell heavily against a small marble table, which toppled over, slowly at first and then much faster, and crashed to the floor, the edge of it shattering and throwing off splinters of white stone.

I was wiping the sweat from my brow when to my astonishment I saw her come at me again, with another, smaller blade in her hand—where had she got it from, where had it been hidden?

'*Maiale!*' she snarled again. 'Pig! Fuck-pig!'

I backed away from her. I was afraid she had lost her reason entirely, and for the first time it seemed that she might manage to kill me. The thought was at once appalling and somehow comical.

I had misjudged the distance to the bed, and now I barged against the edge of it and lost my balance and fell sprawling on my back onto the silk counterpane. I still wonder if it was that miscalculation that saved my life. Caterina stepped between my splayed knees and stood looking down at me, her nostrils flared and her brow glistening. She was pointing the blade of the little knife at me, though it was not so little that she could not have pierced my heart or punctured my throat with it. She muttered something in that new, guttural voice, some words in Italian I did not understand, and then, suddenly, she began to laugh.

'I should cut off your cock,' she said. 'It has crowed enough.' She tilted the knife until it was pointing at my crotch. 'Maybe I will—what do you say, eh?'

She laughed again and tossed the knife over her shoulder. Reaching down, she hauled up her skirts and knelt on the bed and planted herself astride my hips.

'All right,' she whispered, 'now do to me what you did to her.' She fumbled down between her legs, trying to unhook the front of my breeches.

'*Merda*,' she muttered. 'I can't do it. Why do men truss themselves up like a Christmas goose?'

I laid my head back on the bed and closed my eyes, taking long, slow breaths. My heart was pounding still, from all that violence, all that fright.

'Caterina,' I said, 'please.'

'What's the matter? You can't do it now? You could do it to *quella vacca inglese* but not to me?' She put her arms on either side of me and, all sweetness, leaned down and

283

kissed me on the lips. 'Ah, my poor star,' she said, 'you do not shine so brightly now.'

The storm had passed. She sat back on my lap and surveyed me with one eyebrow lifted. 'Tell me, what was she like?' she asked. 'Did she suck your thing? They say Englishwomen love to do that. Tell me.'

I reached up and set my hands on her hips. 'Caterina, I'm sorry.'

'I don't forgive you, I never will—unless you do now to me what you did to her, only better.'

She laughed yet again, making a fat little gurgling sound deep in her throat.

We shed our clothes and lay down together, as so often.

Our love-making was quickly done with, and afterwards we rested quietly in each other's arms. She was gentle, almost distracted, all her wild fury spent. I cradled her in the crook of one arm, and she lifted a hand and played with the lovelock dangling by my cheek.

'Would you really have spilled my blood?' I asked.

She made a pouting shrug. 'I may spill it yet.' She tugged hard on the lock of my hair. 'You are a brute,' she said. 'I let you out of my sight for a day and you mount the first woman to cross your path.'

'She was lonely,' I said.

'Oh, sob sob, I am so sad!'

She pulled my hair again, drawing my face down to hers, and kissed me.

'How did you know?' I asked.

'Sir Kaspar, of course.'

'Ah. So he was your spy, too.'

'He used to be my lover.'

I stared at her. 'That old man?' I said.

She laughed again. 'He was not always old. And I was very young. My father tried to marry me to him. Then Rudi caught my eye, or I caught his.'

I freed my arm from under her and sat up. By shrouding it all in a sort of mental fog, I had more or less come to terms with the thought of her and Rudolf together, but the image of her, in her youth, submitting to Sir Kaspar, that rickety old wreck, with his watery eyes and his bony knees, was intolerable—intolerable and, at the same time, almost, again, a thing to make one laugh.

There were times, and this was one of them, when I seemed to be seeing this woman from a distance, as if she were a stranger, remote from me and unknowable, like that lewd Venus, with her monstrous child by her side, in the painting in the Nuncio's dining room. By what madness had I let her lure me into her arms?

'What are you thinking?' she asked.

She was lying on her side, propped on an elbow, with a hand under her cheek. She never looked her age so much as when she lay like that, naked, with her breasts and her belly flopping sideways and her shiny, mottled shins crookedly crossed. And yet, despite the confusion of images tumbling through my mind—her doughy flesh, Rudolf's wet little mouth, Sir Kaspar's long and bony shanks—I had only to recall how, a few minutes past, she had lain under me in a transport of pleasure, and there would start up a new stirring in my lap.

'Tell me,' I said, 'will His Majesty show himself tomorrow?'

'For his birthday?' She sniggered. 'Of course he will! He loves birthdays, when they are his own. He has two every year, you know, the real one, and tomorrow's official farce.

There will be gifts: princes, legates, barbarian chiefs—all will bring him nice things for him to gloat over. This year he is promised a piece of Christ's—what do you call this thing?'

She reached into my lap and pinched the slack spout of my member.

'The prepuce,' I said, wincing.

'Yes, that—the Grand Vizier of somewhere or other is bringing it in a golden casket. *Certo*, the prospect of that will cure Rudi's melancholy and lure him out of his lair, rubbing his fat little paws.'

She rose from the bed and went to my table, where there was a gilded bowl filled with cherries. Bringing it back to the bed, she sat down cross-legged beside me.

'You know that the Emperor's brother is here?' I said.

She began to eat the cherries. 'Matthias the Mighty?'

'He came a day early.'

'He likes to surprise; he thinks of it as his battlefield strategy. Matthias—ha. You have only to see the Spanish cut of his beard to know what he is. And those eyes of his, the watchfulness behind the bluster. He is the kind who would spy on his sisters at their toilet.'

She was gripping a cherry stone between her front teeth, and now she put a hand behind my head and drew my face to hers and kissed me. As she did so, she pressed the stone into my mouth, as once she had passed me the bone button she had torn from my jerkin, to seal our love pact. Then she let go of me, and laughed. I spat the stone in the direction of the fireplace; it fell onto the hearth.

'And tomorrow will come his cousin Ferdinand,' she said, slipping another cherry into her mouth. 'Young Turnip-head himself. You must—*come si dice?*—cultivate him.'

'I?'

She nodded. Now it was her turn to spit the cherry stone; she had a better aim than I, and the stone plopped into the centre of the fire with a tiny hiss.

'Yes, Ferdinand is our man'—she threw her gaze upwards and made a rapid sign of the cross at her breast—'God help us.'

'I don't understand,' I said. ' "Our" man? Who are "we"?'

She turned her head and gave me a disbelieving look. 'Do you really know so little, or do you only pretend? Have you not talked to the Chamberlain? Has he not explained to you how things are?'

'The Chamberlain tells me many things,' I said. 'Some I believe, some I do not, some I don't understand.'

She sent another cherry stone on a long arc into the flames. All at once I had a clear and specific image of her as a little girl in a pink gown, sitting under a cherry tree in a sunny clime, eating fruit and spitting the stones into the dust. For all of us, even for her, there was once a time of innocence.

'It is very simple,' she said. 'Wenzel and Dr Kroll and their men, they would like to see my poor Rudi forced from the throne and Matthias to be put there in his stead. We—the Chamberlain, I, and you, whether you choose to know it or not—want Rudolf the Mad to grow old and die, and Ferdinand to take his place.' She looked at me and shook her head, smiling ruefully. 'You still don't understand, do you? Matthias would allow the Protestants to thrive and thereby keep the peace—for a soldier, he does not much like fighting—while Ferdinand the Fierce will burn them all.'

'And is that what "we" wish for?'

She thought for a moment, gazing upwards again and sucking a cherry.

'Yes,' she said, 'that is what we want.' She looked at me, and chuckled. 'Think,' she said softly, tapping my forehead with a fingertip, 'think what would become of us—of *us*—if Matthias were to gain the throne. Ah, *mio caro*, think of that.' She held the little bowl aloft, and her voice sank to a whisper. 'No more cherries.'

We were silent then. I was thinking, pondering what she had urged me to think about. At last I said: 'Kroll's daughter—why did she die?'

'What?' she said absently. 'I don't understand.'

'Nor do I.' I sighed. 'Jeppe Schenckel, a little while ago, told me I knew nothing. Perhaps he is right. Sometimes it seems to me I don't know anything at all.'

She was watching me now. She had put the gilded bowl on the floor beside the bed.

'Perhaps,' she said, 'there are some matters it is better not to know about.'

I took her chin in my fingers and turned her face sharply and made her look at me. '*You* know,' I said. 'You could tell me.'

And so she could—but would I want to hear?

'Let go,' she said, 'you're hurting me.' I released her, and she rubbed her chin, pouting. 'What things do I know?' She scowled. 'That Kroll,' she said—'*che lenone.*'

'What?' I asked. 'What does that mean?'

'Pander,' she said. 'Pimp! He pimped his daughter to my Rudi, to be a spy for Wenzel. I'm glad the bitch died.' She shivered. 'I am cold,' she said. 'Will you warm me?'

She put her arms around my neck and rubbed herself slowly against me.

I looked away. 'Something,' I said, 'or someone—I don't know—attacked me in the corridor.'

'Attacked you? When?'

'Just now, as I was coming here.'

'And were you hurt?' She leaned forward and gently licked the side of my neck. 'Show me your wounds.'

'It was some kind of—it seemed some kind of animal, but it was not. It was human, a human monster.'

'Mmm,' she said, 'you have a lovely taste, like salt.' Her mouth was at my ear; I felt her warm, cherry-scented breath. 'Were you frightened?' she whispered.

'Yes.'

'It must have been an evil spirit,' she said, 'flying through the castle, searching for blood.' She took the lobe of my ear between her teeth and bit into it softly. 'A succubus,' she said, 'is that how you say? A succubus, conjured by one of Rudi's wizards.'

She reached between my legs again, and leaned her head down and licked me there.

'Mmm,' she murmured, 'I can taste myself, on you. It is salty, too, like the sea.'

She kissed my mouth. Her tongue was at once soft and grainy, a soft snail coated with sand.

'Mio caro porcellino salato,' she said, pulling back and looking deep into my eyes. 'Tell me again about the Englishwoman,' she whispered. 'Tell me everything, spare me nothing.'

25

It had gone from my mind—is it any wonder, considering the hour I had just spent with Caterina Sardo?—that the Chàmberlain had invited me to take supper with him, and now it was too late. Nevertheless, I rose from the bed and began to dress. Glancing towards the door, I saw something agleam on the floor there. I picked it up. It was a scrap of paper, tightly folded. I opened it.

Come to my house.
Kroll

I crushed the paper in my fist and hurried into my clothes. As I quitted the chamber, Caterina, still naked on the bed, grabbed at the back of my breeches and did her gurgling laugh. 'Don't leave me,' she cried. 'Come back, *dolce porcellino mio.'*

She was still laughing as I stepped through the door. In the corridor I paused, glancing to right and left, in fear that I might be set upon again by the mysterious and terrifying creature that had flung itself at me earlier. A servant had relit the two lamps that before had been extinguished, and I was glad not to have to step again into that awful patch of darkness.

Outside, the night was searingly cold, and there were patches of frozen snow on the ground, but the sky was clear and the moon was high and small and flat as a coin. I walked down through Kleinseite. I had the sense, as I went along, of being close to some large and as yet undisclosed formulation; I was like the lookout on a ship at night, sailing steadily past the coast of a continent he could not see. The mind can know things it does not know it knows.

I crossed the Stone Bridge. Down below, the dark river, on which the ice had thawed, tossed and jostled, showing flecks of foam here and there that were like the silvery manes of a pack of swiftly running horses. The Old Town Square was deserted, the moonlight glinting on its cobbles. I passed the spidery outline of the Týn Kirche and turned into a narrow street, a street I knew. A lantern glowed in the doorway of an alehouse, and I heard the sound of a fiddle within, and someone drunkenly singing. Passing under a balcony, I stopped and looked up. Here was where the whore that day had leaned out and called down to Jeppe the dwarf, and laughed at him, and spat.

Jeppe Schenckel. He was one of the countries of that unseen continent, one of the things I didn't know I knew.

The doctor's house was in darkness. At the front door I crouched down and peered in at the keyhole. Far off at the end of the hallway there was a glow, vague and grainy, like a patch of yellowish mist. I was about to turn away when I heard a very faint creak. A breeze must have moved the door slightly, or perhaps, without realising, I had leaned against it, but now I saw that it was unlocked and open a little way. I hesitated, then put a hand to it, and the door swung back heavily on its hinges. Again I hesitated, listening. I could hear nothing except, from back a little way along the street behind me, the muffled strains of the fiddle and the singer's wobbly notes.

I closed the door silently behind me—why had it been

left unlocked, so late at night?—and walked softly down the hall, remembering that other time I had been here, invited in by Fricka, the housekeeper, and following the dwarf. There had been so many beginnings, of which that was only one. Was an end coming now? I could feel the slow, heavy thudding of my heart.

My ears caught something then, a far-off sound, so soft it was hardly a sound at all, coming to me from deep within the heart of the house, a sound as of someone quietly keening. I walked on, towards that patch of misty yellow radiance.

Around a bend in the hallway another door stood half-way open, throwing a fan of light outwards across the floor. I stood again for a moment, listening. The keening sound was coming from inside the room: someone in there was weeping. I stepped forward, as in a dream when one crosses soundlessly over a threshold from world to world.

It was the room Jeppe Schenckel had led me to that day, where I had waited all unknowing for the arrival of the Emperor. A fire was blazing in the hearth, and in front of it was set an armchair, and there the doctor was seated, just as I had seen him for the first time, the night at the castle, with Wenzel off in the shadows. He was reclining exactly as he had reclined then, his chin on his chest and one arm lolling down at the side of the chair.

Fricka, the old servant, was squatting at his feet, her arms wrapped tightly round herself, rocking slowly back and forth and moaning softly. Hearing my step, she turned up to me a pinched grey grieving face.

The front of the doctor's jerkin was soaked with a deep ruby stain. For a moment I thought he must have spilled a mug of wine on himself. Then I saw the knife wound in the side of his neck.

At once I thought of the two of us in the cathedral, when we had walked there from Golden Lane, and Kroll had stood looking up at the crucifix above the high altar, speaking of blood and of sacrifice.

I unfolded the paper I had found in my chamber and showed it to the old woman.

'Is this the doctor's hand?' I asked. She shook her head. 'Did you write it, then?' This time she did not bother to respond, but turned her face away.

I have no memory of leaving the house. One moment I was in that room, seeing and not seeing the slaughtered man, and speaking to the old woman crouched on the floor. The next I was in the street, under a sky teeming with stars, hearing again that ragged music from the alehouse. The moon was higher, rounder, larger. I stood gazing at it, wondering how it could change its size. It is an illusion, I thought, caused by the air itself; the air must be a kind of lens, a great soft glassy lens. The notion pleased me.

I became aware then of a commotion nearby, of voices raised and the clank of armour and the tramp of hurrying men.

'There he is!' a voice called out. 'There, see! Stop him! Stop, assassin!'

I ran. I ran for a long time. A city is endless: street gives onto street, square onto square; there are houses, windows, doorways, all different and all alike. One might run for ever. At first the soldiers followed me, but I outdistanced them; men-at-arms are not clad for fleetness.

I came to the Church of St Peter, and leaned into the shadow of the doorway, gasping, each breath a blast of fire in my throat.

Kelley's corpse was in a side chapel, laid out on a bier, his clasped hands resting on his chest. The rag that had bound his jaw had been removed. One of his eyes was not quite closed, and I could see the eye itself, filmed over and reflecting a tiny speck of candlelight.

One of Malaspina's big-boned novices, Sister Maria, was seated on a chair beside the bier. She was asleep, softly snoring, her chin resting on a bulging circlet of flesh at her throat.

I stepped quietly into a pew and sat down. After a time, my heart ceased thumping and I could breathe more calmly. My mind was littered with scraps and shards, and I could keep nothing straight. Terror crouched inside me on its haunches, trembling and alert, like a creature at bay, listening for the sound of the hunt.

At length I found the courage to venture forth—Sister Maria continued deep asleep—and skulked along in the shadow of the houses, keeping out of the moonlight. I stopped often to listen, but heard no sound; for now, at least, I had escaped my pursuers.

I went to the nunciature. Although it seemed to me it must be the middle hours of the night by now, I found the Nuncio awake, reclining at ease in his big armchair by the fireside, reading Virgil. Seeing me, he put the book away and rose and came to me.

'*Dio mio*,' he said, 'are you wounded?'

I did not understand him.

'So much blood,' he said. 'Look!'

It was strange: I had no recollection of touching the corpse of Dr Kroll, and yet I must have, for the Nuncio was right: my hands were crusted with dried gore, and the front of my doublet was smeared too.

'It's not mine,' I said. 'It's not my blood.'

'Then whose?'

This was how things happened in dreams, but it was no dream.

A basin of warm water was brought, and I cleaned myself as best I could. How pink the water in the basin was, the pale blush-pink of rose petals.

'I went to Dr Kroll's house,' I said, still gazing into the basin. 'He was murdered—someone stabbed him in the throat.'

'*Gesù!*' the Bishop murmured, making the sign of the cross.

From somewhere far off in the house came the sound of viol music, the same phrase over and over; late though the hour was, one of the novices was practising.

'Mistress Weston,' I said, 'how does she fare—has the fever abated?'

'No, it is bad still,' Malaspina said, 'but she will live. Serafina is with her.'

'Will you take me to her?' I asked.

He led me along the hall and up the staircase. On the stairs he puffed and panted, shouldering the burden of himself from one step to the next, like Sisyphus pushing his impossible rock.

In the sickroom an oil lamp with a red glass shade diffused a dim glow, pink-tinged, like the bloodied water in the washing bowl. Elizabeth Weston lay on the bed with her eyes closed. Her cheeks were livid and swollen and her forehead shone with sweat. I looked at her damp hair spread around her on the pillow, and thought of Magdalena Kroll and the gleaming black halo in which her lifeless head had rested. Serafina sat beside the bed on a three-legged stool. She did not look at me. She was bathing the sick woman's forehead with a damp rag.

On the middle finger of her left hand, she still wore my mother's ring.

Elizabeth Weston groaned in her sleep, jerking her head from side to side, and then grew quiet again.

I stood at the side of the bed. The Nuncio had departed.

Serafina stared at the dark stains on my doublet. She allowed me to take her hand. Her cheeks were wet with tears.

'Serafina,' I said. 'Serafina.'

Elizabeth Weston opened her eyes and stared wildly at the ceiling, tossing her head again from side to side.

'*Ego autem cantabo dissolutio,*' she recited hoarsely. '*In interitum mundi . . .*'

I stayed there for a long time. Serafina and I took turns bathing the sick woman's burning forehead, her cheeks, her throat. She would lie still for long intervals, seeming hardly to breathe. At other times she twitched and thrashed, throwing her limbs about, muttering and crying.

The Bishop sent up to us a bowl of broth and a loaf of bread, dried figs, a round of cheese, a flagon of wine. Serafina laid out the food on a little table in the corner, and we sat down to eat in the gauzy pink lamplight, while Elizabeth Weston slept and breathed.

I dozed too, for a little while, after I had eaten, cradling my head on my hands on the table.

When I woke, the table had been cleared. I straightened, wiping away with my fist a line of spittle that had dried on my chin. Serafina was sitting by the bed again. She had fetched a clean bowl of water and a fresh cloth.

I told her how I had found the doctor dead in his chair and the old servant weeping at his feet. I told her of the soldiers who had tried to apprehend me, and how I had fled from them, racing through the city as in a dream. I knew she understood nothing of what I said, but it did not matter. I remembered her playing with Plato the cat; I did not tell her how I had found the poor thing dead outside my chamber door.

Downstairs, the Nuncio was asleep in his armchair; the volume of Virgil had slipped from his lap and lay open on the floor. *Ego autem cantabo dissolutio . . .*

I raked the embers of the fire and threw on some kindling and a couple of logs. When I turned, Malaspina had woken and was watching me with his gleaming little eyes. I brought up a chair and sat down, facing him.

'Jan Madek came to you,' I said, 'when he returned from Most—that's so, isn't it?'

For a time he made no reply, only went on studying me, sprawled fatly there in his chair. I could not make out his expression. At last he stirred himself and, grunting, struggled more or less upright.

'Madek,' he said, with weary disgust. 'That young fool.'

He turned his gaze to the fire, where white flames were licking at the tinder.

'But he did come here, didn't he?' I said. 'What did he want—was he, too, in mortal need of sanctuary, like me?'

'No. He wished to give me something, something that the trickster Kelley had given to him.'

'What was it?'

He shrugged. 'I do not know. I did not want to know.'

'It was a strongbox, an iron strongbox, containing—'

He held up a peremptory hand. 'Do not tell me,' he said.

'Why?'

He leaned forward, gesturing for me to give him the poker. He took it, and struck the point of it into the heart of the fire.

'So that I should not have to lie,' he said. He let the poker drop onto the hearth, where it made a clatter that jarred on my nerves. 'He was full of wild talk,' he said. 'He was going to expose a treasonous plot, he was going to destroy the High Steward, he was going to bring everything down. And all because of a girl who already had forgotten him, taken up as she had been by a far grander personage. *Follia, follia.*'

I heard Serafina moving about in the sickroom above our heads.

'What did he do with the box?' I said. 'Did he give it to you, for safekeeping?'

He lifted an urgent hand again and wagged it in front of my face. 'No no no,' he said. 'Listen to what I say. I could not allow him to tell me anything, to show me anything. I could not *know.*'

I stood up, and walked back into the depths of the room, pacing the stone flags, one by one. Then I came back and leaned by the fireplace, watching the regathering flames.

'He went to Wenzel,' I said. 'He was mad from jealousy. He made threats—God knows how he imagined he would get away with it. Wenzel seized him and had him tortured. He wanted the strongbox.' I turned and looked at the fat man where he wallowed in the deep chair. 'Did he tell you where it was? Did he tell you its whereabouts?'

The Nuncio shook his head slowly. 'He had something with him,' he said, 'but I would not look at it, though he kept trying to force it on me. He would not heed my refusal, my refusal to *know.*'

'What happened?'

'He left the thing—'

'The strongbox.'

'—whatever it was, and rode away to the castle, to confront Wenzel.'

'And what became of the box?'

'I never saw it. I closed my eyes and told him to take it away. He would not, and put it instead on the table—the table, there—saying I must help him, I must protect him. I turned away, I would not look. He went. I called Serafina and told her to remove the thing. In the morning, Wenzel's men came to question me. I demanded to know what had become of Madek. They laughed. I knew then the boy was dead. *Povero,*' he murmured, '*povero giovane.*'

The distant music of the viol resumed, a plangent, falling phrase.

'They knew he had come to you for help,' I said.

He nodded. 'Yes. They tortured him, and he told them he had come here. They spoke of this box. I said I knew nothing of it, that I had not seen it. Now you understand? I could not allow myself to be compromised, could not be in a position in which I would have to lie.' He paused. 'They threatened me,' he said. 'They threatened *me*, the Pope's envoy! Then they went away.'

'And what did Serafina do?'

He shook his head again.

'I do not know. I told her she must not tell me, that I must not know.' He looked up at me slowly. 'Perhaps you should ask her.'

That was what I did.

I cannot say how I made her understand me, for I don't know; one can do wonders, when one must.

She fetched her sheepskin coat, the one that I remembered so well. I could have wept to see it, so much did it bring back.

Sister Maria was summoned from her sleepy vigil beside Kelley's bier—'The Devil will take care of his own,' Malaspina cheerfully said—and was set to watch instead over Elizabeth Weston, whose fever had begun to abate.

The Nuncio would have offered his coach, but his coachman, who had a secret taste for his master's wine, was in a drunken stupor and would not be roused. Serafina and I thus had to walk across the sleeping town and over the Stone Bridge and up through Kleinseite. It was a long walk. I was full of fear, afraid that at any moment a squad of soldiers would march out of the shadows and arrest me. And yet how the stars shone!

At last we came safe to Golden Lane. It felt so strange, to walk with the silent girl over those familiar cobbles, to the old, familiar door. Serafina had a key—Serafina had always had a key—and we entered. The little house was dark, but she found a candle and lit the oil lamp. There was the table, there the sleeping-couch, and there, behind its bit of curtain, the wooden cackstool, where at morning I used to perch, with my volume of Pliny on my knees.

Now Serafina lifted the china pot out of its hole and put it on the floor, and raised the hinged frame, and there, in the hollow underneath, was the iron strongbox, where she had hidden it the night Madek came with it to the nunciature. I picked it up. It was locked. I shook it, and heard the slither of documents within.

Here it was, in my hands, the evidence with which Madek, in his youth and foolishness, had thought to topple Felix Wenzel, and win back his beloved, and have his revenge on her father the pander. Instead of which he had lost his eyes and ended up in the Stag Moat with a cord drawn tight around his throat.

The box was square, not large and not very deep, with sharp corners, and was rusted somewhat on the lid and down the sides. It seemed so commonplace a thing, an article I used to shit upon of a morning, all unknowing, yet for the sake of it men had schemed and suffered and died.

26

It was the bells that wakened me. They were tolling in towers all over the city, in the lofty cathedral on the hill, in the Old Town Square, in the Týn Kirche, in the little Church of St Peter, where the remains of Edward Kelley lay. I was confused at first, thinking the gears of time had slipped, for I was in Golden Lane, stretched out on my couch as in the old days, with the vague smoke of morning in the air around me and a spike of winter sunlight pale as old gold piercing the dusty window. The couch had not been slept on since I had last lain there; it felt damp and smelt of mould. I was chilled to the bone, having had nothing to cover me in the night except my beaver coat. I had a bad crick in my neck, too, from resting at an awkward angle with no pillow or cushion for support. Even the condemned man chafes at the discomforts of the last night in his cell.

I lay for a while listening to the mingled ringing of the bells. I wondered what could be the occasion of so much solemn clamour, and then remembered what I already knew, that this was the official birthday of the Emperor.

I sat up and looked about. I wished Serafina were there with me, but I was alone. I thought of the terrors of the night, of my discovery of the corpse of another Kroll, of my flight through the city, of what Serafina had shown me, hidden here.

Remembering the strongbox, I sprang up and went to see that it was safe. I had stowed it in my goat-hide satchel.

It was there; a part of me had wished it might have been gone.

There was nothing to eat or drink, and no water in the jug, even, for me to wash with. I could not contemplate using the cackstool, that lowly and yet now so momentous hiding place. Quickly I got dressed and put on my coat and shouldered my heavy satchel, and left the house. I walked along the lane until I came to an inn where I knew the latch on the side gate was always carelessly left undone, and got into the yard there and used the privy.

Afterwards I washed myself under the spout of a water pump. I felt, in my glooms, like a sacrifice preparing itself for the slaughter.

The day was harsh and raw under a louring purplish sky full of snow, and the air was swathed with a dense white mist. I was glad of the mist, as a sort of second cloak in which to wrap myself and hide. It is a strange thing to walk about in the world in the usual way, exercising one's usual limbs, while thinking that by nightfall one will likely be dangling stiff by the neck from the end of a hangman's rope.

In truth, I did not walk, but crept, rather, keeping close to the walls, and stopping every dozen paces to dodge into a doorway and peer back along the street for fear I was being followed. The world had become a vast trap set exclusively for me.

And so I went on, with my cap pulled low and my face sunk to the nose in the collar of my coat.

The birthday festivities were already well under way. A *Te Deum* was being sung in the cathedral, and I could hear within the soarings of the choir and the braying of the organ. In the broad courtyard before the Royal Palace, a squad of the Imperial Guard, gorgeously arrayed in shades of blue and scarlet, was measuring out tight ceremonial squares, the guardsmen's muskets shouldered and their lances bristling and their spurred heels ajingle. In streets off the square, other regiments were going through their paces; there was a great mingling of booted men and caparisoned horses, and echoing everywhere were the sounds of shouted commands and the sharp clatter of iron-shod hoofs on cobbles.

On the balcony above the palace arch, a group of courtiers had gathered to view the manoeuvres being performed in the square below. Rudolf, I saw, had been lured out of hiding, for there he was, at the front of the group, looking cowed and anxious. To his right was his brother Matthias, tall, vigorous, with his plumed hat in his hand, grinning and waving. On the Emperor's left stood a somewhat jaded-looking, slender young man got up in ceremonial black armour, with a jewelled black hat and a deep ruff. This I took to be Rudolf's cousin the Archduke Ferdinand. Caterina Sardo's name for him, I remembered, was Turnip-head, but with his great, deep brow and matching long chin, divided from each other by a stiff brown moustache, to my eye he resembled nothing so much as the sole and heel come loose from an outsized boot. The Habsburgs were not, to say the least, a handsome tribe.

I ducked under an arch and hurried up the stairs towards my chamber. Somewhere in the castle a band of minstrels was playing; I could hear the skirl of pipes and the tapping of a drum. I wondered where Caterina Sardo might be—I had not seen her among the crowd on the balcony. I did not expect we would meet today, for we had a discretionary understanding to avoid each other on ceremonial occasions such as this one; in my heart, I wondered if we would ever meet again.

When I opened the door to my chamber, the first shock was to find Chamberlain Lang, in his long black robe, reclining at his ease on my bed, with his back against a bank of pillows and his ankles crossed, reading my old dog-eared copy of Pliny.

'Ah, Herr Doktor Stern,' he said, looking up and smiling. 'Here you are at last—we have been waiting for you.'

The room around him was in great disorder. My work-table had been overturned, and my papers were strewn across the floor amid puddles of spilled ink. Drawers had been wrenched out and their contents emptied. The cushions on my couch had been disembowelled, and the upholstery had been slashed, leaving wads of horsehair stuffing sprouting from the wounds. A shelf of books had been swept to the floor, carpets had been turned up, and the curtains had been ripped from the window.

In the midst of the wreckage stood a pale young man with a high forehead, watchful eyes, and a deeply receding chin in which was set, like the bud of a rose, a very small pinched pink mouth.

'This is Curtius,' the Chamberlain said to me. 'You have not encountered him before, I think. He carries out for me the more delicate of the necessary tasks that arise from time to time.' He looked about at the wreck of my room. 'Yes, something of a jumble, I fear,' he said, 'but you will understand, there was a certain urgency.'

'What were you looking for?' I asked.

He put his head to one side in his birdlike way and gave me a wry smile. 'Oh, come,' he said, 'we both know the answer to that. We all know it—don't we, Curtius?'

The chinless young man said nothing.

'Then let me ask,' I said to the Chamberlain, 'what it was you found?'

Lang pretended to give serious consideration to this, putting a finger to his chin and lifting up his eyes.

'Nothing very much,' he said, 'to be truthful. Some questionable books borrowed from the Emperor's private library—saucy stuff, Herr Doktor. Notable, too, was a leather riding crop that, I warrant, was never laid upon the flanks of any horse. Also an item or two of ladies' intimate apparel—souvenirs, perhaps, forfeits won, favours given? No, you're right—not my business.' Curtius murmured something that I did not catch, and the Chamberlain nodded. 'Yes yes, of course, I had forgotten that.' He turned his attention to me again. 'And a purse of silver and gold money, pushed to the back of a drawer. We have been saving our pfennigs diligently, it seems, Herr Doktor.'

He stood up from the bed, my book still in his hand. He frowned at it, as if he had forgotten about it, then tossed it across to me. 'A dry stick, old Pliny, don't you think?' he said. 'Or perhaps I haven't got the temperament for it. *Fortune favours the brave*, indeed—and then poisons them in a pumice cloud on the shore below Vesuvius.'

He touched my arm and drew me with him to the door. There he paused and turned, looking from me to his assistant and back again.

'What do you say?' he asked me. 'Shall I tell Curtius to carry on with his search, or would that be a further waste of his not unvaluable time?' I answered nothing; he smiled, and ushered me ahead of him through the door. 'All right, Curtius,' he said over his shoulder, 'you may carry on.'

In the corridor he paused again, still with a hand on my

arm, and looked about cautiously, with an ear cocked. There was the sound of the minstrels from afar, and of the bells from further still.

'We must be careful that you are not seen,' he said. 'We need a little time together, you and I. The matter, as I say, is urgent.'

'And what matter is it?' I asked.

'Why, the matter of Dr Kroll's murder. Along with other things.'

He led me through dim passageways, and across light-less halls I had never entered before and had not known the existence of—the castle was a limitless warren. At last we came to a place I recognised: his little cell, with the prie-dieu and the table and the tapestry showing Actaeon set upon by his dogs.

He crossed to the window and peered out. From with-out came the sound of bugles and marching men, and the loud barking of sergeant majors.

'Such nonsense,' Lang said, clicking his tongue. 'His Majesty detests it all, of course.'

He turned to me. 'Sit, Herr Doktor,' he said, 'sit, please. We shall not be disturbed here.'

He smiled, and joined his hands together and paced the floor a little, with his rapid, skipping step. 'There is not much time, so let us not waste what of it we have.' He paused, humming under his breath. 'You know you are being sought for the doctor's murder?'

'No, I do not know it,' I answered. 'Who accuses me?'

He stopped his pacing, and turned and smiled. 'My dear man, you were seen coming from his house, with blood on your hands.'

I stared at him.

'Who saw me?' I demanded.

'Some drinkers at an inn close by—'

'Impossible—they were nowhere near enough to have seen me.'

'Ah, so you do admit you were there?'

'I admit nothing.'

He nodded. Despite his talk of urgency, he seemed only amused.

'Also the Doctor's servant,' he said. 'Fricka, I believe is her name; she testified that you were there.'

'Yes, I saw her—but the doctor was dead by then.'

The Chamberlain squinted at the ceiling, and rubbed his hands together slowly, making a soft, slithering sound.

'That is not what she says, I'm afraid,' he murmured, pursing his lips.

'And what *does* she say?'

He shrugged. 'That's all: that you burst in and murdered her master.'

'I don't believe it,' I said.

'Well, the Emperor does.'

'Where is the woman now?' I asked.

'The poor creature was greatly shocked, naturally. She was sent away, early this morning, to a convent in the hills. She needs rest; she needs to be cared for.'

My hands were shaking. I had the sense one has on a sunny day when a storm cloud is approaching, that feeling of the light being squeezed out of the air, of a darkness seeping in even as the sun goes on brightly shining.

'Listen to me,' the Chamberlain said, 'listen carefully now.' He came and took me by the wrist and made me sit, and he sat too, in front of me, so that we were again almost knee to knee, as we had been once before, memorably. 'His

Majesty has ordered that you are to be apprehended and charged with the murder of Dr Kroll—'

'Who told him I was seen at the doctor's house? Was it you?'

He reared back his head, in a show of wounded surprise. 'I?' he said. 'Certainly not! I am your friend—surely you know that? I have only your best interests at heart. No, I'm afraid the one who went to His Majesty was—was someone else, whom you know.'

He turned away, tapping two fingers against his underlip. Outside, the bells had stopped tolling, and a solitary trumpet was sounding a slow military lament.

'You have encountered Don Giulio, Mistress Sardo's eldest son?' Lang asked. 'Officially he is Don Julius Caesar of Austria—absurd, I know—but his mother prefers the Italianate form. He was for a long time the Emperor's favourite, and shared many of His Majesty's interests. He has a fascination with clocks, for instance, and—and other things.' He frowned. 'Lately, however, he has become distinctly strange, and difficult—so difficult, in fact, that he, too, is to leave the city this morning. The Emperor has ordered him to be dispatched forthwith to Krumlov, far in the south, to be held at the castle there, for the time being, or until he has recovered his senses sufficiently to be allowed to return to Prague—which, between you and me, will be a long time indeed. Schenckel the dwarf will be his escort. His Majesty is greatly upset, but he sees the necessity of the young man being kept, for now, far, far away from Prague and its—its temptations.'

He paused, and looked hard into my face, nodding. For a moment I was again in that patch of darkness in the night-time corridor, again I felt that foul thing flinging itself at me, all arms and legs and enormous hands. I saw again also my slaughtered cat, my poor Plato, stretched across the threshold in a mess of rusty blood.

'Why do you speak of this person?' I asked. 'What is he to me?'

The Chamberlain steepled his fingers before him and softly closed his eyes.

'Patience,' he murmured, 'patience.' He stopped a moment, casting his gaze towards the ceiling. 'Don Giulio,' he said, 'has always had a special friend, here at the castle. There is his mother, of course, but he has also a protector and—and guide, shall we say?'

'And who is this guide?' I asked.

He fixed on me a slyly sarcastic smile. 'That, my dear Herr Doktor, not even one so shrewd as you would ever guess.'

But he was wrong. At once there came to me, out of the blue, like a bird alighting on a branch, a memory of that first day when Jeppe Schenckel was taking me to Dr Kroll's house to meet the Emperor. We had stopped at the spot where Magdalena Kroll's corpse had lain, and I had described how the girl's throat had been torn out as if by a wild animal. I saw us there, clearly, the two of us, and heard again the dwarf saying how her killer 'must have been playing with her', and saw how he had frowned, in a way, thoughtful and tense, that had struck me at the time as strange.

'It is Schenckel,' I said, 'isn't it?'

'Ah!' the Chamberlain said, opening wide his eyes. 'Shrewd indeed, Master Stern—shrewd indeed!'

He stood up quickly, in that odd, convulsive way he had, and began again his rapid pacing, with his hands clasped before him.

'There were always the three of them, you see,' he said. 'There was Mistress Sardo, there was Don Giulio, and there was the dwarf. A potent mixture, that trio—a lethal mixture. There was little even I could do to control them. The Emperor would not hear a word said against them, being especially sensitive in regard to Don Giulio, as is understandable. When Wenzel and Dr Kroll pandered Kroll's daughter to His Majesty—' He broke off. 'By the way, did you know the Kroll girl was carrying Rudolf's child?'

He smiled at my shocked stare.

'I believed Madek was the father,' I said.

I was beginning, barely beginning, to see my way through this tangled thicket.

He looked at me with a pitying smile. 'Madek was nothing,' he said softly, 'nothing at all—not to *us*.'

Us. There it was again, and clearly I heard the echo of Caterina Sardo, sitting naked on my bed with a bowl of cherries in her lap, smiling into my eyes and saying, '*Us*.'

'Then it was Don Giulio who murdered Magdalena Kroll,' I said. 'Is that what I am to understand?'

The Chamberlain threw up his hands in a pretence of being horrified. 'Ssh,' he hissed. 'You must not be heard to say such a thing.'

'But it's what you're telling me—that Don Giulio destroyed the girl, with the dwarf's connivance.'

He nodded slowly, putting on now a look of tragic sadness. 'Yes,' he whispered, 'with the dwarf's connivance. And more than that, at his mother's bidding.' He watched me keenly. 'Are you shocked? You should be. I know in what high esteem you hold that lady.'

His crimson lips stretched into a crescent smile. Then he tapped me on the knee with the tip of a forefinger, and rose and began pacing again. I could hear the rapid padding of his slippers on the flags of the stone floor.

'She pretends,' he said, 'good Mistress Sardo, to care nothing for His Majesty. She laughs at him and mocks him behind his back. But there are some things she will not countenance. Oh, no. She might have put up with Kroll's daughter as Rudolf's bed-mate, his little playmate. She herself had other diversions, after all'—he turned his head and smirked at me over his shoulder—'but a child, now, a Habsburg cuckoo in the nest, of which she herself was not the mother? No: that prospect was too much.'

The trumpeter outside blew the final flourish of his lament, and into the silence he left behind came the sound of distant cannons: a salute for the royal birthday was being fired from the heights of Vyšehrad.

'And what has any of this to do with Wenzel,' I asked, 'with Dr Kroll—with all of that?'

He broke off from his pacing and in a flurry came and plumped himself down in front of me once more, looking like nothing so much as a large black intently staring crow. This time our knees did touch.

'Nothing!' he said, lifting up his hands to Heaven. 'It had nothing to do with Wenzel, and Wenzel's plots and plans, into which poor Dr Kroll had been unwittingly drawn. That was what Wenzel was so baffled by—that the girl died. He sought to detect my hand in the deed, but failed. And it made no sense to him. Do you see?' He sat back on the chair, hugging himself for glee. 'It made no sense! And Wenzel is a man who must have sense—which is why he fixed on *you* as the culprit. Poor Felix, I almost feel sorry for him: so clumsy, though he thinks himself such a wily, slippery fox.'

He rose and went to a cupboard by the fireplace and took from it a bottle and two glass goblets and returned with them to the table and poured out wine for both of us.

'A toast,' he said, lifting up his glass. 'Let us drink to Hermes, the god of chance!'

He sat down.

'Consider,' he went on, 'consider the unlikeliness of it— I swear, some sportive god must have had a hand in the making of that piece of glorious mischief.' He drew his chair closer still to mine. 'Madek,' he said excitedly, 'hallooing his love for his lost girl, stole her father's box of magic mumbo-jumbo and brought it to Kelley out at Most. They huggered, they muggered, and in the end came to a bargain, by which Madek returned to Prague with a treasure rich beyond his highest hopes: the correspondence between Wenzel and Elizabeth of England. That much Kroll was able to verify, when he went to Most at Wenzel's behest and broke Kelley's broken legs a second time. *Madek had the letters*. And when the young fool threatened Wenzel with them, Wenzel seized him, tortured him, forced what information out of him that he could, then had him throttled and disposed of.' He leaned forward again, showing his teeth in a fierce smile, and jabbed a finger into the centre of my chest. '*And then the girl was murdered.* Why? By whom? It terrified him, the senselessness of it, the unconnectedness. And still the letters were missing—the letters that Kelley's daughter told you about, that you somehow found, and that now—oh, my dear fellow!—that now are so mysteriously missing again.'

We were silent, and so were the cannons. Lang was watching me, waiting for me to speak.

'And Kroll,' I said, 'why was he killed?'

He drummed his fingers on the armrest of his chair. 'Ah, well, now,' he said, 'as to that, I fear I must confess to a certain level of . . . involvement, to a certain level of—of culpability, even.' He smiled wincingly, grimly nodding. 'Yes, I'm afraid it's true. You must remember, however, that he was engaged in a conspiracy, with Wenzel, against the throne. He had to be destroyed, if for no other reason than to clear the line of fire.'

'What do you mean?' I asked. 'What line of fire?'

He put his hands together as if to pray, and touched the tips of his fingers lightly to his mouth. 'Dr Kroll, let us say, was one of the lesser fallen angels, to Wenzel's Lucifer. Do you see?'

'And you are St Michael, of the flaming sword?'

He smiled, almost shyly. 'Ah, no,' he said, 'no, I cannot claim such sanctity.'

'So you murdered him,' I said. 'You murdered Kroll.'

'I?' He lifted high his eyebrows and opened wide his eyes. 'No no no. I do not murder people, my dear Herr Doktor. What a vulgar charge to lay against His Majesty's High Chamberlain!'

'But you cause people to be murdered,' I said.

'No no no,' he repeated, more forcefully this time, with a vehement shake of the head. 'What I did, if it can even be called doing, was to mention to your stunted little friend, Herr Schenckel, that the good—or, I should say, the not so good—Dr Kroll had deduced at last who it was that had done his poor daughter to death, and was about to reveal all to the Emperor. The dwarf, in turn, went with this dark news to Caterina Sardo, and that was all it took for the imperial wolf cub to be unleashed. The rest was—well, the rest was as you saw, all blood and mess and cruel tragedy.'

'And the note,' I said, 'the note summoning me to Kroll's house—did you send that?'

He pulled low the corners of his mouth in a mummer's imitation of guilt and contrition. 'I cannot lie,' he said. 'I know it was wicked of me, but how could I resist? There were the two birds, perched plump and inviting on the fence, and I had the stone in my hand. Who would not seize such a happy opportunity to bring them both down?'

I felt an anger stirring in me, like a beast that had been long aslumber and all at once had been pricked awake.

'You do see it, don't you?' Lang pleaded reasonably. 'It was a way for me to convince you to surrender what I most ardently desired of you. I feared you might try with me what that numbskull Madek tried with Wenzel, and hold the letters over me, for your own gain. Did I wrong you?' He produced one of his actorly sighs. 'I have lived so long at court, I fear I am of a hopelessly suspicious turn of mind.'

'What if you were right to be suspicious?' I enquired darkly, scowling at him. 'What if I were to keep the letters, to ensure my own safety and security?'

He looked at me in silence. His eyes, which up to this point had been bright with merriment, went slowly dead.

'Give them to me,' he said softly, 'give them to me, and you are free. Withhold them, and I have my witnesses who will swear they saw you last night stumbling through the streets with a murderer's blood on your hands. In Prague, it does not take much to have a man hanged—this you know already. Do not give me cause to summon Curtius and his men. They are every bit as brisk as Wenzel's were that night he sent them to seize hold of you. I take it you have not forgotten that night, and who it was that saved your neck?'

Silence fell between us then. I could hear faintly the sounds of the festive crowd out in the courtyard. A thought had been burrowing its way into my mind, silently, secretly, and now it broke through an inner protecting wall.

'Whose son is he?' I asked.

The Chamberlain sat back with a start, then checked himself, and fixed on me a long, large look. 'Whom do you mean?' he asked.

'Don Giulio—whose son is he?'

He held out his hands and spread them wide. 'Why, Mistress Caterina's, of course.'

'But who is the father?'

He drew his head still further back, still staring at me.

I thought of the picture on Malaspina's wall, soft Venus in her great hat, and the stunted Cupid offering her the honeycomb.

The Chamberlain was nodding now, slowly, taking me newly in, with a narrowed eye. 'Ah, you are not so dull as I first took you to be, Christian Stern,' he said. 'You see far, you see deep.'

' "There were always the three of them," ' I said. 'Those were your words. Three of them—Mistress Sardo, the dwarf, and Don Giulio, the son.'

A mandrake root, bristling with tendrils and all caked with marl, its forked form entwined about her white and gleaming limbs.

The Chamberlain went on staring, then lifted his head abruptly and softly laughed. 'Fie, sir!' he said, still laughing. 'What things you do allow yourself to imagine. And yet'— he touched a finger to the tip of his chin—'it's true, there is nothing so malign or misbegotten that it may not catch a lady's fancy, when the moon is full.' He leaned his face

316

close up to mine. 'But tell me,' he murmured, 'this thought that's come to you, have you the stomach to entertain it?'

Abandon Prague, I told myself. Leave now, be gone, tonight.

I stood up. No, I did not have the stomach for it. I had a sick sensation, and in my mouth a taste of bitterness and bile.

The Chamberlain, still seated, with his fingers laced together now in his lap, was watching me. 'Come,' he said, in almost a whisper. 'The letters—where are they?'

27

I proposed to him a bargain. It was quickly struck, since my demands were simple, and few. In return for the letters, he would guarantee safe passage for me out of Prague. I would have a carriage and driver, and an armed escort would accompany me as far as the Polish border. No one was to know which direction I had taken—no one. His Majesty especially was not to be told of my leaving until I was well gone. Further, Curtius would return to me my purse of money, and would be made to stand before me while I counted the sum and verified it to the last coin.

'All that I can grant,' the Chamberlain said, 'easily. And also? For I can see there's more.'

Yes, there was one thing more: Elizabeth Jane Weston was to be afforded the full protection of the Chamberlain's office.

On this the Chamberlain looked at me askance. 'Oh, and what's she to you?' he enquired, smirking.

I made no reply. My satchel was on the floor at my feet. I leaned down and took it up and undid the buckles, and brought out the iron strongbox and set it on the table between us. The Chamberlain stood and gazed at it. Then he laughed. 'You had it with you, all this time that we were here, jawing?' He shook his head. 'You force me to revise my estimation of you yet further upwards. You are not at all the dolt I thought you were.' He glanced at me sidelong. 'Have you seen the contents?' he asked.

'It's locked,' I said. 'You'll have to break it open.'

He chuckled.

'Oh, I suspect not,' he said. 'Wait.'

He reached inside his habit and brought out the gold medallion, the one Magdalena Kroll had been wearing the night I found her in the snow. He placed it on the table and pressed the secret switch, and the Medusa-headed lid sprang open.

'I had a notion about the thing,' he said, 'a feeling that there was something I was not seeing. Then I searched, and found it.'

He dug a fingernail into the paste filling the hidden compartment, and hooked out an object that had been sunk deep in the soft depths. He rubbed it between his palms to clean it, and held it aloft.

It was a key, a small, iron key.

'I did not know what it was meant to open, but I kept it, all the same. So now let us see.' He picked up the strongbox and turned the key in the keyhole; the lock clicked. 'Ah!' he breathed. 'I was right.'

I walked to the window. Below was the Stag Moat. I thought of Madek's body bobbing in the water there, among the shards of ice.

I was putting my trust in Philipp Lang. I had to trust someone.

Behind me he had opened the box and taken out the letters; I heard him riffling through them, humming to himself.

How had Magdalena Kroll come to have the key to the box? Madek must have sent it to her, a token of love betrayed.

'Oh, yes,' the Chamberlain behind me exclaimed under his breath, 'oh, yes, indeed. Now we shall know what things they were hatching between them, those two.' He opened a drawer in the prie-dieu and took out the code-book, then came to the window and shook the letters in my face. 'With this evidence to show against him, I can hang the fellow ten times over!'

I did not shift my gaze from the window and the wintry prospect beyond the glass. I was remembering how, that very first night, Wenzel had instinctively put out a hand to help the dead girl's father as in his grief he faltered. I had taken my stance, I had chosen a side: had I done right? Then the thought returned of Jan Madek dead, with his eyes torn out.

No side is right, ever.

'You are melancholy,' the Chamberlain said, standing beside me with the letters in his hand. He smiled, and shrugged. 'Remember,' he said, 'someone has to prevail.'

I went to my chamber. Curtius had put it back into some sort of order. To my surprise, I found the money purse returned to its place at the back of the drawer where I had hidden it. I counted the gold and silver pieces; they were all there. Curtius was either honest, or too fearful of his master's ire to risk stealing my gold.

I packed my satchel with what few things I judged I would need—some clothes, the purse, my astrolabe. I stood for a moment weighing the volume of Pliny in my palm, then laid it down on the table. Lang was right: the old man was too dry.

I spied a cherry stone on the hearth. Nothing else remained. I looked at the bed. Nothing else.

I had finished my packing when Curtius appeared, bringing food for me, soup with lentils, bread, slices of dried apple, a jug of ale. The Chamberlain's man exuded a curious faint smell, as of candle wax. He was one of those pale clerks whose time of power in the sun—or, better say, under a gibbous moon—would not be long in coming, when Rudolf was gone and his cousin Ferdinand raised up a conflagration in the world. It was from the likes of Curtius that I fled here, to this cold coast, than which there is no further north for me to go, unless I should end up in Ultima Thule itself.

My next visitor was the Chamberlain; he bustled in, in high good humour, rubbing his hands. I was standing by the window, with a plate of bread and the remaining few slices of apple. He cast a quizzical glance at the packed bag at my feet.

'Will you leave so soon?' he exclaimed. 'Won't you wait to see the High Steward brought low? I am putting him in the cell where he put you. You might visit him there, to crow a little. No? Why, sir, where is your spirit of revenge? You told me he threatened you with the rack, and there's no doubt he would have had you broken on it, had *someone* not stepped in to save you.'

To all this I gave no acknowledgement; I was weary of the man, of his skits and sallies. I asked what measures he had made to ensure that Elizabeth Weston should be safe.

'Oh, Elizabeth Weston, Elizabeth Weston!' he exclaimed, with a flick of his hand. 'Why are you so concerned for this female?'

'That is no business of yours,' I answered.

'Ah,' he said, nodding and smiling. 'Ah, I see. By Heaven, young man, you do spread your favours wide!'

He plucked a crust of bread from my plate and began to nibble at it. Outside, a weak sun was managing to shine, even as the first flakes of snow swayed randomly in the air.

'Sir Henry Wotton,' I said, suddenly remembering. 'What has become of him?'

The Chamberlain laughed.

'Sir Henry, learning of what had transpired at Most, suddenly remembered that he had urgent business to attend to in Italy. He is in Venice now, I believe, wooing the Doge and touting for business on the Rialto. A very active fellow, the good Sir Henry. You know his definition of an ambassador? "An honest gentleman sent to lie abroad for England".' He gave a hoot of laughter. 'A polished scoundrel, but witty withal.'

A flourish of bugles sounded in the distance.

'Hark!' the Chamberlain said, lifting up a finger. 'That will be Matthias going home to Vienna. Good riddance. He would keep enquiring for the High Steward, and grew quite testy over his absence. I had not the heart to tell him that his man was even then on his way to the White Tower.' He picked a morsel of apple from my plate and popped it into his mouth. 'I wonder how he will take to a diet of bread and water?' He shot me a merry glance. 'You, as I recall, found it not at all to your taste.'

He stepped past me to the window and looked out at the snow with a suddenly gloomy eye. 'Ferdinand will be staying for some days,' he said. 'There will be revels—subdued ones, I grant you, Ferdinand being Ferdinand.'

' "Our man",' I said.

He cast at me a sidelong glance. 'How so?'

'It's what Mistress Sardo said of him, that he is "our man"—hers, yours and mine, too, supposedly.'

'Well, yes, certainly, she is right. He is indeed our man.' He sighed wistfully. 'I would have had a gayer fellow, given the choice. I blame the Jesuits—they got him early and did not let go. Though, mind you, he is not without a certain wit, young Ferdinand. Not long ago he rounded up a cabal of alchemists who had promised to make gold for him and failed, and hanged them like a line of finches on a scaffold that he had ordered specially gilded for the occasion. That could almost pass for a joke, yes, or a show of irony at least?' I said nothing. 'I see you are not amused,' he said, smiling.

The Chamberlain turned away from the window and smacked his palms together softly. 'So,' he said. 'Shall we say our farewells?' He put a hand to his breast. 'No tears, I hope? His Majesty will miss you, even though he's wrought against you now. He forgives everyone everything, in the end.'

He smiled, and touched a finger lightly to my cheek, and strode busily away.

I put the plate down on the windowsill, and drained the mug of ale.

Time to be gone.

But first I had a last visit to pay, to the place where I had started.

In Golden Lane the cobbles gleamed. Great soft wet flakes of snow were falling hurriedly. I tried the known door; it was unlocked. I stepped inside and stood in the little room among familiar odours, familiar shadows, feeling hardly more than a shadow myself.

Something glinted on the table. Before I picked it up I knew what it would be: my mother's ring.

Serafina.

How had she known I would come this last time? The ring was too small to fit on any of my fingers. I put it into my purse, along with my money, where I had found it in the first place.

It was old, that purse, old and worn. Might it once have belonged to my mother? And might it have been she who had put the ring into it, and forgotten about it, those long years ago, when I was a babe and she was still of this earth? It was possible. After all, the god of chance is ever at our side, shaking the dice in his fist.

I heard a footstep behind me and turned. It was a woman, in a grey cape, hooded, with flakes of snow on her shoulders.

'Serafina!' I cried.

But I was mistaken.

'Is that the name of the little mouse who used to keep you warm here?' Caterina Sardo asked.

She lowered the hood of her cape. Her bronze-gold hair was arranged in the way it had been the first time I saw her, in a long, loose braid flung with artless care over her right shoulder. How often I had twined that lovely lock around my fist and drawn her head back to expose her tautened throat, that pillar of cool, soft marble.

'It's you,' I said.

'Oh, it's me, *certo*,' she answered drily. 'Are you very disappointed?'

The snow-light spread a rich effulgence around her.

'It's cold,' she said, 'as it always is, in this place.' She looked at my bag on the floor, at the purse in my hand. 'You were going to leave without bidding goodbye? *Dio mio*, all is so changed.'

What could I say to her? I looked into her eyes, in which I seemed to detect a new expression, a new uncertainty. 'The girl,' I said. 'Serafina, at the Nuncio's house.'

I stopped. She waited.

'*Sì?*' she said, with a flicker of impatience. 'What of her?'

I paused, for the space of two deep breaths. 'If you harm

that child,' I said, 'I shall hear of it, and come back and find you, and nothing will protect you from my wrath.'

She stood and gazed at me, blank-eyed now. The moments passed. In the open doorway at her back the swift snow fell straight down in silence, like an endless curtain falling. She smiled then, and turned her face away, and sighed.

'Oh, Christian Stern,' she said. She put out a hand behind her blindly and pushed the door shut. '*Quanto sei stupido*—you are, you really are, a fool, my poor sweet fellow.'

She stepped forward, until she was close enough for me to smell the fragrance of her body. There were patches of melted snow on her cheeks, on her forehead.

'Why have you come here?' I asked curtly. 'I know about your son, about Magdalena Kroll, about—about everything.'

'No no no,' she said gently, as if she were hushing a refractory child. 'You know nothing, *caro mio*.' Her voice was a whisper now. 'Nothing.'

'How did you know I was here?' I asked.

'I followed you.' She took my hand. 'Come,' she said, 'come sit with me, for just a little while.'

She led me to the table. We sat.

'The girl, Serafina,' she said, 'you need not be concerned for her safety. Malaspina will protect her—who lays a finger on Malaspina, or any person in his care, lays a finger on the Pope himself. And should that happen, that finger, believe me, would soon be separated from its hand.'

I looked at her. What had changed? She was no longer the enchanting witch whom I had loved so desperately, in such transports of bedazzled terror, these past weeks. Was she, like Philipp Lang, only an actor, one who now had stepped down from the stage? I saw the wrinkles beside her eyes, the straw-coloured wisps of hair at the corners of her mouth, the knotted veins in the backs of her hands. She had become her age, suddenly.

'Why have you come?' I asked again.

'I know all that the Chamberlain has promised you.'

'How did you—?'

She closed her eyes and shook her head rapidly. 'It does not matter,' she said.

'I think it matters.'

'*Io io io!*' she said, making a funnel of her lips and speaking in a hollow voice, mimicking me. Then she smiled, and cupped a hand against my cheek. 'You are such a little boy sometimes,' she said. 'So sure, so stubborn.'

I looked to the window, and the blundering snow outside. 'Tell me how you knew about the Chamberlain and me.'

'Because he told me,' she said. 'As he tells me everything.' She moved her hand from my cheek now and put it at the back of my neck and drew me closer. 'He promised you that you might leave the city, yes?'

'Yes,' I said. 'A carriage is to come for me here at nightfall. By morning I shall be far away.'

She regarded me with a pitying smile. 'No carriage will come, *caro* Christian, there will be no escort to the border. If you stay here, by morning you shall be at the bottom of the Vltava. He will drown you, you and all that you know.'

Still gripping me by the neck, she leaned forward and put her lips to my ear. '*Rudolf has ordered it,*' she whispered.

She released me, and sat back on the chair, nodding.

'I don't believe you,' I said. 'You're trying to trick me.'

'No no no,' she said again, in that softly soothing tone. 'His star has set. He will not consent to see it rise again. This is true. Lang's men have their instructions.'

I scrambled to my feet angrily, knocking over the chair I

326

had been sitting on. 'Why?' I demanded. 'Why would His Majesty do such a thing?'

She was silent for a long time, sitting with her hands loose in her lap and her head bent. At last she looked up at me. 'Because you know who murdered Magdalena Kroll.'

'But it was he who ordered me to discover her killer!' I cried.

Now she, too, stood up. It always surprised me how tall she was, tall enough to look level into my eyes.

'Yes,' she said, 'and you carried out his order, and now my son is banished—'

In a fury, I seized her by the shoulders and shook her. She hung unresisting in my grasp, her limbs twitching like a puppet's.

'You *knew*,' I shouted. 'You *knew* the things he did! You knew he killed the girl. You knew it was him outside the door of my chamber that day, you knew it was he who flung himself at me in the corridor—*you knew!*'

I let go of her, and she flopped back onto the chair. I turned away and paced the floor with my arms folded, trapping my fists—I was afraid I would use them to strike her. 'Look at you,' I said in disgust. 'You cannot even weep.'

She rose again from the chair, drawing her cloak around herself. 'Cold,' she murmured. 'So cold.'

I stood before her, barring her way. She looked at me, frowning vaguely, as if she no longer knew who I was, just as I no longer knew her.

'You should go now,' she said. 'They will come for you soon.'

She stepped past me, turning towards the door. I caught her arm. She stopped and stood motionless, with her head bowed. She would not look at me.

'*Did* you know?' I asked. 'About your son, about the dwarf, about what they did?'

She shrugged, still with her face turned away from me.

'I knew,' she said, 'and I didn't know. What does it matter?'

I let go of her arm, but still she stood there, head down, her shoulders drooping.

'What will you do?' I asked.

'What will I do?' She spoke the words slowly, consideringly, seeming to turn them this way and that to examine them, as if they were in a language she did not understand. 'I will do nothing. Live. All will be as it was before. I will remember you for a little while, and then forget. I will visit my son. I will know and not know.'

She stirred then and drew up her hood and went quickly to the door and opened it, and stepped out into the snow. I tried to call out her name, but I could not.

I went to the Blue Elephant, to buy back my horse. It had died, the ostler told me. I did not believe him, but I had not the time to argue. He offered me a sway-backed mare with a bloodshot eye, asking an absurd price. We haggled, I paid him half of what he had demanded, and he went off swearing under his breath.

Outside, the snow was coming down in swirling billows. I mounted, and the little mare threw back at me an anxious glance. I gave her flanks a prod with my heels, not hard, and we clopped away. A long road lay before us, northwards.

Author's Note

Prague Nights is a historical fantasy. But, then, real life at the court of Rudolf II was entirely phantasmagorical. The definitive account of the period is *Rudolf II and His World*, by R. J. W. Evans. More popular in tone, but no less authoritative, is *The Mercurial Emperor: The Magic Circle of Rudolf II in Renaissance Prague*, by Peter Marshall. I owe an unrepayable debt to the work of both of these fine scholars. Needless to say, they are wholly innocent in the matter of my large-scale distortions of the facts of history.

I also owe it to the reader to separate the historical characters from my invented ones. Among the latter are Christian Stern, Jeppe Schenckel—who appeared in a somewhat different guise in John Banville's novel *Kepler*—Felix Wenzel, Magdalena Kroll and Jan Madek, Sir Kaspar and his sidekick Norbert the page boy, and, my favourite of all of them, sweet Serafina.

The Emperor Rudolf of course existed, however larger than life he may have been, as did John Dee and Edward Kelley, ditto.

Elizabeth Jane Weston was indeed Kelley's stepdaughter, and in later years in Prague she was much admired as a poet—she deserves a novel all to herself.

There was a papal nuncio at Rudolf's court named Germanico Malaspina, but so far as I know, he was nothing like my sly gourmand; I simply could not resist that wonderful surname.

Oswald Croll, one of the emperor's specialists, wrote a highly respected alchemical treatise, *Basilica Chymica*. Again, the historical Dr Croll bears scant resemblance to my 'Ulrich Kroll'.

Philipp Lang was real, and very much so. A converted Jew, he was originally from the Tyrol but quickly got himself to Prague, where he started off as the emperor's valet and rose quickly to the position of chamberlain. Peter Marshall writes that as Lang's power grew, he became increasingly 'impudent and indispensable', feeding his imperial master's already paranoid conviction that Prague was teeming with assassins bent on destroying him, most likely at the behest of his feared and hated brother, the Archduke Matthias. However, when Matthias moved against Rudolf in 1608—Matthias was to become emperor in 1612, in turn succeeded by Ferdinand II, one of the chief instigators of the Thirty Years War—Lang fell from grace, and he died penniless in prison in 1609 or 1610.

Don Julius of Austria—Don Giulio—was Rudolf's illegitimate son, and the favourite among his children. However, the young man was psychotic, and so violent in his behaviour that his father banished him to Český Krumlov, in southern Bohemia. There, according to Peter Marshall, he 'spent his days in hunting and debauchery', while by night, according to another source, his demented screams could be heard echoing along the castle corridors. In 1608 he kidnapped a barber's daughter, whom he raped and held hostage, until the castle servants, alarmed by the girl's cries, forced the door to Don Julius's room and, again according to Marshall, found her 'hacked to pieces with a hunting knife, her eyes gouged out, her teeth broken and her ears cut off', asprawl in the embrace of her captor, who was 'naked and covered in excrement'. Some months later Don Julius died, 'in mysterious circumstances'.

The most grievous calumny in the book is committed against 'Caterina Sardo', who in real life was Katharina Strada, Rudolf's lifelong mistress and the mother of his six children, including Don Julius. Katharina, the daughter of the imperial art collector and curator Ottavio Strada, was by all accounts a perfectly respectable lady, peaceable and self-effacing, and a mainstay in the life of His Imperial and increasingly dotty Majesty. Considering the portrait I have painted of this innocent and long-suffering lady, I felt that the least I could do was to give her a pseudonym, however transparent. *Mea culpa.*

Benjamin Black